VILLAIN

Also by Natalie Zina Walschots

Hench

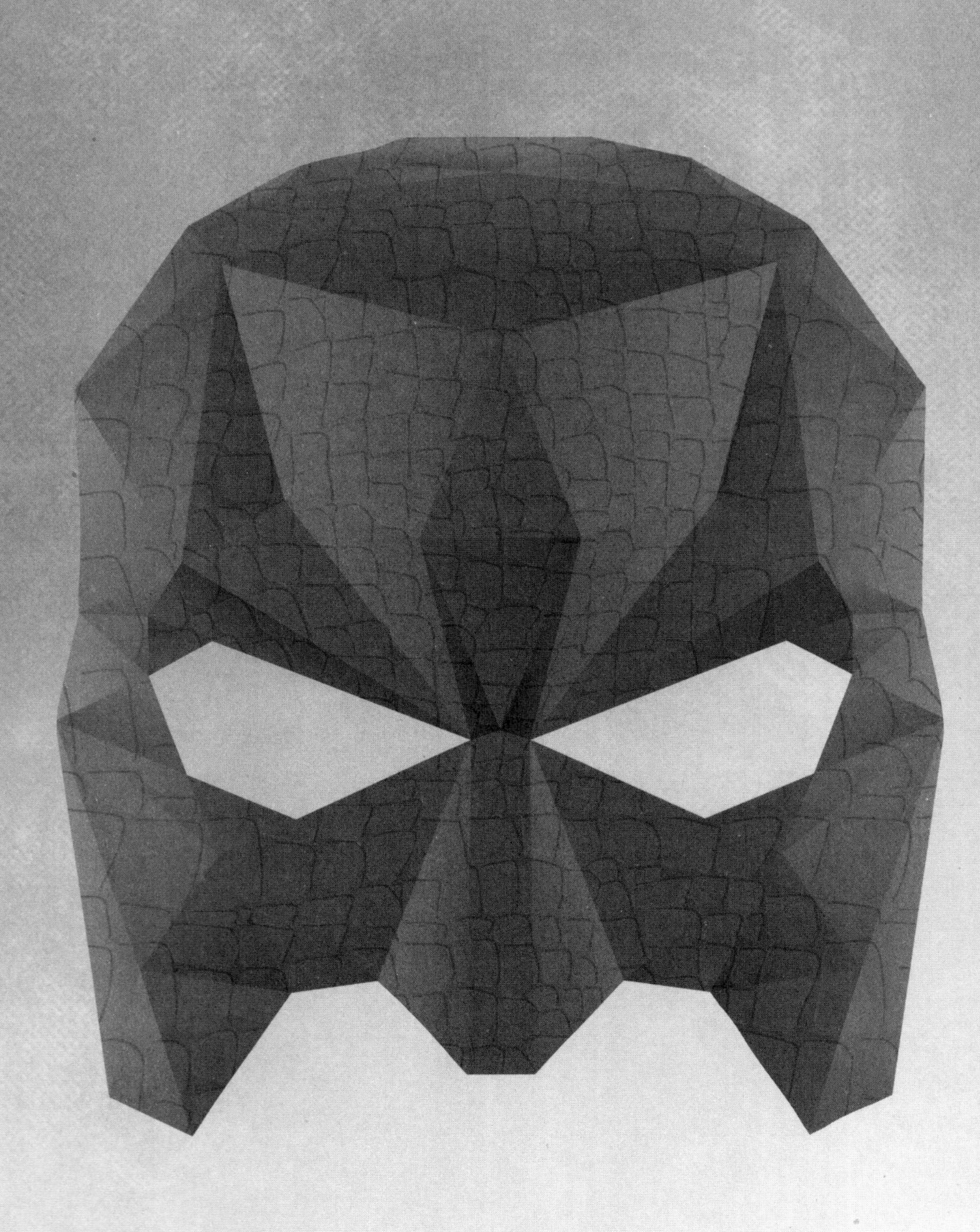

VILLAIN

[*A Novel*]

NATALIE ZINA WALSCHOTS

WILLIAM MORROW
An Imprint of HarperCollinsPublishers

FIRST EDITION

Designed by Lucy Albanese

ILLUSTRATIONS: *Comics Hero font ©Alhovik/shutterstock.com; eye mask ©Sandamali F/shutterstock.com; full face mask ©TheFarAway-Kingdom/shutterstock.com; grunge background art ©one AND only/shutterstock.com; text message bubbles ©Neo/stock.adobe.com*

Library of Congress Cataloging-in-Publication Data has been applied for.

ISBN 978-0-06-323693-6

26 27 28 29 30 LBC 5 4 3 2 1

*For Audra & Haritha, and their Rosefinch.
Without their friendship, and the space they have
built together, I might never have finished this book.*

VILLAIN

— [Part One]

SUPERHEROES ARE BUILT OUT OF LIES FROM HEAD TO FOOT, carved and curated moral products that inarguably do more harm than good. (I know this because I have counted it, calculated it down to the lifeyear, and found the weight of their goodness wanting in comparison.) It's an extraordinary thing to watch an entire institution lie on the scale that the Draft lies.

For months on end, I spent my days watching the Draft lie about Supercollider, as time dragged on and no one outside the maximum-security superheroic medical facility had yet caught even a glimpse of him. I watched them display a fresh batch of fiction every day, their communications department giving cheerful, utterly fabricated updates like a baker producing a fresh batch of muffins every morning. I took note of every new lie, testing its flavor and texture, learning everything I could from what they said . . . and more, what they *didn't*.

"As the vigil outside of the Veterans of Superheroic Conflicts Memorial Hospital entered its two hundredth day," the talking head began with carefully practiced gravitas and weighty optimism.

Their faces all blended together after a while, the rich voices and bright suits blurring as I conducted endless media surveys. "Grateful citizens and fellow heroes the world over continue to visit the hospital grounds, getting as close as they can while the facility remains under enhanced security measures. Some have been here every day, like retired crossing guard Mayla Vernor, who has come each afternoon, regardless of the weather, to visit the recovering hero."

I sat forward as Mayla appeared on-screen, a microphone held up to her face. She was wearing an old purple puffer jacket and a beanie with a pom-pom, an image of such grandmotherly perfection I wondered if she was a plant. "He watched over all of us every day for how many years?" she said, her voice a pleasant, achingly sad warble. "The least I can do is watch over him in some small way."

Definitely a plant.

I took a screenshot of her wholesome face for the reverse-image search and made a note of her name in an endless spreadsheet of loose little strings to tug on. All around Mayla, people gathered outside the gates of the Vet, their arms full of flowers wrapped in cellophane and ugly pink teddy bears. It was a gray day, not raining yet, and there was something funereal about the piles of gifts gathering around the poles of the fences like snowdrifts.

"While the World's Champion continues to recover after the Disaster at Dovecote, where he was injured courageously saving many of his deadliest enemies from an experimental containment explosion—"

A little cinder of anger sparked to life inside my chest. *Like fuck he did*, I thought. She did that to him. Quantum. Not some haywire restraint device, which was a scheme that *I pulled off* way before this.

They were plagiarizing their own malevolence.

"—he has continued to do good in the world, even from his hospital bed. The Citizen Heroes Foundation, a charitable organization founded at the selfless hero's specific request, announced their first major initiative: a mentorship program and educational fund for at-risk youth whose lives have been impacted by the activities of supervillains."

I snorted. The only true statement there was that the Citizen Heroes Foundation did exist and had even been registered as a charity. But it was not at the request of Supercollider; it was the flagship project of the Draft marketing department and the defining moment of more than one bureaucratic career there. I knew all that because Supercollider could barely communicate, as occupational therapy is exceptionally difficult when you've been turned into a piece of chewed gum. He wouldn't have so much as flickered a *DSM-5* textbook eyelash at a hundred villains being reduced to ice sculptures before his eyes, let alone start up a charity.

And the hospital where everyone gathered every day, hoping their thoughts and prayers would be more potent with proximity, dropping off gifts to rot in the rain?

He wasn't even there.

Like everything about this situation, the increased security at the hospital was theater; the wing they had shut down for his treatment and recovery was empty. He was in a Draft facility that didn't have a name, just a building number and branch code, and he was most definitely not recovering. More like in storage.

Part of the problem, of course, was that there was nothing wrong with him. He was healthy as could be, invulnerable as he was, hale and whole and just as strong as he'd always been. It was just that his invincible body has been twisted into an unrecognizable mass of dribbling flesh by his former partner (in both senses of the word) and my once-accomplice, Quantum Entanglement. All the greatest minds working in service of superheroic medicine had yet to come up with a viable way to untangle him from himself. At most they could keep him hydrated, and what they hoped was comfortable, while he worked with a fleet of therapists to give painful one-gesture answers to the questions they asked. They put on whatever television show or music they imagined he would like; I wondered, if because of the way his powers worked—powered by expectations—if that meant they were always right.

I swung between grudging admiration and disgusted pity as I watched the lengths the Draft went through to hang on to whatever was left of their most valuable IP. He had been the cornerstone of not just their industry but the very idea of heroism for so long that they didn't yet know how to live without him.

Well, they knew one thing, actually: how to keep lying.

The lie was so vast, so complicated, multiple industries—and every one of the Draft's esoteric departments—bent toward making it a reality, that it in turn bent my mind to have to look at it all day. It felt like a propaganda campaign designed to gaslight me specifically. With each update on the hero's progress ("unfortunately slow, but definitely positive!") I felt a little more like I had imagined it: the sounds he made as we dragged him through the depths of the prison, every pound of his wet flesh a key we needed to get through the biometrics and to Leviathan. I wondered sometimes if I had just made up the way the few fingers he could move above the surface of his flesh clawed at the air when we left him, blindly hunting for one last inch of violence. I clutched jealously at what I knew to be the truth, and relished being one of the relatively few people on earth who knew what his real situation was. At the same time, I felt perpetually furious, marinating in the Cassandra-like bitterness of knowing the truth while being unable to speak it. I refused to be manipulated by an entire comms strategy that felt specifically designed to destabilize me.

It was a strange time, living in a different world from almost everyone else on the planet. To the average person, Supercollider was wounded but recovering, and they had no doubt he'd make it in full. He'd been eaten by the Void Wyrms once, and had almost been lost in the Time Slime. He'd survived both encounters—and so much more—so of course he'd be back on the job. Not to mention that Leviathan, the biggest bad to have plagued superheroics in several generations, was "safely dead" and had been ever since Supercollider heroically slayed him on the grounds of his own evil Lair. So there was allegedly no true threat to either Supercollider's *or* the public's safety. They just needed to be patient. To hold the line. To keep believing. To hold on to those lies so tight they could mistake their own grip for proof.

IT'S EASY, EVEN as someone who has made it their life's work to ruin the lives of superheroes, to make the mistake of believing some of the Draft's lies. It's easy, for example, to think of heroes as autonomous entities, people acting on their own free will. The Lone Hero, struggling against the darkness. Someone set apart by their extraordinary talents and unimpeachable moral compass, making the kinds of decisions and doing the kinds of deeds mere mortals could never conceive of doing. This image is no accident. Heroes, and the forces behind those heroes, have worked incredibly hard to preserve that image of the individual hero or perhaps the found family of the superhero team, each their own little island of justice.

But the truth, as it always is, was much more bureaucratic and ugly. Heroes were never truly on their own, no matter what the propaganda would have you believe. Someone was funding the construction of all those secret bases and developing the technology for the cutting-edge gadgets; someone was training those heroes in the most advanced combat and interrogation techniques; someone was exposing them to just enough trauma to ignite their superpowers to full potential. That someone was, in fact, a *something*: a vast, multifaceted organization that found, formed, and supported every hero worth knowing. Behind every conveniently tragic backstory, every dead relative leaving a hero an untold fortune, every childhood best friend who was secretly an electronics genius making gadgets in their basement—behind them all was the Draft, the Department of Superheroic Affairs, crafting each hero's narrative to perfection. An incredible engine of lies, the source of the money and marketing, with a not-for-profit face and a paramilitary lack of soul.

Heroes might be built of lies, it but it was the Draft that constructed them.

Villains, while we are very good at lying with purpose, are on the whole much more honest. We wear our hatreds on our chests and scream them from the rooftops. We point to the people we loathe and declare them our enemies, and gleefully admit to the horrors we inflict on them. We calculate the damage our vengeance will cause, weigh the cost against our causes, and choose to do bad anyway.

At least, I do. And I have decided the harm is worth it. I've come to accept it and, eventually, revel in it. Because I know, at the very least, I am not a hypocrite. I own the harm I do. You won't find villains like me making moving speeches about justice and clemency while spiriting off our detractors to black sites.

(We'd still commit the abductions, of course, but at least we'd properly take credit for them.)

The role of the Villain, of course, is to fight the Hero. For each of us, for our own pitiful or glorious reasons, are cast as the Adversary, the opposing forces the heroes must fight in order to do good. We provide the schemes to be foiled, the disasters to avert, the victims to save, and the darkness to beat back. It's noble work, in its own way, fueled by enmity and our own personal ambitions and personal grudges. It's a pattern that has held since time immemorial. But for me, and for my boss, it was no longer enough.

After the defeat of Supercollider, Leviathan and I had stood next to each other and pledged our hatred to a new cause. We were ready to look beyond the heroes; it was time to fight the Draft. Leviathan had long been called "the monster lurking beneath the surface of the world," and if the Draft occupied the same position, just behind all the heroes, then the organization was the only true enemy worthy of him.

Of *us*.

His enemies were my enemies, and I'd bound the full force of my mind and malice to whatever cause he directed me toward. It helped that I had my own bones to pick with (not to mention flesh to take from) the Draft in the process and together, I thought, we would extract every ounce of revenge that we were due. And I knew what we were due—I am very good with numbers. I had meticulously calculated them, obsessively refined the figures of our malevolence. And more than anything, I wanted us to collect, together.

The problem was, in the days and months that followed, I found myself working almost entirely alone.

At first, there was a lot I enjoyed about targeting the Draft. It was work full of deep quiet and unstructured time to plot and balance equations to my dire heart's content. I could turn my entire focus on taking down the Draft brick by brick, secret by miserable secret. I could hone and refine, take all my blunt instruments and turn them into blades, so they might not even feel it by the time they were bleeding out. Sometimes there was nothing between me and the limitless hours to imagine every terrible thing I could dream happening to my enemies and see how I would carry that fate to fruition in perfect detail.

I ran the numbers and I laughed at where they fell. I studied each variable and decimal point like they were drops of poison and the tips of knives. I turned them over lovingly in my mind. I plotted. I came up with exquisite plans, beautifully choreographed and carefully balanced. For a time, I was content to let my mind loose like an army of termites into the foundations of the Draft and eat it alive.

But I grew increasingly frustrated. The plans took shape, yes, but I was never allowed to deploy them. I sent endless proposals to Leviathan for approval and was praised for every one, but he would never commit to putting any directly into action. The villains we sponsored could torment the Draft to their heart's content, and we could endlessly plan and plot and research, but he refused to give the go-ahead to launch anything substantial. At first, his excuse was that he wanted to watch "what harm they would do themselves." Who would fall apart, who would be fired, what systems would fail in the wake of Supercollider's defeat.

As time went on, though, that evolved to him waiting for the "right moment to strike," to an indeterminate and ever-shifting target. He wanted the data we collected and the reports we turned out, and above all else he wanted the plans we dreamed up to bring about their downfall.

He just would not act. And, worse—he would not let me act.

I was the one to bring him these plans—many of them my own, others the evil dreams of the rest of the Disruption team and our allies—and I knew he relished all of them with great pleasure. It was the only time I saw him that he seemed at all happy, as we went through the details of our latest iteration of his enemies' collapse.

But still he refused to let us put these great schemes into motion. He would cite some indefinable "right time" that never arrived, and disappear again into a fog of despair until our next meeting. It left all of us working for him in a special kind of liminal hell, unable to deploy the nightmares we created. Because *he* was the villain; we were there to serve his ambitions. So we could only polish and refine and fretfully wait, a legion of spreadsheet snipers with our fingers all on our formulas, waiting for the smallest bit of movement so we could release all the tension.

Except it wasn't coming.

I WAS OFTEN lost in a maze of my own frustration. I lost track of time more easily, falling into the cadence of watching, recording, pulling new bits of data and new tangles of falsehoods. Which was why I was already twenty minutes late when the steady vibrations on my desk penetrated my hyperfocus. I glared down at my phone, which I thought I had set to silent, and discovered I most certainly had—except for priority contacts and reminders . . . like the Friday morning Departmental Sprint Review.

The meeting I chaired every week.

"Fuck's *sake*." I threw my presentation laptop into a tote bag and hoped that 67 percent battery would be enough to carry me through it.

When I finally walked into the conference room everyone looked at me with expectant glee instead of annoyance. When I pulled the first few bags of candy out of my bag, there were unrestrained cheers. Bribery always worked.

"Fuck yeah, late candy!" A data analyst, Sanouk, happily reached for a small bag of mini eggs while I was still laying out treats in the middle of the table. It was a little ritual I'd developed as a way to balance the inevitability that I'd get lost in what I was doing; the later I was, the better the treats.

With the positive association between my tardiness and sugar reinforced, I waited for everyone to grab something before dragging their attention back to the meeting itself. It was a better than average attendance, with participants from Data, Research, Comms, Information & Identities, and my own Disruption team filling the seats. I'd been tipped off that the Data team had pulled off some solid skullduggery over the past week and asked them to go first, to set the stage.

"We have good news, great news, and . . . something else," said Molly, adjusting their plastic-framed glasses. They fired up a slide deck titled "The Stages of Grief; or, the Current State of Draft

Leadership." There was even a GIF of flowers sprouting next to a gravestone, so I knew this was going to be good.

"Let's begin with the great," I said. I opened a mini Twix and started gently separating the top layer of caramel from the cookie below with my teeth.

Molly nodded gravely. "Let's get this out of the way: Our strategies are working. The D is in the midst of a full-scale leadership meltdown. They're obviously being quiet about it, but it looks like a total shakedown and restructure of the C-suite positions and a good third of the directors."

"Fan-fucking-tastic, they'll finish our job for us," Jav said. I wondered if Jav sounded strangely flat or if I imagined it. I was focused on Molly, though, and would have to consider that another time.

"Who's in and who's out?" I asked, cartoonishly rubbing my hands together.

Molly nodded. "CDO and CVO are both stepping down; they're planning to stagger the announcements, but inside, it's all happening at once." The slide that accompanied this data point showed both of them looking downcast, making that strange, thin-lipped, puff-cheeked expression usually reserved for married conservative politicians whose Grindr profiles had just been discovered. The chief development officer, Stephanie Bulwark, apologized for nothing and looked vaguely pissed under the shame, while the chief vision officer, Michael Zhang, openly wept.

"Don't let their expressions fool you," Molly said, as though reading my mind. "Their severance packages are nauseating."

"I want copies," I demanded, and Molly nodded. "*Investigating* why they're being given golden parachutes is currently the top contender for your focus for the next two weeks," I said.

Molly nodded once and continued. "There's a lot more. Compliance is resigning, effective immediately. The chief branding officer position is safe for now, but there's been some chatter about a 'new role' being created for her in Marketing." Compliance was Draft code for "muscle," and their realm included security, enforcement, and any and all non-superpowered violence. After the complete disaster at Dovecote, I expected the now-former CCO would be out on his ass and was disappointed it was a resignation rather than an out-and-out shit-canning. He was broad, bullish man with an over-developed sense of Boomer entitlement, and I doubted he'd be missed. Nor did I think he'd learn anything from the experience. I wondered what role he'd fail up into next.

The fact that Branding would escape relatively unscathed matched my expectations as well; her work was exemplary. This would make all our jobs harder, as any worthy adversary would, but I couldn't suppress a little grudging admiration.

Molly continued. "Both the CTO and CIO have been offered 'early retirement' packages and have a week to accept. There's a new job listing being prepared for a chief mindfulness officer, so that's also going to go great, whatever that is about." A GIF of a brain exploding into a galaxy of sparkles accompanied the draft job posting.

I couldn't help snorting at that.

"Who's even left?" Darla had been diligently taking notes but looked up, their eyebrows so high they'd disappeared under their bangs.

Molly was physically incapable of taking a question as rhetorical if there might conceivably be an answer and started looking through their notes. "No one's mad at the CFO; sponsorships are as robust as ever, and that new partnership with 'defense technology innovators'–aka, weapons manufacturer Isengard–is flourishing. So Finance seems safe for the time being. Hmm. Marketing's coming out of this looking the best by a long shot. Oh, and their head of Communications is definitely going to be promoted, maybe moved in the process."

I nodded in grudging respect. "Their crisis comms are impeccable."

My team made little noises of annoyed agreement around the conference table.

"Who's in line for CDO?" I asked pointedly. Despite the bland title, the CDO was immensely powerful. Everything from screening kids for powers before puberty and interacting with their families to developing the curricula and running the training facilities that turned people with powers into supercops fell under their domain.

It was also the closest thing to a singular leader that the Draft had. The CEO position had been symbolically vacant for decades, a foolish gesture toward their commitment to rejecting the "rule of the individual." But no governance structure is truly flat, no decentralized power structure perfectly balanced, certainly not one as fundamentally rotted at its center as the Draft. The CDO position was always set apart, just by nature of the responsibilities assumed. They would always have more power and influence than their colleagues.

This, of course, also made them the largest target for me and mine.

Molly waggled a finger at me. "They're the 'something else.'"

I raised my hands apologetically. "Didn't mean to skip ahead."

They gave an uncharacteristic smile. "Let's pivot." Molly advanced quickly through the next several slides, a blur of official headshots and highlighted documents, until they found the slide on Development, with the CDO now on-screen.

"Stephanie Bulwark," Molly said, pointing at the picture, "is currently missing."

I sat up straighter. "Like, not showing up in reports? Or missing-persons missing?"

"The latter." Molly had selected a photo of Bulwark at a podium, speaking to one of the Draft's recent cohorts of baby superheroes. She was an imposing woman, powerfully built and incredibly intense. She had a kind of authoritative gravity about her that was like a physical force—even in a photo—and had been almost universally lauded for her liaising between superpowered kids and their parents and the Draft. She framed herself as a social worker while operating as ruthlessly as any military recruiter.

"How long?"

"Coming up on a week. Her staff is covering for her, but her assistant is getting antsy."

"A week and no one's reported it," I murmured. Molly, as they were wont to do, heard it and responded.

"Everyone's so terrified of her that they're afraid if they do, she'll immediately appear and destroy them for being too stupid as not to know she was officially sequestered for something."

"Is that possible?"

"That she's missing on purpose? Of course. The fact that no villain has claimed her kidnapping or murder—and we certainly didn't do it—means it's most likely Draft initiated, or she's wandered off on her own. Which is why this is the 'something else' category. Could be just some miscommunication and turmoil, but could be extremely interesting."

Molly started speeding through the slides backward now, picking up where we'd gone off course. "While this next—well, last—section is merely 'good,' that doesn't mean it's not juicy." They'd come to rest on a slide of three superhero teams. The photos were clearly part of their respective press packages, with all three sets of heroes in carefully choreographed poses and heroic scowls, contemplating the seriousness of their responsibilities.

"All these bands suck," one of the researchers said, and half the room laughed.

Molly cracked a smile. "You'll be pleased to know they all seem to be breaking up."

"Ah, very good," the researcher said, leaning too far back in his chair. He almost toppled over and scrambled to right himself.

"I recognize Siegeworks and Ossuary," I said. The former team loved the law enforcement aesthetic and had adopted charming names like Rubber Bullet and Tear Gas; the latter team were of the brooding, gothic variety who were all named after bones. The third, however, were entirely new to me. "But who are the other fashion disasters?"

"They're, uh, Atmosphere."

"What."

"They are called Atmosphere."

"What Captain Planet-ass nonsense is this?"

"They're very young, very earnest, and seem to have vaguely weather-themed powers."

"How unfortunate."

"The good news is all three teams have been called in and officially disbanded very quietly, no reasons given."

Someone from I&I, one of Menachem's new hires, openly cheered. Everyone hated Siegeworks.

"What makes it more interesting, in my opinion, is how little reason there seems to be." Molly advanced to a compilation of action shots. Siegeworks visiting a cop who was recovering in hospital; one of the Atmosphere heroes being presented with an award at their graduation ceremony from the Draft's shiniest new academy, the Workshop; the four Ossuary members being interviewed while several bedraggled, recently arrested henches were loaded into a van in the background. "They've all been active less than three years; Atmosphere were barely in action eighteen months. No obvious fuckups, by Draft standards, and no dramatic conflicts. None of them have really been tested, but they've at least performed at or above expectations."

I frowned in thought. "Do we think it's a power struggle? Are they someone's protégés, getting the boot along with their mentor?"

"Was someone unhappy with the fact that they were made in the first place, and is trying to undo that now?" Tammy added, and I pointed at her in approval.

"We don't know," Molly admitted. "But there's a lot of digging yet to be done here, if we wanted to. It's one of those things that struck me as just odd, and pleasant from our perspective . . ."

"But there could be a lot more going on under there," I said, finishing the thought.

"Bingo."

I rubbed a hand over my mouth, thinking. "I suppose I can't say 'I want you to follow all of these leads,' can I?"

"Not if you want a deep dive into any of them." Molly was firm, not apologetic.

"Alright. Digging into the CDO race—and what happened to Bulwark—are your priorities. After that, I want you to keep as close an eye as you can on the rest of the leadership situation, as that all shakes out. If you have any resources or time at all—"

"We won't."

I sighed. I knew they'd say that; I also knew they'd be correct. I pushed aside my instinctive irritation. "Okay, well, if anything changes, then, or if something gets weirder about the three teams, let me know and we can discuss a pivot."

Molly thought for a second, then nodded. "We can do that."

We spent the rest of the meeting strategizing. Eventually, we got too hungry to focus (chocolate alone can only do so much), and I adjourned. As we were standing up, I caught Jav's eye and inclined my head meaningfully. He gathered his stuff slowly, so in the end we were the last two in the room.

"Did I piss you off somehow?" he asked, grinning in such a way that I knew he didn't think he was in trouble at all.

I shook my head. "No, I'm afraid I'm going to have to ask how you're doing."

His face fell. "Come on." There were few people who hated talking about his feelings, even professional ones, more than my Excel Pervert. It was easier to check up on him when we worked out of the same office, but ever since I'd moved up and away, I wasn't able to keep an eye on his body language and energy level the same way as I had before. So I was forced to ask, which neither of us loved.

"Look, I can leave you alone if you want but you just seemed . . . less enthused than I expected."

He was quiet for a moment, considering. "Yeah, that's fair."

"Is everything alright? Have I pissed *you* off somehow?"

"I'd tell you if you had."

He was deflecting weakly, and I refused to let him. I just stared expectantly until he sighed and looked down.

"It's genuinely nothing. But. Well . . ."

"Tell me.

"This is just less fun."

"This?"

"Yeah. Like, trying to fuck up the relationships between the Draft board and their shareholders or whatever. This corporate stuff just . . . bores me a little. I mean, it's fine, and it's necessary."

"But you don't love it."

"I really miss ruining the lives of superheroes."

"We're still ruining their lives, just indirectly. The Draft—"

"I know. But it's not the same. This is so . . . impersonal. Three steps removed. I miss being able to *see* the impact. You know?"

I felt a little pang in my chest. "I miss it too." He looked up at me, startled. He hadn't expected that.

"Does that mean . . . you're ready? We can do something?"

The eagerness in his voice, the way his eyes lit up, almost broke what was left of my heart. I was going to have to let him down, again, by saying no. I dug my nails into the palm of my hand, trying to contain the surge of resentment that moved through me. As terrible as it was to have my own schemes and strategies held up again and again, it was just as bad—arguably worse—to have to let most of my colleagues think that the problem was *me*.

As much as I was in a state of frustrated agony waiting on Leviathan to dig his way out of his feelings, no one else actually *knew* that.

After his rescue, Leviathan had been adamant that only his closest inner circle be made aware he was still alive. I thought this meant a few days at first, while he recovered from the worst effects of his captivity and grieved missing Supercollider's defeat. But along with his refusal to act, his insistence on remaining "dead" dragged on much longer than I felt it should have. Most of my coworkers believed that our entire organization was being run by Leviathan's lieutenants, primarily Keller and me, and that we were limping along with what we had until I got my shit sufficiently together to unleash mayhem properly again. This meant I was constantly saying things like "As I've said before, we aren't currently equipped to act on our own" or "Our best strategy at the moment is relying on subcontractors" and other phrases that made me want to throw up in my mouth. And I found myself facing down another moment where I was going to have to say something like that again, to Jav, who deserved a lot more from Leviathan, and from me.

So instead, I said, "Can you look into these teams for me?"

He frowned, confused. "But you need me on the—"

"I need you exactly where I say I need you." He grinned at that. "Let's see what we can find. Even if it turns out they just sucked and are getting thrown out with the rest of the trash, it'll be fun to watch.

"Let's fuck up some superheroes."

"Whatever you say," Jav said, a brightness returning to his voice. He held the door for me, and as we walked back toward our offices, I thought there was a little more energy in his stride than there had been recently.

I found myself wishing that little pep talk had revitalized me as much as it did him; I wanted, more than anything, to tell him to do whatever his heart desired. To leak their nudes and browser histories, or give them E.coli before their next media appearance. But I couldn't. And that meant while I could dole out the odd morsel of dopamine for my subordinates, I was left clenching my jaw in frustration.

But I worked through that, for Leviathan. I found quiet victories to savor. And though I might not be able to do it openly, I took whatever shots I could. The media landscape might not be set ablaze by a Draft executive's infidelity being exposed to their long-suffering partner, or a promising junior administrator having their allegedly scrubbed social media accounts sent to their superiors, but it ruined their lives all the same. It threw wrenches in the Draft machinery. I took a lot of solace in that when the work just felt like wheels spinning in the mud: deserving lives were being ruined all the same.

I tried very hard to adhere to Leviathan's orders (or lack thereof), but there was only so much stillness I could tolerate. It was a wrestling match between obedience and ambition, and I allowed myself some creative interpretations of "following up" and "completing tasks already in motion." So it wasn't as if nothing was getting done. Especially when some of my earlier actions had set up prospects that couldn't be ignored.

We hadn't just released Leviathan when Quantum Entanglement and I blew several impressive holes in the walls of Dovecote while she fought Supercollider. In total, thirty-seven villains at the Supermax managed to escape. We didn't try especially hard to free any of them, but we did make a considerable mess and disabled most of the security, so aside from a few of the incredibly unlucky or uncreative or unpowered (the gadget-based villains), most of the residents saw their opportunity and ran for it.

As far as I knew, only two had been picked back up. Caiman, still wearing a prison jumper, made her way to the new workplace of her former second-in-command. They had double-crossed her and ultimately turned her in; the lieutenant did not survive the reunion. She had been almost gleeful after being caught, content with that particular revenge. The phrase "death-roll" showed up in most of the reporting and I turned down the opportunity to look at the crime scene photos. She let herself be taken relatively quietly, though cybernetically enhanced sharpshooter Deadbolt's kick lost a couple of fingers, so that there could be no doubt in anyone's mind who was responsible.

Geode, who was never very bright, got picked up soon after for "geology-related crimes."

That left thirty-five villains who found themselves suddenly back in circulation, most of their strongholds empty and staff dispersed, but nonetheless free to pursue their evil aims. And we were prepared, eager, even, to help anyone capable of significantly moving the needle on superhero lifeyear counts.

So one of the initiatives I spearheaded while Leviathan was on his emotional sabbatical was to put out a request for proposals, soliciting any villain (or villainous collective, if they were feeling spicy) for their best plots—not to be aimed at the heroes themselves, however, but at the organization that made and managed and controlled them. It wouldn't be Leviathan's organization alone who were tormenting the Draft, but many villains with fresh bones to pick over their recent incarcerations. I pitched it as a kind of thought exercise, a test of ingenuity and might, and we offered considerable material support for the best of them.

I was extremely proud of how the RFP turned out:

Taking on the Draft is like fighting a hydra. Not the fictional monster, but the little invertebrate that might be effectively immortal. If the problem was just that for every head you chop off, another grows back, that would be a difficult but simpler, solvable problem. We know how to cut off heads. But not this. Not the Draft.

Like the real hydra, essentially a tube and tentacles, the Draft have almost infinite regenerative properties. Because it's not just that a hydra can come back from any injury. Cut one in half, you get two little animals that will grow back whatever they're missing. Chop it in pieces, each segment grows into a new, complete hydrozoan of its own. No piece is too small or too specialized that it can't reorganize and rebuild itself; even a single cell can become a new creature.

That is the Draft.

It has no head. Instead, it is a mass of collaborative but competing departments, every decision made by committee, a horrific and complex process made entirely out of manipulation, intrigue, and vibes. It would be easy to assume it is a multiheaded monstrosity, pulled in different directions by the whims of the entire C-suite, but it is worse than that. It is more of a nerve net, a collection of impulses that could move its whole body when aligned. Removing any part is not enough; the whole thing has to be annihilated.

I don't know how many responses I'd actually expected. I wasn't sure how much weight the call would actually carry, signed by only my name, even on the company letterhead.

But I got replies. And, unfortunately for me, one of the good proposals came from Putrefy.

I STEELED MYSELF before walking into the conference room. I'd had the distinct displeasure of meeting Putrefy only twice before, just enough for a mutual dislike to gain traction.

Despite having the personality of week-old roadkill, he was very good at what he did, and had been a rotting thorn in the side of the B-tier superhero collective the Alchemists for most of his career. He had a proven track record, so setting him up was certainly to our advantage. With a final deep breath and a roll of my shoulders, I affected the most confidence I could and walked into the room.

Putrefy, in a slate-gray suit and nausea-green accessories, all but leapt to his feet when the door opened, then sank down in visible disappointment when he saw it was me.

"So it's true," he said before I could get to any pleasantries.

"I'd love to know how I've managed to disappoint you so much already."

"He really is dead."

I sighed deeply, as though this was an exhausting and painful conversation. "Did you think you'd be meeting him were he alive." I hoped my carefully practiced grief would conceal my amusement that he would think he rated a one-on-one with fucking *Leviathan*.

Putrefy scowled, sitting up straighter, haughtily offended. "I held out hope that had your former employer survived, he would do me the honor of taking this meeting to reveal himself." He huffed and brushed some imaginary lint from his lapel. I took a moment to arrange myself comfortably in a chair well away from him.

"Ah," I said, wistfully. "I'm afraid you'll have to make do with me."

He gave me a quick, sour smile. His teeth were too long. "One does what one must."

"Oh, come now, it'll be fine. Pleasant, even!"

"So you're . . . what. Administering the estate?"

This was not idle wheedling. He wasn't the first villain who was starting to get ideas about seeing just how much space there was in the perceived power vacuum. While I was not afraid of an attempted coup actually succeeding—Keller could handle almost anything and Leviathan would certainly rise from the grave if it was absolutely necessary—villains turning on each other was the last thing I needed.

"Carrying on the legacy is how I like to think about it."

"Mmm."

"But that's not why we're here."

"It isn't."

"We're here to talk about your proposal."

He leaned a little closer, conspiratorially. "I do have to say. The RFP? Great work."

"Thank you, I feel seen."

"Do you often work in the medium of corporate memoranda?"

"It's one of my favorites." I was starting to think he wasn't as awful as I remembered. "And I have to say, your response immediately stood out."

His response could only be described as preening. "Of course it did."

I bit back a smirk. "As a connoisseur of violence via inconvenience, 'give them all food poisoning' is a plot after my own heart."

He made a noise of disgust. "A gross oversimplification. Simply giving them"—he put the phrase in scare quotes—"'food poisoning' would not only have limited impact, but repetition would almost certainly lead to exposure."

"Oh yes, I got that—and did not mean to minimize. I just wanted to convey that I appreciate the . . . practicality of the idea."

He crossed his arms and settled back, visibly bristling less. "What, tired of plans to blow up the moon?"

I gave an exaggerated sigh. "Desperately bored of them. Also? Too many rays."

"Rays?"

"Death rays, freeze rays, giant orbital rays. You know."

"Ah yes. Big science guns."

I snorted. "Hate them."

"What about a good mind-control ray?"

"Mmm. I'm biased, had a bad experience once."

"Understandable."

"I do see how it's different," I conceded, "just not for me."

"But some nice old-fashioned listeria . . ."

"Now we're talking." I pulled up the proposal he'd sent on my tablet, looking for a specific quote that had stood out to me. "With that in mind, I want to hear more about 'cascading gastrointestinal distress.'"

He leaned back and waved a hand theatrically. "It's all about the timing."

"Go on."

"Obviously, if you're going after the Draft's catering, the problem can't all come from the same place."

"Of course."

"You have to distribute your interference among suppliers and events, but that's still not enough. You can't develop a regular cadence of incidents."

"Too predictable."

"And easier to recover from. You want to stagger the problems, then lay low for a while, make them think that everything is resolved." He snapped his fingers. "That's when you hit them with new strains from different sources in quick succession."

"Would you sync that up around a specific event, or do you think it's better to let tragedy strike completely randomly?"

He made a thinking noise. "I prefer randomness."

"Mmm."

"However." He leaned forward. "If you were careful, you could orchestrate that final flurry of contamination incidents to fall at a time when it would be quite terrible to find themselves short-staffed."

I nodded. "When everyone calling in sick would be a special kind of disaster."

"Exactly."

I nodded, pretending I hadn't already made up my mind. Finally, I smiled.

"What do you need?"

FOR A WHILE, I held things together. I managed our "independent contractors," inflicted pain (or at least inconvenience) on my enemies in whatever small ways I could, and managed my own feelings as effectively as I was able. I kept the teams running and the lights on and the paychecks signed. But it wasn't the logistics that failed first, and I didn't notice the first cracks until they started to leak.

It started with Tamara. Or, rather, it started in how I didn't notice how badly Tamara was doing. I was so wrapped up in my own work—and my complicated, ugly feelings that I had no desire to discuss with anyone—that I didn't notice she was getting quieter and quieter. She'd never been bubbly, exactly, but she was much more reliably pleasant and positive than I ever was, more so than most of the people I worked with on a regular basis. So when she stopped making eye contact and spoke more timidly, I wasn't looking up from my screen either, and the difference in her tone didn't register for a long time.

It took her walking into my office with the air of someone going to their execution for me to furrow my brow for the first time. She had a report in her hands, a survey of Draft press releases she'd been picking away at over the last few weeks, and I could see the edges of the pages trembling.

The tension gathered between us, and while I didn't fully understand it, I knew I wanted to defuse it immediately, so I said the very first thing that popped into my head.

"Whatcha got there, sport?"

Tamara didn't laugh at my cringeyness, as she had every right to, just stared at me, wide-eyed.

"Yeah, you're right, that was terrible," I said, maintaining both sides of the conversation as though she'd spoken and made fun of me.

"I wasn't—I didn't mean—" She couldn't seem to form a sentence.

"No, I know," I said. "Nothing is wrong, I just—"

Tamara took a shuddering breath and sank to the floor.

I got to her as quickly as I could and crouched down on front of her.

"Sit down, try to breathe. Do you need Medical?"

Tamara shook her head wildly and threatened to stand, but I gently shushed her back down. I looked at her gray face and the hand clutching the front of her shirt, and it dawned on me I was looking at a different kind of emergency than I originally thought.

"Look at me. Can you look at me?"

Tammy shook her head again, made a weird gasping sound and then started to sob.

I hunched awkwardly in front of Tamara while she tried to get her breathing under control with minimal success, making what I hoped were soothing sounds, telling her to take her time, do whatever she needed, her body knew what it was doing. She didn't answer me, but eventually I got a nod of acknowledgment. I tried to remember what had helped me the most the last time I had a panic attack. I asked her to notice things in the room, ordinary physical objects, things she could touch. Gradually her breathing deepened and slowed.

I fished a bottle of water out of my mini fridge and handed it to Tammy, told her to drink slowly.

She struggled with the cap. I took the bottle back and opened it for her, and then she dutifully took a small sip.

"Great job," I said, and immediately felt stupid.

While she slowly collected herself, one sip at a time, I got her some tissues and stood nearby, but not too close to be threatening or oppressive.

She risked a quick glance toward me, and I tried to talk to her again.

"Do you . . . want to talk about it?" Neither of us wanted this to be happening, but I tried very hard to be open to it.

"No," she whispered. "But. I guess. I have to?"

"You don't, you can just leave for the day—"

"No!"

I held up my hand to make it clear I wasn't threatening her.

"No," she said again. "I'm not—I'm fine. I don't want to leave."

"I understand."

I did not understand.

"What's stressing you out?" I gently prodded again.

"I'm not . . . doing anything."

"Okay."

"Like at work, I'm not doing anything."

"Is that your recent search history? Online shopping receipts?" I gestured toward the report that was on the floor next to her chair where she'd dropped it.

She made a coughing sound in place of a laugh. "No."

"You're here. You're showing up. Everything is fine."

Except that was the wrong thing to say; she immediately became agitated again, one hand gripping the fabric of her leggings.

"It's not—it *can't* be fine. We're not doing anything. Nothing is happening, the needles aren't moving—we're not—there's not—"

I held up my hands to gently encourage her to slow down.

"It's a weird time."

"We're failing," she whispered. She met my eyes for the first time, and she was clearly terrified.

"We are *waiting*." A little bit of confusion tinged the fear in her face. "I know it's weird right now; I'm feeling it too." I felt around inside myself for a minute, looking for all the discomfort and sharp edges that might help. "I hate being this still and quiet. It makes me anxious as fuck. But it's all about keeping our heads down and not raising suspicion. The quieter we are, the more successful we're being."

"Is that true, though? What are plans without execution? What are *we*? There's no point to us."

I risked a small smile at her. "I know it feels like that right now. But as soon as I can get things moving again, we're going to do our finest work. It's going to be fantastic."

"But until then . . ."

Rest is a weapon, I heard inside my head, in a warm, low, buzzing tone. "Until then we continue to plot and prepare, and when we can't, we rest so that when we can move again we'll be ready."

She was trying to hear me, I could see her struggling to hold on to the words, but they were slipping past her, not giving her purchase. "But what if." She looked away, not able to meet my eyes. "It looks like we're useless."

"No one here thinks that. We're all in the same boat."

"*They* might," she mumbled.

I cocked my head a little to one side. "Who is 'they'?"

While she tried to process the question, a shape for her panic was slowly coalescing in my head. "I want to be very clear, Tamara: no one is going to get angry with you for only doing the parts of your job you are capable of doing because of their explicit instructions and the circumstances. I promise."

She looked over my face carefully, trying to pull apart if I was fucking with her. I watched her, reverse-engineering the tension in her forehead, around her mouth, the tightness in her jaw, and imagining where it came from. "I know *you* won't."

I calculated the angles of the stress I found there and made a guess. "I know some places . . . aren't like this."

She flinched. "I'm sorry."

"It's fine, this isn't my first job either."

She nodded, like she remembered something. "Your old job . . . they fired you. When you got hurt. Right?"

"Yeah. They sent a fucking fruit basket to my hospital room and never filled out the unemployment paperwork."

"That's . . . brutal."

"What about you?"

She was quiet for a while, and went back to looking at the floor. "At my last place . . . It wasn't me, exactly. But I was in an elevator, and . . . Well, he was my boss, but I didn't know him, we'd never talked. He got in and was furious; the henches with him, they'd fucked up a job. They were talking about it before they got in but then went quiet." She folded her hands together neatly. "Then right before the door opened, he set one of them on fire."

I made a weird, hiccupping sound of shock. "With, like, lighter fluid?"

She laughed once, a single sad bark, but it was a real laugh. "No, he had some powers. Kindling. His name was Kindling."

The name struck a sour note. I'd met him at a networking event that ended up being a complete bust. I remembered thinking how uncomfortable his assistant looked all night, avoiding eye contact and flinching when he laughed. "I've heard of him."

"He wasn't very good."

"That's fucked up."

She shifted a little. "They put him out in the lobby. With a fire extinguisher. After the elevator stopped."

She wasn't entirely in the room with me when she said that. She was in that elevator, for those few seconds, listening to her colleague scream. She could smell it. Feel the heat. She was watching them run past her, falling, when the door finally opened, seconds that felt like years later, watching him roll on the ground until someone in business casual had the presence of mind to rip a heavy extinguisher off the wall and douse them in powder or foam. She was listening to them writhe and moan afterward, while a monster watched dispassionately, or maybe just walked away and went to have a three-drink lunch.

"That doesn't happen here," I said, hoping to anchor her in the present.

She looked back at me, snapping back into the present moment.

"I'll try and remember that."

"It's okay if you can't. I'll remind you whenever you want."

I kept her talking a little longer, letting her slowly put herself back together, sneaking in whatever assurance I could. Then all of a sudden she was more embarrassed than upset. I suppose that was at least something. I refused to accept her apology and insisted she'd done nothing wrong, and let her leave with as little fuss as possible.

It was suddenly very hard to return to my desk—I was pinned in place by an intense bolt of anxiety that wound its way into my stomach and coiled wetly around my guts.

As I groped my way back to my chair, I knew that I had to talk to Leviathan. Not schedule a meeting to go over a new proposal, not ask for his approval or opinion, but *challenge* him. His refusal to act, and even more so to engage with his staff, or even let me do so on his behalf, had moved beyond the frustrating into the actually harmful. If Tamara was having a panic attack in my office, she wasn't the only one who was starting to fray at the edges.

Standing up to him was a terrifying prospect. He hadn't spoken to me for weeks immediately after his rescue, and even after we had reconnected, he had remained much cooler and more distant than he'd ever been around me. Though he'd claimed to have "ascended" past his emotional reactions, he was still grieving deeply. And while that was so incredibly obvious to me, it was just as clearly *not* obvious to him.

More, while I was still one of the very few people he had direct contact with—like Vesper, Ludmilla, and Keller—I was called into his presence much less than I ever had been before. It made me question whether I had been wrong about what might have been between the two of us, something I had taken for deep, genuine caring. I remembered what it felt like when he affectionately wrapped his hand around my neck; or was it just possessiveness, a sense of ownership that had spurred him to rescue me? Whatever might have been there, it was unquestionably different now, distant and fractured. Without any certinty about his affection, having a difficult conversation was a lot more frightening a prospect than it had been in a long time. I'd told Tammy that it wasn't like that here, that she didn't have to be afraid, but then wondered if I believed it myself.

I sent an email to his assistant, requesting his first available time slot for a personal conversation, trying not to think of the smell of burning hair.

IN THE MEANTIME, I did what else I could to improve morale. It had been a long time since I'd spent off-the-clock time with the members of my original team. Too long. It was easy to just let one day bleed into another, working until I was too tired to keep going and then watching pirated premium television on my phone until I fell asleep. I was no longer working in my old goblin hovel of an office, surrounded by the sounds of the team typing and talking to themselves as they planned to do terrible things to superheroes. I was now in a beautiful, custom-built suite with multiple monitors and a door that locked, several floors away. All those little incidental moments of contact didn't happen anymore; neither did the spontaneous invitations to grab a drink or just walk part of the way back to our apartments together. I realized I had to make it happen, so a few days later, after what felt like a respectful amount of time, I startled the crap out of the team by appearing in person and inviting them out to dinner.

"This is one hundred percent not about work," I told them, after we'd gotten menus and ordered drinks. "Like, obviously if you have a burning question or something, go for it, but—"

"Did the lizard make it?" Darla blurted out.

"Who?" I squinted at them, as I thought that would help me hear them more clearly over the noise in The Hole. The place had been remodeled since the last time heroes had trashed it, and in the process renamed from Dr. Willicker's Wholistic Wonder Bar to the Holy Carnation, all of which meant no one stopped calling it The Hole.

"You know, the lizard."

"Chameleon, the shape-shifting little guy? Was something wrong with him?"

"No, the pet lizard." They leaned closer and said more quietly, "Leviathan's."

Jav and Tammy had been having their own conversation, but both snapped to attention as soon as Leviathan gossip was about to take place.

"Oh! Right, of course. Shannon."

"That's her fucking name!" Jav said, slapping his leg. "I couldn't remember."

Tammy looked disgusted. "You forgot Shannon's name."

"I kept thinking Susan, but I knew that was wrong."

"Obviously," Tammy said.

Darla glared at both of them to shut them up. "Yes, that one; now, *is she alive*?"

I nodded and took a long swallow of winter melon bubble tea. "She's fine, yeah. A couple of her staff carried her out and kept her safe off-site until everyone was called back."

Darla was visibly relieved. "I was so anxious."

"Iguana's got staff," Jav muttered. "I don't have staff."

Tammy poked him in the arm. "You want someone to make sure your enclosure's temperature is properly regulated?"

He looked at her haughtily. "As a matter of fact, I do. It's a bit drafty where I sit."

"I thought she might have been left behind," Darla said, trying again to ignore them.

I shook my head. "There was a whole contingency plan for her. They drill and everything."

"Like part of the standard hero drills?" Jav was swirling the last of his Tom Collins and ice in the bottom of his glass, contemplating ordering another.

"Yep. She doesn't love being carried around or anything, but she's not a biter, and they made sure she was comfortable enough with someone scooping her up when a lot of activity and loud noise was happening, so she wouldn't freak out."

"I just have to toss some hard drives in a vault, not wrangle a damn iguana."

"Honestly," I said, "I think the support staff have the roughest jobs of all of us."

"Here, yeah." Tammy said it quietly.

I nodded. "I do mean here. I think in most places 'roughest' is equivalent to 'how much close proximity you have to the villain.'"

"Under other circumstances, that'd be you, then," Jav said, grinning at me. I threw a squished lemon wedge at him.

"But under these circumstances," I said, still glaring, "I think it's got to be the custodians and the servers."

"Why them?" Darla asked. I was watching Tammy carefully, making sure this conversation wasn't upsetting her too much. While Tammy looked watchful and uncomfortable, it was a manageable kind of tension from what I could see.

"Aside from the usual stuff—it's hard work, it can be boring and repetitive, you get treated like you're less than or invisible by assholes in your vicinity, all the classic service role garbage—first of all, it's weird."

"You just said it was boring and repetitive."

"And weird."

"Uh."

"Like you're mopping the floor here or at a bank, same basic job, right? But what about after Mucosa comes over for a meeting? Now you're cleaning up secretions."

Everyone at the table gave a small shudder.

"Right. Boring but weird."

"Same job, different circumstances." I sucked up a stubborn boba through the wide plastic straw. "And they don't even get to be evil in the process."

"Uh, I think if you're sponging up a supervillain's snail mucin, you know what side you're on."

"Oh, sure, but you're not, like, *evilly* cleaning the snail mucin."

"The job itself isn't about evildoing."

"Exactly." I laid a hand on my collarbone. "Unlike me, or anyone else at this table, who has the opportunity to channel their worst and their best into their jobs every day. I get to express all my terrible qualities as part of my job description."

I tapped the table in front of Tammy, and made eye contact when she looked up, startled. "Why did you take your first villainous job? Be honest."

I saw her brain scramble for a reason, something that made a good origin story. And then I saw her abandon it, and with a sigh and a bit of weariness creeping into her face, she told me the truth.

"Student loans," she said, picking another bit of citrus off the rim of her cup and dropping it onto the table.

"A classic." I nodded. "Making payments and watching that balance stay the same."

"I fucking wish." A rare anger flashed across her face. "The balance kept going up."

I grimaced. "Even worse."

"And then I saw this ad for a PA job that paid, like, two and a half times what I was making, for a few less hours, and they had a debt counseling program."

"No shit. Who was that with?"

"Visigoth. I mean, it was a bad deal for other reasons—they bought your debt from the creditors when you enrolled so it was a lot harder to get away. But they were honest about it."

I almost admired aloud how smart that was, but caught myself.

"It was an awful job." She took a sip. "In a lot of ways better than what I'd had, though."

I nodded, then elbowed Jav gently. "What about you. How did you start building diabolical spreadsheets for the unworthy."

He grinned at me. "I have a bad answer."

"No such thing."

"It's going to sound fake."

"Try me."

He made us wait another moment, adjusting his posture and stretching like he was about to do something physically strenuous.

"I worked for a bank for a while."

"You. The Excel Pervert."

"Yeah, exactly. Banks have a lot of internal processes that need people exactly like me."

"Alright."

"I was working mostly with mortgage brokers and their systems—and I got real familiar with their internal mortgage-approval algorithm."

"Did you, like, steal it?" Tammy was already invested in the fanfic she was writing in her head.

Darla slammed a hand dramatically on the table. "Jav, did you rob a bank?"

He rolled his eyes at us. "Come on."

"So you found an algorithm—that is your origin story?"

"You know those things are racist as fuck," I said.

He pointed at me. "They are racist as fuck. And you are both correct *and* you both stole my punch line."

"Sorry! I didn't know that was it!"

"Well, it was, and it was enough. I'm, like, doing the thing I'm supposed to be doing, fucking going to work. I sometimes need a suit for doing all this white-collar-respectability-politics shit, and these fuckers are doing real-ass actual evil all the time, either deliberately or accidentally because they're both greedy and don't know how to open a pdf without help."

"So you stole it."

He looked disgusted. "*Please.* I started working on my own algorithms that were at least transparently evil instead of pretending to be all virtuous."

A server came to the table and we all took a moment to order another round and a sampler platter of whatever deep-fried things they had on the menu. There was a pause after they departed while we all imagined which pieces of fried dough or battered vegetable we were going to eat first.

"To be clear," Jav said, like he'd just remembered something, "I also stole it."

"I am trying to imagine you as a banker and I am having a really hard fucking time," I admitted.

He raised an eyebrow at me. "Next time you need someone to put on a suit and be charming for no reason, hit me up, and I'll show you."

"Deal." I looked over at Darla. "Alright, your turn."

They made a face and hunched their shoulders, clearly hoping I'd forgotten they had yet to contribute. "It's boring."

"Dude, I had student loans," Tammy said, rolling her eyes at herself.

"I wanted a couple more bucks an hour while not putting on pants," I said.

"Yeah, but you have a proper origin story now."

"This is not about me, Darla—don't change the subject, and tell us your terrible past."

They sighed, resigned to us not letting them weasel out of the conversation. "You're going to make fun of me."

"Oh, probably."

"I mean, I needed some dental work and while I pretend insurance was why . . . in reality, there was a boy."

"That's not so bad," Tammy said.

"Yeah, I was bracing for something really stupid and egregious."

"Trust me, it was both."

"As are most relationships. So, what, was this a handsome piece of Meat, or . . ."

"No, we were, like, doing this night class on technical writing together, and he was always stepping out into the hallway to take calls on his phone. Which was much more annoying than it was mysterious, and one day I called him out on it in the hallway, like 'why do you always take this class if you spend half the time on your phone.' And he looked mega-guilty, and admitted that it was for work, he was on call, and I felt like a complete asshole."

I thought about all those months Greg spent doing on-call tech support for villains, how we could barely have a conversation and certainly not even grab breakfast without him being interrupted a thousand times by someone who didn't know how to reboot their own death ray. I felt a pang of guilt—it had been a long time since I'd spoken to Greg, not since we'd been back at the rebuilt office. I thought of his confused face the last time I'd seen him, being driven away from the safe house. I made a mental note to catch up with him.

"So I bought him a coffee to apologize, and we kind of hit it off," Darla was saying.

"And he slowly brought you over to the dark side."

"No, fucker hid it from me for months! Eventually we moved in together and he couldn't anymore and he admitted that he was doing remote phone fraud for one of The March Hare's side hustles."

"He's the one who gets super pissed if you make a White Rabbit reference around him, right?" Jav asked.

"Him having a meltdown about it at the Christmas party was an annual tradition, yes."

"So what happened when you found out?" I said.

Darla slid a little lower in their seat. "I was really pissed. But he offered to get me a job. I'd been looking and having a hard time anyway, it was mostly why I moved in with him, so I . . . took him up on it."

"And that was it, huh?"

"Honestly?" They took a sip of sangria to fortify themselves. "It was the best job I'd ever had, to that point. Coworkers were hilarious, we hung outside of work all the time, and they even had a monthly Tea Party that was catered."

"Aw, that's nice!"

"So whatever happened to Hench Charming?" Tammy asked.

"His contract ended and wasn't renewed . . . then mine was and he couldn't handle it."

I could practically taste the toxic masculinity from here. "Ah, tale as old as time."

"He wanted me to quit in solidarity, I didn't want to, and that was the end of that romance. Kept the job—and the apartment—for two more years, though. Then came here."

"That was way better than I was expecting based on your preamble," I said encouragingly.

"Yeah," they said, perking up. "I wish he'd been better, but the journey wasn't so bad."

"That's a three out of ten origin story. Not enough trauma," Jav said.

I glared at him. "Rude."

Darla gave a theatrical sigh. "But Jav's right, isn't he? I have barely any excuse to be a menace to society at all."

"Don't listen to the guy who worked in a *bank* over here," I said, and pressed on over Jav's protests. "It's funny to think how small those steps are. Like, such a small nudge in a different direction and any of us could have been one of the good guys." As I said this, I peered in the general direction of the kitchen, hoping to catch a glimpse of our sampler platter as it made its way to our table. When I saw the tray in our server's hands, I sat up a bit straighter.

Jav scowled at me. "You're getting philosophical again."

"Sorry."

"No, you're not."

WHILE I MIGHT have been able to assuage my team's immediate anxieties about their safety and well-being—mozzarella sticks are surprisingly good for morale—I faced the looming threat of my meeting with Leviathan, where I was determined to confront him for all these months of disengagement.

I was a little surprised by how quickly my invitation to a meeting was accepted; I was still at the restaurant when my schedule updated. Which meant for the next week, every time I looked at my calendar and saw "L +A," a shiver of anxiety ran through me. I couldn't tell if it was good or not.

I rehearsed over and over what I was going to say to him. I had to convince him it was time to resume his role as the archnemesis of the superheroic world. I would talk about how his enemies had breathed too easily for too long, mistakenly believing that before he was "injured" in the "jailbreak," Supercollider had slain the monster lurking beneath the surface of the world for good. But while their Saint George was out of commission, the Dragon was very much still alive, as viciously imaginative and horrifically powerful as he'd even been. All he had to do was expose one of the Draft's crucial lies, and reclaim his position as the great bane of the self-important and cape-clad. I even practiced my speech to him in front of a mirror, carefully controlling my expression, so he would see enthusiasm instead of anxiety.

Under all that healthy fear, I was also just worried about him. For all Leviathan's posturing, the primordial terror himself was having a pretty bad time of things, emotionally. He made a show of relishing the fact he held the truth, enjoying immensely being in sole control of the sword dangling above the Draft's collective heads. And while this may have been part of our extended period of dormancy, I knew it was not the primary reason for it. That he was still grappling with the immense grief of the loss of his nemesis, and it was a fight that he was not winning.

I had given him as much space as I could, and tried to let him heal at his own pace. It hurt to have so little contact with him, but there was also a sense of relief. Since the day we rescued Leviathan from Dovecote, things between us had been . . . strained. Quantum had tied up the hero's body like a sailor making knots out of rigging, and when I (and the Meat who helped me) dropped that sodden mass of skin and misery at his feet, I meant it as an offering. A gift. I wanted to give him the thing he wanted most in the world.

It turned out I had instead taken it from him.

Captive, vulnerable, he had been unable to free himself, unable to triumph over his single greatest adversary. He was at his weakest, possibly in decades, and at that moment, he had to confront the fact that not only had he failed on multiple counts, but now that victory would never be possible.

He wasn't the only one with a claim on Supercollider. Quantum deserved to shred him down to his atoms too, of course. She deserved the catharsis of pulling him like taffy, ruining the rest of his life and career. I also deserved my own piece of him. But whether or not we were a deserving instrument of reckoning didn't make the experience of that loss any less painful for him.

It was out of respect for that pain I hadn't pressed him up until that point. I wanted to avoid causing him any additional stress, lest it block whatever healing he was doing and damage our already tenuous relationship further. But after the incident with Tammy, I took a long look at myself and my colleagues, and knew that some pressure was necessary.

IT WAS IMPOSSIBLE not to get anxious approaching the massive doors to his office. They were as huge and imposing as the doors of a cathedral, and I felt as intimidated as any sinner in front of them. I couldn't tell, in that brief, eternal moment before knocking, whether I was so relieved to finally see him again, or whether I would have given anything to put off this reunion even further. In the moment, the feelings were eerily similar, a cold longing, like a coin still flipping through the air that had not yet chosen on which side to land.

I crossed the threshold and immediately made the terrible mistake of consciously thinking about what I should do, rather than letting my muscle memory take over. Did I usually cross the entire room immediately, or wait by the doors until he acknowledged my presence? Did I speak first, or clear my throat to draw his attention, or was he the one who broke the silence first? I ended up second-guessing myself, repeatedly stopping and starting again as I made my way across the room to his desk. I found myself clinging to my cane hard, just to give my hands something to do.

Leviathan watched me as I walked toward him. He was eerily still, his chitin a dark shape in the already dim room. He'd kept the lights lower after his captivity than he had before; very bright lights were one of the few things that could hurt him, and they blasted his cell with every lumen they could every moment that the Draft had him. The lower lighting made the space feel more intimate and more threatening that I remembered, which made me even clumsier than I usually was. While he stared at me with all of his usual distance and dignity, I had no idea what to do with any of my limbs.

I tried to will myself not to show any outward signs of my incredible embarrassment, which I am sure was wildly ineffective. When I came within a reasonable distance I just held still, waiting for him to speak and save me from myself. Of course, he left me hanging, his head tilted slightly in alien curiosity, so I gave up and initiated the conversation myself.

I swallowed, which somehow made my voice more scratchy, not less. "Thank you for making time for me; I know it is extremely valuable."

"Do not waste it with formalities," he said. He may not have meant it as threatening as it landed. But he may have. "What do you need?"

I had intended to approach the subject sideways, more diplomatically, but he'd both frightened and irritated me into bluntness. *You*, I wanted to yell. *I fucking need* you. What I said wasn't too far off.

"We need to start taking direct action against the Draft," I said.

He left the space for a sigh, but didn't make any noise. "As I have told you, the time is not–"

"I have to disagree,"

He tilted his head. "Do you."

There was a threat there, but I stepped over it. "Your teams are struggling. We are holding course, but it is difficult. Your apparent death is deeply troubling to everyone. We need to be *doing* more, and they need to know they are being led."

I seemed to have finally got his full attention. "Do you not often counsel patience?"

"Yes. But this time we are playing *too* passive; we have evaluated their threat surface many times over, and we should start taking shots."

He regarded me for a moment. "And why now? What has inspired this particular petition."

I tried to find a way to say *you are stressing everyone the fuck out right now* that I would survive.

I went with: "I believe the Draft are beginning to stabilize. Their leadership is still in turmoil, but the restructure has already begun. We are at risk of losing our window. We can't let them regain too much balance. And all the while our own people are feeling increasingly lost."

He was utterly unmoved. He drew in a breath as if to dismiss what I had just said.

"The lack of action and clear direction is having a negative impact on morale," I said quickly. "Your employees are deeply impacted by your absence."

He made a dismissive sound. "They don't need me. Every part of the organization can function fully independently, whether I am present or not."

"But without your presence and guidance, the organization is—"

"You make it sound as though I have abandoned my post." I flinched internally. "Yet here I am, hand on the wheel."

Which no one can see, I thought. "I don't mean to say you aren't performing your duties."

"Then say what you mean."

"They can function, yes. And you are leading—in secret."

"Yes."

"But they need to *see* you. They need *you*."

"I am disappointed. I thought you, of all my lieutenants, would best understand the value of holding an advantage."

I should have been more frightened than I was; disappointing Leviathan was a dangerous thing. But there was something odd in the way that he said it, like he was trying to sound more threatening than he felt, so I would leave him alone. It gave me the courage to push harder.

"I don't want to disappoint you," I said, with a patience I did not feel. "And I *do* understand. However, most of your staff don't have the same level of comprehension. They can't."

That seemed to mollify him. "Don't concern yourself with their shortcomings. I don't require their understanding, only their obedience."

He turned slightly away from me, indicating that the conversation was drawing to an end.

Feeling more desperate, I reached down and tried to find a different kind of appeal, a more honest one, even if it would be more vulnerable.

"I *am* struggling, though."

His eyes snapped back to me. "Then I ask again, what do you need?"

"I want to—I wish I was serving you better."

That seemed to irritate him. "Your performance is exemplary. You know this."

"I don't need an employee evaluation."

"Then what is it?"

"I want to see all of our plans to come to fruition, like you promised."

"They will."

"I want us to destroy the Draft. Together. Just as you said."

"We will." It sounded so empty, almost hollow.

"I am starting to worry that all these beautiful plots will start to rot and wither before we can make them real."

"You are not one to fret."

"I'm actually very good at fretting." I'd hoped to squeeze a drop of amusement from him, but nothing. So I pressed on, refusing to allow too much silence to gain momentum. "I want us to work more closely. As we have in the past. I want to be doing this *with* you, not just for you."

"Stop. Continue to do what you do best. Serve me as well as you always have. Stay on your own path and I will stay on mine."

Frustrated defeat clenched a fist in my chest. "If those are my orders."

"They are."

I swallowed. "In that case, that's all I had to speak to you about."

Something changed in him then, a small softening in his shoulders. And he didn't turn around. So instead of leaving, I waited.

"We have not . . . spoken much." He let the words hang there, as though wishing them to convey more meaning than they could possibly hold. "Of late."

"No. We haven't." I stared at my hands, gripping the handle of my cane. I found myself wishing feverishly that I could phase myself out of the room, out of reality, like Quantum could. Whatever was about to happen, whatever excoriation of our respective emotional states was about to occur, was something I was wholly unprepared for.

"Why is that." He was observing me, in the wary, scientific sense, as though he had just combined some volatile compounds and was not yet sure what reaction was about to occur. I had no idea where he would want to take this, or why he would bring it up—his emotions were unfathomable to me—but some deep-seated instinct told me that wherever it went wouldn't be good. No matter how this conversation went, once it was started it could never be undone.

"I don't think this is a good idea," I said.

I'd never seen the expression that moved over his face before; he looked confused, and unsure if he should be affronted. It was the closest thing to an outright no I had ever said to him. I briefly considered softening my earlier words but resisted. I did think it was a bad idea and he needed to know that before proceeding.

"I am not sure by what measure you are defining 'good,'" he said, infuriatingly, "but I believe that it should happen."

I felt my lips break into a tiny smile. Even now, scared and irritated and certain that things were about to go very badly, the way he said everything was just so *weird*.

"If you think it should happen, then . . ."

He nodded, recapturing some authority over the situation, but I recognized a bit of relief in the way he set his shoulders. He walked forward and ushered me over to a chair near his desk, gesturing for me to sit. He came to stand quite close to me, his hands clasped behind his back, in a position that would have seemed supplicating in almost anyone else.

He spent a long time staring past me, at the wall; in a recessed nook there, like one that might hold the statue of a saint, and illuminated from above by a single small light, were the remains of Entropy's shattered mask. I imagined he must be staring at it, as he often did to focus.

"Things have not been the same," he said.

"I think there is a second clause beginning with 'since' that is missing from that sentence," I said.

He flinched, and turned to hide it. I watched him struggle around the words he needed to use. "Since you—since my imprisonment and return."

I disliked the choice of words, as though he had freed himself, but I left it alone for the moment. "They haven't," I agreed.

"I don't like it."

I blinked. There was something very bare and vulnerable in those four words, in their simplicity, that was deeply unlike him. I swallowed hard, and decided that if he was going to try, I would too, even if it was stilted.

"I don't like it either."

"We should." A pause. "I would like to—attempt to—move past these difficulties."

My throat started to tighten. "I am not sure—" I cut myself off and took a breath. "That will be challenging."

"I am prepared for that."

Something bubbled up to the surface, something I didn't immediately recognize as anger. "I am not certain that you are."

His mandibles rippled. "Are there consequences you think I have not anticipated?"

I chose my next words very carefully. An ugly emotion was welling up in my chest like black sludge, but for the moment my self-preservation was still intact. "Once we have this conversation, we can't . . . un-have it. At the end you might find something you would rather not know, and there will be no way to take it back."

That seemed to calm him somewhat. He straightened. One of his hands swept around to the front, and he posed as if holding an invisible orb lightly in his fingertips. "There is nothing I would rather not know." It was clear he assumed my concerns were ordinary human nonsense, from someone who was still capable of finding knowledge frightening. It was frustrating he still did not know me well enough.

I gave up on my attempt to protect him from whatever awful emotional hot spring was now active in my body. Whatever conversation he wanted this to be, we would both have to live with the consequences.

"Alright."

He returned his hand behind his back and turned more fully toward me. "When you first saw me, as my captivity ended, I comported myself . . . quite badly. There were, of course, extenuating circumstances, but that is explanation and not excuse." He paused for a moment while he turned his next words over, like coins. "Clearly, my behavior that day has had a negative impact on the way you perceive me."

I stared up at him for a long moment; I wanted to ask him if he was joking, but I knew he wasn't. He had so deeply, so profoundly missed the point, and the weight of it was so painful, that I almost wished he was fucking with me on purpose rather than being so far away from what I meant.

"You are . . . spectacularly wrong." It seemed like someone else was speaking using my mouth.

He stayed very still. "How so?" His voice was completely calm, but I couldn't tell if it was genuine or dangerous; I decided to proceed as though it didn't matter.

"Just to make certain I understand: you believe that I think less of you, because I saw you at a weak point."

His whole body tensed. I watched him fight past the word "weak" in order to answer me. "Correct."

"That's not right . . . at all."

He looked over me carefully. In just a few moments he'd gone from standing over me protectively, almost humbly, to looming. "It's a perfectly logical conclusion."

"No, it's not."

We stared at each other. Neither of us were used to me being this combative. I pressed forward quickly, while he was still a little off-balance, before he could wrestle complete control of the conversation away from me again.

"You were exhausted and grief-stricken. Your emotions were overwhelming and complicated. You behaved the only way you could. No one can tell you what an appropriate reaction would have been, including you, because it doesn't exist. I understand, and deeply respect, those feelings." I paused briefly, but when I caught him stirring to speak again, I added, "I would never think less of you for that."

He was struggling to grasp what I was saying. I could see him trying to hold the words, to find a grip in them, but he couldn't manage it. He couldn't imagine that I was telling the truth, so he dismissed it when he couldn't find purchase. "Your behavior toward me would suggest otherwise."

I gritted my teeth; he would not turn this around on me. "The only one whose behavior has changed has been yours."

He did not like that at all. "I have been nothing but professional since my return."

"You have been *absent* since your return."

"I have not so much as left the compound."

"I mean with *me*. It's been months and you've barely written me an email."

"Had you requested a meeting, I would have accepted it."

He was really starting to piss me off. "You asked me for privacy during your convalescence, and I respected that."

"I did not want to see anyone."

I shifted my cane in my hands to force myself to loosen my grip. "Are you genuinely saying you have not been avoiding me."

"Neither have you sought me out."

"I *did* seek you out." My voice was definitely raised now. "I moved the world to get to you. You have no idea what it took, because you never asked me or tried to find out. I don't have your resources or your powers, and I risked everything I had, everything that everyone had, over and over again.

"For *you*."

This was not how I had ever wanted this conversation to go. I wanted it to be about the organization, not me. I paused for a moment to breathe, to try to keep some control of the awful feeling that was taking over my body. Like an upswell of sludge, the horrible anger there felt like it was leaking out of my eyes and bubbling out of my throat. In those moments I expected him to end the conversation, to kick me out of his office immediately—or worse—but he was still. He was watching me with a weirdly detached, almost academic interest that did nothing but make me even angrier.

I decided, one last time against my better judgment, to keep going. As I did, I wondered if this might be the last chance I'd have to say anything to him ever again.

"I know the way . . . things happened was awful for you. I can't imagine what that felt like. But it *also* feels awful that you resent me for it."

His mandibles twitched; I had come to recognize that particular movement as something akin to a brow furrow. "Preposterous. I gained respect for you."

"You've barely looked at me since I found you."

My voice wavered. I tried to keep it steady, but I was suddenly dangerously close to tears. I dropped one hand to my lap, dug my nails into my leg to distract myself, to try and keep the tightness in my throat from reaching my eyes. Luckily, while I was fighting myself, I could see he was completely taken aback and had no idea how to respond. I took advantage of the moment and, with a colossal effort, regained my composure. I still felt deeply unsteady, but at least I also felt like I could speak again without making a complete fool of myself.

"I don't know exactly what created this . . . rupture. I don't know if it was because you feel I stole something that you thought would be a moment of glory; or because I engineered the downfall of someone you hated so much; or if I succeeded while you were failing. But it's clear to me your feelings for me changed in that moment. And I . . . hate it. It has been very painful for me. Any . . . distance that you feel, it is only because you asked for it first. Then I stayed away because I did not think I was welcome back."

After the last words spilled out, I felt a deep exhaustion. The anger slowed from a thick torrent to a trickle, and as it cooled it felt a lot more like anguish than rage.

Leviathan, for his part, sat completely still. Whatever he expected from me, it was absolutely not this. Maybe he thought I'd admit, under some pressure, that I did think less of him after he wept in the basement of Dovecote when I threw Supercollider at his feet, that he seemed pathetic in that moment and the image of him then now superimposed itself over him every time I looked at him. But that was a lie I would not tell him even if it would have been easier. Cruelty he could understand. This raw emotion? He had no idea what to do with it.

So he seized the only part of it he could cling to, the only shape that fit and made sense to keep him afloat: something he could be insulted by.

"You are mistaken. I am incapable of such weakness; the implication is disrespectful." His voice was hard but hollow; he was trying to protect himself with anger but could not quite shore up the necessary emotion.

I, on the other hand, had no problem summoning the necessary anger. I would not let him invalidate my entire experience of the last several months to make himself feel better. "That isn't what's happening," I said.

"Are you saying I am lying?" He sounded much calmer; this was now becoming dangerous.

"I think you are deceiving yourself."

"Is that a yes?"

I looked him straight in the eyes.

"Yes."

"Do not tell me what is going on inside my head."

Anything I might say now was a roll of the dice; I had no idea how he would react or what the larger consequences might be. But just like I had foreseen, now that the conversation had begun it couldn't be undone, and I felt a kind of momentum fused with panic, like I would not be able to stop it now even if I tried.

But I tried, my god, did I try. As calmly as I could, I said, "This is what I do. I see patterns. They help me understand how things work, and I have come to understand, in part, how you work. I think in this very specific situation where you're just—where you're hoping to annihilate your feelings, and denying they exist—I might have a better idea of your emotional landscape than you do."

He stared at me, his eyes both furious and carrying a kind of venomous disappointment. "You think so little of me."

"What?" I was completely at a loss.

"You think I am capable of this . . . pathetic response."

"I think you are in incredible pain."

"And you think I am frail enough that I would respond to something as meager as pain this way."

I took a breath. "I think I have a great deal of evidence to suggest that either you are reacting because of grief, or because—you no longer feel about me as you once did." I swallowed hard, and fought down the tremor that desperately wanted to take over my voice. "I find the idea of the latter too difficult. I am hoping it is the former."

"This conversation is over."

I sat very still for a long moment, staring at my hands rather than meeting his eyes. I'd been waiting for this moment, bracing for it, even, but when the walls came down and he ended the conversation in my most vulnerable moment, it still set my chest on fire. I wasn't sure whether it was rage or screaming panic that ignited somewhere between my ribs, but whichever it was, the feeling was awful.

I tried, for longer than I should have, to come up with some kind of a response, a protest, but nothing emerged. There was nothing inside me but knives and heat and bile, and I was sure I would deeply regret anything that came out of that place. I was also not sure if I would survive it. Eventually, I gave up. I nodded once, stood, and made my way to the doors, never looking at him.

I didn't flee the room, but I walked quickly, needing to put whatever little distance between us that I could. I didn't trust that, if I waited too long or fumbled too much, I wouldn't be able to control myself and would say something awful. I did take my time at the doors, forcing myself to carefully work the mechanism and leave as gracefully as I could, so I wouldn't flail or stumble as I was walking away from him.

I knew what it felt like to be near Leviathan when he was angry. I had felt it before, the way fury radiated off him like heat from an incandescent metal bar. But that anger had never been directed at me. It was now. I could feel the heat on my back as I left; when I ran my hand over the back of my neck, safely on the other side of the doors, I expected to find blisters.

I groped my way to my apartment on autopilot and sank into the couch, almost afraid to move even in that place of relative safety. I didn't know how I was supposed to face him again, not after I'd shown him an ugly part of my soul in an attempt to appeal to whatever soft feelings might be left for me and been utterly rebuffed. I was also blazingly furious, and acutely disappointed, in his decision to overwrite reality to protect his vision of his ego. In that moment, I liked him less than I had at any point since I'd met him.

I'd always known, on some level, that one day I would find myself backed against the place I was in, with nowhere to go, like anyone who found themselves in any kind of fucked up and complicated relationship like ours. There was no way for us to have conflict, in our current configuration, that wasn't entirely one-sided. If he wanted to, he could always win.

It was an easy thing to overlook when we were aligned, even imperfectly. He might disapprove of a specific choice I made, he might say something careless that bothered me, but minor points of friction were navigable. We magnified each other, made each other better, knew how to close ranks and plot in unison and make incredible things happen. And in that space, something else had grown between us, like moss between paving stones. Something alive and surprising, green somehow thriving in concrete.

But when the bond between us ruptured, when we were out of alignment—as we clearly were now—there was no compromise; he got exactly what he wanted, and I had no recourse. More, I didn't have to just consider whatever our relationship was, but also my livelihood. While it was never something he threatened, the fact remained he held my job and the place where I lived in his hands, and could effortlessly take them away with no consequences whatsoever beyond his own sense of justice. It was something I was usually able to avoid thinking about at all, but now, wrung out and anxious and so, so angry at him while sitting in an apartment he'd given me, I couldn't look away from it.

I also had to consider my own mortality. It was grotesque, and felt like a betrayal, but I would be lying if there wasn't a base, physical fear of him as well. If he decided he didn't especially want me to be alive anymore, there was absolutely nothing I could do to stop him. I wouldn't so much as be able to leave a scratch on him.

So when he told me the conversation was over, and I could tell by his tone this was no longer a conversation but a command, I left. It was the only thing I could do.

And I hated it.

I THREW MYSELF back into the work however I could, attempting to transmute that nervous energy into accomplishable tasks. There was no other fallout from our argument, no terrible consequences, just an awful silence. Working didn't exactly make me feel better, but it gave me something to focus on other than the ever-growing certainty that whatever tender strangeness had once grown between us was over for good. When I ran out of work, I often found myself turning back to Supercollider, to both soothe and torture myself by checking in on his always horrific situation. It was something I only reserved for my worst moments, when my mood was terrible and my ability to be wise sufficiently eroded. It came from the same place of terrible judgment as checking in on a toxic ex's social media accounts.

It wasn't the Draft's lies I was looking through this time—everything about "the best doctors are working with him" and "we continue to be optimistic about his progress" and "the rest of the world's heroes are shouldering the burden of his absence with incredible grace." Instead, I combed through impossible amounts of publicly available data in order to see what I could glean from it. And as is the case with any open-source data analysis, I searched for what was missing. I was happy to find what scraps of truth were out there for me to pick over. But more than anything, I went looking for the blanks, the empty spots, and tried to divine the shape and volume of those voids.

I didn't share these research deep dives with Leviathan. He never asked me for updates about Supercollider (or much of anything else at that point), and I never offered them. That felt like its own kind of disloyalty, but bringing up the reason for all of the taut, unspoken distance between us seemed far more awful. I never wanted to remind him about the reason for that space, why he now liked me so much less than he did before his enemy fell. I imagined he had his own ritual too, possibly augmented by one of our talented hackers or a payment through a third party, but no less a private indulgence.

Most of what I turned up was small but valuable. I knew when one of Supercollider's catheters failed because of a flurry of new requisitions from new suppliers; I knew which psychologist they acquired when a new vegan caterer was engaged, and confirmed it when she left an esteemed position at a spinal cord injury research facility. All these little spaces that added up to a kind of photo negative of his current state. It pointed to a patient with no progress, just small adjustments and accommodations. As long as I knew the truth, they could not lie hard enough to make him anything but what he was: a twisted mass of flesh, and a victim of his own rude endurance.

It wasn't any of these details, though, that told me things had changed. I'd been vaguely following an upcoming research conference, hosted in a nearby city: "Exceptional Medicine: Treating the Superheroic." Half a dozen speakers pulled out on short notice within a couple of days of each other, every single one of them having published papers on invulnerability medicine, with the exception of a lone ethicist. We looked into it, and with a bit of patience and luck we discovered a number of them had made last-minute hotel reservations, all within a few miles of the facility where Supercollider was kept.

All at once I knew something was horrifically wrong. I knew it the same way I knew that Leviathan wasn't dead, despite seeing his shattered "body" in person and then again, over and over, on surveillance tapes. It would take my conscious brain a long time to catch up to that certainty, but I trusted it. In that moment I knew a true thing, and how I knew it mattered much less. This was the same feeling, that fundamental certainty, that despite no change in the Draft's outward messaging, no sirens or rising smoke, we were about to witness something catastrophic.

I spent the rest of the night researching. I startled a cleaner who walked in humming, headphones on, who almost leapt over their cart when they saw me still hunched over my desk, which was the only time I was conscious of time passing. Soon I could no longer focus effectively enough to be of any use to myself, it was midmorning and I could just start to see the awful, empty spaces where the tragedy was taking place. It would take days until I had a clearer picture, days of pulling records and pouring over notes, and there would always be emptiness I couldn't see into, an interiority of the Draft I couldn't penetrate.

I knew this: Without intervention, he would have lived. He would have stayed a lumpen mass of dribbling flesh, but that's the problem with invulnerability, isn't it? He was trapped and abject, but he was healthy.

I knew that there were endless pitch meetings, where doctors and C-suite execs and consultants all brought potential solutions. Some of them were even good. The one that got the farthest, that I thought had a real chance, was pitched jointly by Comms and Marketing: with a sophisticated full-body prosthetic and a psychic interpreter, he could have lived a full life. Just as crucial, he would have been useful for the Draft. He could have given moving motivational speeches, become the cornerstone of their mentorship program, retired to the academy and trained baby fascists for the rest of his days.

In the end, the board couldn't allow it. If Supercollider couldn't be Supercollider, he was worse than dead to them. He was a reminder of a loss. So after hearing all the solutions about hydration management and the custom controls he might be able to operate with neural uplinks and tongue movements, the Draft could not be satisfied with what was left of him.

I had long suspected that there had to be a *way*. The Draft weren't stupid; if they were going to take on the risk of training and supporting a hero as spectacularly powerful as he was, they would have to control him. In this case, that control could only mean one thing: If he turned on them, how could they take him down? For every hero that they took on, they spent considerable resources researching weaknesses, a glass they could break if things really went sideways.

I don't know exactly when the glass was broken here, but I know there was a different series of meetings after it happened. I knew from the way schedules lined up. From travel to and from the facility. From the small bits of silence in the news cycle where a decision needed to be made and someone was told to hold off for a moment.

I knew they took whatever hallowed weakness of his they'd carefully guarded out of cold storage, took it away from the scientists and gave it to surgeons. People who specialized in medical care for the superpowered. People who didn't live nearby, but were surreptitiously flown in.

They turned that sword into a scalpel.

I don't know exactly when they carried him from his room to the operating theater. The fewest number of people possible were told. But there's always a trail, somewhere. Certainly the doctors were brought up to speed and conferred—that took some time. And once the surgeons announced they were ready, the date and time were selected at random. Again, random is only so random—with enough data, you can find the way the pattern emerges (or doesn't, which is, in turn, its own sort of pattern). The team assembled in secret, effectively sealing themselves off entirely from the outside world until they worked a miracle.

I had no sense of what happened in that room once the doors were locked. I tried through every means that I had, but there were no communications that emerged—certainly no videos or recordings—and any debriefs, if they existed, remained out of reach of my digital fingertips. I didn't know if the experimental delivery method for the anesthesia worked; I only knew they had brought in the best anesthesiologist in the world. I didn't know if things went south from the first moments they began to try and untangle him from himself, or agonizing hours into the process. I didn't know if one thing went catastrophically wrong, or one thing after another in an unstoppable cascade.

But I did know that Supercollider entered that room as healthy as a meat sack could conceivably be, as well as he was when I left him on the floor of the prison. And I knew he never came out again. As they sliced or burned or burrowed into his seemingly invulnerable flesh, he died on the table.

There are thirty-seven hours lost in that void, obfuscated by silence and security. I don't know precisely when they pulled the trigger on the procedure, at what hour or minute he went under the gamma knife or plasma lance they built just for him. At some point, though, an alarm was raised, but only very few heard it, and no one who did was capable of making any difference. Somewhere in that liminal space, after minutes or hours, everyone in that room, everyone who had anything to try, failed; and they all, one at a time or all together, had to accept that whatever had once lit the flesh now empty before them wasn't coming back.

They held his body in that room a long time before even releasing him to the morgue. I can't imagine what it was like to be there for those hours, where no one even dared move him because it would mean he was really dead. That time would have been as dense and impenetrable as the fog of war; the rage in that room, and all the panic, the consequences that raised careers from their bedrock—or let them crater into a bottomless pit—would have never left those walls.

But what was left of Supercollider did leave that room, and once he did there was only so long they could keep it from me. The slab they kept him on was more secure than most bank vaults, but I could still see the shape of the space he was about to leave in the world. I didn't know if he was already gone when I first noticed something was amiss, or there was still a chance, if he still drew breath. I found myself hoping that I was awake and already working the moment he died, that I was there, in some distant way, to witness it.

When I had proven it to myself, when I was sure the augury of email autoresponders and road closures cemented my insights into certainties, I did the only thing I could do in that moment: I logged out of my computer and left. At that moment, I still retained some measure of plausible deniability. It was still possible to an outside observer (or one outside observer, the one who mattered) that it might look like I hadn't yet recognized what I was seeing. Because the moment I officially knew that he was dead, I would have to tell Leviathan. Immediately. I also knew that under no circumstances could I be the one to tell Leviathan that Supercollider had died.

It's not that I would lie to him—I couldn't, even if not telling him wouldn't have been tantamount to treason. He deserved better than that. He deserved to be the first to know. It's just that *I* couldn't be the one to tell him. There was no way I could deliver the news that his nemesis had committed the ultimate betrayal: dying, and not by Leviathan's hand. I knew he would hate whoever or whatever delivered that message to him, rational or not, and whatever still existed between us could never bear the strain. Even if our last conversation had not been such a disaster. Nothing would be able to separate my existence from that moment of grief.

I spent the rest of that day alone in my apartment trying miserably to sleep, my mind unable to shut off. For those few hours, I was the only person outside the Draft who knew Supercollider had died. The Invincible Man, the world's greatest hope, a hollowed-out thing—every version of him was gone. I was entirely alone with that knowledge, and those hours were mine to carry.

By early evening, I knew that while I could not tell Leviathan, I could lead him to it. I would have to build a path of data in front of him a step at a time, and stay just far enough ahead that he might not see me laying the bricks.

I WAITED UNTIL morning to send the first message. Not as soon as I sat down at my desk, but after I would have had a chance to get settled. To buy into my own fiction, I made myself read over every document again, carefully, as though I was seeing them for the first time, and combed through the data that had been scraped overnight. Part of me was hoping I might even find something that proved I was wrong.

I didn't.

When I finally wrote my note, it would look like I reached out to him at the earliest opportunity.

~~t,~~

~~Sir,~~

Leviathan,

I've turned up several data points that suggest heightened security/possible lockdown at medical facility D.117 as well as a crisis comms team mobilization. (see attached)

   None of our active or allied disruption efforts correspond— with your permission, I would like to pivot my efforts to investigating this opportunity, and request additional support from Research.

~~Yours,~~

Loyally,
A

The response wasn't instantaneous, but within half an hour I had his assent—and an immediate summons to show him what I had so far. I gathered the most compelling documents I had and tried to remind myself I wasn't going to my death. I chose the pieces that had zipped the body bag shut for me, hoping that they'd do the same for him, and took the long, dreadful walk to his office.

"Show me what you found," he said, the moment the doors shut behind me. He did not wait for me to walk over to his desk, but instead he strode over to a smaller table near the door so he could get his hands on whatever I held a few seconds earlier.

I gave him my tablet. "I highlighted the most relevant, but everything I have is here. I've put in a request with Research, but don't yet have a timeline."

He hunched over the screen almost protectively, slightly turning away, so I could see the ultraviolet eyespots glowing on his shoulder blades.

I swallowed and looked down. With my hands empty, I suddenly felt very exposed, and still raw from how awful our last interaction had been.

He was looking at a commercial satellite photograph of the Draft's medical facility—or rather the grayed-out classified space that covered it. Outside the redacted image, a network of road closures and rerouting filled in the blanks. "He hasn't been moved." It wasn't a question.

"He's still at the facility," I answered anyway.

He was quiet for a moment then, reading over the same pieces of data I had hours earlier. My stomach was a bag of ice. I realized this was what knowing the future would be like and was fervently glad that particular power did not exist.

"Any changes to personnel?" His voice sounded as though it was thinning.

"This is the troubling part." I gathered myself, and hoped he took it as the stutter of things sliding into place in my own head. I looked down at my phone, checking a detail. "Additional security was added, but none left. It feels like a lockdown."

"This is your current priority," he said. He was speaking quietly, with a warmth and calm that would have been soothing if I didn't know the place it came from. "I want to know what is going on in that building."

I nodded, and rose to leave.

"No." He reached out toward me, fingers tense and palm down. It was a command; but I felt a pang when he reached for me, even brusquely. "You will work from here." He made a few sharp, sweeping gestures across a touch screen set into the table. "IT will be bringing your work station in momentarily."

"In . . . here."

"Is there a problem?"

His voice had a threatening grate to it, and I suddenly remembered that the last time we spoke we'd been furious with each other.

I tried hard to soften. "Not at all, just making sure I understood."

His shoulders relaxed the smallest fraction. "Good."

"May I—"

"Your requests, current and future, regarding this matter are approved."

I tried to find the appropriately gracious reply, but he met my eyes and I froze. The same grief I saw in his eyes when I'd rescued him was still there. "You will be here as the truth takes shape," he said.

I was mercifully freed from having to reply by IT arriving at the door with my computer and monitor; someone followed behind carrying my chair. In the bag resting against my hip, I could feel my phone vibrating as a flurry of notifications came through. I was sure the rest of my team were sending me frantic DMs trying to find out if something catastrophic had happened to me, like being fired or disappeared to a black site (again). After sending off a few reassuring messages, I used my carte blanche permission to completely ruin the entire research department's day.

I requisitioned a pull of any outbound communications that Research could get their hands on—even a catering order or receipt for office supplies. I asked for a review on the surveillance on the entrance of the Draft medical facility, looking for footage or other data on anyone who might have gone in but then not left. For each request, I attached a handful of examples from the files I did have, just to be thorough.

All the while, I watched Leviathan and I slowly fed him the data I filtered, like yarn into a spindle. I hoped he would start to see the patterns I had and would follow the golden thread into the labyrinth. He caught on fast—more quickly than I intended, and I was afraid he would notice me unspooling clues in front of him.

I saw the moment he knew. The instant that it registered in his body, before the words formed in his mind for the first time, that was his and his alone. There may have been time when he pushed that physical dread into a corner, demanding more evidence before he allowed it to rush in. I don't know if it was a carelessly phrased email, or the particular medical staff assigned to the surgical wing, or the ever-increasing number of hours that no one has passed through the medical facility's doors. But in among those things, the knowledge found him, and he could hold it down no longer.

I'd never heard him make that sound before. It was like a quick, shuddering intake of breath, but with the ghost of his voice within it. A word turned inside out. He gripped the edge of the desk tight enough that the wood creaked.

"Sir?" I stood, and walked toward him slowly. He did not look at me

"Leave, please." He said it gently, and did not look up. I was grateful for it; whatever was going on inside his head, he wouldn't associate it later with the sight of my face.

The soundproofing in his office was very good. If the doors had been completely closed I doubt I would have heard anything, but the lock had not fully engaged, and I was still too close to the gap.

And so I heard the first wet rasp of his weeping.

"WE SHOULD JUST leak it."

Jav was trying to keep his voice casual, but I could hear a tremor of excitement. I could hear it because I was already attuned to it—I felt it too. I leaned back in my chair. He hadn't even let me formally start our team meeting before pouncing. Tammy and Darla were suddenly on high alert, looking up like a pair of meerkats to see what I was about to say.

"It?" I knew exactly what he meant, but I needed a minute to think. The only communication I had received from Leviathan since I'd left his office was the order that under no circumstances were we to release any information about Supercollider.

"You know." Jav drew his thumb over his throat and made a *skkkktch* sound. "When do we get to tell the public that the flesh dumpling shall dumple no more."

"Ask not for whomst the skin bag dumples," Tammy said gravely. "It dumples for thee."

Darla turned away, snort-laughing.

I stayed uncharacteristically somber. "Not yet."

There was a palpable deflation of the mood in the room. Jav crossed his arms over his chest, preparing a rebuttal. Finally he said, "Don't you think we deserve this?" gesturing with an extremely chewed-up pen. "In the grand scheme of things, we've earned breaking the news that Supercollider has suped his last, no?"

He had a point; of course we deserved this, and had it been any other superhero whose death we were responsible for, I would already be cackling in a meeting with my favorite writers from Comms. But this was not any superhero. It was Leviathan's nemesis, possibly the closest relationship to another person he had ever had. I needed to tell my team something satisfying, but I also couldn't tell them the naked truth that our boss was not only alive but probably face down on the floor listening to Dead Can Dance.

"Just give me a little more time."

Jav looked like he was about to explode. "If we give them much more time, the Draft will announce it *themselves*."

"What if they *never* announce it?" Tammy mused.

Jav nodded toward her. "Right, they might just conceal it indefinitely, never tell the world he's gone to the big pierogi factory in the sky."

Darla started wheezing.

I tried to ignore them. "We need to see how they are going to handle it and react to that. What they do next will give us invaluable information, and if we act too quickly we won't get that opportunity back."

Darla managed to collect themselves sufficiently to speak. "Even if they want to keep it secret forever."

I wrinkled my nose. "Here's the thing with indefinite secrets, especially something this big: they're impossible. If they say nothing long enough, people will just start making shit up, and eventually no matter how damaging the truth might be, it's still better than the inevitable conspiracy theories."

"I want to see those *Bigfoot: Confirmed* videos now," Jav said. That was good, I was winning him over.

"Can you imagine trying to get him a body double?" Darla asked.

"Casting call: one sentient hemorrhoid, nonspeaking role," I added.

Jav flinched. "Gross."

"Don't play squeamish with me, I've seen you give too many people scabies to be fooled."

Tammy cleared her throat, unwilling to let the subject drop. "Okay, but back to the matter at hand here. It seems like such an easy win for us. The Draft is thrown into crisis comms chaos. Isn't that a win? Isn't that what we're supposed to be *doing*?"

Darla and Jav stared at me, waiting for a response. The balance in the room was tipping again, unfavorably. I suppressed my bristling irritation.

The problem was she had a point. They'd lost their hero and there was no longer any hope for a miracle. And it didn't seem like the Draft had anything resembling a contingency plan for him inconveniently shuffling off his mortal coil ahead of schedule and in such spectacularly terrible fashion. I'm sure they hadn't thought he was actually immortal, but they must have assumed he'd live to be 102 and then die conveniently in his sleep on Christmas morning. It was a delicious opportunity for us, and we were going to squander it.

I tried to change tactics. "There's a lot of potential harm we wouldn't be taking advantage of."

Jav perked up a little, eager to find what he'd missed. "Like what?"

"Right now, they're a united front. Everyone was pulling for the same goal, hoping to be a part of a miracle: save Supercollider. Up until he bit the bologna."

Darla wrinkled their nose. "That is not a phrase."

"Now, all that camaraderie and morale is a complete shambles. The miracle is a real impossibility now. And sure, not everyone inside knows what happened, but enough do and they're all having their own personal breakdowns about it. And as more people inside find out he's dead, the higher the likelihood becomes someone has a complete crisis of faith, blames the Draft for putting him into an atom smasher, and decides to send all his medical records along with half of their database to Superleaks. If we leak it now, we take all that potential damage away. But if we give them enough space, they might tear themselves apart for us."

Tammy was nodding slowly; Jav had turned away a little, not ignoring me, but thinking. I knew I'd at least given them something to consider, and I started to relax a tiny bit.

"When that happens," Jav said quietly, "I'm immediately posting one of those photos you have of Skinbag whimpering on the floor."

I grabbed the armrest of his chair hard, startling him. I summoned the firmest, most menacing voice I could, which admittedly wasn't much but I worked with what I had. "You are absolutely for-bidden from ever posting any of our data about him, mine or other-wise."

He blinked at me. "Whoa. Hey."

"I am serious. This is for your own safety."

We stared at each other hard for a minute while he tried to fig-ure me out. When he finally nodded once and broke eye contact, I looked over at Darla and Tammy, who both now seemed deeply uncomfortable. "That goes for you too."

"Oh. Yes, okay."

"Whatever you say."

I knew neither of them were seriously considering it, but I needed to make sure they knew they were implicated. Convinced they were both sufficiently intimidated, I turned back to Jav, about whom I had no such illusions.

"This is not a power trip. I am saying this because I want you working here, with me, making a lot of lives very miserable long into the future. I don't want some crisis comms fuck who hasn't slept in three days deciding that you're the particular thorn in their side who has to go."

He looked down again briefly, and I pounced on that tiny open-ing of grudging agreement. I tapped the side of my head, where there was the knotted scar that curved back from my temple and ran up into my hairline. I had kept that side of my head shaved ever since the incident, long after the incision healed and the staples came out. I'd earned that scar. Everyone who saw me deserved to see it too. Especially if it made them uncomfortable. In this moment, the scar gave me the advantage of an indisputable, terrible experience.

"Trust me on this," I said.

His shoulders tensed, and while I didn't think I'd conclusively won, he seemed to at least be taking me seriously. "Fair."

I tried to hide my relief, and turned a little toward the others so they knew I was addressing everyone in the room. "I promise when they do announce his death, willingly or otherwise, we'll make that experience as excruciating for them as we possibly can. Deal?"

Darla smiled a little. "Promise?"

"Cross my heart." I drew an *X* over the left side of my chest.

I broke the tension by jumping into the meeting's official agenda. After a few awkward minutes, the tension seemed to dissipate, though Jav was a lot quieter than usual.

I hadn't been truthful with him. While I would have been concerned that someone at the Draft wouldn't hesitate to take out a hit on my Excel Pervert, that wasn't the possibility that made my blood run cold. I knew that if Jav, or anyone he could easily get his hands on, leaked the news of Supercollider's death without his direct order, Leviathan would kill him.

It was the most obvious fact imaginable, and also something I could never say out loud.

Announce it soon, you fucks, I thought furiously while Tammy went over a progress report. Right now, impatience was an enemy, both mine and especially that of my team, and every moment that went by only increased the tension. The longer they delayed, the greater the chance someone on either side of the line would jump the gun.

Someone inside the Draft needed to fuck up, and soon, I decided. An internal leak would do a great deal of damage, further our cause effectively, and keep Leviathan's fury directed entirely outward. Despite knowing better, I began to wonder if there was any way I could exert enough pressure in just the right places to make sure that happened.

Quietly, on my own, I started looking for those pressure points.

HER NAME WAS Aoife, and she just wanted to know where her husband was.

Niall had the great honor and misfortune of being an exceptional surgeon. During the Low Earth Orbit Crisis, he'd been on the scene when Horseshoe and his sidekick, Lucky (he wasn't), were partially digested by Tarantula Hawk. He'd managed to stabilize them both until the rest of his team had put the villain down and could safely transport them to the Vet. Both of them lived; it was hard to say if it was because of Niall's intervention, but he unquestionably saved most of Lucky's fingers and kept Horseshoe's face intact, which was enough to earn him the honor of becoming a Caped Citizen (the Draft's highest award for non-superpowered heroism, which you didn't need to die to earn).

There was a last-minute crisis the night Supercollider's procedure was attempted; one surgeon and their backup were temporarily incapacitated when a hero came into the hospital delirious and misfiring their powers. Both were hit; they would live, but neither of them were going to be useful to anyone for the next few days to weeks. After what must have been the most stressful debate of several careers, the decision was made to attempt to commandeer a civilian surgeon rather than scuttle the attempt entirely; and when Draft officials accosted Niall in his hospital's parking garage, he was just comfortable enough with this kind of fuckery to agree.

Everyone else on the team had lives specifically set up to accommodate their disappearing. Their families were briefed and trained, knew what questions to ask and which to never think of asking. They were accustomed to unexplained absences with zero explanations—it was all part of the important work their partners or parents or siblings did at the Draft. So when the rest of the surgeons and anesthesiologists and phlebotomists didn't come home the day of the procedure, it meant something serious had happened, but it was no cause for alarm. Their families just needed to do what the families of the peripherally heroic have always done: wait.

Aoife had no such training. She was not intimately familiar with the demands placed on the loved ones of trusted Draft employees. She knew what it was like to be married to a doctor in a city where superheroes regularly fucked shit up, and while that might involve seeing her husband on CCTV tying a tourniquet on someone wearing a carbon-fiber codpiece, or coming home with utterly wild stories about what came through the emergency room, it did not require her to cope with disappearances.

When the Draft came for Niall, they had him sign all the same terrifying NDAs everyone else had to, but no one followed up with Aoife. I'm convinced they didn't actually know that she existed (someone really dropped the ball on that one). From her perspective, her slender, dandelion-blond husband just kissed her goodbye one afternoon and never came home again.

He was fine, of course. Physically, anyway; I am sure that killing Supercollider personally—whether or not he was at all ultimately culpable—was an unpleasant emotional experience for him. But he and the rest of the surgical team were wearing freshly laundered new scrubs every day, enduring the boredom and uninspired catering of the lockdown after the surgery.

All the while, Niall had no way to contact the outside world, no way to tell his wife he hadn't been rendered down to plasma by someone's powers going haywire while they returned to or departed from consciousness, or just mundanely mugged walking to his car. She knew that his work was unpredictable, that there were hundreds of scenarios that could keep him away much longer than expected. But she was not someone who was accustomed to being close to Big Secrets, so when hours turned into days, and then more days, and no one was able to give her any answers whatsoever, she started to panic.

She did everything she knew how to do. She contacted his hospital, who were able to tell her when his last shift had ended and that he hadn't shown up for the next, nor any since. She started smoking again, for the first time since she quit in college. When she called the police to make a missing person's report, she waited seven hours for a bored officer to show up to yawningly take her statement. He refused to believe Aoife and Niall hadn't had a fight despite everything she said and just kept repeating that he'd probably be back "as soon as he cooled down." She talked to her best friend and her brother, both of whom tried to console her but didn't know what else to do.

Now, it was around this time that someone at the Draft realized their mistake. That missing persons report in Niall's name must have triggered an auto-alert and the Draft took over the report. When Aoife called for an update she was met with platitudes and avoidance, and then the worst possible follow-up call from a Draft agent, who I was sure thought they were going to make everything better and ease all of her fears.

"Your husband is a hero," they said, or something equally obscene, when Aoife begged for any information about her husband. They told her nothing, less than nothing, only that he'd bravely volunteered himself for a mission of the utmost importance and secrecy. They told her how brave she was, how unimaginably thankful they were, and refused to so much as tell her whether Niall was alive or not. They ended that call with the sobbing partner of their commandeered doctor thinking they'd done an excellent job. They'd reassured her how important this was and confirmed his heroism. What else was there to do?

The lack of research on their part was their undoing. Because Aoife's entire direct experience with the Draft up to that point had been the horror stories her husband had told her about working on the damage superheroes did while going about their business, and the harrowing hours he'd narrowly escaped being partially digested by a villain's secreted digestive juices. She white-knuckled through the ceremony where Niall had received his Caped Citizen award, knowing in her gut just how close she'd come to receiving a slightly different award on his behalf, after his funeral. She didn't want a hero, she wanted her husband to come home. And after that phone call, she was all but certain that was never going to happen.

Aoife knew what she did next was a bad idea, but she felt bad ideas were the only ones left to her. Any thoughts she might have had about not wanting to get Niall in trouble were utterly obliterated; whatever was happening to him now was so much worse than any trouble she could possibly cause. She went about it as well as she could. She took their dogs and drove to her brother's place, and then did what a lot of people did as a last resort once they'd been stonewalled by customer service and traditional channels failed them: she told the entire internet what was happening.

She went on social media, tagged every Draft-affiliated account she could find, and demanded publicly that they tell her where her husband was. She put together a thread of the timeline of his disappearance, from the last moment she'd seen him, the way her nose had wrinkled when he kissed her through his scratchy new beard. She noted everything that she'd done since, every attempt she'd made to get someone to just tell her where he was and what had happened. She relayed how she'd contacted the police and how they'd been less than useless, tagging the city PD scathingly in the process. She included her best attempt at a line-by-line transcription of the call she'd had with a Draft agent. When she'd finished her story and gotten down every detail that she could, she spent hours tagging every person she could find who had the Draft listed as their employer in their bio, as well as every journalist she'd ever heard of.

I caught it all only a few posts in, and watched it spool out like gold strands from a bundle of straw. I knew, instantly, that I had found my way in. I am sure it would have been picked up anyway to some degree, had it been a slowish news day or been boosted by the right people. But I was not going to take the risk her story would explode on its own. Despite the certainty I was dangerously close to subordination, I saw the tiniest slit of light and immediately diverted my entire team's energy toward tearing it open. We fired up the bots and sock puppets, we tagged and hashtagged and threaded. I leaned on the journalists who owed me favors and threatened a couple who owed me more than that. As we worked, I was certain any moment I would be summoned to Leviathan's office to explain myself, but it never happened. My relief at this was tinged with the smallest bit of sadness.

I told myself I wasn't directly disobeying Leviathan, while I knew in my heart that was a technicality at best. Every post felt like rolling the dice, every direction I chased the story a new moment of risk. As I worked I kept hoping I'd escape his notice for just a few more minutes, that by the time he did notice, the tendrils I'd sent out would be too embedded to make him do anything but act—to once again *be* Leviathan.

In the meantime, I kept pushing my luck and in that weird, rhizomatic way data has of spreading, it soon reached critical mass and carried on with its own momentum. And suddenly, instead of being met with silence, *everybody* wanted to talk to Aoife.

There was a tense day where I was medium-sure the Draft would just kill her. To be honest, if she had stayed in the pretty little bungalow she shared with Niall by herself, they very well might have. Just a quiet little gas leak to solve all their problems.

But Aoife was smart. Once she reached her brother's place, she was in a house with two other adults, her toddler nephews, and a total of three trained Belgian shepherds. That would have been a disaster to wade into, and things very quickly got much worse for the Draft the more people were paying attention; before long, there were just too many watching. And the scrutiny meant there was almost no chance for the Draft to do something more permanent.

Soon, Aiofe wasn't just a thread of desperate social media messages, she was the main character of the week. She played the role exceptionally well; she had a tiny gap in her front teeth that somehow gave her an air of vulnerability, and her voice had a warbling lilt to it that made her sound lost and pitiful. I made a point to put extra work into elevating any posts or articles that included video or audio of her speaking. "I just want to know where he is," she said, over and over again. It seemed like so little to ask, something so reasonable, that the unknown *why* behind the Draft's silence grew uglier and uglier by the moment.

One of my favorite journalists to work with, an absolute shark named Sacchi, kindly agreed to suggest to Aoife that she make an official video appeal to the Draft. I helpfully sent a script for Sacchi to suggest Aoife use, and she barely changed a word. It was a little eerie, a few days later, to listen to my words come out of her mouth.

"I know his work is important," she said, sniffing. She was trying to stay composed but couldn't quite do it, and her lips kept trembling and causing her to stumble. This was the kind of thing I couldn't script, and it was exquisite.

"I know that *he* is so important. I understand that, and that because of whatever is happening, he might . . . I might not be able to see him. It might be for a long while. You don't even have to tell me where he is. I just . . . I need . . . I need to know he is safe, he is alive. Because he's so important to *me* too." The tear that had been threatening to spill over finally slid down her face.

"Laying it on a little thick, isn't she." Jav had materialized next to me, watching the video on my monitor over my shoulder.

I scowled up at him. "How dare you."

"It's just a bit much."

"She thinks her husband is dead, you asshole."

"Yeah, but the crying."

"Wow."

He shrugged and wandered back to his desk. "Don't be mad; you didn't write the crying."

"She's perfect," I yelled after him, queueing up a fresh batch of posts with links to her video. It was the only video on her otherwise empty YouTube account, and her profile photo was one of her dogs. Her little appeal was barely a minute long, but it did all the work it needed to. It wasn't just her tragic face and breaking voice, it was how utterly reasonable her request sounded. The more people heard her plea, the more they wondered why wouldn't the Draft just reach out to her. Why wasn't a charismatic PR representative already at her house or on the phone with her, apologizing profusely for the miscommunication and insisting that Niall was safe? All they had to do was confirm he still had a pulse. With every hour that went by and her tearful, infinitely reasonable request went unanswered, the more deeply suspicious their silence became.

It was incredibly difficult to resist the urge to press the issue even further, but I knew patience was a weapon I could not afford to squander. So many times my fingers ached to comment here, to nudge there:

Goodness gracious, it's probably a coincidence, but it sure seems like no one's heard any news about Supercollider in a very long time. I wonder if these things could possibly be related . . .

No, surely not.

Unless?

I fantasized about it repeatedly but fought the urge, knowing the best (and safest) course of action, now that I'd helped set this in motion, was to let things fester and explode in their own awful time. Patience was not one of my virtues, but a hard-earned, well-practiced skill.

An unfortunate side effect of Aoife's brilliant narrative was that it suddenly became harder and harder to monitor Draft activities, even for me and our incredible team of skullduggery experts. Devices were replaced and encryption protocols shifted; like airlocks closing off parts of a sinking ship to keep the unfolded compartments from going under, internal communications were restricted and segmented. Still, some info still came to me, such as the fact that everyone in Draft PR and Comms was frantic for any official word on the messaging, but nothing came. The medical facility, and everyone inside it, remained in complete lockdown, and the very few in leadership who knew what had happened were a silent void.

And there were other trickles, just enough around the edges that I could still pick up on a bit of the tone and tension. I didn't need a direct line to know that inside the Draft real panic was mounting. For those who knew, any hope that they might have been able to just lie forever—throw what was left of Supercollider into a neutrino bath at the bottom of a mine shaft, and issue vague updates about his distant recovery for the rest of an average mortal lifespan—had been dashed to smithereens. There was only so much of the narrative left that they would be able to control. I counted on them to decide they wanted every scrap of that control that they would be able to claw back; and in the end I was not disappointed.

"I OWE ALL of you an apology."

A woman I recognized from her headshots and surveillance photos as the chief branding officer stood in front of a ring of mics in an iron-gray suit, quite matching her pallor. Her skin seemed to hang too loose on her face; I wondered if it was the work of an excellent makeup artist or actual exhaustion. It should have been Stephanie Bulwark, the CDO, standing at that podium, looking like shit, but she was still extremely missing. Instead, the woman

I knew as CBO, Carmel Gentileschi, was introduced as the interim chief development officer, a fact I immediately wrote in my own notes before DM'ing Molly.

"I offer it now, unreservedly," the woman continued. Standing to her right and a little behind was Aoife, her face lowered and inscrutable. A low rumble of voices rose from the gathered crowd of journalists, who all shifted restlessly and muttered to each other. The interim CDO was quiet for a long time. She waited for the susurrus of the crowd to stop and the shuttering of digital cameras to fall quiet. She let an uncomfortable stillness settle on the room before taking a sharp breath, as though she were in pain, and continued.

"Our relationship with the public, and with the media, is built on a strong foundation of mutual trust and respect."

There was an audible snort behind me, and I grinned without turning around. A dozen or so of us were watching together in a conference room I'd booked for the afternoon. Jav had brought his laptop and was pretending not to care what was happening on the huge screen, making a show of working through it with his headphones in, but his head involuntarily cocked to one side at that line and gave him away.

"Over the last ten days, we have not been honest with you. To be more specific, we have not been as forthcoming as we wish we could have been, and, many will soon say, as we *should* have been. On a personal note, I wish we could have spoken to you sooner. None of this is an excuse; a sin of omission is no less severe.

"In not sharing the whole truth with you, we know that we caused harm to the trust that lies between us. The Draft takes that trust very seriously; we hold it sacred. Today we know that we failed to protect that trust, and we caused innocent parties"—she looked behind her toward Aoife and nodded; Aoife kept her head down. I wondered if they put little strips of gaffer tape on her shoes to remind her to keep her eyes in the right place—"significant distress, and for that we can only humbly apologize."

Darla vacuumed up the last of the Diet Coke from the bottom of their Big Gulp, rattling the ice aggressively. "I should be taking notes on this," they said.

I nodded. "This speechwriter is good."

"I hope, once you hear the full story," the interim CDO continued, "you will come to forgive us. That you will understand why we had to keep things as close to our chest as we have. The news I have to share with you today is grave."

"More like gravy than of grave," Jav said, who I guess had decided to stop pretending he wasn't interested. He was still mad about not being able to directly leak this before the Draft could respond, but it was better to have him angry and alive than briefly satisfied and annihilated.

The acting CDO took a moment to meaningfully adjust the mic nearest to her, as though taking a moment to compose herself. "I wish I could say we 'had no choice' but to keep it from you. We had reasons, and we believe—*I* believe—they were good, justified reasons. Kind reasons. We had to make sure those closest to this tragedy were informed first, and for reasons that I am sure will become clear, we took every effort to ensure that news was delivered as swiftly, respectfully, and privately as possible. This was difficult work, and it took time. It is not impossible we could have done better, and it's clear now that in protecting those few we recognize we have harmed many. This is, and always has been, the exact antithesis of our values.

"We also admit that, for all of us at the Draft, this news is deeply painful. On some level, we did not want to even speak it out loud, if only because in telling the world, this awful thing would somehow become more real. If, in our own grief and human imperfection, we have done less than our best in serving all of you and treating you with respect, we can only apologize. I solemnly promise to do whatever I can, put in whatever work is necessary to regain your trust and repair the damage we may have caused."

Aoife shifted from one foot to the other, looking suddenly guilty.

I pointed to my screen. "This is a master class in delivering an apology that is designed to make the injured party feel shitty for being harmed."

One of the researchers cupped a hand around her mouth, like a megaphone. "Just say it, my god, I have aged ten years already,"

Instead, the CDO paused again. Gripping the podium, she seemed to gather herself, like a diver at the top of a cliff. I didn't want her tactics to work on me, but even as I intellectually deconstructed what was happening, a string of tension wound itself tighter in my chest. For all that this was theater, she had said something true. Once she delivered the news she was still barely holding, once everyone knew, the whole world would be different. I put a hand on the back of my neck, bracing for it.

Finally, with a last breath, she said, "It is with a broken heart that I tell you the unthinkable has happened: Supercollider is dead."

When it was finally spoken, the tension leaving my body was like a physical exhalation. His death was out in the world now, and no one could undo it. For ten days a few of us had held that knowledge as a secret, spent time with the impossible weight of it, and suffered under it in various ways (a large percentage of those people were still in a secure medical bunker somewhere, bored and disoriented). But it wasn't just ours anymore. With the burden of that knowledge redistributed, it was suddenly so much easier to breathe.

That relief came at the direct expense of everyone else hearing it for the first time. At the press conference, the scene was complete pandemonium. A collective noise of horror, a combination of gasps and shouts and even screams, erupted from the press room. The crowd surged forward, as the inarticulate sounds of shock gradually coalesced into a cacophony of desperate questions. Security suddenly looked like they were working the fence of a heavy metal show, trying frantically to keep a bunch of sweaty, hysterical kids from climbing onto the stage, except they were all adults in suits wearing pancake makeup.

The acting CDO stood motionless at the podium, a point of stillness in the chaos. With her head bowed, she looked like a statue in an ancient mortuary. The announcement seemed to have utterly exhausted her, as though now that her purpose was fulfilled she could finally return to stone.

Aoife shrunk back, looking out wide-eyed over the crowd, completely overwhelmed by the noise and uncertain what to do. She looked around frantically for one of the members of Draft security for safety, but they were all more than occupied trying to get the room under control.

"Safe to say they aren't going to take questions." That was Tammy, one hand pressed to her chin, shaking her head.

"What answers could she possibly have?" I added.

As though she heard us, the CDO reacted with an incredible power move: she turned, took Aoife gently by the arm, and walked out of the room with a frankly eerie level of composure.

"We should order our catering now," Darla said. We were all in for our own long night, watching the world light itself on fire in grief. Most of the room stood up, chairs scraping.

"Yeah, great idea. Would you like to do the honors?"

Darla pulled out their cell phone, one-handedly putting the order in.

I reached out to disconnect my laptop from the projector, but stopped—to my surprise, the acting CDO walked back out to the podium, reigniting the chaos in the press gallery. She took up her place behind the mic with the air of a singer who'd just emerged from the wings for an encore.

"It's not over," I said, too quietly.

"Make sure you order a bunch of that sports milk or muscle juice or whatever it's called," Jav suggested. "The protein and electrolyte stuff. It's important to stay hydrated."

Darla raised an eyebrow. "Yeah I am definitely going to type in 'sports milk or whatever' into this form and assume that will be fine."

I projected my voice properly this time. "Shut up and *look*."

The chatter around me died down. A couple of data scientists had already scurried off to their office, but the rest of the room grew quiet again, retook their seats. Darla put their phone down and perched on the very edge of a chair, tense.

The CDO stood impassively, waiting for the crowd to settle enough that what she had to say would be audible. It seemed for a horrible few moments the journalists and camera operators wouldn't be able to get themselves under control, but with a mighty effort and a lot of jostling, they reined themselves in just enough.

"I know you have many questions. I do too. I can't speak to all of them, or even most, but I will give what I can. I know what is on the forefront of your minds, because it was on the forefront of mine when I first heard the news: *how.*

"This news is as difficult to convey as the loss itself—no, perhaps worse.

"What I am about to say will seem impossible. But I am so sorry to tell you it is nothing but the stark, awful truth. There are very few things in the world capable of taking Supercollider from us, one of which we thought was neutralized forever. But we were wrong." She took a moment to gather herself, to swallow in a way that looked annoyingly genuine.

"I wish I did not have to be the one to ever speak these words. But I have to. You all—you deserve to know.

"Supercollider is dead—and Leviathan killed him."

I closed my eyes as the room around me erupted into chaos.

AN INCALCULABLE LOSS

K. McKinnon

In the early hours of May 17, the Veterans of Superheroic Conflicts Memorial Hospital was as silent as it ever was. The machines still whirred and beeped; specialized medical staff still dutifully walked the halls, their voices carrying words of comfort. But there was a peace to the building that was never present during the day, with most of the superpowered patients recovering in its wards finally getting the rest they needed and deserved.

But in the basement, something stirred. Like a scene from a horror movie, a steel door in the morgue slid open, and moments later, the former occupant walked out. It was not difficult to do—after all, why would any door in a morgue lock from the inside?

The location of the Villain Leviathan's body has been one of the Department of Superheroic Affairs' (known colloquially as the Draft) most closely guarded secrets of recent months. While most suspected the body would have been moved from Dovecote Super-max after the prison break that badly damaged the facility last autumn, no one knew where the mortal remains of Supercollider's nemesis had come to rest. That question, at least, has now been somberly answered.

"The Vet was the most obvious choice," said facility director Hogarth Simms, speaking exclusively to the *Megacity Megaphone*. "It was both incredibly secure and offered researchers access to cutting-edge medical facilities for their research."

When asked if anyone suspected such a move was putting the patients and staff of the Vet in danger, Simms was adamant that the move was supposed to be incredibly low-risk. "While the threat can never be zero, especially when something like Leviathan is involved, you must realize that, until the events of this morning, we believed he had been dead for months.

"He shouldn't have been able to hurt anyone."

"This aspect of his powers was entirely undocumented," admitted Lin Hassar, one of Sanctuary's leading hazardous powers experts. "While the Draft were aware of his damage resistance and regenerative capabilities, no one had any idea he could become 'dormant.' And certainly not for this long."

Hassar believes now that Leviathan was able to effectively shut down most of his body's systems as a last-ditch resort to survive. After Supercollider's unprecedented victory over the Villain, after a climactic battle that rocked the supervillainous world, he was able to slow down his metabolic system to the point where life signs were undetectable.

"I have to believe there was no way we could have known," says Stan Carraway, the coroner who pronounced Leviathan dead at the scene and ultimately signed off on his death certificate. "I keep going over those moments in my head wondering what I might have done differently."

After a pause, the shaken doctor continued, "While I know I followed all the protocol, this will haunt me forever."

While everyone believed the body lay inanimate in a secure freezer, below their feet, behind steel and concrete, the Villain Leviathan slowly healed from his injuries. When he finally woke, he not only found that he had survived the impossible, but that the very hero who had orchestrated his downfall lay in the hospital mere floors above him.

"The irony is almost impossible to bear," said interim CDO Carmel Gentileschi, when questioned about the attack. "Supercollider was brought here, to the Vet, to recover after the Dovecote break not just because this facility is the best, but because it is supposed to be the safest in the world. This was the one place he should have been able to find the peace and relaxation to heal undisturbed.

"Instead, he was sleeping in the lion's den."

The attack was swift, targeted, merciless. The Villain fell upon Supercollider as he slept. "He knew he couldn't take out Super in a fair fight," said head of security at the Vet, Eleanor Vandry. "He never could. So he found him at his weakest, like a coward."

The Draft's forensic teams are still piecing together the events of the murder itself, which took place around 3:30 a.m. But one thing is clear: when the Villain attacked the high-security ward where Supercollider was being treated, even while injured, the hero sprang into action.

"Security had no idea what was happening; the alarms went off, so we went in," says Vandry, in her official statement to investigators. "It was chaos, complete chaos. Our guys had no idea what they were up against, and by the time we knew, it was too late."

One fact about the attack does seem clear: Supercollider placed himself between Leviathan and the security team who went in to protect him. The hero's final moments were what everyone around the world expected of him: selfless.

"He died doing what he always did," Vandry said.

"Fighting to protect us."

"What happens now?"

I looked up. Darla was in my office, standing behind my chair, wearing a look of deep concern I'd never quite seen before. I wondered how long they'd been there. I'd lost track of time again, trying to process the deluge of information and messaging that came pouring out like an opened vein.

"It looks like we're going to war." I picked up a squishy stress toy on my desk, one in the shape of a snail, and started kneading it between my already aching fingers. "Maybe a hot one, maybe a cold one. This was the first real shot."

I had wondered how they were going to spin Leviathan's extremely inconvenient resurrection, whenever he inevitably resurfaced. They were so certain of their victory after they'd captured him, so absolutely sure that they'd be able to kill him whenever they wanted, that they created a massive PR hole for themselves that they were eventually going to have to shovel back in.

This was a significant amount of dirt back in that pit.

"But at least it's out there," I said. "We'll see their whole comms strategy they're rolling out now."

"Did you know?" Tammy asked.

All the air seemed to have been sucked out of the room. She did not have to finish the sentence for me to know what she meant, and the immediate shift in energy let me know that even if I lied, my team already had their answer.

"Yes," I said mechanically. "I knew he was alive."

I expected them to give me shit about it—Jav at least, if no one else—but they were all quiet. I saw their expressions change as they processed this new information, watched the ways they each looked at me differently afterward. Before that moment, we had all been on the same team: a group of henches just trying to solider on in the face of tragedy and the possible collapse of our organization. We were all in it together, trying to find a way forward.

Now, they knew I had kept all of this from them, I had been operating in a completely different reality from theirs, and that was not the kind of betrayal I could come back from. I was on a different side now, the same side that Leviathan was on. I was no longer like them, and I was no longer the same kind of safe person to them.

It was Darla who eventually broke the silence. "What do we do next?"

Darla's tone was different, cooler, more respectful. It was also clear that I was not included in that "we"; they wanted to know what *they* were supposed to do, not what we all were doing together. They weren't looking for commiseration, just instructions.

I didn't have an answer for them. I hoped one would surface, but my brain felt like an overstuffed crypto mining rig and nothing but waste heat came out, no matter how long I thought. Darla left eventually, and might have said something else, but I'd fallen back into my own thoughts and didn't notice.

I couldn't find a way to articulate this out loud, but we were in real and very grave danger. Since Leviathan's escape, the Draft had a vested interest in leaving us all the hell alone. Even before that, before Supercollider and I warmed the old and half-dormant conflict he and Leviathan had nursed for two decades, the Draft hadn't had a reason to antagonize Leviathan directly for a long time. After all, he'd initiated plenty of confrontations for the both of them, and going out of their way to attract his attention was never a smart move.

But now, we had become the biggest target for heroics in recent memory. It wasn't even that they had a motivation to go after Leviathan and, by extension, anyone associated with him; they would have no excuse not to. The heroes and the public would demand it. Our work had become exponentially more dangerous, and more damning. And unlike Leviathan himself, few of us were conveniently invulnerable.

I wondered if Leviathan was capable of realizing how much danger everyone who worked for him was now in. Not that it wouldn't occur to him under most circumstances, but he was in such a pit of despair I wondered if the idea could reach him there.

It had been a while since I had felt this kind of ambient fear, and so much awareness of my vulnerability. It had been easy, for a long time, to feel protected by my proximity to Leviathan. Working for him and falling under the auspices of his control drew a kind of shield around me, and to some extent, all of us. But that felt much more fragile now, both because Leviathan was out of his mind with grief and also because, if every hero and citizen were suddenly looking at him as something that needed to be exterminated, would he really be capable of protecting me?

I felt a sudden, irrational need to talk to Quantum Entanglement, and immediately felt ashamed about it. She'd offered me a similar feeling of utter protection when I was near her, so I shouldn't have been shocked, I supposed, when my traitorous brain reminded me of her powerful forearms, the beauty of the tattoos on her face. She was, of course, the one who actually deserved the share of blame (credit?) for Supercollider's death, and I slowly found myself getting angry at the way she was being cut out of that narrative.

I can't believe they'd do this to her, I thought while I read. Story after story, press release after press release with the entirely fictional accounts of the hero's final moments, and not a single mention of Quantum Entanglement. In all the accounts, they gave the horrible glory of Supercollider's death to someone she'd hated. I didn't mean to, but I felt awful for her, wondering how she must feel after having suffered so many consequences of turning him, and her own life, inside out, and then having it all obliterated by another lie.

I wondered if she was in her own kind of mourning, too. She'd hated Supercollider, maybe almost as much as she hated Leviathan— and as much as Leviathan hated Supercollider. And a hate that deep has its own unbearable kind of intimacy. Was she also writhing in confused agony at his loss, racked by the kind of enmity that shared so much of love's surface area? I missed her deeply in that moment, and didn't push the feeling away, like I usually did.

I MISTOOK IT for a headache at first, a weird throb that gathered behind my left eye, the one that had been replaced. I'd fallen asleep at my desk, or near enough to it, sifting through the never-ending memorial articles and social media posts, the blue of grief and monitor static blurring together. The sensation woke me, and after a moment I realized this wasn't pain but the subaural tone of Leviathan calling me. His was the only number that rang in my head, part of the upgrades Leviathan had gifted to me while rebuilding a good part of my head and face. His own bone-conduction ringtone.

I groped around my desk for a communicator, and answered.

"I must speak with you." His voice was an open wound.

I inhaled to reply, but the connection was already severed. I stood completely still for a moment, shaking from the sudden surge of adrenaline that now had nowhere to go, then put myself together, grabbed my cane, and went to his office.

The lights were even lower than they usually were. I wondered if he had a headache; then wondered if he even experienced headaches, if that discomfort was a part of his physiological repertoire.

He was seated when I entered, and he did not immediately stand. He was usually on his feet when I arrived, as it was his preferred way to think, either pacing around the room or standing extremely still, head slightly tilted as though listening for something. This time, though, he was perched on the very edge of his exquisite, spinelike chair, turned slightly away from me so that I saw him in profile. The armored mandibles around his mouth were very still, and the bioluminescent glow of his armor—some of it his skin, I still needed to remind myself—was muted, turned down to a low incandescent throb.

He didn't move at all when I entered, giving no indication he was even aware that I was there, so I walked over to his desk and waited. I stayed standing; usually I would have sat immediately and without invitation, but at that moment it felt wrong somehow, even if I was having a bad leg day. I shifted more of my weight to my better leg, adjusted my grip on my cane, and gave him time.

From the angle of his shoulders I knew he was critically exhausted. I wondered if he'd been sleeping much at all these last few days; I wondered how much he needed to sleep. When asked by my colleagues, long ago, I had confidently said that he never took any downtime, never unwound. Whether or not I had been right, I could tell that now he desperately needed it. I tried to imagine what that space might be like for him, what he would look like at rest or uncoiled. While I had a very hard time even picturing it, reaching for that space made me feel a weird longing and loneliness I couldn't entirely place.

It took him several full minutes to speak. "They are all grieving now."

"They said you killed him."

His head turned sharply. "Kind of them."

His voice was acrid and hollow, but he meant it. He was taking solace in the blame, drawing it around him as something comforting.

Seeing that made me panic internally. I worried he could not see the severity of the threat that being blamed for Supercollider's death represented. "This is probably a grotesque understatement, but this is a critical—"

He waved a hand dismissively. "If they wish to place the responsibility at my feet I will not reject the gift."

I didn't reply, taking a moment to untangle and suppress the surge of frustration I felt. The threat he was hand-waving away was massive; I had no idea what it meant for me, or him, or any of us. And the responsibility *wasn't* his, as much as he might wish. I wanted him to call it out, make note of the fact he didn't deserve all of the blame *or* the credit. But I managed to shove it down, and if he noticed my struggle, he ignored it.

"You are no longer burdened with secrecy," he noted, forcing me back into the conversation.

"It feels strange," I admitted slowly, "that suddenly so many people know, having lived with it awhile." It felt like a weirdly intimate thing to say in that moment. I had never been sure how much of my thought process to share with him; I was no longer certain my inner life was a subject that he was interested in. Once it was out, I was worried I had overstepped, but decided to crush that anxiety and let him be the one to pull away.

I was rewarded with a slight incline of his head toward me, a small gesture of curiosity. "Does the nature of secrets still surprise you?"

"No. Just this one."

There was silence instead of the hum of acknowledgment I was used to. I put my hand on the back of the chair in front of me for additional support, both physical and emotional.

"How are you?" I knew it was an absurd question to ask, but not asking seemed worse. I knew the answer and I also knew he would lie about it.

"My equilibrium is undisturbed."

"You don't have to say that."

He stood and turned suddenly, snapping from reverie to aggressive hyperfocus. "I have constructed my life in such a way that I do not 'have' to do anything."

I held out a hand. I should have been scared, maybe, but instead I was just tired. All the anxiety I had brought with me into the room was uncoiling in his presence. Sharing space with him, I no longer saw him as a specter to focus all my worry; he was someone I cared for, in pain.

"I simply mean you can be candid. Not that I would put you under any duress."

A little bit of tension left him, as though it evaporated, and while he didn't look away from me his focus softened somehow. His eyes were liquid and deep, and I wondered if he would say something honest to me.

"Sit," he said, gesturing to the seat in front of me. I chose to believe his voice was truly a few degrees warmer rather than the work of my imagination. I gathered myself into the chair and he slowly rose, coming around his desk to stand closer. I felt a squeeze in my chest as we assumed our usual, more comfortable position around each other, while feeling embarrassed at myself that it even mattered.

"There will be a funeral," he said, folding his hands together behind his back.

I felt a sour spike of anxiety. This was news to me; I was suddenly worried I had missed something huge. "Has that been announced already? I was watching—"

"No. But there must be. There always is."

I relaxed a little. I opted to wait for him to continue rather than attempting to anticipate where he wanted the conversation to go.

"They will want to lay him in state," he continued, pacing away from me and looking toward the ceiling. "So half the world can walk by him and perform their grief."

"One last spectacle," I agreed.

"There will also be a Night Service," he said.

When I had first heard about the concept of the Night Service, like a lot of things that villains whispered about, it seemed too fantastic to be real. Anything I had heard, or overheard, was told with a kind of conspiratorial condescension that made me feel like I was being fucked with. But as often as not, or maybe more often, really, the most absurd rumors turned out to be true.

Whenever a hero of merit died—one who'd had a career of note, with whom the public had a significant relationship, and most important, who had amassed a significant rogues gallery in their time—it wasn't only the other heroes who were afforded the opportunity to pay their respects. After all the heroes and Draft officials and civilians and journalists had said their goodbyes, the villains would make their peace. Sometime after midnight, the wake would reopen for select mourners who could not show themselves during the day, and the Night Service would take place.

Sometimes only a few villains came; this was especially true for the older heroes, who would have very few nemeses still alive to celebrate their demise. But if they could or were free to do so, a few grim survivors would trickle in to reminisce about their enmity once more time. In the case of a younger hero cut down in their prime, the building might be full of mourners and celebrants brimming with ill intent and complicated grief. Either way it was a chance to pay their respects or spit their final insults at the recently departed, and it was held as sacred as anything could be by the villains of the world.

The apocryphal story about the Night Service and its origin was that in prior generations, the villains would just break into the buildings themselves, thwarting whatever security happened to be in place, in order to see their dearly departed nemeses off one last time. Over time, it became an unspoken but deeply respected tradition, with the heroes putting up only symbolic resistance or just turning a blind eye, allowing the gathering to take place. The villains kept their part of the bargain as respectful trespassers, who made a show of leaving the place as pristine as they found it, save perhaps for a few additional floral arrangements with questionable aesthetics. Any upstart who thought this was an opportunity to desecrate the building or the body wouldn't survive the misstep.

"We will have to prepare," he said, voice distant and sad.

I tried to process what that meant. "You plan to attend."

"Of course."

"Will that . . . be a problem."

His head moved slightly.

"You are officially his murderer," I said, hoping I kept my voice neutral.

"Ah." He almost sounded like he'd forgotten again. "That is much more a problem for them than it is for me."

I tried to be more pointed. "Do you think the Draft will attempt to stop you?"

He was unable to repress a small twitch of aggression in his left hand. "While I would prefer they maintain some semblance of dignity and decorum, no one will prevent me from celebrating his death as I see fit."

I had no idea if what he was saying had anything in common with reality, or whether his ego had just entirely blotted that out.

"It seems the only fitting occasion for my reintroduction to the land of the living." He looked at me with an expression I had not seen in a very long time: it was fragile and brief, but he smiled.

"I would like to go with you," I said. I wondered as I spoke if this was a terrible idea; I second-guessed almost everything I said to him now, sure I was about to put additional strain on whatever tenuous connection remained between us. I was also certain that if I took no risks, never reached for any intimacy, we were already doomed.

"Of course. It is only right that you, the crux of his downfall, should be there to see it through."

My throat felt tight. "Leviathan."

Had I ever called him by his name like that before? I typically used an honorific; the word felt very strange in my mouth. His reaction, the sudden tension in his body, indicated he was as unused to hearing it as I was to speaking it.

I swallowed and continued. "I want—to apologize. If I had known how—"

He sharply raised his hand, and I stopped. A moment ago he had been staring into the middle distance, thinking; despite the fact that the direction of his gaze hadn't really changed, I was suddenly aware he was avoiding eye contact.

"You are forbidden from apologizing."

I was at a loss. "What . . . can I say, then?"

"Nothing, if you intend to express remorse."

"Regret, then. For the impact it had on you."

He sighed. "You should not have seen it."

"You had been through a lot."

"I have no excuse for my reactions. I have . . . done a great deal of reflection in the past weeks. I have progressed past such undignified displays of emotion."

He was, of course, completely full of shit. Pain was pouring off him like lava from a gouge in the earth, so thick and heavy it was almost visible. He was devastated, mourning the loss of what might have been the closest connection he had to another living thing on this planet. Denial would not reverse that loss or make it any less painful, but by god he was going to try.

"I should have said this earlier," he continued. "You took on vast responsibilities that were not yours to bear. You claimed that power instead of allowing it to fall. Your role in that, and in the fate of . . . the recently deceased, is commendable."

I was not prepared for praise. "Thank you." It came out as a grainy whisper.

He waited a moment for more, but I could not form words coherently. "You may attend the celebration of his death in whatever capacity you feel is appropriate."

"Going is . . . important for me," I managed.

Leviathan nodded. "You hated him very much."

"I hated him as well as I could."

"I know," he said, softly, as though I had said something kind. I had hated Supercollider with every atom in me; who he was and what he represented in equal measures. Leviathan recognized that, and respected it. Not going to his funeral would have felt obscene, and even if it hadn't, there was no universe where Leviathan attended that funeral and I did not go with him.

THE EXTENDED VISITATION was streamed and broadcast around the clock for almost a week before the funeral itself. The procession lines never stopped, a never-ending stream of mourners walking past the massive stone monument that held Supercollider's body. It seemed like he was really there, though already sealed away from anyone who couldn't teleport through concrete and lead and a matter-distortion-proof alloy. Photos of his chiseled, perfect face were everywhere, beaming out the benevolent-seeming smile that had died with him. Even had it not been my job to watch, there was no escaping the infinite coverage of his death.

While the outside world performed its grandest theater of grief, everyone inside Leviathan's compound seemed to be holding their breath, waiting for the consequences. So far the Draft had made no further moves, only announced a "policy of containment" they intended to enact. "Supercollider would not have wanted us to act rashly and put any innocent lives at risk," the acting CDO said in response to pressure for immediate retaliatory action. It was tense and far too quiet, and everyone was certain it was only a matter of time before some superheroic loose cannon slipped out of the Draft's rigging and decided to personally blast through the ceiling.

For Leviathan himself, Supercollider's death was an existential crisis, a moment where the very meaning of his life and work, his very identity, was in a state of flux. I had my own ugly, complicated feelings about it, worry for Leviathan battling with grotesque pride, and a weird sort of longing. I'd hated deeply and well; it was a relationship that helped define me and provided infinite psychic fuel. A dawning sense of true loss finally crashed inside me. In quiet moments, I found myself wishing I could have hated the living man just a little longer.

For most of Leviathan's staff, a very different series of internal conflicts was taking place. Not only was their boss suddenly alive again, he was more hated than he had ever been. Their personal heat score had just been raised exponentially, and for a lot of people, this meant considering whether the on-site housing and extended drug coverage was worth being indefinitely marooned from the rest of society. Many of them still had the option to leave, to join other legitimate or gray industries, rather than hitch their fates to Leviathan's for whatever came next. While for most of my colleagues Supercollider's death was a Big Deal, possibly a critical turning point in their career, it represented a question of livelihood rather than something that threatened to redefine their state of being.

A few even had the luxury of being flippant. When I ventured out of the secluded island of my office, I discovered someone had added a funeral poll to the nearest break room's glass whiteboard. The first two voting axes were "Casket: Open" and "Casket: Closed." I stood for a while and stared at the options, wondering if I was upset, and if so about what. Eventually I abandoned trying to sort it out, and after considering both options for a moment, I added a third, "Casket: Absent," along with my initials. Two folks from R&D, who had been animatedly rubberducking at each other before I arrived, watched me and then nodded sagely. While I shoveled a selection of protein bars (lemon and birthday cake flavored respectively) into my bag, one of them stood up and changed their vote to my suggestion.

"You're just trying to throw everyone off," said Vesper, directly behind me, and I jumped. He was quiet and sneaky (and cyborgy) enough to still give me a mild heart attack whenever he chose.

I attempted to regain my cool by turning slowly, and I hoped menacingly. "I think it's entirely plausible that they've already dropped whatever bag they scraped him into in the Mariana Trench, just so no one with such ambitions could get their hands on the body. Besides, even if they keep his real meat sack off-site, they need to put something out there for people to gawk and weep at."

He was standing in the doorway behind me, arms crossed, his multi-jointed metallic fingers folded seriously over his elbows.

"Are you saying there should be a fourth category, then?" He pointed at the board. "'Casket: Symbolic'?"

I thought about it. "You know what, yeah, I am."

He picked up the green dry-erase marker and wrote it in the poll. He pressed too hard and the marker squeaked.

When I left, he followed me. I was glad to have his company; he was one of the very few who had always known Leviathan was alive, and therefore was not treating me differently after the recent revelations.

"Are you going?" he asked, once we were out of eavesdropping range.

"To the funeral?"

"The other funeral."

I swallowed. "Obviously."

"Are you . . . sure?"

There was a lot of meaning in that short pause, most of which profoundly irritated me for reasons I could not fully articulate. "I am."

"You think that's a good idea?"

"If you are implying Leviathan might have a problem with my attendance, I can assure you it's already greenlit."

"That's not it—it just seems like a lot for *you* to deal with."

"I mean. Fair." I shuffled my thoughts around like a deck of cards, trying to feel for the right one. "I was there at the beginning of his death; it seems right I should be there at the end."

"The beginning of his death," he repeated.

"Would you prefer 'present as he was turned into flesh macramé.'"

He shuddered. "Wow, never use those words together in that order ever again."

"How about 'flesh crochet'?"

"Auditor." He held up one hand in a gesture of I'm-going-to-puke supplication.

"I give you gold," I grumbled, but elected to be merciful. We walked for a quiet and comfortable few minutes back toward my office.

"I'm serious, you know," he said quietly. "Are you going to be okay?"

I looked over, and realized what I'd taken for companionable silence was him nervously trying to figure out what to say next. I slowed a little to give myself the time to come up with an acceptable answer.

"At the funeral? Or is that a larger and more terrible question."

"Let's go with 'at the funeral.'"

"Of course I am."

I heard the mechanical whirr of his eyes narrowing suspiciously.

"If that sounded unconvincing, that's because I am easily distractible, not because I suffer from human emotions."

"I see," he said. I had never heard anyone less convinced of something.

"Look. I know I have a lot of reasons not to be okay."

"That's an understatement."

"I think the . . . closure will be good for all of us. The finality of a funeral. He's dead as a doornail and sealed in a vault. There's nothing else to wait for. It's done."

I took the opportunity to disengage myself with half a smile. He watched me, pensively, but for a moment I thought I'd given him enough to let me off the hook. When he spoke again, it was quiet enough that I pretended I could no longer hear him.

"When you say 'all of us,' who do you mean?"

"HAVE YOU EVER been to a Night Service before?" I asked, pausing putting my earrings in and shifting my gaze to Melinda's reflection. She was behind me, leaning on the bathroom doorframe, arms crossed rakishly. She was wearing a fantastic suit, beautifully tailored, even though she would be driving and not setting foot in the building where the funeral was being held.

"Sort of. Chauffeured, but never gone in. As is my lot in life."

I focused back on my own reflection. I'd spent an embarrassing amount of time trying to settle on what was a funeral-appropriate level of eyeliner. No, not just funeral, but funeral-of-my-nemesis-appropriate. Choosing clothes had also been an agony, and for the first time I was jealous of every villain who had a stupid signature outfit they could always fall back on.

"This is what the cloaks are for," I said, critically evaluating my jacket. I'd gone with a green velvet so dark it was almost indistinguishable from black—until I stood next to Leviathan, which would illuminate the color by contrast, and make his chitin seem even more light-swallowingly dark. Suddenly I was worried that I'd overthought it and now just looked drab.

"You're not tall enough to pull off a cloak," Melinda said, and I glared at her. "You'd look like a high fantasy maid all forlorn in the wood."

"I would look powerful and dignified."

She placed the back of her hand against her forehead. "'Tis that my love the woodcutter? Oh, I hope 'tis not the evil wizard.'"

"Do you think you are helping right now?"

"Now, a capelet you could pull off."

"Absolutely not."

"They're subtle and chic."

"I'd look like an heiress leaving the courthouse after eloping."

"So specific."

I examined my face critically. "I'm trying for 'widow who most definitely poisoned her husband for the money,' minus the husband part."

"Your skirt should be sluttier, then."

I glared at her, "I am about as slutty as a gnome."

"Wear some fishnets at least."

I grudgingly admitted that was an excellent suggestion and started hunting through my drawers. Melinda gallantly turned her back.

"What are the odds I could fake a cryo-sleep accident in the next couple of hours," I said, gingerly rolling on the fishnets.

"You know, you don't have to go," she said over her shoulder.

"You are both correct and utterly wrong."

"Yeah."

"I wish I could send some kind of replicant or hologram instead."

"Molly might be able to arrange something."

"Don't give me hope. You can turn around."

Melinda looked at me again. "Remember, you actually went through the effort of ensuring you could go."

I suddenly wished I hadn't told her so many details about my conversations with Leviathan. "I know, I definitely did this to myself. And I do want to be there. Need to be there. I need to . . . put him in the ground."

"I get that."

I walked back to the vanity mirror in order to more efficiently stress myself out while poking at my face. "I also can't stand the thought of him . . . going alone."

"Is that because the Boss needs the support, or you *think* he needs the support?"

I made eye contact with her reflection. "What kind of question is that?"

"The important kind. I mean, I know what you think you're doing; I am just trying to figure out if you're lying to yourself."

"You could be a little less honest today."

"He has been saying he has 'ascended' or whatever."

"He told you, too, huh?"

"Yes. He is no longer 'troubled' by 'trivial emotions.'"

"Ugh."

"So maybe he'll be just fine at suppressing his feelings."

"He absolutely will not be fine."

I pointedly did not meet her eyes, despite the fact she was boring into me with her bullshit-destroying laser vision. "Yeah?"

I thought about shutting her down, but for some reason I didn't. If I was going to have so many imaginary arguments in my head with Leviathan about bottling up all of his emotions, I couldn't hypocritically do the same thing.

"He's . . . devastated, to be honest." I immediately regretted saying it out loud, but I knew I wasn't telling Melinda something she didn't already know. While he was never going to be chatty or forthcoming, he would let slip just enough that, coupled with some careful observation, Melinda would be fully capable of getting an extremely accurate read on him.

"He hasn't been himself," she agreed, confirming my suspicions.

"So . . . exactly. I want to be there, and I need to be there. But I'm dreading it."

"While I can probably guess most of the answers, tell me anyway: What's making you so avoidant now?"

I did have an answer, or rather a series of answers, all tangled together in an ugly, undifferentiated mass inside my head. *Like a rat king*, I thought. I tried to pull them apart, separate each wriggling feeling from the other, but it was nearly impossible.

Ultimately I landed on "I don't want to remind him that he hates me."

Except I felt like someone else had said those words; I did not make the conscious choice to speak them but suddenly there they were, out in the world, hanging between Melinda and me. Melinda's entire face seemed to furrow, like it was turning inside out in the effort to make sense of what had just been said.

"That's the stupidest thing I've ever heard."

"Oh, come on, not the very stupidest, I'm sure."

"No, definitely number one."

"Wow, I'm honored."

"He's fonder of you than anything on this hell planet."

"Except Shannon."

"Auditor, shut up."

"You know he loves that lizard."

"Are we going to really have this conversation or—"

"I recognize I started the conversation, but now that I'm here—"

"No, fuck it, overruled." She actually sounded a little irritated, something I was not used to. Melinda usually indulged my whining with remarkable stoicism, but I'd finally gotten a rise out of her and I instantly regretted it.

"Sorry. It's a defense mechanism."

"Just listen to me, then. I'm around him a lot. More than you, at least since he's been back."

That stung more than I wanted to let on, so I didn't say anything.

"He's different about you."

I swallowed. "He was, or might have been, but I don't think that's still true."

"I am telling you. The only thing that lit him up like you was defeating his mortal enemies, and—"

"But that's it, that's *exactly* it! I took away the one thing that was most important to him in the entire world."

"You mean Supercollider."

"The possibility he could have beaten Supercollider."

"Auditor—"

I started pacing. "And now we're about to spend the night in a room with his fucking body, at a ceremony specifically designed to evoke every awful emotion Leviathan might have about that loss."

"So when you say 'took away' you realize you are referring to saving his fucking life."

I let my anxieties take the floor. "I might have overreacted. He probably would have escaped, eventually."

"The fuck he would have, and even if he did, what would have been left of him by then?"

I knew what she was saying was true, it was what I had said to myself countless times and what I absolutely believed at the time, but I felt like I doubted those certainties more every day. I didn't know how to argue with both her and myself.

Melinda, however, was having no problems at all when it came to finding words.

"I want you to listen to me very carefully. Got it?" It occurred to me that she was really quite angry.

I stopped pacing and stood still. "Yes. Okay."

She nodded once. "Whatever he's dealing with, whatever his I-don't-have-feelings feelings are—nobody knows what's happening in there. He sure fucking doesn't. So quit thinking about it. That's his problem."

She had taken a couple of steps toward me, intense but not aggressive, though I felt like I was being backed into a very specific kind of corner. I resisted the urge to back away.

"What you did was—and I mean this positively—heroic. Bordering on impossible. No one else could have done it. But *you* did it and you did it *for* him. You are not responsible for managing how he feels about you opening the doors of hell for him. Whatever he's feeling, let him process it in his fucked-up way. You need to be proud of what you did, because right now? All you're doing is robbing yourself of your own victory—and don't let him rob you of it."

I felt like she had stabbed me in the chest. I looked down, half expecting to see blood welling from the point of pain in my rib cage, but I found I couldn't see anything—tears were pouring out of my eyes like a faucet had been turned on. I wasn't crying so much as I was leaking, alarmingly. I tried to speak, but the only thing that came out were ugly, heaving sobs.

Melinda's anger evaporated. She was suddenly apologizing, hunting around the room for a box of tissues, reaching toward me and then hesitating. I took the wad of tissues from her hands and tried to say she had nothing to be sorry for, but what came out wasn't exactly a coherent sentence. I collapsed into my vanity chair and blew my nose.

By the time I was able to get my face back under control, my makeup was completely destroyed. The tissues were no longer absorbing anything, so I wiped my eyes one more time on the backs of my hands, leaving huge streaks of melted eyeliner. I wondered how long that explosion had been building.

"Fuck." Melinda was wringing her hands, not sure what to do. "Shit. I was a real asshole there. I'm sorry."

I shook my head, not quite able to talk yet. I struggled out of my jacket, unwilling to get tears or makeup on the velvet.

She turned in a little circle, and then left the room for a moment, returning with a glass of water. I took it gratefully and, holding it with both hands, took several long swallows. The storm had passed. My entire head felt strange and cold, and a deep exhaustion gathered in my chest.

"It finally happened," I gasped. Melinda took the glass from my hands and placed it on top of the dresser.

"I'm so sorry," she repeated.

"This isn't your fault."

"I was being a shithead."

"You were being honest. I needed to hear some things." I stood up shakily. Melinda extended a hand toward me, but I waved her off and tottered to the bathroom, sniffing.

"That was a long time coming," I said. I looked in the mirror and groaned; my face was red and puffy, my eyes swollen. There was no choice but to completely start over.

Melinda followed me and stood guiltily in the doorway. I squeezed a few pumps of an oil cleanser into my hands, rubbed them together to warm it, and slathered it on my face and neck.

"You, uh . . . You want to talk about it?" I could tell she was deeply uncomfortable with this turn of events but felt obligated to offer. I was about to let her off the hook, but changed my mind while ruining my face.

"Yeah. Maybe a little. Thank you."

She didn't say anything. I dried off my face, looked at myself in the mirror again, and frowned. I retrieved an ice pack from the kitchen and wrapped it in a damp towel, holding it against my swollen face.

"You're right, of course," I said.

"About what?"

"Everything you said. About. You know. Me wrecking all my own shit."

She flinched. "Well. I hate being right, then."

"Sucks, doesn't it. I'm right all the time."

"Tragic."

"Yeah."

"What are you going to do?"

"I'm going to reconstruct my makeup and then go to the funeral. I might hate every second of it, but I will live and then it will end. If Leviathan . . . If my catastrophizing isn't pathological, and my worst fears come true, well. That's his problem. And I will deal with it."

I said the words, and while I knew they were technically correct, I still couldn't feel them. I tried to lay my emotions out, look at them as though they were objects, things with interesting characteristics I could dispassionately observe. I saw the awful disappointment that Leviathan, in his grief, hadn't been able to give me the recognition for what I had done, recognition I knew I deserved; the fear that, in saving him, I had severed whatever the delicate connection between us had been; and behind that, the haunting fear that there had never been anything between us, that I had just imagined it and allowed my friends to convince me it was there, because I wanted it to be so badly.

I suddenly felt like I couldn't bear another person looking at me for another moment. "Hey. I think I need–"

Melinda immediately leapt away, seemingly thrilled to be released. "Of course. I'm really–"

"Please don't. We're totally good. I just need to fix my face." I laughed. It almost sounded genuine.

She nodded once, and disappeared as quickly as she could. She shut the door so quietly when she left, it was as though she was trying to just sublimate out of my apartment without a trace.

When I was sure I was alone, I walked out into my living room and sat down in the middle of the couch. It felt completely alien to me, unfamiliar, like I was in a hotel room I'd never seen before. My desk felt like home; my apartment still felt like I was staying in a stranger's house.

When the Draft left Leviathan's compound, after his battle with Supercollider in the courtyard, they'd wrecked as much as they could on their way out; my apartment had been one of the casualties. Since then, most of my furniture had been replaced, both because it was damaged and for security concerns. The mattress, which had been thrown on the floor, the one I slept on in a state of shock in the immediate aftermath, wasn't there anymore. The couch, whose cushion had been cut open and stepped on by Draft paramilitary boots, had been incinerated. The new couch was a different color, less firm and with plusher arms. The holes in the walls had been patched and painted. It barely resembled the room I'd recovered in twice, where I'd reinvented myself and created a new career, where I had once come home from to find an orchid from Leviathan waiting for me as a get-well present.

If it's all different, then I need to be different too. I would adapt to this, like I had to everything else. I returned to the vanity to paint myself into a new person.

KELLER SOMEHOW MADE every suit I'd ever seen him wear look like a military dress uniform. Didn't matter the cut or the fit, it was just something about the way he inhabited the formal clothes.

The two of us walked to the rear doors of St. Byrd's Cathedral with careful purpose. We were to approach openly and find the way unblocked; that was how it was supposed to be done. While the vigil still held outside the cathedral, and throughout the city and far beyond, inside there would only be whoever was keeping watch, and the body.

Everything we carried was ceremonial. In place of a handkerchief, Keller had a set of gold lockpicks arranged in a leather case; I held the bolt cutters. They were beautiful, made just for the occasion, the sterling silver head engraved with skulls and roses. Neither were meant to be used (the lockpicks were too soft a metal), as the door would be unbarred. Symbolically, we were prepared to break in, but it wouldn't be needed if everything went well.

"There's still a chance this all goes to shit," Keller said casually.

"Yeah." I adjusted my grip on the dark walnut handle.

He shrugged. "Probably it won't. But don't let your guard down."

The massive wood doors loomed in front of us, their handles cast in bronze. Keller gave one an authoritative pull but met almost immediate resistance. He looked at me with steely concern, and I leaned closer to see the problem.

There was a thin chain looped around the door handles, linked by a tiny, almost jewelry-like padlock. It wasn't meant to stop anything, not really; Keller probably could have given it another firm tug or two and it would have given way. It certainly wasn't meant to stop anyone who could splinter the door with a psychic blast or shoot acid out of their eyes, but the message was clear: if you want to come in, you're going to have to break in.

"Do you want to do the honors?" But I was already adjusting my grip on the bolt cutters, and found myself hoping he'd say no.

He shook his head, though. "It should be you."

I nodded. Keller held my cane while I lifted the bolt cutters with both hands and snipped the chain in half. It was pathetically easy, and the chain and lock slithered to the ground. I took a moment to very deliberately pocket the cut chain and lock before nodding to Keller to open the doors.

A feeling of something like relief, but much more complicated, washed over me as we walked into the narthex. There was no ambush, no trap sprung, just the echo of our footsteps and the vast loneliness that lives in mostly empty places of worship. Keller relayed back to Leviathan that we'd made it in the building, and we started to turn on the lights.

"I thought it'd be you."

I recognized his voice but still turned slowly anyway, while Keller both looked back casually and had his hand on whatever nightmare device he was carrying at his hip.

"Hi, Doc," I said. "I'm sorry for your loss."

Doc Proton stood in the doorway to the nave, silhouetted by the lights behind him so the shadowy outline of the hero he'd been was briefly visible. He'd taken off his tie and jacket, and his shirt was open at the neck. His massive shoulders had a slight stoop, like the weight of responsibility he carried had grown a bit heavier since I'd seen him last.

At his side, rather than his usual medical attendant, was a young hero in a black, formal version of her official heroic outfit. She was taller than Doc and much lankier, with an intense, sculptural face. I recognized her as Thundersnow, someone I had barely heard of. I tried to pull up a single fact but every slide I'd ever seen about her escaped me. The only thing I could remember about her was that once when someone had asked her about her (objectively weird) name, she'd simply answered "I'm Canadian," as though that explained anything at all. She stood to one side watching him closely for guidance, her stance wide and ready to spring into action.

"I'm sure you are." There was an acrid bitterness in his voice I hadn't heard before.

I softened in response. "I mean it."

His eyes got wet then and he nodded, looking down at the floor.

"You're on Watch," Keller said, reaching out a hand toward Doc. Thundersnow watched it like he was holding out a cobra, but after a moment Doc took the handshake and the two squeezed hard.

"No one else," Doc said.

"That's rough."

Usually, when a hero died, their sidekick would stay up all night the last night of the visitation, keeping vigil over the body before it would be laid to rest. Usually that kick would be a proper hero in their own right by then, assuming their old role as one last service to their mentor.

Supercollider didn't have a sidekick, of course. I'd made sure of that. And with Quantum Entanglement in exile and no obvious successor, it had fallen to Doc, his aging mentor, to fill the role. I felt a dull stab of anger. They should never have made him do it; the burden was too cruel. But standing in that cathedral, I was suddenly glad for my own sake that it was him.

"You should know," I said, wanting to broach the subject as quickly as possible. "Leviathan is coming."

Thundersnow's faced darkened, anger overtaking her. "*Leviathan*. No! We can't let–"

Doc Proton held up a hand to cut her off, then said to me, "That's not wise."

"Regardless of the wisdom of the idea, he most definitely is coming."

Thundersnow was almost vibrating, clearly caught between being furious and terrified.

"He wouldn't dare to show his face here," she said, falling back on her heroic repertoire of stock phrases in a crisis.

I couldn't completely suppress a sneer. "You'd be surprised what he'd dare to do."

It landed even more like a threat than I intended and Thundersnow's face screwed up angrily. Doc put a hand on her shoulder, the permanent shunt he had in that arm briefly visible.

"Of all of them, he's the one who deserves to be here. They hated each other the most."

Thundersnow's eyes were wide. "But I—we're supposed to guard—"

While she spluttered, I reached into the pocket of my jacket and produced a gift I'd brought for Doc: a pack of the filter-less cigarettes he regularly smuggled into the Hadron care facility for retired heroes where he now lived.

"I thought you might need these." I held them out.

He let out a raw little cough of a laugh. "Are you trying to be nice, or are you saying 'die faster'?"

"It was meant to be nice, but you can take it however feels better."

He took the cigarettes and bounced them in his hand. "Thanks."

"I'm not supposed to let you smoke either," Thundersnow said.

All three of us looked at her, exasperated. Doc recovered first and put both his hands on her shoulders.

"Let's go outside a moment, champ. I need to explain a few things."

Thundersnow thought about arguing, but after looking me and Keller up and down allowed herself reluctantly to be led away. I could see how exhausted Doc was by his gait, and turned away before I felt too much sympathy for him.

"How much of a problem is this going to be," I asked, half addressed to Keller and the other half to myself.

"Depends." Keller had pulled out his phone. I watched him laboriously text a few words back to headquarters. "If you've got anything you want to do, do it now before anyone shows up."

I knew what he meant: if I wanted my own moment alone with Supercollider, this might be my last chance to take it. I nodded through the sudden cloud of dread that descended over me, and trying to keep my shoulders straight and confident, I left the entrance and walked into the largest room of the cathedral.

I knew what to expect: the black stone ziggurat with its smoked glass panel, the snaking lines leading the mourners past it defined by heavier velvet ropes laid directly on the stone floor. I'd watched the news stories with the endless lines of mourners shuffling past, each allowed only a moment's pause by the monument. I'd been wrong about the casket—he really was there, whatever was left of him.

It was different to be there in person, in the huge vaulted space now mostly empty but for the monument in the center. I felt like I was walking inside the body of a fallen giant, flying buttresses like a rib cage arching above me. The monument itself was huge and imposing, requiring superstrength of the pallbearers who would carry it, but it was all the empty space that seemed full of ghosts.

I expected my feelings to be complicated, but I saw them as dry and acidic, made of ash and sand, baked by the heat of all my hatred. But all the emotions I felt, standing alone where Supercollider's body lay, were wet, slithering things I could not hold or control. Pride and grief writhed together in a slick, entangled mass, and I felt as though I were about to vomit sea water.

I wish we had more time, I found myself thinking. I closed my fist and placed my knuckles against the stone. *I could have hated you so much longer. I could have done so much worse.*

A deep sense of loss sloshed around in my chest. Without Supercollider to focus on, there was a great void left behind, a huge volume of hatred without a focal point. Of course there was the Draft, but it's hard to hate an organization, even a very evil one, with the kind of passion you can hate a person. I knew no one could ever take his place, that what we'd had, what he'd taken from me and given in return, was special.

I could have wept then, but I chose not to. I swallowed it all, the brackish anguish, and left him there.

As I rejoined Keller in the narthex, I fantasized briefly about leaving, sneaking out a side door and hiding in the back of Melinda's car all night. But then the doors groaned open again and the villains began to arrive.

I recognized Defense Mechanism immediately. I hadn't spoken to him since I'd hired him and Denial (though he would describe it as us "working together") for one of my first successful operations. The whole thing had gone swimmingly, with only a few third-degree burns, and we'd efficiently ruined the hero Glassblower's whole life. However, despite us upholding our end of the bargain to the letter, he always felt he'd been short-changed somehow, and complained bitterly about being kept "out of the loop of our greater ambitions." He was right on the second point, but he got all the fame he'd wanted at the cost of only a few horrifying injuries to his own henches, so it always felt like little more than a tantrum to me. In my opinion, he hadn't done enough on his own to capitalize on the incident and so his bump to fame had been extremely temporary, something he wanted to make everyone else's fault.

Denial, I noted, was nowhere to be seen. Instead, Defense Mechanism was flanked by Manticore and The Choir, who each looked smug and spoiling for a fight respectively. All three of them were well-connected, loved to gossip, and were terminally bad at keeping their mouths shut when doing so wasn't to their immediate benefit. I assumed they had nominated themselves as a scouting party, first on the scene to the Night Service.

Manticore pointedly avoided eye contact with me (we'd never gotten along) but the other two made a beeline for me directly so he was forced to follow. Defense Mechanism didn't even try to hide his shit-eating grin while The Choir adopted an exaggerated look of sympathy.

"I knew I'd see you next at a funeral," The Choir said, opening his arms for an uninvited embrace. I leaned forward stiffly and he kissed the air near both of my cheeks

"I'm so glad you could make it," I said, as chilly as I could manage.

"Wouldn't miss it for the world," The Choir said. He put a hand on my shoulder, an awkward pinch. Defense Mechanism took a theatrically noisy sip from the straw of his iced coffee. The Choir shot him a look. "How are you holding up?" he asked me.

"This is the best thing that ever happened to her," Defense Mechanism said before I could answer, looking around the mostly empty foyer as though trying to find someone more important to talk to.

The Choir pretended to be scandalized. "She has been through the wringer; you could try and be polite."

"I've kept busy," I said.

The Choir tutted. "I can only imagine. The entire headquarters must be a powder keg."

"I'm surprised you decided to stay on, considering the heat." Defense Mechanism was clearly trying to goad me into some kind of a reaction.

I smiled. "I think my lot's been cast, don't you?"

"Indeed it has," The Choir hissed, glaring at him.

"So, what, you're a proper villain now?" Defense Mechanism gestured toward the foyer ceiling, indicating the entire funeral and my role in it.

"My job title hasn't changed."

"I told you, she's still a hench," Defense Mechanism said to Manticore, who openly laughed.

"You say that like it's a pejorative."

"I just think it's sweet, how you're so content to be in his shadow forever."

"I'm sure you're making all the best decisions for yourself," The Choir said, patting in the general vicinity of my arm.

I made meaningful eye contact with Keller, who had been keeping half an eye on the situation. He strode over almost immediately.

"Defense. Good to see you." Keller stuck out his hand and Defense Mechanism took it hesitantly, grimacing at the older man's grip.

"The pleasure is entirely mine," he said witheringly, withdrawing his crushed hand.

"You the Meat here, then?" Manticore said. He made it clear he considered the word to be derogatory. Then he had the gall to light a cigarette with an intricate Zippo.

"You bet your ass," Keller said cheerfully. Keller immediately yanked the cigarette out of his mouth, like a snake striking, and dropped it into Defense Mechanism's drink. It hissed when it hit the watery iced coffee.

"Have a good evening, gentlemen." Keller turned from their three stunned faces and led me away from them toward the doors, where more villains and their entourages were beginning to arrive.

"That was spectacular," I said, no longer able to keep from grinning.

"That little shit lights up again, I will drag him outside and make him say 'Meat' with some respect."

"His lighter isn't even shaped like a fucking manticore—it's a griffin."

"Maybe you two can play Dungeons and Dragons later."

"Fuck off."

For the better part of an hour we served as an awkward receiving line, greeting the villains as they came in, letting them rant and gesticulate as they needed, and then letting them pass into the huge chamber where Supercollider's body lay. Most of them were there to be seen, and it was obvious.

"Who's the wizard?" Keller had appeared next to me again, and was wrinkling his nose in the direction of a villain who was sweeping through the foyer in black and purple taffeta robes, holding a huge staff topped with a coiled snake.

"Oh my god, it's Constrictor."

"Wasn't he in jail."

"He was. I think we let him out."

"Shame."

"He had the *worst* proposal."

If there was one thing Keller loved as much as military strategy, it was gossip. "Did he want to TP the headquarters?"

"He wanted to put poppers in the ventilation system."

He glared at me. "And you didn't fund *that*?"

"It didn't move the needle. Although, on reflection, it's funnier than I gave it credit for."

I watched Constrictor greet Thespian with nauseating fondness, the two of them holding each other at arm's length and spitting compliments at each other. Thespian was wearing a full-body black leotard, almost like a morph suit, with a huge white tragedy mask covering his entire face. While they loudly performed their grief, I found myself bristling in irritation; neither of them so much as had a fingernail broken by Supercollider in their middling careers, and their presence here seemed somehow blasphemous.

On the other hand, the few who had legitimate relationships with Supercollider were, for the most part, much more understated. Many even wore their civvies, opting for black suits or robes. Thessalonika, who had once caught Supercollider in a chronodisruption field that slowed time around him and very nearly brought down a Draft satellite while he was delayed, wore a Victorian mourning gown. The Abbatoir wore an all-black version of his signature suit, complete with a leather butcher's apron. He was gravely polite but also seemed suspicious of me, examining my face with a surgical intensity I found unnerving. We caught each other staring and both offered a grave nod.

"Don't look so nervous, you're at a funeral," Keller said, recapturing my attention.

"Everyone here has about thirty-seven competing motives operating at a time. I'd say my 'nervousness' is just awareness."

"This isn't so bad."

"Compared to what."

He had a twinkle in his eye that suddenly made me deeply worried. "You should have heard what Leviathan *wanted* to do."

". . . What."

"He was going to steal the body."

"*What.*"

"Yep. Just show up with a crane and pick it up like a claw machine."

"Why the fuck are you telling me this? Is this supposed to calm me?"

"I talked him out of it. I think. You know how he is."

I stared at him in horror, then just turned and walked away, glancing up at the ceiling as if I could see through the roof to find a skycrane hovering above.

As I glanced around, I saw him sitting by himself in a nondescript corner, one of the last people I expected to attend. He wore a suit without a tie, in a style that was a good thirty years out of date, and seemed to have arrived alone. I made my way over to him slowly, so as not to surprise him in any way, keeping my hands visible.

"Can I join you?"

The legendary supervillain Decay scowled preemptively, but his face relaxed as soon as his eyes swept up my body to my face and recognized me.

"By all means." He gathered his jacket a little closer to him, though there was plenty of room, and I bobbed my head in thanks, sitting in a folding chair next to him.

"Thank you for coming," I said. "I didn't think you were someone I would ever meet in person."

He snorted. "Frankly I'm as surprised as you are."

"A hell of a trip from Antarctica."

"Oh, hardly. Truth is, I've been here for a few months now."

That was shocking. No one had heard from Decay in decades;

under other circumstances his reappearance would have been head-line news. Which, it occurred to me, was probably the point. "I sup-pose this would be the time to return, if you wanted to stay under the radar."

"I should thank you somewhat for that."

I smiled a little. "Happy to be of service."

"Are you?"

"I'm sorry?"

"Happy. And to be of service, specifically."

"I don't—"

"Feel free to tell me where to stuff it, of course, but it seems odd to me that you would at once be so ambitious and so happy to serve the needs of someone else, so devotedly."

I was catching up. "There's a lot of space to be ambitious when Leviathan is the only person above you."

"That's entirely fair. Has it been worth it, so far?"

"The word 'it' could mean a lot of things."

He waved a hand dramatically. "The left-hand path. The 'de-scent into villainy' or however you want to call it."

"Ah." I looked around the room for a moment. Most of the villains in the foyer were huddled in tight little groups, having hushed con-versations and, very occasionally, shooting glances to where I was sitting. "So far, it's been the best thing that ever happened to me."

"Really."

"To be fair, it was a pretty low bar."

He gave a tiny, wet chuckle. "Sounds about right." The laugh seemed to have unsettled something in his lungs, and he coughed. He produced an inhaler from his pocket and took two hits, his breath rattling. I waited until he was fully recovered to continue.

"It's still true, though."

"Do you intend to stay where you are forever, then?" His voice was not unkind.

I was starting to hate this sort of question. I looked down. "I don't have all the answers yet."

"Of course. Forgive me for pressing you."

"No, not at all. They're good questions, but they might not be the right ones."

He nodded sagely. "Whatever you choose, just make sure it's all worth it." He coughed again, a damp and stringy sound. "If you want to get out of this life, this could be your chance. And it might be your last one."

"To what, leave Leviathan? Stop being a villain entirely?"

"Surely you can see the narrative. The hero dies at the hands of the villain, you regret your role and repent. Good story there."

I turned in my seat to face him a little more directly. "Are you, as someone who spent decades in a possibly mythical base at the South Pole, telling me to consider walking the straight and narrow?"

"I am saying the door to the outside rarely opens, and as someone whose face is not recognizable on sight to the average civilian—yet—you should at least entertain the thought. Unless you aspire to retirement at the extreme end of this planet."

"Sounds peaceful."

He frowned again, clearly disliking my playfulness in the face of what I am sure he considered important advice.

I pulled back the cheek a little. "I appreciate what you are saying. Genuinely. But I've run the numbers. I know what it will cost."

He looked at me with deep pity, then. "Young lady. The devil's rates have never changed: everything you have, for everything you want. It's the fairest bargain there is, and anyone who says otherwise either expected to be able to cheat or never understood the deal to begin with."

I felt a chill come over me, as though I was surrounded by ghosts. I huddled down and tried not to visibly shiver.

He picked up my hand, like it was a small creature all on its own, and held it in both of his. His hands were thin and damp, and the skin had an odd fragility to it, like he might tear. "You have paid dearly. I am sure of that. But you have so much more yet to give, and to earn in exchange. In these rare moments when our contracts might be canceled, just be sure this is still the bargain that you want."

I tried to come up with something clever to say, but all the words turned to sand when they reached my mouth. Eventually I just nodded, which he seemed to accept; I imagine he knew he'd unbalanced me and thought it only fair to give me some time to recover.

Mercifully, before I had to figure out how the hell I was going to respond, or if I was just going to slap my legs, say "welp" and exit the conversation awkwardly, there was a small flurry of activity near the door. A brief change of the guard; a fresh supply of our Meat came in, and a few who'd been working inside left; Keller rematerialized from wherever he'd been lurking and scanned the room, clearly looking for me.

"I have to go now," I said, not taking my eyes off the scene in front of me. "I'd just like you to know that you have absolutely no cause for alarm, regardless of who may or may not be about to arrive. I've always been a great fan of your work."

Before Decay could manage a coherent reply, I quickly rejoined Keller. Together we walked over to the doors, trying not to draw too much attention to ourselves and only moderately succeeding. When I looked back over my shoulder toward Decay, he was gone.

Then, Leviathan walked through the doors.

There was no great fanfare, no trumpet blasts, no herald loudly announcing his name. He simply walked through the doors, and all of the energy in the building bent around him.

First, the room went quiet. It didn't happen instantly, but like dominoes falling, as conversations fell into stunned silence and then another villain turned their head to see what everyone had gotten so quiet about, and saw him.

He looked magnificent. His body might have been covered in natural armor, but that didn't mean he would not dress for drama. He'd draped epaulets over his chitinous shoulders, leather straps wrapping around his arms and chest. Around his waist he'd wrapped an asymmetrical skirt in impossibly heavy velvet, gathered up to one side. Around his neck, on a thick platinum box chain that evoked chain mail, was the only thing on his body that wasn't utterly black: a broken shard of porcelain, held in a setting shaped like eagle talons.

After a few beats of silence, there was a frantic scurrying as everyone scrambled out of his way. No one dared approach him directly yet, but rather stood a respectful distance off. Leviathan, of course, barely acknowledged the shock he provoked. He scanned the room imperiously, not rewarding anyone with eye contact. Ludmilla appeared behind him a moment later; Keller and I took that as our signal to join his retinue, Keller on the left and me on the right.

Ludmilla was there as his personal bodyguard, exuding an air of complete unfuckwithability, wearing a black jumpsuit like something a jewel thief would wear to the opera. I watched her scan the room for exits, vantage points, and ad-hoc weapons.

"The place is safe enough," Keller reported, I'm sure also noticing her. "They're watching but keeping distance. Should be fine."

She nodded, not taking her eyes off a balcony that she apparently didn't like very much. "Did you sweep?"

"I'll check again," Keller said, turning to investigate for what would have been the third time.

"No. Stay here." Leviathan's voice was deeper, more resonant than it often was; he was speaking in his Villain Voice, I realized. I'd gotten used to what he sounded like in private, when he didn't need to command the maximum amount of fear and respect. Here, though, he would be on his high-test alert level, using every ounce of his formidable ability to intimidate. My legs suddenly felt much less steady than they'd been moments before.

"How have the . . . guests behaved themselves so far?" He directed the question to me.

"Decent manners, terrible attitudes. None of them expected you would come."

"I am thrilled to disappoint them." He glanced down at me in a way that made me feel lightheaded.

He started walking suddenly, and all of us parted around him, reassembling in his wake into a proper entourage. I stayed closest to him, while Keller dropped back with Ludmilla and they brought up the rear like a proper honor guard. It was a wonder to watch all of the other villains practically scurry out of his way; all of the posturing and ridiculous confidence every one of them had been lobbing around at each other vaporized in his presence.

I was so focused on Leviathan, so caught up in the wonderful menace he exuded that I didn't see Doc until it was too late. He stepped in front of Leviathan just as he was approaching the door to the nave. His assistant was nowhere to be found; he'd clearly given her some task to keep her from interfering with what came next. He stood with his hands on his hips, shoulders back, like the statue of him that decorated the front lawn of the newer Draft headquarters.

"Step aside," Leviathan said. It was not kind, but there was a gentleness that no one else would have gotten.

Doc shook his head with great weariness. "I'm sorry, son. I can't do that."

"It is my right to see him gone."

"It is my duty to keep him safe, at the end."

Both of them sounded rehearsed, or like they were reading from a holy book, but I could tell from the incredible tension building between them that this was not part of the plan.

"You will not be able to stop me."

Doc sighed. "Of course not. But it's my job to try."

I realized with slow horror that he might really do this, might actually raise a hand to Leviathan and make the villain go through him. That Leviathan could and would was no question; he could have fought Doc to a standstill in his prime, but that time was decades gone. Doc's resistance would be entirely symbolic—a weak chain tying shut doors that we would nonetheless be forced to break to get through.

Please don't do this, I wanted to say out loud, but I knew it wasn't my place to do so. Leviathan gave him a long moment, but the old hero just stared him down, and with a mighty grief Leviathan gathered himself to step forward.

There was a cough to our left, and both Doc and Leviathan turned to look. Decay stood there, a hand raised to his mouth, smaller than any of us but still capable of incredible presence.

"Let him pass, Proton."

Doc's throat moved as he stared at his former archenemy. The last time they would have seen each other, decades before, was when Decay was leaving the world for Antarctica. Doc had gone to stop him from boarding his submersible escape vehicle, to crush his routed foe once and for all—but Decay got away, managed to slip beneath the gelid water and retreat to whatever peace he was capable of. Doc had been roundly criticized for standing aside and letting his enemy go, but Decay had kept the peace he promised.

"I can't do that," Doc said. "You know I can't."

Decay took a step closer.

"Beta," Doc warned, using his foe's old name, back from when there were three Decay siblings still living, before Alpha died in jail and Gamma was killed by Atom Bomb at the Battle of Pittsburgh.

Decay put a hand heavily on Doc's shoulder. "Step aside one more time. As you once did."

Doc looked down at the small, slim figure in front of him and I wondered how many times they'd tried to kill each other over the years. How many times they each had almost succeeded. I wondered if they counted, if it was possible to keep count. It all hung in the air between them for a moment; then Doc nodded once, and got out of the way.

"Thank you," Leviathan said.

Decay took Doc arm's then, and the two withdrew back into the foyer. I watched them while Leviathan briefly regained his composure. Decay said something quietly to Doc, still gripping the taller man's arm. Doc's entire body sagged as he started to sob, and Decay pulled him into an embrace. Then Leviathan stepped forward again, and I followed him.

The huge antechamber that held Supercollider's body was buzzing as we walked in, but as soon as Leviathan's presence was noticed, it grew quieter and quieter in waves rippling out from the door. It was a strange sensation, to have so much attention fixed in my direction, even by proxy; but while I felt its weight, the concentrated focus of everyone in the room pressing like a physical force, it was another thing to watch Leviathan react to it. He was like a black hole, all that energy just vanishing into him, and whether it was feeding him or just lost into the void it was impossible to tell. It felt like being in a submarine, in the deepest trench in the ocean; without his presence holding back the weight all around me I would have been crushed. But inside his orbit, I was safe.

There may as well have been no one else in the room then, for all the other visitors mattered. There was only Leviathan and the body. I felt real only in that I was close to him, as though his presence made me solid at the same time it turned everyone on the periphery to a pale shade.

Leviathan walked toward the monument slowly, so keeping pace with him felt like being a part of a procession. His cloak was long enough that it dragged the ground, spreading behind him like a train, and I was terribly afraid I would accidentally step on the hem. He stopped just a few feet away from the monument, and somehow all four of us close to him knew that this was our signal to pause and wait. After a second, he approached the monument alone.

The room was eerily quiet now. I caught myself holding my breath as he took those last few steps to the pyramid, and wondered how many people in the room were doing exactly the same thing.

After staring into the porthole for a long moment, he lifted one hand and placed it flat on the concrete, right next to the glass. He leaned forward, visibly pressing on the surface, as though he suspected it might give and allow him to sink inside.

"I should have been there," he said to himself, so softly I knew I wasn't meant to hear. "I should have watched the light go out."

THE WINEGLASS I held was plastic. I grasped it by the rim rather than the stem, feeling the carbonated bubbles of the ginger ale fizz against my palm. I tucked myself more deeply into the corner of the love seat, whose aging, threadbare cushions suddenly and vividly reminded me of the couch that rested in the courtyard behind our old safe house.

I'd hated the place. The weeks I'd spent there were unrelentingly awful. I was always on the verge of collapse from exhaustion, sick with worry for Leviathan and trying to subtly manipulate Quantum Entanglement into helping me rescue him. But I loved that couch; I almost came to think of it as a friend, something that was stalwartly there to offer what little support it could. It was the one thing I regretted having to destroy when we cleaned the place (and by "cleaned" I mean "razed to the foundations and bleached the ashes"). It was made of secrets (and probably rats), the fabric as worn out as the coat of the Velveteen Rabbit. Some of my most desperate and unlikely plans were born there while I watched pigeons fight over pizza crusts. It was the best thinking spot I'd ever known. While most of my plotting and subsequent success I knew realistically was attributed to collective, preternatural effort, being pushed to the edge of my capacity trying to save Leviathan's life, I entertained the foolish little idea that the couch had its own kind of magic.

At the funeral, I'd retreated here to the love seat for a few minutes alone. Leviathan was holding court in the cathedral, having taken up his role as widower for the event. It was glorious to watch, but exhausting, as I was being useful and attentive and steering conversations in a way that kept things as pleasant as possible for him. Eventually my energy flagged to the point where I excused myself, trusting Keller to do a satisfactory if more blunt job, and tried to sit for a few minutes in silence.

I was watching the doorway absently as mourners continued to drift in and out—Larvomancer finally showed up wearing more eyeliner than a stage magician, and Perchta and Scylla walked out together, deep in conversation. Then, it was as if reality glitched.

In a moment more vivid and uncanny than any incident of déjà vu I'd ever experienced, the next memory that came to me lined up perfectly with what happened. I remembered the day I was sitting on the warehouse courtyard couch, when Quantum Entanglement walked toward me like a hurricane. It was the day the Draft pinned the murder of Melting Point and his partner on her, and I thought for the first time that, if I wasn't very careful about my next words, she might actually kill me. At the same moment this memory came to me, the real Quantum Entanglement walked through the door.

The Quantum in my mind was furious, incandescent with betrayal and injustice and utter terror for her future. She was ready to take apart whoever was responsible, bone by bone if necessary. The Quantum I saw today was overlaid by her for a second, but then the memory dissolved. This woman was not angry. She hesitated at the threshold and scanned the room, every plane of her unmistakable face showing the tension she carried. She was wearing a rented suit that didn't quite fit her, and the tattoos on her face made the frown she wore seem more solemn. Both in my mind and now in the flesh in front of me, she was radiant.

Her eyes brushed over me briefly, then locked on, and I realized

I must be gaping back at her. I struggled to get my face under control and gave her a tiny nod. Her eyes widened in what might have been panic. Instinctively she glanced around the room, looking for anyone else she knew, but of course there was no one there she'd ever spoken to outside of trapping them in a force field or hauling them in for a stint in a Supermax facility. And they were starting to notice her, based on the sudden jump in the volume of conversation around me.

So, I got up, and as casually as I could manage, I walked over to her. She watched me, both alarmed and resigned, letting it happen.

I came to stand beside her rather than in front of her, and together we moved out of the doorway and the direct flow of traffic. I escorted her to a corner of the room so she could compose herself. I also hoped my presence next to her would offer some tiny modicum of protection, so some shithead wouldn't take the opportunity to say something horrible to her.

"You look good," I said out of nowhere.

"This was a mistake." I could tell by how eerily calm and even her voice was that she was panicking.

"I don't know if it was a mistake, but it's definitely a statement." I leaned a little closer. "I'm impressed you knew when to come. Sleuthing was never your strong suit."

"Are you trying to give me a compliment? Because you are still terrible at it."

"Sorry, I don't get much practice."

It was so easy, talking to her like that. The banter was right there; the exact degree of caustic and self-deprecating I knew she'd appreciate. I realized I'd missed talking to her, and it hurt me.

"I had to see it," she said. She used her real voice to say this, lower pitched and richer and in pain.

"I understand."

"It . . . He really is . . . That really is *him*. In the next room."

"Are you asking if he's really dead?"

"Not many people would know for sure. You would know."

I swallowed.

"He is."

"Did you—"

"No."

A new, weird tension grew between us. I concentrated on the set of her shoulders, her breathing, trying to puzzle out what she wanted.

"Do you want to see him?" I tried very hard to make my voice kind. I wondered if that was something I was still capable of.

She didn't answer for a long time, and I began to wonder if I had read her wrong.

"I have to," she said at last.

"Would you like me to take you?"

"Yes. Thank you."

I took a step away from the wall and she mirrored me. All around us, villains were openly staring, and not in a particularly friendly way.

She followed my gaze, saw the hostile scrutiny, and stopped. "I don't want you—"

"It's fine." I risked putting my hand on her arm. She flinched a little but didn't pull away from me. "This way. I'll show you." I gave her sleeve a light tug, and she allowed herself to be led out of the huge foyer to the central room, where the body was.

As we walked down the short corridor between the two main funeral spaces, it occurred to me I should warn her.

"He's here, of course. Leviathan."

She nodded in a way that made it very obvious she was trying not to freak out. "I expected as much. How is he?"

I decided to be honest. "Terrible."

"I'm sorry. He must be . . . hard to deal with."

I realized that we were talking about different things. "He's not terrible to me. This is . . . a catastrophic loss for him."

Her lip curled. I couldn't tell if it was dark amusement or disgust. "What does that say about Collider? That the person who hated him the most in the world is the one mourning the deepest?"

I picked up and discarded several responses in my head. *Hate is less than an inch from love*, or *It's all obsession in the end*. I settled on a kind of toast. "May we all leave someone behind who hates us so well."

I couldn't call her expression a smile. It was a splitting, like the edge of a razor drawn across scar tissue. I gestured for her to step through the arched entranceway into the next room.

It was a long walk, from the door to the sarcophagus. All of the velvet ropes that were used to control the daytime crowds had been moved aside, piled in one corner of the room like loops of intestines. Without those snaking lines of people, waiting interminably for their moment in front of the monument, it seemed so much more ominous. Horrific, even. There were many more guests in this room than the foyer, but the room was so huge it gave the illusion of being much more sparsely populated.

I walked Quantum through the room, and then we stood together in front of the slab of concrete and lead and glass that would be Supercollider's final resting place. Somewhere inside the massive block he was curled up, embryonic, flesh still entangled. Quantum stopped only a few inches away and stared into the circular glass panel, fitted in the slab like a porthole. It was opaque but gave the illusion of a window; I was convinced that behind it was more concrete. I thought I could see her face more clearly in the glass than I could in real life, as though I was scrying. She looked anguished.

I pulled my eyes from the glass; it suddenly felt voyeuristic to watch her. Instead, I stared at the rough surface of the concrete, imagining him somewhere inside it. *I hate you so much*, I thought at him. *You're dead and still hurting them.*

You toxic wasteland of a person.

I was so wrapped up in hating him that Quantum scared the crap out of me when she grabbed my arm. I started and instinctively tried to pull away, but there was something in her grip that was oddly protective, and made me go still.

I followed her line of sight to Leviathan, whom she must have laid eyes on for the first time. Knowing he was in attendance and actually seeing him were doubtless very different experiences for her. He was holding court in a far corner of the room. A coterie of braver villains was gathered around him, offering both congratulations and comfort; he was, at once, the victorious and the bereaved. He was turned away from us and clearly deep in conversation with Sleep Paralysis.

Everything about Quantum's physical presence had shifted; she was suddenly humming with potential energy, like a pressure-fed engine. As though he felt it, Leviathan turned slightly and looked toward us, and their eyes meeting changed the gravity of the room.

They seemed to stare at each other for an eternity, but it must have been only a few seconds. They'd been adversaries for over fifteen years, and I doubted had ever shared space where one of them wasn't trying to kill the other. All that muscle memory, the backstory of every blow that had ever been exchanged between them, hung in the air for a moment.

The tension made me feel physically unbalanced, and I swayed a little in her grip. That tiny movement seemed to remind Quantum that I existed. In that moment her energy changed again, from aggressive to protective. She shifted her body so that she was more solidly between Leviathan and me—even though there was half a room between us—and gave him the smallest, almost imperceptible nod. A heartbeat later, he inclined his head just as subtly. It was enough to break the magnetic violence that held them both, and

Quantum took a step forward. She held me by the elbow instinctively, making sure I didn't fall, and the feeling of her cold, strong hand holding me up opened a fresh wound in my heart.

Leaving the room felt like running up the basement stairs when you were little, certain something was chasing you, something you didn't turn around to see; reaching the door felt like escaping. The monster wasn't either of them individually, but both of them together, and I felt like I had just barely escaped something.

Quantum didn't stop when we made it out of the room but kept barreling directly for the main entrance. I thought she would stop to collect herself, that I would have another moment to talk to her, to look at her beautiful, tragic face. But now I was looking only at her back I realized that this might be it; once she left I might never see her again.

My brain reached out desperately for anything I could possibly say that might make her stay a little longer. Anything but asking her directly.

"Do you need anything?"

"Not from you."

I flinched at her sudden hostility. "We don't have to be enemies."

"Don't we?"

"Why are you suddenly being an asshole?"

She grimaced at that. It felt good, knowing I could get to her, that I could make someone like her uncomfortable with just the right amount of withering annoyance.

But now her face was freezing over. I was about to lose her for real, and I knew I had to let go. Yet I could not keep from taking one more shot at her, making one more stab for somewhere soft. I let the loneliness I'd felt over the last few months reach my eyes, the betrayal of her leaving settling into the set of my lips.

"It was good to see you again, Quantum." She was ready for me to match her icy sarcasm, but the warmth and vulnerability in my face hurt her. I watched it land, then turned and walked away slowly.

Part of me screamed to turn around, to go back to her, but I smothered it. I wasn't sure if she was watching me or if she had gone, but I refused to turn around and check, resisted the impulse as though I would turn to salt if I looked back. I kept my pace measured, my shoulders relaxed; she would not see me upset. I let my heart freeze over and rejoined Leviathan's side.

NO ONE SAID anything on the long drive back. It was just before dawn when we finally arrived back at the compound. The sky was the swollen violet of bruised knees, the odd wisp of cloud a luminous, wet orange. Melinda pulled the eerie, oil-slick car in front to Leviathan's building first, all the cars behind us following her lead. When we pulled up directly behind, I watched Ludmilla elegantly open the door for our boss.

Once Leviathan had unfolded himself from the car, he stood perfectly still for a moment, thinking. Ludmilla stood a few steps away, a toothpick resting indolently in her red lipstick, waiting without impatience. She was extremely good at waiting; arguably it was the most important part of her job, the ability to be in any place she was needed with nothing to do however long she was needed there. Melinda, who was almost as good at waiting as Ludmilla, sat behind the wheel with her head cocked slightly toward them, observing closely without staring.

After a long moment deep in his thoughts, he came back to the surface and dismissed them both by name, asking Ludmilla to let the rest of our grim motorcade know he would no longer be in need of any form of escort. She nodded and touched her earpiece, speaking rapidly, gesturing with her free hand.

Then, startling me, the door next to me opened. Leviathan had come around to my side of the car and said, softly, "I would like a moment."

I got out of the car too quickly, and barely recovered without tripping. Melinda nodded to me with an oddly significant expression, as though silently wishing me luck. Ludmilla got back into the car and the entourage pulled away, every engine either too loud or eerily quiet, as everyone else's duties had finally ended.

I stood next to Leviathan on the sidewalk in front of the central tower, but he did not go inside. Instead, he started to walk toward a narrow path, lined by slim, recently planted trees and rock gardens, leading behind the building. I kept pace with him, leaving an arm span between us so that I was obviously close at hand but not uncomfortably in his personal space. We made our way to a small parkette behind the building, with a dry fountain and a low stone bench, out of sight of any of the main walking paths. Even the odd, solitary early-morning jogger or security detail was unlikely to interrupt us.

He sat down on one end of the stone bench, and I sat on the other. It was shockingly cold to the touch, and the chill seeped through my clothes and into my joints almost immediately. But the sun was rising now, very warm on the front of my legs and backs of my hands. I felt like a moon, illuminated on one side and cold on the other.

Don't fucking say anything, I thought viciously to myself, as I caught myself picking up and discarding conversation after conversation. *All you have to do is shut the hell up. For the love of fuck, don't ruin it by saying something.* While some part of me writhed in panic at the prospect of just waiting for Leviathan to speak to me, if he was going to at all, I turned my focus on the moment itself. Onto the person next to me. My emotional discomfort aside, he had asked for me. We were here, both warming and chilling ourselves, while the sun came up. If what he needed from me in that moment was to be present and quiet, that was something I could happily give. I let my mind grow quiet.

He was sitting so still, his face angled slightly away from me. I followed the sharp lines of his neck and jaw, the sharp plates that joined where a collarbone would theoretically be, or have been. The new light gleamed off his shoulder, where the prominent, bladelike shape of his carapace was particularly reflective. Here, he was iridescent, not just smooth black but blue and purple and green.

"You are staring at me." A cool, quiet observation he made without turning.

I let the anxiety rear up, and then shut the door in its face. I took a full breath, and in the calm that followed said, "It's not very often I get to see you in sunlight."

A tension slid into his face and tightened his jaw. He didn't turn any further from me, but I saw the effort that took.

"Why would you." He was trying to sound understatedly threatening, but for once it didn't ring true. Or maybe I was just too exhausted for my self-preservation to be functioning the way it should be, so it wasn't working on me.

I looked out over the green space around us, a kind of reverse quad where the backs of several buildings came together. "I don't want to make you uncomfortable."

I hoped releasing him from my direct scrutiny would dispel the tension, but it only seemed to increase it. "I am comfortable."

"You're usually a much better liar than this." It was like listening to someone else speaking. *All you had to do was not say anything!* I wondered what the ever-living fuck had come over me, if I was finally having some kind of breakdown. Some part of me frantically searched for my anxiety, to activate my filter, but it was nowhere to be found.

He turned then to stare at me. "Are you ... deliberately antagonizing me?" He sounded completely baffled rather than angry.

"No. The opposite." I met and held his eyes. "I like looking at you. That's the only reason I was staring. But if you don't want me to, I can stop. I don't want to cause you distress. So if there is something you need from me, or need me not to do, you need to be honest with me."

He looked even more confused and it was hard not to enjoy it. "I am not distressed."

"I am not sure how that can be true. We just came from—"

I stopped when I saw Leviathan's left fist twitch reflexively, expecting me to say the deceased hero's name. "Don't." It should have been a warning, but it came out like a plea.

He glared at me, and I smiled at him. I knew that I looked terrible. The deep violet circles under my eyes seemed to be permanent now, and no amount of sleep or skincare could mend them. My eyeliner was no longer in my signature, razor-sharp wings, having smeared at the edges. My face was coming apart in a thousand tiny ways: fine lines, fading makeup, silver ghosts of scar tissue. I watched him trace the emotional cartography of the last few years with his eyes.

I watched him soften. It started in his neck and shoulders; he leaned forward just a little, letting the exhaustion in. One of his hands was locked onto his thigh, just above the knee. I reached out and pried it off, cradling his hand in both of mine. He didn't return my grip but didn't pull away either, staring down at our fingers.

"I want to make this easier, not harder," I said. "What can I do?"

"You've done enough. Too much."

I closed my eyes for a moment as a little spike of pain came back. "I'm sorry."

He shook his head. "You should . . . should never have had to . . ." He swallowed. "To come."

We were both lost in our own woods, I thought. We were speaking past each other, each of us trying to navigate private miseries. As the sun crept a little higher, it occurred to me for the first time that I might have been wrong about the way he felt, what he thought of me, what he might or might not blame me for. We were just in very different places. For the first time in a while, I felt something a little like hope. Maybe we could grope our way out. Maybe we could find each other again.

I paid very close attention to my hands. His fingers were covered with tiny plates overlapping each other like fine-scale mail. There was give and warmth to his grip, and in some places where the scales were not at this moment tightly together, there was a softer connective tissue visible. I found myself absently tracing over some of these lines on his wrist and toward the center of his palm. A rigid surface is much more brittle than a flexible one capable of redistributing force.

"There wasn't a moment that you were gone that I wasn't trying to get you back." My voice was a thin and ragged thing.

"Auditor."

I didn't trust myself to say anything else. After a moment, I felt his fingers move, returning my grip with a subtle pressure of his own. I could feel a roughness to his fingertips, all the tiny, Velcro-like hooks that gave him extra grip.

"They must be furious," I said.

"Who?"

"Them. All of them. The Draft. They must all be so furious, every day that we're still alive."

His grip tightened just a little, and he sat up a bit. "They must be."

My lip curled. "Can you imagine it."

"Tell me."

I swept one of my hands out in front of me, as though gesturing toward a majestic vista. "Some senior administrator is touring the smoking husk of Dovecote. Two cronies desperately try to explain what happened, how it could have happened. The whole time, he is just radiating fury because we are both still alive."

He nodded gravely, his eyes sparkling. "The sheer audacity."

"Every day they have to wake up and know we're still here, we're already making their lives worse."

I watched him savor the idea; it was genuinely cheering him up. "We cannot waste this opportunity."

"Not a moment of it."

We sat together for a long time, each exploring our own personal revenge fantasies while he drew his thumb back and forth across my knuckles.

[Part Two]

She actually printed it out, a physical sheet of paper, and thrust it into my hands as soon as I arrived at my desk. I'd come in late, after a few pitiful hours of sleep, and I could tell she had been waiting furiously the entire time.

"Wait. Let's talk about this." I reached around her and pulled my office door shut so we could have some privacy. She looked alarmed, so I adjusted it to be open a crack, and moved away so that there was nothing between her and the door.

"I understand that you're freaked out right now. Believe me, I'm freaked out, too."

"It's not the same." Her face was intense and focused, but her voice came out unusually soft.

"Sure. We all have different risk profiles and tolerances—"

"No. I mean, you're here for life."

"With Leviathan?"

"With the villains."

I was taken aback. "I mean. I do know what side of the line I'm on, yes."

"I'm not as sure. And this might be my last chance to walk away."

"Do you *want* to walk away? You're incredible at your job and you've always seemed happy here. If this is the final straw or something, I'm sorry I didn't see—"

"No. It's not even that I want to leave." She looked up at the ceiling for a moment, trying to find the words. "I love it here. But if I don't leave now, I might not ever be able to again."

I found myself haunted by the memory of Decay's soft, reedy voice in my head: *If you want to get out of this life, this could be your chance. And it might be your last one.* Tammy could now see her own door closing, and was making the opposite decision that I had.

On some level I knew I shouldn't try to change her mind, but it seemed wrong to just wish her well without letting her know, definitively, that her leaving would be a one-way trip.

"You won't be able to come back." I said it as softly as I could, hoping it came out as a statement of fact rather than a threat.

She looked pained at that. "I know. And I'm sorry. I know I did good work here, and I am proud of it. But if I leave now, there's a chance I could do something else. Anything else. If I stay after this … no one will let me do anything but this ever again."

I thought I could see this moment from her perspective. She was making a choice, even if it was a bad one, while there was a choice left to make. It made me wonder if I had any choices like that left to make, or if all my apertures for other possible futures had closed long ago. I pushed the thought away, hard.

"Can I ask you to think about it? Even for a day."

"No. The longer I hesitate, the worse I look to everyone else."

Which I knew was true as well. Still—something kept making me try to convince her otherwise. "Sure. You leave now, it looks like a pang of conscience forced your hand. I get it." I tried to keep my voice soft, conversational. "But you don't need to make a huge decision right now. No one out there is going to care if you quit today or next month. If you're good enough—and you are—and pass through the security checks, it doesn't matter who you were. It's not like your average district manager is more virtuous than Dragonbreath. You'd be surprised how few people care who your boss used to be."

"No one else's boss killed Supercollider."

I swallowed. She stared at the floor.

I gave myself a moment to think. I leaned my cane against my desk carefully and pulled myself into my chair. Exhaustion vibrated through my body like an especially cruel tinnitus.

"So your mind is set."

"No . . . but yes."

I took a breath. "Leaving won't be an easy process."

"I know."

"It will take a little while to get you cleared to permanently leave the compound."

"That's okay." She looked back up at me. "I'm not afraid, exactly. I don't think I should be."

"No. They'll let you go. You've certainly seen some things, but I don't think anything that requires a full security audit."

She flinched and I wished I hadn't chosen the word "audit," even though it was accurate.

"The process is annoying, but you'll be fine," I said.

"So I can go."

I sighed. "You don't need my permission. I don't want you to leave; you're a great part of this team, and you'll be hell to replace. But if this is what you want, then I wish you all the luck in the world."

"Thank you," she whispered.

"I'll even be a reference if anyone would take my word for it."

She smiled without any emotion, an anemic expression. I didn't need her to say it to know she was never going to mention my name again once she was finally cleared to leave the building.

I put her resignation down on my desk. "It's been a pleasure working with you. Truly. Let me know whatever I can do to help."

There was enough finality in what I said that she took it as an invitation to leave, awkwardly pulling the door shut before opening it in the right direction, fleeing the office entirely. I listened as the sound of her high-tops squeaking on the floor got quieter.

I sat listlessly for a while, trying to sort out what the arduous process of releasing Tammy and hiring someone new would look like. For the first time in a long time, I thought about Nour; when she'd left the team, it made a different kind of sense. She'd taken on an incredibly dangerous assignment at great personal risk, both physical and emotional. At my request, she'd become a sidekick's lover just to help destroy him. It was an awful assignment, one she'd accepted willingly, but also one she could never come back from.

This felt different, and not just because Tammy's role had always had her infinitely more sheltered. While Tammy's social engineering was exceptional, she worked very differently and much more conservatively than Nour had, keeping herself and her psychic well-being far more insulated from the things we did to heroes and those close to them. But there was no insulating herself from this. She wasn't willing to destroy herself for this job the way Nour was—the way I was—and the worse parts of me resented her for it.

THE NEXT FEW weeks were a time of peak chaos, with almost every department scrambling to hire and everyone stretched too thin either covering for whoever was lost or desperately trying to get new talent up to speed—or both at once. After the long torpor of doing nothing, it felt like we were doing everything in a frenzy. Our admin staff and general service positions—anywhere that, most of the time, you could absolutely ignore what your job actually was and who you were doing it for—were hit the hardest. I could imagine what those henches were going through, as I had once been in their place. I remembered that state of willful ignorance, back when I was picking up odd data entry and analysis jobs, just filling out spreadsheets mindlessly and keeping myself divorced from any significance that might have been gleaned from the rows and columns. I could imagine how jarring it must have been to suddenly and dramatically be confronted with the reality of what we did, and had done. Many couldn't get the blinders back on.

They walked.

Our communications department was also having a rough go; not because they were ever really able to lie to themselves and pretend we weren't the bad guys (seeing as they were so precise and eloquent in describing exactly how monstrous we were), but because they were imminently hirable on either side of the line. The Draft themselves, and anyone who worked with superheroes, were always hiring crisis comms wizards who knew the vocabulary and rhetoric of superheroism. For anyone who wanted to take a crack at working for a different kind of evil, and look like saints for doing so, it was a golden opportunity. Like with Tammy, if they left now, it looked good; they could spin their quitting as a crisis of faith, point to Levithan's recently revealed "unthinkable sin" that finally shook them from complacency. You know, typical redemption-arc shit. I grudgingly respected the narrative they were going for, even as I felt growing contempt for them for writing it.

As my stress mounted, I asked Menachem out for a drink at The Hole to commiserate; he'd been my first sort-of-supervisor when I first landed with Leviathan, freshly hired and with the titanium rods and pins still in my leg from my first "meeting" with Supercollider. He was a kind of patron saint of the information and identities department, a weird mad-scientist uncle who got many people like me settled into their first niche. I imagined he was dealing with a similar deluge of frustration and stress and loss as some excellent talent lost their taste for the work we did and walked out the door. I imagined, considering how much longer he'd worked for Leviathan, and how many more people he'd mentored and supervised, that he'd be having a much rougher time than I was.

Instead, I found him remarkably nonchalant, even jovial. He ordered a neon-pink cocktail in the middle of the afternoon and grinned at me as he folded his grasshoppery body into the corner booth I was anxiously brooding in.

"This is your first time, innit," he said, infuriatingly.

"How can you be so happy?" I seethed. "I have deadlines, Menachem, emphasis on 'dead.'"

He waved a hand. "The pressure will equalize."

"What the fuck does that mean?"

He took a sip, and made a happy little *ooo* noise. Whatever was in the glass smelled something like a watermelon Jolly Rancher. "You're on the wrong end of the vacuum right now, but trust me, it'll sort itself out."

"You are making less sense, not more."

He nodded a few times, brow furrowing, as though I had said something illuminating. He thought for a minute and I could practically hear pistons and levers shifting in his head. "Right. This is new to you."

I took a cleansing breath. Despite my frustrated impatience, I knew that this conversation was going to take exactly as long as it needed to, regardless of my feelings on the matter. I flexed the hand that had been gripping a heavy ceramic mug too tightly and willed some of the tension to leave my body.

"It happened a bit around Accelerator, too. You lost Nour, but the rest of us took some hits as well. The difference was you were so busy at the time, and I bet you didn't see the larger thing. No reason you would."

"By 'it' you mean the quitting."

"Yes! Exactly. Not just a person or two but a whole shift. Some big, some smaller. Accelerator was a small blip, but it registered. But this one, now. This is a doozy."

"Big, but not surprising to you."

"Not at all."

"You're are saying this is a pattern."

He looked at me more closely, cocking his head to one side like a little kid. "It's easy for me to forget you haven't been here very long. You've done so much. I barely recognize you, you know. And I mean that as a compliment."

He sounded so proud that at that moment I felt like a spectacular asshole for being so impatient with him (not that he seemed to have noticed). I smiled awkwardly and looked down at the table.

"Thanks. I was . . . not at my best."

"You were a different person. Don't be embarrassed!"

"I wasn't until you said that."

He laughed. "Be nice to the old you. She has a long way to go yet and hasn't had nearly as many of the breaks you got."

He was being extremely kind and I hated it. "But you're right. I haven't been here long."

"Well, I have."

"How long?"

"I've been here almost seventeen years."

"Holy fuck."

He shrugged. "I haven't changed much at all. Pay goes up, job stays weird, get to see all these bright-eyed and bushy-tailed little devils on their first days go on and do their worst. But being around's got its own set of advantages, such as knowing the patterns."

I sighed. "And this looks familiar."

"Terribly." He grinned. His teeth were lightly stained, lived in, someone who'd smoked a bit and quit and drank coffee their whole life. Comfortable teeth.

I gave up and decided to trust him. "Alright, wise mentor, what the fuck is happening now, then?"

He slurped his drink. "Big events in the hero-sphere like this? Always leads to a big shift. On both sides. We're at the wrong end of the exchange right now; a light got flipped on in the basement and all the cockroaches who can't handle the attention are running for cover."

"And this doesn't alarm you."

It wasn't a question, but he answered anyway. "Nah." He leaned back, tossed a lean arm over the back of the booth's seat. "It'll suck for a while, of course. But the shift's happening Over There, too, just slower. Before you know it, a whole new group of disillusioned former good guys will be showing up on our doorsteps."

"That doesn't make sense. Why would they want to ally themselves with the people who are 'responsible' for this tragedy?"

He waggled a finger at me. "Ah. Because a lot of them know the truth."

I sat up a little straighter. "Some of them know the Draft is lying?"

"Oh, a lot of them, probably. Some of them are even writing the lies, or building them, or what have you. If they were ever going to get sick of it, now is probably the time to do something about it."

"So you think, in the near future, a bunch of them are going to cross the line."

"That's how it goes. Something happens, everyone gets uncomfortable on both sides, folks leave first one and then the other. Clockwork. Do you remember when Molten Core threw Minotaur Man's wife into a volcano?"

"I heard about that. Wasn't there some cover-up?"

"Rumor was someone tampered with her restraints, so a classic threat-and-dangle turned into a scandal. Bunch of people on both sides quit over it."

"Okay, while that's reassuring, what do we do in the meantime?"

He shrugged. "That's up to you. When it's me, most of the time I wait. Do what I can. Soon enough, new folks start walking through the doors and I find spaces for them." He looked at me critically and rubbed a hand over his chin. "Something tells me you aren't really in the mood for waiting."

I gritted my teeth. "I can't. There are too many things in place, too many things moving, and we've lost so much time already. They'll never be this weak again. This disorganized. If this window closes . . ."

He looked out over the mostly dead bar, watching the dust motes in the slanted late-afternoon light while he listened to me. There was music playing but only in the kitchen, too dainty to make out what it was beyond the vague shape of guitar and power ballad vocals.

"How can you use it, then?" He sipped thoughtfully. "All the shifting. Everything that's happening here, it's about to happen there. Sure, they got a head start this time but it'll still be bad for them. Do your job and ask yourself:

"'How can I make it worse?'"

A slow grin spread across my face, like the pink and orange light of a sunset. "You always know exactly what to say."

He raised his half-empty cocktail glass in a toast, sloshing the green liquid around in the process. I got up and walked out immediately, without saying goodbye; our drinks were already paid for and I knew he'd never consider it rude.

MENACHEM'S ADVICE HELPED me envision a positive future, even with the losses to our staff, but that conversation alone wouldn't have been enough to buoy me for long. I would have easily slipped back into a miserable froth of anxiety if it wasn't for a much quieter, much more significant change I soon noticed happening: Leviathan was becoming himself again.

After months of frustration and imposed inaction, everything was happening at once. After the funeral, the world's grief transmuted into fury. There are few things that feel better when you're in pain than having something, someone, clearly to blame, and the world had Leviathan. They all thought they knew who had taken their hero from them, and could redirect all that mourning into righteous anger. The moment the mausoleum was set in place in the cemetery, the collective consciousness turned toward vengeance.

Mercifully, a parallel transformation took place in Leviathan. With Supercollider in (well, on top of) the ground and every hero who mattered announcing their intention to pin Leviathan to an oversize specimen mat, he seemed to wake up and come back to himself. Our meetings were no longer one-sided affairs where I would update him on whatever progress I'd made while he barely listened, and which would end when he told me to "hold, for now." They were no longer exercises in lonely frustration. He looked at me when I was speaking, eyes bright and alert, the ultraviolet spectrum on his carapace vibrant. He asked me to tell him again all of the plans I'd begun to disrupt the Draft's tradition of power; and to my delight, he began saying yes to things.

When I described some of the ideas I was brainstorming—I was hoping to destroy the reputation of one CDO candidate and cause the mental breakdown of another, then pit the two who were doing the best and collaborating the most against each other—I saw him become animated in a way I hadn't in a long time. He was attentive and curious, leaning forward and making little humming sounds of approval when I explained how I planned to get the interim CDO's therapist to fire her. He demanded I explain what an "emotional affair" was, and told me chilling stories of his own encounters with the former chief compliance officer, who was designing combat drills for young heroes in training back when Leviathan was still in the Draft himself. He was engaged in a way he hadn't been in so long, and when he told me I could act however I saw fit, I had to take a break and regain my composure in the bathroom for a few minutes when a wave of joyful relief threatened to wreck me in the middle of our conversation.

For all the logistical horrors that lay before us, I had him back. While I had known that I had missed his active involvement, it wasn't until he was right next to me again that I truly felt how much. He held the reins of this project with as loose a hand as he always had, but he was at last holding them again. That renewed interest, and retaking of control, gave me a surge of hope and productivity I didn't know I needed.

IT WAS DURING those overjoyed but understaffed next weeks, when I was already feeling like reality was fraying and stretched too thin, that the first invitation arrived. When I got the call, I assumed it was a joke. The caller ID alone was enough to elicit a weird laugh out of me: DRFT-CMO.

While the phone vibrated away in my hand, I looked around the office, expecting to catch Jav or Darla just outside my office door, trying not to laugh. Frowning, I answered.

"This is—"

"The Auditor, hello!" The voice on the other end of the line—baritone, jovial—sounded genuinely thrilled I had actually picked up.

"To whom do I owe the pleasure?" I made a great effort to sound the opposite of thrilled.

"I'm a fan of yours, big fan."

"That's great, Big Fan. Do you have a real name as well."

"Ha! I'm the chief marketing officer over here, but that's a real mouthful, so call me Mom."

"What?"

I opened a chat window and started frantically chat messaging my favorite digital surveillance guy, whom I knew only by the initials AR in our chat client.

AU Some fucking Draft bureaucrat just called *me*.

"I know eh? That's what the staff call me—they're a hoot."

AR On your line?

"By 'over here,' you mean . . ."

AU Yes on my actual fucking line, can you record it?

AR On it. Stall.

"Come on, you don't need to play coy."
"I just want you to say it out loud."
There was the faintest hum, and a barely audible click on the line.

AR Got it.

A laugh. "Alright, fair enough. It is I, CMO of the Draft, calling you, the Auditor. There, got it recorded for posterity?"
"That will do, yes."
"Now, listen. I don't want to talk your ear off or anything, but I did want to get in touch. As you may have surmised, there's some pretty big changes going on in this organization."
"I sure can imagine," I said, glancing at a massive surveillance folder that had recently been delivered to my desk.
"And it's important to me that, as part of all that change, we do some things here differently."
"Okay."

"I sense a reasonable suspicion."

"Oh, you know, it's part of the job description."

AR *It's really them.*

"Of course, of course. So are back-channel conversations, right? So! I see no reason why folks like you and me, well, why we can't have much more collegial relationships. We're not wearing the capes after all."

"I can think of several reasons why I would want the exact opposite of that."

He tried to sound serious. It seemed genuinely hard for him. "I am sure that you do. Listen. I know my former colleagues and predecessors, and even some that are still around . . . Well, they really bunged some things up. Dropped a lot of balls, and believed that their omelettes were worth breaking however many eggs might have been in reach. And well. I want to do things differently."

"Admirable."

"So in the spirit of doing this differently, of fresh starts, I was wondering if you'd like to come by the office, have a chat, maybe get to know each other a little better."

"You're serious."

"Absolutely!"

"Wow. I mean. I appreciate the audacity, I really do, but that seems like, and you will pardon me for saying so, a colossally stupid idea."

"Hey, listen, I absolutely can understand why you would think that."

"Glad to hear it."

"But the thing is, it's actually a great idea."

"Oh, well, in that case . . ."

"Auditor, think about it. We don't need to be like them. We have desk jobs. We believe in our work, I'm sure, but we don't have to become it. We can learn to . . . disagree and still respect each other."

I fully started laughing. I wasn't sure he intended to be funny, but it landed just right to crack open a genuine cackle. "While referring to my relationship with the Draft as a disagreement is genuinely hilarious, I must still decline your request both on principle and practicality."

"Okay, let's start with the second objection."

"That was a no, in case that was too complicated for you."

"Hear me out."

I wanted to hang up on him very badly, but AR sent a push notification to the message client, as though he had heard me think.

AR   Let him keep talking.

"Oh sure," I said. "It's not as though I'm busy."

"Great!" he said, and the enthusiasm in his voice was horrifically grating. He asked, as if this was a regular recruiting call, "What are the practical barriers?"

"Well, to be blunt, this not only looks like a trap, but an extremely bad and obvious trap. Like, box with a rope tied to a stick, leading behind a bush where I can hear you chuckling, with a fresh bag of Doritos perched under the box lid."

"If it looks like a trap, smells like a trap, and walks like a trap, it's a trap!" There was genuine laughter on the other side of the line, and I wondered if I'd have any molars by the end of this conversation. "Yeah, I can see that."

I decided to be as big a downer as possible in revenge. "And since my last visit left me—"

"Auditor." His voice sounded significantly subdued, almost conspiratorial in its guilt. "Listen. The way some things were handled . . . Well. I don't like to speak ill of anyone, but let's just say it's not how I would have done things or intend to do things now."

"You have considerably more reasons to wish me harm now than they did then."

"Not according to my metrics."

Metrics? A spark of curiosity raced through me, and I had to quell it before I said something unfortunate.

"Right, you're better than they are."

"I'm more of an optimist."

"Uh-huh."

"And those old methods? Well, they got us here."

"Where's 'here'?" I liked how ominous that sounded. There was a lot of meaning in that "here" that spoke to exactly how badly things were going for him.

"I mean. It's hardly a secret that the Draft's in . . . Well. Rather a pickle, wouldn't you say."

"I would say you're fucked."

"Mmm, I wouldn't say we're there yet."

"No?"

"We might have a trick or two under our capes. But I'm not going to lie to you and pretend that everything's sunshine and roses."

"Then . . . you're fucked."

"If you say so." He said it so good-naturedly, without even a hint of frustration in his warm, welcoming voice.

"Why else would you be talking to me, if things were any better."

He chuckled. "Look, I'm not going to pretend I'm not up to my elbows, cleaning up all the messes here as best I can. I'm sure you can relate."

"I've seen my share of your messes."

"Here's the thing: I think the time for tricks and subterfuge is over."

"How enlightened."

"I hear that healthy skepticism. And that's good! This sounds too good to be true. But I even have some folks here agreeing with me, or at least willing to see what happens when we're operating aboveboard. According to our values, the way we're supposed to."

"And I am the perfect guinea pig for this charm offensive."

"You got to admit that you'd make an ideal first candidate."

"Which is why I'll be staying right here in my corner office, so thank you."

"Wait—"

I didn't reply, but I didn't hang up. I let him hear me sigh quietly.

"I know this invitation must stink to high heaven. But you're no stranger to welcoming heroic ambassadors through your own doors—heck, you've worked with some directly."

I knew he meant Quantum, and I shoved down how angry that made me. For all I knew he'd been instrumental in utterly ruining her life, in driving her to me, and he at least allowed it to happen. To invoke that in an attempt to win me over was a terrible misstep. But I decided I didn't necessarily want him to know that yet.

"We've had successful parlays, yes," I allowed, thinking of our meetings with the Ocean Four, or the time Blowtorch and The Spark visited our offices. "But none of them had just released a statement about how we had killed their hero. Let me ask you something, then. If you knew this call would come across to me as so sus . . . why make it at all?"

"Listen, you can't take those press releases so seriously. But to answer your question honestly? Curiosity."

"About what."

"No, *your* curiosity."

"What?"

"I'm banking on this being so suspicious you won't be able to resist."

I sat back in surprise. "So you're just showing me your hand, is that it?"

"I told you—no tricks. I have nothing to hide whatsoever."

"Well, I am sorry to disappoint you."

"You've done nothing of the sort."

"Oh?"

"You answered and didn't hang up on me. We're talking. That alone is a win in my book."

"I needed to know who would dare to just fucking call me."

"See? I know we'll get along just great."

"I wouldn't count on it."

"Just give me a chance."

"I disrespectfully decline."

"Come on."

"You just declaring 'gee, this sure must look like a trap, huh' doesn't neutralize the threat; you haven't magically de-trap-ified this invitation by calling it out."

"You know what, that's fair. We could meet at a neutral location, like—"

"No neutral locations."

That seemed to genuinely surprise him. He sputtered and had to pause before speaking again. "Sorry, say again?"

"If I am going to meet you—and to be very clear that is not a yes—I want the opportunity to walk right through the front doors."

"You're really something, you know that?"

Anyone else would have said that venomously, dripping with bile and suffused with every awful thing that person thought about me. His voice was genuinely admiring, still open and warm without a trace of sarcasm.

"I do know, actually. But thank you."

"Would a hostage help?" He said it like he'd just asked how I took my coffee, and I must have been silent for a while, because he eventually followed up with, "I mean, you're right; our track record is terrible, especially with you, and while I can say anything I want to you right now, at the end of the day I need to put my money where my mouth is.

"So let's do this the feudal way: exchange prisoners, trade hostages, whatever works for you."

I pulled my phone away from my ear and stared at it, like it would reveal more data about what the actual fuck was going on. There was just the caller ID and the timer for our call, slowly counting up.

I returned the earpiece to the side of my head.

"You have my attention."

I heard him clap his hands together in glee; he must have been wearing a headset. "Great! That's just fantastic. I am so glad we can work it out."

"Don't get too excited; I've haven't told you who I want yet." I was so bewildered by the call that no one immediately sprung to mind, but I was sure I could think of someone I wanted out of prison badly enough, or someone from the Draft who was valuable enough, that risking my harm might not be worth it.

"I'm sure we can make it happen." He sounded for all the world like I'd agreed to sneak him in for a haircut even though technically we were booked up for the day, but I'd make an exception just this once, because he asked so nicely.

"I'll send you an email today so we can figure out all the deets," he continued. "Thanks for your time, you've been a real peach. I just know we're going to be able to make great things happen!"

He hung up then, good-naturedly somehow still, before I could reply; I was left wondering what the fuck had just happened to me, and wondering how I was going to convince anyone else that I really should attend this meeting.

In exactly the amount of time it would take a tall, powerfully built middle-aged man to storm from his office to mine, Keller burst through the door.

"There is NO WAY—"

"Not even a hello."

"On god's GREEN EARTH—"

"Here we go."

"That you are going anywhere near—"

"Keller."

"That fucking building."

"I didn't commit to anything."

"Don't give me that horseshit." He was pacing back and forth across my office. He was radioactive with anger, in a focused, protective way that felt weirdly comforting. "I *know* you. I know you're thinking about it."

"Of course I'm thinking about it."

"Well, fucking STOP."

"Maybe I'll just string him along, see what I can get—"

"But you won't do that, will you? So don't pretend like you are."

"It could be worth it, Bob."

"Don't you fucking 'Bob' me, you little shit."

I grinned at him. "Remember when you wanted me to do field-work, when you actively schemed to—"

"Yeah, I was an asshole, and also I was in control of that situation." He slowed in his pacing, then stopped in front of me. "If you go in there, you're on your own."

I frowned; that stung in a way I wasn't expecting. "I'm not asking you to—"

"I'm not saying I wouldn't help you, I'm saying I *can't*."

I realized it wasn't a threat but an expression of limitation. "I doubt they'd let me take in a bodyguard you'd be happy with."

"Even if they did, and you're right, they won't, there are too many variables." He started pacing again. "The exit logistics alone are a fucking nightmare. You may as well be on the fucking MOON the entire time you're in the building. And no matter what they promise, what the deal is, as soon as you're in there, they can do whatever they want to you."

He was still agitated enough, and that prospect was unpleasant enough, that I started to get more serious. "I am not fighting you on this right now, but I want to think it through. Could we set something up that would be watertight enough, have them offer someone or something valuable enough, that the risk surface would be small enough to risk it?"

He wanted to just yell at me, but with a mighty effort and a deep, stentorian breath, took a minute to think about the problem. "Let's say we do. Let's say, yeah, there's a deal we work out that would be so catastrophically stupid for them to break, that it would make sense."

"What would that have to look like."

"That's not the problem. The problem is, whatever the odds actually are, once you go in, they're fifty-fifty."

"I'm not sure that math checks out."

He glared at me. "Fifty. Fifty." He overpronounced each word to make it very clear he meant exactly what he said. "You come back out, or you don't. That's it. And I fucking hate coin flips."

"Alright. So it's Schrödinger's meeting, which I may or may not survive. Is that what you're saying."

"That is precisely what I am fucking saying, and as the person in charge of security and enforcement of said security on this godforsaken property and anywhere else our boss determines is his sovereign domain at that moment, I am not allowing this to happen."

"You're right."

"I am?

"We should ask him."

"What?"

"We should ask Leviathan what he thinks we should do here."

"So you're going to fucking go over my head. Is that it?" He was still furious, but he genuinely seemed hurt that I would disrespect him that way.

"No. I am not going to go myself, I am saying *we* should go, present the option–"

Keller threw up his arms. "He'll let you do whatever the fuck you want and you know it!"

That surprised me. "Uh, no, I don't know that."

He stared at me a moment, with the penetrating analysis of someone who was trying to work out if I was fucking with him. He determined that I wasn't. "I thought you were smart."

"Fuck off."

"Eat shit. I'll tell you exactly what will happen. You'll say your piece, I'll say mine, it won't matter a damn, he'll pretend to seriously consider all angles and then just let you do whatever you want while making it seem like it was his idea to begin with."

I was surprised by the resentment, the venom with which he spoke. "I'm not trying to—Like that's not how I want it to go, and I don't think—"

"Just shut up for a minute."

I obliged. He sat on the edge of my desk and mopped his sweaty forehead with a cotton handkerchief that he then folded back up into the inner pocket of his jacket.

"Look. I'm not saying you're . . . doing anything wrong."

I stayed quiet.

"But you can't pretend like he's—objective when it comes to you."

At first I didn't reply because he asked, but now I genuinely had no idea what to say. "I . . . know it's weird between us. Weirder than it's ever been. But I didn't think that would have an impact on his decision-making."

Keller snorted. "I can't tell which of you is worse."

"I liked this conversation better when you were yelling at me."

"And I liked this day better when you weren't thinking about walking into the Draft under your own power, but here we are."

"Okay. So what do you suggest?"

"Tell this fucker to shove his invitation up his dick and have a considerably longer life than you would otherwise."

"You think I should squander this possibly unique opportunity to get a look into enemy territory?"

He looked at me like I was an idiot. "If you don't think I have every air vent and surface elevator mapped—"

"I don't mean physically."

He crossed his arms at me. "What, then?"

"I mean the whole *feel* of the place. The tone. Body language. How miserable everyone is. How friendly or hostile they are. What they don't want me to see, what they avoid talking about. I will learn more in five minutes in that building than ages of surveillance."

He shook his head and muttered, "You think you're the only one running math here."

"What?"

"They know *exactly* what you're going to get out of them. Whatever you're going to learn, it's worth it to them."

"It could still be worth it for us."

"It isn't worth your life." He looked up at the ceiling for a minute. "Do your own math. Run it. Tell me it's worth you maybe dying over."

He had me there. It didn't take long, even thinking about it casually, to know that the scales were wildly imbalanced; I could do infinitely more to them alive than dead, especially if everything I would learn could only be put to use if I survived.

"I am considering this matter settled." He stood up, graciously not gloating, and prepared to leave my office.

I raised a hand to stop him. "If I can come up with something that would make it worth it," I said slowly, "we will have this conversation again."

He snorted. "Yeah, sure. If you can actually come up with a reason to go that might be worth dying for, give me a call. Until then—" He flipped me the bird and left, shoulders back and chest thrust out.

I settled back in my chair to think. His reaction drove home for me that I would have to frame my plan to Leviathan with utmost care if I had any hope of it being greenlit. That framing, I was convinced, would come down to what we could get out of the exchange. I might see the value in just being able to get through the door, but I would need something concrete if I didn't want the entire thing shut down instantly.

Reaching for my keyboard, I started a new file, thinking of what, or who, we could get out of the Draft that would be valuable enough to warrant the risk.

What is a realistic assessment of how important I am?

THE NEXT TIME I led our weekly sprint, I got to the meeting room before anyone else. Which, sadly for my colleagues, meant I did not come bearing any emotional bribery treats. I only had a cappuccino the size of a depth charge rapidly cooling on the desk in front of me while I obsessively reorganized my notes. I'd thrown myself into researching the CMO immediately after our deeply unsettling conversation, and was eager to share what I'd found. I felt much calmer, much more secure, than I had in some time, despite the fact that things were objectively more fucked up than they'd been for some time.

"How are you coping?" I looked up. Veronique, one of the researchers I frequently worked with, had taken a seat across from me. She looked over at me sympathetically enough that I cringed. She had no access to my interior optimism.

"I thought I was projecting much more 'calm and collected' energy than I seem to be giving off."

"You're here early. There tends to be a pretty direct inverse correlation to how well your work's been going and what time you arrive."

"I realize this is what you do, but could you point your analysis elsewhere."

"Hmm. I could pretend to." She took a seat at the opposite end of the conference table, arranging her tablet on a small stand with a wireless keyboard. "But I don't think that's what you mean."

"It isn't. And you're right."

She smiled briefly, just a quick acknowledgment of her correctness, a punctuation mark of an expression.

"I hope today gets better from here."

Before I could reply, Molly bustled in with more of their team in tow, and we soon called the meeting to order. I was uncomfortably aware that in addition to Tammy's empty spot, several other members of the data team I expected to see were absent.

"Well, it certainly has been a week," Molly said in a robotic emcee voice that made me groan reflexively.

"How many did you lose so far?" Jav asked, twirling a stylus between his fingers.

"The exact composition of the research and data team I lead is currently in flux." Molly's voice was upbeat and chirpy, so I knew they were already pissed off.

"Let's save the lamentations for after the meeting." I hunched over my laptop like an angry buzzard.

"Fantastic. Let's." Using a small remote fitted with a laser pointer, Molly queued up the first slide in their presentation, this one titled "Worth Two in the Bush: When One Mystery Solves Another." A GIF of a pair of birds holding a ribbon between them floated back and forth across the slide.

"A quick aside to begin: you may recall wishing we could follow all the suggested research areas."

"I do, which I recognize as unmitigated greed."

"You will be pleased to know that in researching Bulwark's disappearance, we may have answered some bonus questions along the way."

I let myself slouch a little lower. "You are now my favorite person of the day. Proceed."

Molly advanced to the next slide. It was a photograph, clearly taken surreptitiously with a long-range zoom lens. It wasn't exquisite quality and the subject was wearing gigantic sunglasses, but they were instantaneously recognizable. Bulwark was wrapped in a black lace bathing suit cover-up and holding a drink that seemed to have half a pineapple attached to the rim.

"Where is she, Ibiza?"

"Portugal."

"Nice beach."

"It seems that Stephanie Bulwark, our wayward former CDO, was offered a severance package, the details of which were most certainly not disclosed to any of her colleagues, and in a truly clichéd move is spending time in Europe with her former personal trainer."

"I assume that's the oiled-up fellow holding all of the bags and umbrella."

"His name," Veronique said, trying to keep her voice from sounding too giddy, "is Chad."

"*No.*"

"Hand to god."

"Incredible." I started to daydream about whether it would be more fun to send that photo directly to her husband or try some blackmail first.

"Yes, she seems quite taken with this handsome Chad," Molly said vaguely, and I couldn't contain a real laugh.

Molly wrinkled their nose and continued. "Let's get the first thing out of the way: the race for CDO is not over."

"Carmel Gentileschi, who was chief branding officer before Bulwark's departure, may have the title temporarily, but she's going to have to defend it," Veronique added.

"'Anyone's game' not over or 'there's a chance' not over?" I asked.

"Closer to the former than the latter."

"Interesting."

"The interim CDO was given the position with remarkably little fuss—they needed someone in the seat immediately—and with extreme emphasis on the 'interim.' Her term cannot exceed six months, then there's a full internal review. Lots of stopgaps in place to keep her from keeping it via inertia."

Molly advanced a slide, showing a photograph of the temporary CDO taken after the recent press conference announcing Supercollider's death. Despite her curated exhaustion, Gentileschi looked remarkably serene for someone being screamed at by an entire parking lot full of journalists. "I'd argue that putting her in this position is a disadvantage—she's going to be dealing with a colossal amount of shit."

"Shame," Veronique said, deadpan.

"But also probably the point," Molly noted.

"We'll have to make it worse for her," I mused, and I could see a few heads nodding.

Molly advanced to a different angle of the acting CDO standing at the podium, moments after announcing everyone's favorite hero had died. Her head was bowed, as if in prayer, and she was the sole still point in a chaotic image. In front of her, journalists roiled and heaved like a medieval painting of sinners condemned to the lake of fire, the security personnel trying to control them appearing as devils. Molly had included a pair flaming wall sconces on the slide to heighten the effect.

"Let's take a closer look at Carmel Gentileschi," Molly said.

"Her work has always been great," Sameera, a crisis comms specialist, added, "but it's a huge jump."

"Agreed. Her role has always been strategic, not focused on leadership."

"Let alone a role with teeth," Darla said.

Molly raised a finger. "You know, it's very interesting that you mention teeth."

Darla flinched. "There is no way this sentence goes anywhere I want it to go."

Molly advanced several slides ahead to one titled "Bite a Gift

Horse in the Mouth." It looked something like an organizational chart, but out of order and grouped oddly; I realized that Molly had pulled apart the C-suite and other important positions within the Draft and roughly organized them into three groups, with an internal hierarchy that didn't necessarily represent anything official.

"Now. A good deal of this is inference and conjecture, which I don't usually like to share, but I was feeling naughty."

I grinned. "You know I love it when you guess."

They winced at the word "guess." "Please—'data-driven hypothesis.'"

"I apologize."

"Based on the *information at hand,* I've changed my mind about something: I don't think that the C-suite are going to do an external search for a new CDO."

This was news. "No?"

"I think they're only looking internally. And by 'looking,' I mean letting the execs go complete *Lord of the Flies* and see who survives."

"While I genuinely love this idea, how can they allow this to happen."

Molly cocked their head. "Who is going to stop it from happening?"

I looked back at the dissected organizational chart. Three rough clumps, spheres of influence that overlapped here and there but for the most part were functioning as their own little fiefdoms.

"So let the games begin."

"It looks like they're well underway. We don't have a complete picture when it comes to who is allied with whom right now, but we have some general ideas. And we know who the three top candidates are for the job."

"Let's go on this journey together."

Molly nodded and reversed back through the slide deck, back

to Gentileschi at the press conference. Then she advanced one forward, to a much less chaotic image of her in a summer-weight suit, smiling widely while shaking hands with someone I recognized as a super-rich civilian technologist. Next to that image, Molly had placed one of the Renaissance painter Artemisia Gentileschi's masterpiece depicting Judith as she murders Holofernes, sawing through the Assyrian general's neck while gouts of arterial blood spray from the partially severed stump.

"Carmel has made a career forming relationships with powerful civilians and their organizations—hence her former title. Not all of her colleagues appreciated these initiatives, but those that did *really* did. And there's no doubt she's been incredibly effective; this partnership with Lars Steiglitz four years ago, for example, allowed for massive overhauls of the Draft's prepubescent testing programs. Steiglitz's R & D allowed for better, more accurate testing earlier, meaning a greater chance of catching powers manifesting much earlier than the more common puberty barrier."

A few bells in my head started to ring. "So she's the one who was doing all that outreach to new parents?"

"Bingo." Molly advanced to a slide composed of a piece of Draft propaganda: an idealized portrait of a pair of new parents, holding and cooing over a bundle that presumably held a baby. The blanket fell in such a way to suggest, with the folds of the fabric, a tiny cape, and from the baby's face there was a golden, beatific glow. Above them, a pair of storks held a sign in their beaks that read: "Every Child Is Special; But Yours Might Save the World." In smaller print, below the family, were the words: "If you're a new parent who suspects your child may be exhibiting early signs of superpowers, we are here to help! Contact your local Draft office today."

"Has your child showed signs of radioactivity?" Jav put on a voice like a circa-1950s radio announcer.

"Have they set the cat on fire by thinking it?" Veronique added.

"Do you suspect your infant is mind-controlling you?" I said.

Molly waited for us to stop giggling at how much we each liked our own jokes. "That was her. And the reception means she's a force to be reckoned with."

"Real talk, though," I said. "Does this just look really good, because babies, or is something actually being done here?"

"Oh, a lot is being done. Veronique researched this most intensely. V, would you like to take this on?"

"Absolutely." Veronique spent a moment looking through her notes, making a little "ah ha" noise when she found what she was looking for. "So, unsurprisingly, most of the screenings turn up nothing. Doesn't mean the kid is a dud, but it does mean that nothing significant shows up on any of the early-sign scans. And there isn't enough data to suggest that these kids are more likely to manifest later because, well, they're not old enough yet."

"Righto."

"Where it gets interesting is when there *is* something of note. There've only been a dozen or so cases where it turned out the kid was on the verge of a full-blown power manifestation, but in those cases . . . Well. They did probably save more than one baby's life."

I managed to stop myself before I said "that's unfortunate" out loud. "What happened."

"Two successes got big press. So did one failure. And the failure reinforced the 'necessity' of the project more than the success stories, honestly."

I frowned. "Failure on whose part?"

"Partially the tech, partially the parents." Veronique spent a few more minutes frowning at her monitor. When she found what she was looking for, she asked Molly if she could take over the share-screen briefly. She was about to press a button, but paused.

"How squeamish are y'all?"

"My tolerance is pretty high, but let's keep the 'not safe for life' images to a minimum." I could feel Darla's palpable relief; they did not do well around gore.

"Gotcha." Veronique made some changes, possibly swapped an article or image out, and then began sharing her screen. "I'll start with the happy ones."

She showed us an image of a woman, her face obscured by a privacy blur, holding up a tiny girl in a swimsuit. She had shockingly chubby legs and a gummy smile.

"To protect their privacy, somewhat, in all the case study literature this kid is referred to as Baby G. Baby G's mother entered treatment for postpartum depression when G was thirteen months old; late for something like that to manifest, but not unheard of. She spoke to her doctors extensively about her concerns that her baby was 'mad' at her, that she could feel it. Eventually she confessed that, while this had started off as a feeling, she had begun to hear her daughter's voice in her head, telling her she hated her and she was a bad mother. We think her therapist referred her to the program to prove to her it was a delusion."

"It wasn't," I guessed.

"It wasn't. Turned out this little one was a full-blown telepath beaming all that furious-baby energy into her mom's head whenever the baby had a tantrum. Draft got her mom a fleet of therapists, assigned them some telepathy specialists, and by all reports the kid's going to be a world-class interrogator before she starts the first grade."

"Wonderful," I said flatly. "Go on."

"This little bundle of joy is Baby W."

A new image popped up on screen and I wrinkled my nose. "That is the ugliest baby I have ever seen."

"He does look like a gremlin," Molly said seriously.

"This gremlin," Veronique said in mock offense, "blew out a babysitter's eardrums when his powers manifested at eleven months."

"Oh, good, a screamer."

"A dangerous screamer," Jav corrected me.

"This one was especially good for PR, because no one had to contend with any difficult feelings surrounding mental health."

"Right, harder to blame the mom here."

"Not that much harder—some people had a problem with her leaving a baby under one with a non-family member—"

"Oh, fuck directly off."

"But yeah, a seventeen-year-old with burst eardrums was generally considered a less controversial consequence."

"Charming."

"Anyway, they got the family all fitted with custom earplugs, a specialized speech therapist for when the little screecher started talking, even a good audiologist for the babysitter."

"At least they did something for them," Darla said. Sometimes they were still a bit idealistic, which could be irritating or refreshing in a melancholy way depending on the circumstances.

"Now, for the bad one." Veronique stopped sharing her screen for a moment, presumably to check she'd censored her documents.

A cold, sick feeling started to gather in my stomach. "Was it a firestarter?"

She looked up at me grimly. "How'd you know."

"Spoilers," Jav scolded.

I shuddered. "The worst ones are always firestarters."

Veronique nodded. "It's about what you imagine it to be. Baby L was by all indications completely normal and happy until the age of twenty-three months."

"Very late," Molly noted from the sidelines.

"It looks like there might have been a minor incident or two before everything really went sideways; a couple weeks before, the fire department got called out for a small kitchen fire with no discernible source. The only thing that went up was the high chair."

I grimaced. Even with minimal description I was already dreading the details.

"Forensic investigation after the official manifestation incident showed Baby L was having a fussy night, so her parents eventually took her into their bed to co-sleep with them. The whole bed went up in the middle of the night. None of them survived."

"She didn't have any resistances?" Not everyone with superpowers was also durable enough too safely use all of them; part of what made Supercollider's deceased kick Accelerator so exceptional was the fact that he was able to withstand friction, g-forces, and wind resistance to effectively travel as fast as he did. As I'd learned from his official records, he was capable of traveling much faster than his body could safely withstand.

Veronique looked at me with an unfathomable expression. "She was immune to the fire. Not to the smoke inhalation."

"Jesus."

"The Draft did a shockingly effective job, I am sad to say, of spinning the incident into an exceptional piece of PR for the program. Because as much as success stories are compelling, nothing motivates like fear."

"Especially to a new parent." I had to grudgingly admire the effort even as I hated it.

Veronique nodded gravely. "It was an exquisitely well-timed tragedy, and Carmel capitalized on it brilliantly. It's unquestionably why she was promoted to acting CDO."

"She seems . . . too dangerous to be just handed the position. Strong enough to keep it."

Veronique looked over to Molly, who took the signal and resumed control of the meeting. After taking a moment to reconnect her laptop, she moved on. "It'll make more sense when you see who else is in the running. Our next contestant is the new chief compliance officer, aka the recently resigned CCO's second-in-command."

Molly displayed a slide with two photos of a steely-eyed man with an aquiline nose and a scar on his top lip that forced his face into a perpetual smirk. In one photo, he was standing next to the former CCO before his recent resignation. The latter was delivering a speech while the former stood nearby, his body curved inward in a slightly servile manner. In the second, he was shaking a hero's hand (it looked like one of the Ocean Four), smiling broadly with his chest puffed out. Molly had added a GIF of Starscream with a speech bubble over his head that said: *In your . . . absence, someone had to take command.*

"Looks like someone saw their opportunity and struck."

"We don't have all the details, but it appears this charming fellow sold his boss up the river to take his place."

"No," I said, attempting to sound as unsurprised as I possibly could.

"I know it's hard to believe," Molly said, absolutely destroying my attempt with an icy delivery of their own. They even paused to polish their glasses on their shirt before continuing.

"This charming fellow is August Chisholm, who is much cleverer than and has, if possible, fewer scruples than his predecessor."

I tensed at the name. Leviathan had shared some genuinely horrific memories of the "training simulations" Chisholm had designed for the young heroes in his charge. He'd especially enjoyed pitting the inexperienced and insecure heroes against each other, encouraging them to compete directly and report each other for any behavior that might suggest "villainous tendencies."

Molly continued. "General consensus is he was the real brains behind Compliance. While it's clear he's wanted his current position for the better part of a decade, now that he's finally achieved it, he might not be content to sit on those hard-won laurels."

"You're saying 'might' more often than usual," I pointed out.

"His motivations beyond his current position are more opaque," Molly said.

"We have no idea what this fucking guy's deal is," Veronique offered, and I cracked a smile. I was starting to like her quite a lot.

"He's been making some noise about 'what he'd do if it were up to him,' and doing some sniffing around for potential allies. But he might also decide to just fuck with everyone, abandon his CDO ambitions and focus on making Compliance his own terrible little fiefdom."

"Either way, I look forward to fucking up his life at every opportunity and then siccing Keller on him," I said, fantasizing about delivering him to Leviathan personally, and alive.

"We have one more key player to go over," Molly said, advancing to a slide I had prepared. This one showed a wider shot, with a slew of Draft execs and staff in front of one of their newest buildings on a summer afternoon. One figure was circled with a bright pink digital marker: a bearded man, smiling broadly, clapping his companion amiably on the shoulder as the two of them talked. He had a wide, jolly face and was wearing an absolutely hideous floral print shirt.

Molly looked over to me. "You're up."

She passed the presentation remote to me like a sacred conch, and we switched places.

"This is Mom."

There was a confused volley of laughter across the room.

"Otherwise known as the chief marketing officer. In the spirit of full transparency, I am presently engaged in a … conversation with this charming gentleman."

"It's so weird," Darla added.

"So I have an even more vested interest than usual when it comes to figuring out what his deal is."

I advanced to a photo of him at a Draft staff picnic in a local park. He was wearing a bright yellow T-shirt with a hot dog on it, radiating genial charm.

"The chief marketing officer has held his position longer than any of his colleagues', and is by far the most firmly entrenched, and well-liked, member of the C-suite. When he took the position almost twenty years ago now, Marketing was very much stuck in the eighties. Heroes were a product that the Draft wanted the public to buy.

He ushered in a new era with a completely new approach: selling the public ideas."

I displayed a slide of some of his best campaigns: portraits of heroes wearing rainbow-themed capes for Pride Month, with the phrase "Inclusivity Is Our Superpower" arching optimistically above them. A younger Doc and teenaged Supercollider on the cover of a magazine with the tagline "The New Nuclear Family." And his latest, a yet-unveiled initiative that he was seeding through a viral marketing campaign. All the released images were examples of simple but stunning graphic designs, warm gray backgrounds with the words "Are You Ready for the Future?" in perfect pink font.

"He has sold people on the *idea* that heroes make their lives better. They are sources of Safety and Justice, as though these were natural resources that they dutifully mine at great personal expense. He and his team are in many ways responsible for the level of buy-in most people have toward superheroics."

I clicked through to a photo of a memorial pamphlet from Accelerator's funeral. The kick's portrait, of him in perpetual, glorious motion, just a smile and enough blur to know he's moving, is slightly desaturated, as though he was ever-so-slightly beginning to fade. Below, in a devastating serif font, "Our Hearts Stand Still."

"He's also the mastermind behind most of their narrative-crafting. He works incredibly closely with the crisis comms team—that means Gentileschi—and his storytelling ability is perhaps his greatest strength. He turns scandals into tragedies and tragedies into triumphs."

Finally, I clicked through to a partially redacted screenshot from my own email. It was a follow-up sent from Mom, with the saccharine title "Auditor + Mom: RSVeeP!"

"He also makes everyone call him Mom . . . and is trying to have me over for a lunch date."

"To murder you, obviously," Jav added.

"One can only assume."

"What a weird play," Veronique said, frowning at the screen.

I cleared my throat. "Whether due to our interference or their own infighting, the competition for leadership has been narrowed down to these three: Gentileschi, Chisolm, and … Mom. Our complicated—but extremely fun—job now is to learn about their strategies, how each of them is going about their various bids for leadership. And, of course, decide the most advantageous way to fuck with it all."

As the meeting evolved into questions and brainstorming, I found myself frequently getting distracted, my eyes wandering back to the final slide still displayed on the wall screen. As much as I wanted to send over some malware masquerading as a calendar invite in response to that "RSVeeP!" I hadn't replied. I hadn't given up on the possibility of meeting him face-to-face, which was only that much more compelling as I slowly became convinced he was the most potentially dangerous of all three CDO candidates.

It wasn't just his skill set that made Mom a problem; he was also remarkably resistant to being fucked with. He wasn't married and never had been; he had a sister and while her family might make decent ransom candidates, the payment would be made out of obligation rather that real affection; they only talked at Christmas and birthdays. He had very few significant relationships to speak of that weren't directly tied to work; he seemed to embody the position of "colleague" more than anyone else I'd ever encountered. I couldn't tell if he'd become skilled enough in his own narrative-building that he'd somehow bamboozled himself into believing it—or, worse, whether the messaging was that good to begin with, and fueled his work as a result. It was like he was grown in a tank, which was mostly a joke, but I made a note to investigate his background more seriously, just in case.

It was a strange thing to try and dismantle someone who had poured all of themselves into their work and had been doing so for a very long time. I had nothing to exploit, nothing to ruin but his own plans, which at the moment were surprisingly opaque. Marketing had some of the best security protocols outside of actual super-hero secrets, which made him much less susceptible to the data breaches and security loopholes of many of his colleagues. Mom understood the importance of a good product launch, and how important controlling the flow of information and messaging cadence was to that success.

All of which only made me more dangerously curious about the invitation optimistically sitting in my inbox, waiting.

OF COURSE HOSTAGE exchanges are delicate. The stakes are high, emotions are often higher, and things either go off seamlessly or catastrophically bad. But that's only half of the problem. They're also underpinned by extremely complicated psychosocial math. It's not just a matter of swapping a couple of people with a handshake while snipers watch serenely from a distance. You've got to run the numbers, and you better be damn sure about your calculations. Everyone involved on both sides has to be weighed and measured, meticulously compared in substance and value to the other person or people in the equation. Miscalculations are, of course, fatal.

It was immensely difficult to apply that kind of math to myself. Since I was the only thing the chief marketing officer was currently interested in—my temporary presence at least—that was the only thing I personally had to bargain with. I had to estimate what I was worth—to the world, to the organization, to my colleagues, to Levi-athan himself—and determine what they could possibly give back that would not only make the risk worth it, but ensure that I could get back home. It was a complex and ugly process, and in the days following Mom's invitation, I struggled to bring that value into focus.

Kindly, Mom solved my problem for me. Not deliberately, of course (though I suppose I shouldn't dismiss the possibility it was a variable in the plan), but very conveniently nonetheless. I had redundant noti-fications on all the official Draft-affiliated social media accounts, and so when the announcement was made my computer, phone, and several other devices all started squawking in a dissonant chorus.

It wasn't the announcement proper, of course, but the announcement of the announcement, twenty-four hours' notice of a scheduled livestream to give as many people as possible the chance to watch. Across all of the accounts was the same placeholder image, in the same pink and gray design as all of the ads I'd seen: "Come See the Future."

I did not reserve a conference room, electing to watch whatever was coming alone in my office. I had windows open across all three of my monitors, ready to divert my attention along whatever path was necessary.

I expected another press conference, another room full of journalists and pantsuits and flashbulbs. Instead, it was a prerecorded video that showed five young heroes, all in immaculate dark gray uniforms with the same pink logo on the front: a crystal ball. They were clearly on a soundstage that was made up to look like a vaguely pastoral scene, the grass and sky of a fake idyllic anywhere.

I recognized four of them immediately as members of the three superhero teams that had been disbanded: Ossuary, Atmosphere, and Siegeworks. From Ossuary were a pair of identical twins, both with extremely short brown hair and mournful chestnut eyes. From Siegeworks was a young man built like an offensive lineman, a certain determination in his face and a strong cleft in his chin. There was also a woman with striking red hair I recognized from the back line of several photos of Atmosphere. The fifth I had seen at Supercollider's funeral, the young hero who had accompanied Doc; she was standing slightly in front, taller than the rest of her teammates, her face seemingly sculpted for staring meaningfully into the middle distance.

But this time, she was looking directly at the camera. "We know that we can never take his place."

"No one can," said one of the twins.

"It hurts to think about a future without him," said the young man from Siegeworks.

"But tomorrow comes whether we face it or not," said the other twin.

"And none of us have to face that future alone," said the woman with red hair, the only time she would speak for the rest of the video.

"All of us are still grieving."

"And we know many of you are afraid."

"But we are here to face those threats for you."

"There is a void that no one can ever fill."

"And while no one person can ever fill it—"

"We can make new spaces together."

"We know you want answers."

"We hear your calls for justice."

"We will do whatever we can."

"Whatever is necessary."

"Whatever is needed."

"To make the future brighter for everyone."

"We are *your* Future."

The video ended with a pan up to the nonexistent sky, a serene backdrop blue that slowly faded to black. A link popped up to the new superteam home page: the Future.

"That son of a bitch," I said out loud.

I texted a single line to Keller.

> I know what to ask for.

Then I put my phone down and ignored his furious responses, and started to pull a proposal together.

I WAS PREPARED for a war. Keller was torn between being furious and impressed I'd met his terms. He didn't hate the idea of my meeting with Mom any less, but after letting him cool down and read my arguments he admitted, very grudgingly, that I had made my point. I expected that part of what mollified him was the strength of the chance the Draft simply might not go for it at all. Risking one of their greatest hopes for the Future, all for an under-the-table lunch date, seemed like a much worse deal for them than it could have been for us, looking at the two organizations holistically. While I might not be 1:1 replaceable, enough people could do my job reasonably well, whereas none of the heroes in question had their equivalent. Besides that, if they did refuse, that in and of itself was invaluable data.

Leviathan was a different story. I gave myself even odds of getting permission to accept Mom's invitation—maybe less, if I was being entirely honest with myself. I had prepared my arguments and backed them up as well as I could, and was prepared to pretend I'd annihilated whatever vestigial stump of self-preservation instinct I had left, but he could feel very different about the risk/reward proposition and completely dismiss the entire venture.

But he approved my request almost immediately, after barely enough time had elapsed between my submitting the full proposal and the length of time it would have taken him to read it. He called it a "briefly open door," and agreed that it would be "wasteful" not to take advantage of the opportunity.

And it . . . stung, in a way I hadn't expected. I'd braced myself for his resistance, for having to convince him to allow me to put myself in danger. I'd expected him to protest even if it wasn't entirely rational—no, especially if it wasn't rational. Subconsciously I thought he would have worried about my safety more than squandering a potential opportunity for leverage—but instead, he looked at an equation, whose balance was predicated on the value of risking my life, and accepted it without hesitation.

I was deeply embarrassed that his easy acceptance hurt as much as it did, especially since Keller had all but predicted it. It felt so infantile, that I wanted him to chase after me, to try and prevent me from doing a dangerous thing out of nothing but his own care for my well-being. I felt stupid when I found myself in pain just because he did exactly what I asked. I sent a blithe, formal thanks and pressed those feelings down into the smallest and most shameful corner of my head that I could find.

From: Auditor@Leviathan.org
To: CMO@DRAFT.SPR
Re: Re: Auditor + Mom: RSVeeP!

MOM,

Regretfully, I have decided to accept your invitation. Despite my reservations and the objections of several of my trusted colleagues, upon weighing the options it's clear to us, as I am sure it also became clear to you, that under our current circumstances, building bridges may be a wiser course than burning them.

There are, of course, significant conditions around my in-person attendance at any Draft-controlled location. While our respective legal departments can work out the details of the exchange, here are the terms: for the duration of our visit, one of the members of the Future (any of them, your choice) will remain in Leviathan's custody until my safe return. For the duration of the visit, they will not be harmed in any way and we will endeavor to make the experience as pleasant, even useful, as possible. If everything goes well for me, that will be all that happens. I won't insult you by discussing any possible alternatives, because I am sure that you, like me, are completely confident that's the only possible outcome.

We eagerly await your response,
The Auditor

From: CMO@DRAFT.SPR
To: Auditor@Leviathan.org
Re: Re: Re: Auditor + Mom: RSVeeP!

A,

GREAT to hear it, can't tell you how thrilled we all are over here,
I'll get the paperwork started today and we can let the experts
work out the deets.
   Keep an eye out for a calendar invite!!!!

All My Best,
Mom <3

"Red Sprite is the lucky winner."

There was a mumble of acknowledgment from the roomful of henches, all of whom I had commandeered to help directly with the hostage exchange. It wouldn't be the first time I had been a part of an operation like this—supervillains liked to kidnap each other's scientists like it was an amateur sport—but it would be the first time I was one of the hostages in question.

"Why her?" Veronique asked, not looking up from the brief I'd handed out.

"No idea," I said cheerfully. "What matters right now isn't why, but that it *is* her, and what we're going to do with that."

I looked over the room, which was more sparsely occupied than it would have been a few weeks ago, but filled with faces I trusted. Jav and Darla would be instrumental in making the exchange go the way we needed it to, but I'd also enlisted Veronique, as well as several Meat to serve as security and liaisons to the rest of enforcement (Keller was still being extremely shirty about the whole thing), and (still lacking a new social engineer since Tammy left) I had asked Vesper to step in.

"I wish I could be here to witness your efforts in person," I admitted. "But sadly, as the second body involved in the exchange, I'll have to trust you all to make this as memorable as I would.

"Vesper"—he sat straighter in acknowledgment and casually saluted—"will be our Virgil, guiding our hero through her various circles of hell." I made eye contact with him. "You are to be charming and merciless."

He laid a hand on his chest. "You know me so well."

I raised my voice so it was clear I was addressing everyone. "The goal here is simple, but not easy: I want her to have an absolutely terrible time, and yet not be able to say a single negative thing about how she has been treated."

I directed everyone to flip to a photograph of Red Sprite in the brief; there was her official Draft headshot, where she was holding her chin up and giving an easy smile, and a candid shot of her leaning away, tense and furious, while a reporter shoved a microphone in her face.

"This is who the Draft have offered up as their sacrificial lamb," I said. "That means one of two things: she is either the weakest link and therefore expendable, or they are most confident that she's going to get out of this alive. Our job, barring some catastrophically stupid actions on her part, is to make sure that she is returned safe and sound, having had an absolutely miserable time despite the fact our hospitality has been impeccable.

"I can hear you now: 'Auditor, that's implausible; how can we make her time here miserable while also being gracious hosts?' So I will answer myself: We make it a perfectly bespoke discomfort. We tailor the experience to her, so that almost anyone else she describes the situation to couldn't see anything we did wrong. Now, we do not have perfect recon here, as she's very early in her career and generally very introverted—that will be important later—but I'm confident we have enough that we can give her something really awful to take home with her.

"When she arrives: security checks should be long, boring, and thorough. The name of the game here is redundancies. That means she signs in and out everywhere she goes, is given a visitor badge as well as UV ink stamps. I want checkpoints to be in constant communication with each other in earshot. Make everything a hassle, a process. Nothing is easy. If she has to go to the bathroom, give her a cartoonishly oversize key with 'HERO' stamped on it."

There were a few audible chuckles at that. Jav turned to someone from I&I, a young man I didn't recognize, and informed him, "She's not kidding. I'd fire up the 3D printer."

I smirked and continued. "Moving on to security: it's key we make her stand out in any way possible. We know she's the least social of all the Future and she, by all accounts, finds the public scrutiny the worst part of the job. I might even say she's having some trouble adjusting. As such, I want as many eyes on her as possible at all times, and in a way she will notice. Any lanyards, guest passes, or other identifying markings she is given are to be as obnoxious and high visibility as possible. Anytime you enter a room, I want a nonemergency alarm tone to be triggered and everyone to turn and look at her.

"If *she* enters a room, I want it to be excruciating. You and your colleagues should all stop what you're working on, make it really obvious you are doing so, regardless of the actual security protocols around your work. Watch her. Stand up for a look. Take a minute to pop your head up over your cubicle. Make it very clear that she is interrupting someone and you are painfully aware of her presence and waiting for her to leave before you can do anything else.

"I want her to walk into a hum and then have to stand there in our silence.

"Finally, anyone who has the opportunity to talk to her: Ask her as many questions as you can. Reframe the question if she decides to deflect. Wait for her to answer and stay attentive and expectant. Force her to participate as much as you can. Let her off the hook if she's getting too flustered—we want her to have the panic attack at home rather than here—but otherwise if there's a way you can wring some awkward conversation out of her, go for it.

"I want her to leave here confused, exhausted, and above all viciously resentful that she was chosen. We know she was picked, that she did not volunteer. I want her to be thinking endlessly, obsessively, *Why me?* Why did they make her go, especially when the visit was so utterly pointless from her perspective? What does it *mean* that she was picked? I want her to hate every single answer that she comes up with.

"Any questions?"

LATER, WHILE I was decompressing in my office, I was interrupted by a single knock at the door that happened at the same time the handle started to turn. Without greeting me, Keller strode into my office and shut the door firmly behind him.

I frowned, assuming he was going to try and persuade me to abort my interorganizational luncheon. "We've been through this."

"Open your email," he said, marching over to stand behind my shoulder while I read.

At the top of my inbox was a message from him without a subject or body text, just a link.

"You're being awfully mysterious. Also, doesn't this violate that anti-phishing training Security had us take—"

"Do it."

His voice was calm and even in a way that made a cold tension start to gather in my chest. Without another word I clicked the link.

It opened a window to a live video feed, showing the inside of an employee's apartment—*my* apartment. At first, I saw nothing but my empty living room, several abandoned cups of tea scattered over the coffee table. I drew a breath to ask what I was looking for, when a sudden movement on-screen caught my breath in my throat.

A woman stepped into view, then stood in the middle of the room, shifting awkwardly from one foot to the other. Her back was to the camera, and but I could see her thick hair gathered into a low ponytail. It had once been bleached but over the last several months she'd let it grow out. She had her head tilted slightly to one side, as though listening intently for something. The breadth of her shoulders, the unconscious strength with which she held herself, was unmistakable.

"She arrived a few minutes ago," Keller said. "Hasn't done a thing, just seems to be waiting."

"You haven't sent anyone in." It wasn't a question.

"No. Thought you'd want to see it first. Besides, I just ate."

"Good. Thanks. Don't tell anyone."

"Which anyone?"

"You know which *anyone*, the only *anyone* who matters. Let me handle this if I can."

"Let's pretend I'm not going to tell him. What's your plan?"

"I'm going to go talk to her."

"Yourself?"

"You think having someone in the room with me would make a difference?"

"Fair enough."

"Can you make sure we aren't disturbed?"

"Sure. Unless the Boss wants you disturbed, then all bets are off."

"Don't tell him unless you have to. Give me as much time as you can."

"If it goes at all sideways, I'm calling him."

"That won't be necessary."

"Because you'll be dead."

"Because it will be fine," I said, with a lot more conviction in my voice than I felt.

"I'll be watching."

"I'm counting on it."

Keller offered an arm to help me up, and we both left my office. Two of his Meat were lurking in the hallway.

"Go with her, and wait outside the door until the all-clear," Keller said. He then quick-walked away as the Meat and I headed off toward my living quarters. I heard Keller bark something into his comm before he was completely out of earshot.

When we reached the door to my suite, one of many identically laid-out clusters of rooms lining identical hallways, each of the Meat took up a position on either side of the door. I didn't insult them by telling them to stay outside no matter what they heard, but instead I said, "If it's at all possible, let me handle this."

I knocked once, softly, to let her know I was about to come in, and opened the biometric lock with a hand that shook no matter how hard I tried to keep it still. I opened the door just wide enough to step inside and shut it quickly behind me.

She was waiting. She had turned to face me, her hands at her sides and loosely curled. Standing in front of her was as breath-taking as it always was; I built her up in my head to the point I was sure I would be disappointed, but in the flesh she always exceeded my imagination.

"I hoped it would be just you," Quantum Entanglement said, and I felt my stomach flip.

"It might not stay that way for long."

She nodded. "Your security knows I'm here."

"Keller probably knows what your blood pressure is at the moment, so yes, I knew."

"He's good."

"Quantum, what—"

"I know I shouldn't be here."

"You're goddamn right you shouldn't be here," I said, a bit surprised at the heat in my voice. "Do you have any idea—"

"This isn't dangerous for me."

I felt anger start gathering in my jaw. "I know. But it causes a lot of fucking trouble for *me*."

A grimace flickered across her face.

"Did that not occur to you?" I pressed.

She seemed to affect an air of indifference but wore it badly. "What if I just don't care?"

"So you came here just to fuck with me. Real nice."

She didn't reply.

"Look, if that's what you wanted, mission accomplished. Now, if you'll excuse me, I have a panic button to press and then a colossal amount of paperwork to start."

But I didn't move, and neither did she. There was an awful tension in the room between us, but the implied violence I might have expected didn't materialize. Just a crackling energy between our bodies, not yet coalesced into a coherent shape. We stared each other down until she finally broke eye contact.

"Look. I know this is a terrible fucking idea."

"And yet here you are."

"It's important."

"To whom?"

"To you."

"So tell me."

She hesitated. I realized that she was on the precipice of something, that whatever she had to tell me would push her over some edge that even now seemed unfathomable. I tried to gentle myself a little. Gathering the nerve to phase herself into her former enemy's— was he a "former enemy" now?—headquarters was a lot already, but whatever was happening now was infinitely more difficult.

"Would you like to sit down?" I managed not to sound entirely exasperated.

She watched me suspiciously for a moment, as though she wasn't sure if I was making fun of her; when I gestured toward the couch, though, she nodded once and gingerly sat down on the edge of the cushions. Since the only other chair was an armchair across the room, and it would be incredibly awkward to try and sit and speak so far from her, I pushed all of the cups to one side and sat on the coffee table.

"It must be important for you to risk phasing yourself in here," I said cautiously. "I'm sure Keller would love to know how you did it so he can plug that hole."

The corner of her mouth quirked up a little, affectionately. "Yeah, I bet he would. Maybe I'll get the chance to tell him."

"For now, though—" I said, making a sweeping gesture for her to continue.

"Yeah." She looked at the floor. "So. It's been. Not great for me."

"Since the funeral."

"No, since the . . . Well. 'Rescue,' I guess."

Something softened in my chest, which I hoped was invisible to her. "Of course. You know. You didn't need to take off so fast."

She looked at me as if I was stupid. "Of course I did."

"We could have worked it out."

"Bullshit."

"I—" I caught myself and reevaluated exactly what I wanted to tell her, in which order.

"Look," I said. "We haven't been honest with each other. Both of us have a reason not to trust the other. But I will hear you out. I owe you that. I owe you . . . more than that."

I watched a tiny bit of curiosity creep into her face, and saw it as an opening. Weaponized vulnerability, in the right doses, had always worked on her. "I should have told you sooner. About Melting Point."

She flinched when I said his name. They had, after all, been lovers; I hadn't thought about it much at the time—the fallout from her infidelity to Supercollider had been the thing that toppled her life, but losing him must have been painful. "So you found out who did it? Who killed him and his partner."

"I knew before . . . well, before the fight. I should have told you, but I didn't want you to leave."

"Who was it."

"His name was Harold, he was a handler for—"

"I know him, the weaselly fuck."

"*Knew* him."

She started to pick up on the significance of my past tense. "What did you—"

"Nothing he wouldn't have done to himself. He had a lot of gambling debts and used too many tranquilizers. I just made sure it caught up with him quicker." This, at least, wasn't a lie.

She looked both queasy and grateful.

"Why would you do that? Let alone tell me?"

"It was the least I could do." I figured at least feigning magnanimity would get me farther in this conversation than honest bitterness; and who knew, I might actually mean what I said. "We were both desperate and doing what was necessary. I would be a hypocrite to hold too much against you."

She searched my face, and whatever she saw allowed her to continue. "I wasn't prepared for *him* to—for Leviathan to be alive."

I tried not to flinch at the way she said his name. "And I wasn't prepared for him to be dead."

"I couldn't . . . It would have been a bad idea to stick around. But. Sometimes, I wish I had."

"Where have you been?"

"Just . . . That's not important. What is, though, is the Draft. They came to me."

I sat up straighter. "They came after you?"

"No. Not exactly. They—"

I looked around the room, as though that would tell me anything useful. "How much trouble are you in right now?"

She shook her head. "They tried to get me to come back."

I sat back, shifting my grip on my cane from one hand to the other. This was news to me. Despite watching for it, I'd never seen anything suggesting the Draft was going to allocate resources to chasing her down, or any kind of an intent to repatriate her after Supercollider's defeat.

"I am assuming, since you are here, that it went poorly."

She was quiet for too long.

I pressed. "What happened, Quantum?"

"Decoherence."

"What?"

She held my gaze for a moment. "My name is Decoherence."

I smiled. So she'd officially changed it; I'd liked the name since she first told me she was thinking about it. I wanted to congratulate her. It meant she wasn't a hero anymore, and maybe that I could trust her more than I'd been able to. But before I could say any of that, I needed her to tell me why she was in my living room.

"Decoherence. What happened?"

"They told me I could come home if I killed Leviathan."

I suddenly felt like there was no oxygen in the air around me. "Is that why you're here?" It sounded in my own ears like I was speaking from another room.

She looked away. "I turned them down," she said. "Eventually."

I felt relief as intense as a physical sensation, a sudden melting. "They took out a hit on Leviathan." Once I said the words out loud, I surprised myself by starting to laugh in complete shock.

She almost looked hurt. "They did."

"I believe you!"

"Then what's so—"

"It's just . . . ridiculous."

"I could do it."

My laughter died. There was a dead, icy quality to her voice I hadn't heard before. She didn't sound upset, just hollow and matter-of-fact.

"I know you could." I thought for a minute. "You're . . . probably the only one who could."

"I thought about it. Seriously, too. I thought about it for a long time."

A new withering panic started to grow in my stomach. Her voice was still cool and empty, and I was suddenly worried she was regretting the decision she'd made.

"Why didn't you?"

She took a minute before she answered. She rearranged herself on the couch, leaning back into the cushions and crossing a leg over her knee. She stretched out one arm across the back of the couch and rested it there almost languidly. I swallowed hard.

"Two reasons. Despite what they, or you, or anyone else might think, I'm not a fucking murderer."

"I never thought you were."

"And I am certainly not for hire. Not for them."

"But there's a third reason."

This time she was the one who broke eye contact. "I knew if I did, you would hound me for the rest of my life. You'd spend every minute of every day gouging out your revenge. It would be your new purpose."

I let myself feel, just for a moment, the edge of that imagined grief and betrayal. At finding him gone and knowing exactly who had done it. It was almost enough to choke me, the billowing ash that was belched up into the atmosphere of my soul just thinking about it, like the fallout from a volcanic eruption. I would become a nuclear winter, a permafrost, a sunless traumatic ice age. There would be nowhere she could hide.

"You're right," I rasped, the ash still clinging to my throat.

She nodded. "So. I'd have to kill you, too."

We both let that hang there for a moment. The energy shifted between us a little. She had decided not to kill me, even if it would have let her begin rebuilding her life. That meant something.

"I could justify removing him from the world," she continued, running her nails over the fabric of her leggings. "You, though. You didn't deserve that. Not from me."

I tried very hard to remind myself she'd spent all of her adult life believing the world would be infinitely better without Leviathan in it; and probably her life would have been. "Thank you," I said. "That must have . . . not been easy."

"It wasn't." She gazed back up at me. Her eyes had dark circles under them, and she looked deeply tired. "And then, my window closed."

"How so?"

"Well, he's 'alive' again now, and everyone knows."

A few things clicked into place. "Of course. Killing him while he was conveniently already 'dead' would mean the Draft never had to admit they'd lied or fucked up."

She nodded. "They wanted to make the fiction real while they had the chance."

"Why are you telling me this now?"

She stared a bit past me, apparently wishing I had not asked this question.

I refused to let her off the hook. "You could have just said no and not told me."

"They might send someone else."

I scoffed. "You're the only one who stands a chance."

"They could still."

"He wouldn't be in any danger."

"No. But."

She stopped herself from saying it, but I could almost hear the three words she left hanging:

You might be.

"Does the 'why' matter?" She brought her arm back down to her side. I could see this was making her uncomfortable.

So I pushed harder. "Quite a lot, actually."

She raised one of her eyebrows "Would you like it if I told you I couldn't stand the thought of them winning?"

"I mean. It would further solidify something I've always liked about you."

Her smirk became something else, and suddenly I was painfully aware of where my hands were, somehow both dangling and clutching awkwardly at the same time. I wondered in horror if she thought I was flirting with her, while trying to figure out if I actually had been in the first place.

"Because I wanted you to keep being alive. And because fuck them."

"I . . . appreciate both those sentiments."

I knew that the next thing either of us said would be the end of the conversation, a doorway she would step through, and neither of us wanted that to happen. At least, I hoped she didn't. As the tension in my chest wound tighter, I decided if there was no way I could stop her from leaving, I could at least take whatever control of the situation I could.

"How can I get in touch with you?" I asked. "I owe you a lot."

"No, you don't." She stood. "You helped me at the funeral, even when I was an asshole."

"Hardly seems even."

"Talking yourself deeper into debt is a bad strategy, and not like you."

I looked up at her and scowled. "If you're going to be stupid enough to turn down the offer, it's rescinded."

She smiled. I fought down the impulse to spit insults at her and instead rifled through a couple of my drawers until I laid a hand on one of a handful of burner phones.

"At least take this."

"Seems like a bad idea," she said, but let me put it in her hand.

"Take it anyway."

"This is where I say something cavalier, like 'just whistle when you need me.'"

"Fuck off."

"You got it."

Before I could retort, she turned and, with an ultraviolet crackle and a smell like ozone, she vanished into the wall.

"Fucking shit balls!" I threw my cane across the room in disgust.

I was loud enough that it summoned the Meat that Keller had sent, who in turn irritated me by insisting on sweeping my apartment before they'd leave. By the time I locked the door behind them my heart was threatening to hammer through my chest.

I needed to talk to Leviathan, immediately, to tell him what had almost happened, what Quantum—no, what *Decoherence* had so narrowly turned away from. As it was, I was too distraught to send as much as an email heralding my arrival.

Despite my lack of an appointment, the high-security elevator in Leviathan's building still slid open for me. It made my heart ache, the implicit trust there, that I could just walk in whenever I wanted. Guilt ran me through like the point of a rapier as I remembered asking Keller not to tell Leviathan about the meeting I'd just taken, to give me time. I'd wanted to protect her from whatever reaction or retribution he might have wanted to visit on her, without even knowing if that was a certainty. I would have lied to him to protect her—when she had very nearly agreed to kill him.

I'd been so wrapped up in the distance I perceived he'd been placing between us, and how upset I was at him for it, that I'd missed the ways I was also disconnecting from him. He might not have been as affectionate with me of late, but what did that really matter when he continued to support me? He'd given me access to almost any of his resources that I'd needed or wanted, trusted me to lead the projects he was most deeply invested in, and despite his complicated feelings did not hesitate to place me in an unparalleled position of trust at his right hand. The absolute least I could do was reward him with loyalty—and that meant trusting his judgment. I shouldn't be protecting anyone from him.

By the time I reached the massive doors to his office, I was almost hyperventilating. For one awful moment I stood outside of them, unable to move. Did I do something as ridiculous as knock, and then wait for him to open them for me? I'd always just walked in, but then again he'd always been expecting me. In the end, I let the fear carry me forward and awkwardly shouldered my way into the room.

He didn't leap up when I entered, but he turned extremely quickly. He had only two types of movement: an eerily languid slowness and an almost preternatural darting speed. Something like a spider, either slowly unfolding itself limb by limb as it crept across the web, or moving lightning fast to secure a kill.

"Leviathan, I—"

He seemed to almost teleport to my side then, hovering around me with deep concern.

"She didn't harm you," he said. He ushered me into a chair while looking me over sharply, I assumed for any signs that I was hurt. I was surprised he already knew that Decoherence had appeared in my room but probably shouldn't have been; Keller had probably tipped him off.

"No, I'm fine," I replied though he hadn't asked a question. I took a couple of deep breaths, which didn't help me feel better at all, and ended up gulping like I had gills instead of lungs. He lowered himself into the chair opposite me, staring into my face the entire time like he was trying to scry what I was thinking from the fine wrinkles and sheer panic written there.

I swallowed. "I need to tell you something."

He was oddly patient while I struggled for a moment to find the words.

"They told her to kill you," I managed to blurt out. For a moment, there was nothing else.

He nodded, slowly. "I know." I felt a huge rush of relief, knowing that I didn't have to explain everything.

"She thought about it, very seriously."

He nodded gravely, but didn't appear angry at the idea. "She was an intelligent opponent. I would not have assumed she was weak enough to turn down such an opportunity without careful thought."

I could have left it there, my duty of disclosure done, and trusted that any surveillance footage and Keller's timely reporting would cover enough of the details. But that would not have been fully honest. *This is your chance to start doing things differently,* I told myself, and forced myself to hand over facts I would have kept to myself only hours before.

"I gave her a burner phone, as a means of contacting me."

"You did." He folded his arms.

"I will, of course, deactivate it if you feel maintaining a connection is unwise. But I saw the potential advantage."

"It is a risk. Especially now. But it is a risk you have managed in the past. I trust you."

That landed like a needle in my heart. "Leviathan."

This time he didn't flinch but the tension in her shoulders softened at his name, and invited me to continue.

"I felt. I thought." I took a deep breath and started again. "When she—when Decoherence—told me what they asked of her. I learned what I always should have known."

"What is that?" he said softly

"There are no rules. There is no honor. There is no such thing as a fair fight. They would have had her sneak in here and murder you in your sleep."

He waited while I paused to gulp in a few breaths.

"Keller may have told you this already. But at first I—I asked him not to tell you she was here. I wanted to handle it myself. Without you knowing."

He said nothing, but his head tilted ever so slightly to one side.

"I should never have asked him that. I should have told you myself, before going in."

"You should have," he agreed, but was still unreadably gentle. "What did you think you were sparing her from?"

"You."

"You don't trust me."

"I didn't."

"Why not."

"I didn't . . . recognize you, when you came back. I wasn't sure I knew you anymore." I would have lied to him if I could, if only to be less brutal and blunt, but I couldn't bring myself to say anything but the absolute truth, no matter how ugly or awkward it was.

"Did I disappoint you so much?" There was a woundedness in his voice that destroyed me.

I shook my head. "It wasn't like that. It felt like—I couldn't reach you."

"But you changed your mind."

"She could have killed you," I whispered. "And then I knew it shouldn't have mattered. That is a mistake that I won't repeat. Whatever I thought I was protecting her from doesn't matter. The only person I should be protecting, whose interests I should be serving, is you."

He looked at me then like he had not seen me in a very long time. There was a particular kind of focused attention, and a kind of deep warmth, that I had not seen in him since the initial rupture between us, and all of the longing and emptiness I'd been carrying crashed over me in the same moment it was alleviated.

"I am so glad, my Auditor, that you have arrived here again." He took up both of my hands. "Back to me."

Hearing him use the possessive pronoun with my name broke some sort of a dam inside me, and I started openly weeping. I would have been mortally embarrassed just an hour earlier, but now there was nothing but a quenching relief.

"I will not stand in your way. It's not a mercy, it's spotting them an advantage. And they would never extend such a mercy to us."

"No," he said, reaching toward my face. "They never will."

"If she had agreed, and they had succeeded, and I hadn't—" I stopped, unable to even articulate aloud the horror of losing him because of my own squeamish stupidity. He held my face until I could speak again. "I will never forget this. They will never be fair. So I won't be either."

He was kneeling on the carpet in front of me then, pulling me forward until I was on my knees with him.

"They'll try again," he said sweetly. "And you'll have every opportunity to show me how merciless you can be."

My entire body felt like it was becoming undone, little bits of tension and anxiety that I didn't know I was carrying falling apart like unraveling threads. When I'd imagined a moment like this, I assumed he would have more sharp edges, that I would have to be careful, but his chitin had a warmth and a give that was deeply comforting. I leaned my head against the plate that covered his collarbone, and it felt like laying my cheek against warm porcelain. "If I don't give you every possible advantage, every opportunity to defend yourself, then I might as well be turning the knife myself."

"Knives cannot damage me."

"That was a figure of speech."

"And that was a joke."

I looked up in shock, and he was looking down on me with that same unfathomable affection. There was a gentle amusement, too, as he searched my face, cataloging everything he found there.

I placed my hands on his chest, palms flat against the armored plates there. The armor, the real armor he wore, was carefully built to match and often indistinguishable from most of the chitinous plates that covered his body. The armor felt distinctly different from his body; the plates I touched at first had a ceramic-like coolness, smooth and inanimate. But closer to his throat, where the organic plates were visible, they were much warmer, with a slightly rougher texture. Touching him reminded me of the way you tested to see if a pearl was real: you rubbed it against your teeth to see if it would catch. That minuscule roughness, the surprising catch against something that was also so smooth.

He took one of my hands and pulled it away from him; for a moment I thought he was going to break the contact between us, gently but firmly putting the usual distance back in place. Instead, he looked at my fingers. I kept my nails very short, and my hands were completely unadorned. He studied them a moment, with what seemed like a close academic interest, then brought my fingers up to his mouth.

I held my breath as his mandibles closed around my fingers. It felt like a dozen knives trying to hold me, gently. Everything was sharp and complicated, so many unexpectedly moving parts, all brushing against my skin and making an extraordinary effort not to break it. His mouth moved over my fingertips and to the back of my hand, tracing a small circle before finally letting go.

I wasn't sure what would happen, but I leaned closer to him and lifted my face, closing my eyes. There was a moment's pause, and a rustle of movement; then something extremely delicate touched my face, something almost feathery but with a deliberate precision. I opened my eyes, slightly startled, and saw he'd removed a piece of armor I'd never seen him without before, a piece that fit around the back of his skull and over where his ears would be, like a cap with a pair of ridges. With the armor off, he freed a pair of prehensile antennae, each about as long as my forearm, and was using them to explore my face.

I breathed in sharply. He grew still for a moment, watching me carefully, as if trying to gauge the value of my startled reaction. Almost instantly, I felt a completely involuntary smile break over my face, like a welling light. It felt like something genuinely magical; everything about him was surprising, but that never dulled the delight of uncovering a new thing.

Seeming convinced that my reaction was positive, he relaxed and moved slightly closer to me again, allowing the tips of his antennae to once again glide over my face. They were jointed, incredibly delicate, and precise in the way that they moved, much smoother and more tentative than fingertips. They were also shockingly fluffy, the tips ornamented with something that looked closer to feathers than hair. He alternated between extremely light brushes with just the feathery ends and firmer, more exploratory taps with the "body" of the antennae themselves.

I made a little humming noise of my own. "This tickles a little."

He laid one antenna against my throat and brushed the end of another over my ear, making me giggle. I realized he was feeling me laugh though my throat, like you might place a finger under a cat's chin to feel it purr.

He put his arms around me in a practically affectionate kind of way, holding me still as much as it was an embrace. I obligingly kept still, wondering what new data this was giving him, what he was able to learn about me from the texture of my skin, the flutter of my eyelids, all the tiny lines and pores and bits of makeup that came together into the shape of my face.

"Why do you hide them."

"They're extremely sensitive."

I lifted up a hand. "Can I?"

"Carefully."

I held my hand still until he placed the end of an antenna into my palm, then curled my fingers around it very slightly. He didn't pull away so the contact was at least tolerable, so I risked moving my fingers a little over the fluff. After a few brushes, he suddenly pulled it back with a whole-body shiver.

"Did I hurt you?"

"No," he said. "But it's . . . a lot."

"Is it better if you do the touching."

"For now."

He let go of me and leaned back a moment. I wasn't sure if he was thinking or just needed a moment without contact; it might have been both.

"I don't know what you're expecting," he said quietly.

"Neither do I." I held still until he gave me some indication of if I should pull away or move closer.

"Of me."

"I don't have any expectations. Just curiosity."

He reached out with both hands and I gave him one of mine. For a moment he just held me there, turning over my palm, considering it.

"How unusual for you." Then, with seemingly no effort whatsoever, he lifted me to my feet with him. He led me to the back of the room, behind his desk, where there was an alcove and, I could see for the first time now that I was close enough, a door. It wasn't designed to be entirely invisible, just very hard to notice, with tight seams and no visible handle. He touched a biometric pad and with the smallest blip of acknowledgment, a tiny piece of the door jutted out—a handle. He twisted it and guided me in through the door; all of his movements had the mechanical ease of someone operating entirely on muscle memory.

There was a small spiral staircase, twisting upward like a seashell, and the soft light and pale-colored ceiling above me only increased that impression. The wall was an eerie purple, a color that almost always appeared with iridescence, and long before I reached the top I could smell something tropical and green.

The room at the top of the stairs was full of enough not immediately recognizable equipment that it could have passed as a lab, and was pervaded by the server-hum sound I had come to associate with his office. There was even a partially rebuilt energy cannon on a workbench he'd been recently tinkering with. But there was also a wide-armed upholstered chair with a mid-century modern reading light hanging over it, like a massive amber drop of liquid, and an overstuffed bookshelf twisting organically up and around that corner. A frosted partial room divider kept a section of the space out of immediate view, but I could see the foot of a bed, with wrinkled black linen bedding. An archway led to a hall, from which came the sound of running water from what must have been a small waterfall in Shannon's enclosure.

A sense of unreality descended over me, a diving bell made out of a looking glass. This wasn't something that was ever supposed to happen. We were supposed to be weird with each other forever, tangled messes of frustrated longing that we sublimated into our various hyper-fixations. But we'd found the right moment, strange and raw enough that a tiny pocket universe had formed around us, and I would stay within it as long as the delicate bubble of its structure held.

Undressing is slow and complicated for supervillains. We began separately, Leviathan unbuckling one piece of armor at a time in a slow cascade, the removal of one pauldron loosening a chest plate. My clothes were much easier, and after a moment it felt more comfortable to help than watch. His antennae quirked toward me when I offered my hands, a tiny unconscious gesture that gave me such a rush of affection it almost knocked me over. I was a lot slower than he was, which became its own sort of lovely thing, discovering which piece of armor was connected to what, where his body was underneath it. Then all of a sudden there was only his body, an intricate mosaic of flexible chitin plates and all the softer joinery holding them together.

He was much more slender with the armor off; the only other time I had seen him without it was when we broke him out of Dovecote, and found him sitting on the floor in that empty, over-bright cell. He had a new daintiness to his shape, the planes and angles of him gaining a sort of delicacy with his antennae framing his face. Without the layers of fabric and tailoring I felt a lot smaller, and softer, than I usually was, if not nearly as physically remarkable.

The surfaces of him were hard but not uncomfortable, warm with unexpected give. We had to find the ways in which we fit together, a question unlocking an answer and another question, like a braid or links in a chain. I came for the first time against his thigh, grinding against a plate shaped like a tasset, while he bit down on my shoulder with his chelicerae, drawing pinpricks of blood in a starburst. Later, draped over his back, I tried to brush one of his antennae gently, and he wrapped his fingers around mine to make me squeeze harder.

"Pull," he whispered, and then whined when I did, arching under me.

"You'll have to show me all the places I can hurt you," I said, and pulled harder.

We stopped fucking gradually, moving on to different questions, different kinds of touch. We were both sore and tired and I needed a minor amount of first aid for puncture wounds; he found us some antiseptic and dark chocolate, and then for a while we were both quiet, and still, breathing next to each other. I wondered, briefly, what was supposed to happen now, and if I should offer to leave, but he was drawing something on my back with the tip of one finger, and I dismissed the thought he might want me gone.

The deep weirdness of my surroundings once again settled over me. His office had always been the epicenter of his existence for me, the inner sanctum from which he worked and exercised power. Of course there was somewhere he retired in private, where he slept, but I'd had no mental image of that space. And now I was falling asleep in a room that was as much a workshop as it was a bedroom, a place of stark intimacy.

"You should confess things to me more often," he said, waking me up a little.

"But my plan is to be perfect now, so I'll have nothing to confess."

"Make something up," he said languidly, and I laughed.

"Should I have Keller throw me under the bus again for dramatic effect."

"He told me nothing."

He tilted his head slightly. I saw an emotion play across his face that reminded me of amusement, but deeper and sharper. "There is not much I don't know, when it is nearby and interests me."

"So I interest you?"

"Deeply."

"Did you look in on the surveillance feed, then."

"Are you asking me so you can refine your systems of deception?" His tone was gentle, almost humorous, but it was also a question I knew I had one chance to answer correctly.

"No," I said. I settled a bit closer to him, hooking one of my ankles around the plate of his shin. "I won't keep anything from you again."

He sighed deeply and shifted under me, getting more comfortable with a few little clicks of contentment.

"You won't, will you."

"No."

A deep peace settled over me, a kind of contentment too pure to sleep through. *I belong here*, I thought, and it was true. I'd never allowed myself to feel it before, always held some part of me apart, in reserve, so that when I was inevitably abandoned or betrayed there would be something left. But as soon as I let go, as soon as I went all in, I finally felt what it would be like to fit somewhere perfectly. A tooth in a socket. A hand in a hand. A grave dug just for me.

"I'll tell you," Leviathan said.

"Hmm?"

His fingers on my back grew still.

"How I knew."

One side of my mouth quirked up. I thought I detected a tiny bit of playfulness in his voice, a rare mood I decided to encourage.

"Tell me."

"You have one of my eyes," he said. "When it is necessary, we can look out at the world together."

For a moment, I didn't understand. I would think about that moment with an awful jealousy for years into the future, the last time there was nothing but a little eddy of confusion to disturb the still waters of my belonging. But then my brain caught up with me, and time caught up with me, and with a piercing clarity I knew what that must mean.

Time slowed down. I sat up suddenly, my entire body reverberating with an entirely new kind of panic. I thought back over all the time since my kidnapping and subsequent reconstructive surgery. I thought of everything I had done, everything I had said or read or looked at in what I was certain was a private moment, and wondered if he'd been there. I felt a kind of nausea in my soul. The idea was excruciating; I couldn't tell what was worse, the thought of him eavesdropping on a personal conversation where he would absolutely hate whatever I was saying, or the idea that he might have observed any of my clandestine google searches while I was alone in bed.

"You. You can watch . . ." was all I could manage.

"I can." He sounded surprisingly calm for someone who had just destroyed my dignity and sense of self. "It is a means of observation I use only when absolutely necessary."

That did not reassure me in the way I think he intended. "Can you turn it off?"

"No. But I am the only one who can access it, of course. And I respect your privacy."

He looked me over carefully and then sat up as well, kneeling in front of me while I panicked. He reached out slowly, trying not to startle me, keeping his hands visible as long as he could so I could see they were empty of ill intent. I swallowed hard and realized I had started shaking.

He cupped both his hands around my face. The pads of his fingertips and curve of his palms gripped my skin, slightly rough and always surprisingly warm. With two fingers, he traced the skin at the outer corner of my left eye. Buried in the fine lines there were a few incredibly delicate scars, remnants from the vision-saving surgeries I'd undergone to replace the damage the Draft had caused.

I closed my eyes. His grip gentled, and I was sure he took that for an expression of relaxation or surrender rather than the overwhelming distress that it was.

"After all," he said, that gentle amusement returning, "you said you would never keep anything like this from me again. So I won't have any need to look, will I?"

[Part Three]

SOMETIMES, I WOULD STARE AT MY MONITOR FOR A LONG TIME, paralyzed. I knew how to behave when I was certain I was being surveilled, or when it was a distinct possibility. Most of this experience was rote by now, simple muscle memory that I rarely had to think consciously about. Only during extremely stressful situations did I plan out each of my moves carefully, or think about likely camera angles or what might be picked up on a microphone. Both consciously and unconsciously, I was good at it.

But now I had no idea how to act. This was not a mic or a camera in the room; the vulnerability was, essentially, inside my own body. Despite saying he did not "need" to watch me anymore, he made it immediately clear he had no interest in changing my current settings. He promised not to use the eye more than was strictly "necessary," but my now deeply ingrained hypervigilance had to assume that it was on and transmitting 100 percent of the time. I found myself examining everything I did, voluntary and involuntary, and wondering how it would look. How it would read. Would a spike in my heartbeat register? Would a GPS tracker ping that I was in a part of the complex I didn't usually visit?

I needed to tell someone; I couldn't tell anyone. It would be monstrous of me to bring someone, especially any of my colleagues, into the mess I found myself in. They were as dependent on Leviathan, and as subject to his frequently absent mercy, as I was, if not more so. Burdening them with the secret I carried around, in my own body and looking out one of my eyes, would be profoundly unfair, especially considering that Leviathan might be aware from the moment I told them. I couldn't inflict that on anyone, as much as I desperately needed the commiseration and, potentially, the help.

I went so far as to actually meet up with Vesper, but as soon as he was sitting across from me I knew I couldn't tell him. Doing so would just be sharing a curse, spreading the surface area of the danger out farther while doing nothing to dilute it. So I let him grumble about my invitation being "ominously unspecific" and treated the conversation like I really just wanted to catch up. When he told me about some new modifications he was considering, an upgrade to his aging accelerometer, I had to excuse myself from the table and spend a few minutes in the bathroom trying not to vomit.

With nowhere else to go, I found myself reaching back out to Leviathan. I asked him to explain the surveillance system, and he took my interest for acceptance and curiosity rather than the horror that it was. It wasn't just my vision that he had access to; as I suspected, he could tell all kinds of things about my physical state, from my temperature and heart rate to my blood sugar and cortisol levels. The same mechanism that allowed him to communicate with me via bone conduction could also let him hear what was happening very close to me, if necessary, though he admitted there were "unsatisfactory limitations" to this system. I knew that he'd replaced the GPS tracker under my skin the Draft had ungently removed, which also rested somewhere in the structure of my skull.

I'd never really been frightened of Leviathan the same way that most people were. He'd intimidated the hell out of me the first time I met him, and he certainly registered with my sympathetic nervous system as a Very Dangerous Person. But it wasn't the same physiological terror many of my colleagues experienced or his enemies reported. Susan, one of the doctors who took care of me while I was recovering in Medical, told me once that she felt something like an arachnid response when he was around, a nerve-deep revulsion. I'd never really understood or experienced it, but suddenly I was catching myself holding extremely still in a new kind of horror when he was nearby, or having to suppress a shudder instead of a smile.

It was all made so much worse by the fact that he was so fucking happy. The warmth I had missed with every fiber of my being was back and multiplied, and I desperately wanted to sink myself into it. It no longer felt like we were avoiding each other, looking for an excuse to cancel our meetings and feeling a sense of relief when one or the other did so; whenever we spent time together, it was suffused with devious joy. I would spread my notes out on his massive desk and walk him through the plans I was making, and he hovered right behind me, pleased and eager for me to continue, resting a hand on my lower back. His engagement, his attention, his weird affection was everything I had wanted back, and now I had it. When I could forget, for a moment, he'd turned my eye into a camera and could analyze my heartbeat, I was happier than I had ever been.

It was almost enough. I tried very, very hard to make it enough, as hard as I could. I pressed down my discomfort and disgust and humiliation, the way I'd reduced and compartmentalized so many things. I turned forgetting into an active practice and tried to move through the world as the same person I'd been before he'd told me what he'd done to me. It even worked, for a while. I avoided looking at myself closely in the mirror, in case my own eye reminded me about what I actively ignored. I spent more time with him, when I could, to remind myself what I had at last regained and how good it felt to be there. But the horrified revulsion I felt about being watched, about my own body betraying my confidence, was something I could never shut out completely. At these moments, I did everything I could to stay calm, still, collected, so he wouldn't notice anything was wrong.

There *were* advantages. Mixed in with the profound discomfort was a kind of invulnerability—while I might not have been safe from him, I was safe from everything else. It's impossible to be a hench without being keenly aware of your abject human fragility, how your little bones and twists of muscle are nothing to someone who can stop heavy machinery with their hands. I wasn't helpless, and between the visible scars and my reputation for ruining people's lives, I was more than capable of being intimidating when I needed to be. But I was always aware of my own comparative delicacy, how easy it would be for someone to take me off the board with a casual, glancing blow.

Some part of that exhausting, constant hypervigilance was extinguished by the knowledge Leviathan would know the moment something was truly wrong. It wouldn't be days until I could be rescued the next time; it would be as quickly as his reflexes and resources would allow. There was a deep security there I found myself falling into, and a certain register of my anxiety quickly dissipated. Suddenly, things that had seemed like huge personal risks were much easier to walk into with a sense of invulnerability.

And that wasn't nothing.

"THERE YOU ARE! So glad you could make it, really thrilled."

Mom wore a cardigan and a collared shirt, in muted blues and browns that looked like something a kindergarten teacher would wear. He had a thick but trimmed beard that emphasized a broad, toothy smile, the centerpiece of his jovial face. He was leaning in the doorway at the security checkpoint with a casual theatricality that made me feel like he was about to be the cool adult talking to me about how lame drugs are.

"We're just on the way to processing, sir," the guard on my left barked, unnecessarily gesturing toward me. I gave a little wave.

"I'll take it from here, guys."

"Sir, she hasn't—"

He clapped the guard on the shoulder. "I insist! You kids work too hard. I got this one, trust me."

The guard turned, and the senior security staffer on duty gave a small shrug that made it clear this might be against policy but it was not a winnable argument. His younger colleague nodded and abandoned the laborious check-in process.

"They're really something, eh?" the Draft CMO said, patting another of them on the armored back like a car salesman showing off a sweet deal.

"They sure are."

He grinned a little wider and stuck out a hand, broad palm out and stubby fingers splayed. "Call me Mom."

"That's not weird at all." But I took his hand, which he squeezed and gave a single, affectionate shake.

"Ha! It's because I'm the CMO; that somehow turned into Mom. You know how it goes. Come on, I'll show you around!" He tossed his head over his shoulder, gesturing into the larger office beyond the security station.

"Lead the way."

Instead of taking me through the scanner, he let me around behind the security counter, silencing the protest of the Draft security officer on duty with a single pat to her shoulder before it could be voiced. Then, he opened a door and gestured expansively toward the huge, open-plan office we'd just stepped into.

I could feel his physical excitement, Wonka about to show me his favorite room in the factory. "Here's where the magic happens!"

I wasn't quite sure about the magic, especially when taking everything in. Because there are two aesthetics that define workplaces you never leave: Rec Room and Waiting Room.

While the decor was generally a lot more sophisticated than what might be implied by Rec Room, Leviathan's compound was unquestionably the former. The entire facility was not only designed around the fact that most of the employees lived onsite at least part of the time, but assumed your workspace was where you spent all of your time. All that comfort and convenience came at a cost, of course: every easily accessible snack bar or lunch-break massage therapist exerted a quiet kind of pressure to keep you there, and focused, longer. The psychic pressure of a foosball table can't be overstated.

The aesthetic of the Draft was unquestionably Waiting Room. As much as I bristled sometimes at the way working at a supervillain's lair shrank my world, I hated this approach much more. Everything was chosen to be inoffensive: the neutral color palette, the functional furniture, the industrial upholstery being the softest surface anywhere. These places made professionalism ideal, a very specific kind of masking that required business casual and pathological pleasantness. Despite the attempt at a harsh separation between the personal and the professional, these places were no less demanding than Rec Room, and *also* often required that you essentially never leave. The building just *pretended* you didn't, and made no accommodation for the frail, fallible people moving between the gray walls.

In a kind of unconscious desperation, these spaces were inevitably restructured and repurposed by the people who worked within them. A particular conference room would be designated the nap room; there would be a second-floor crying bathroom; an unoccupied meeting room would be where people would go to pump their breast milk. The rooms might be indistinguishable from any others, the same gray furniture and chemical air freshener and chairs stacked in the corners, but they would be pressed into the service of the grim necessity of human comfort.

The marketing department had the same awful foundation as the rest of the building, with a fresher, more colorful surface layer of framed posters and a few beanbag chairs. It was bigger than I expected, with high ceilings that I supposed were to make it seem airy and expansive but instead gave the room an industrial loft/airplane hangar quality. Desks were laid out in little clumps, like cells from a beehive, with minimal dividers between them. Nearly everyone sitting at a desk had someone standing next to them sipping a coffee, or hovering over their shoulder as they frowned at something on a monitor together. In the center of the space were a few conference rooms with enormous whiteboards and made entirely of glass, so everyone could see (if not hear) the meetings taking place inside. There was a dull hum of conversation that hung over the whole place like an aggressive air conditioner.

"Isn't it something?" He was looking at me eagerly, examining my face for excitement.

"It is."

He nodded vigorously. "We've grown a lot in the last couple of years. Absorbed parts of some departments. Made a bunch of new hires. Big changes!"

"You wouldn't know it."

He tapped the side of his nose like he was telling a secret. "Not yet, but lots of great things coming down the pipe. Great things. Can I get you something? Would you like a coffee?"

Without waiting for a reply he strode down one of the aisles between the desks. I followed, trying to stay in the force field he seemed to exude.

He led me into a kitchenette. There was a coffeemaker that looked like it came from a diner in the sixties, but also a brand-new espresso machine, a huge water boiler, and other appliances that looked extremely new. A woman with an Afro and a thin, nervous-looking man were standing in front of the massive espresso machine while a shot drained into a mug. They stopped talking as soon as Mom appeared, but smiled at him while he beamed back.

"Sigmund! You try the oat milk yet?"

"Not yet, just making myself—"

"Here, I got this." Mom sidled up to the machine and the two employees made room. He grabbed a milk frother and slapped a towel over his arm like a barista. "I know you'll love it." Sigmund put up no protest as his boss took over making his coffee for him.

"And what can I get you?" It took me a moment to realize he was addressing me.

"Whatever Sigmund here is having." I nodded to the man in question, and Sigmund's smile faltered slightly.

"You got it." A burr grinder roared on.

"Are you new?" the woman asked cautiously.

"Just visiting."

"A fellow expert," Mom said, clearly not wanting me to say anything. "Here for brain exchange, that kind of thing." After a final theatrical pour, he presented Sigmund with a drink. "You'll love this, I promise."

He handed me mine with a thumbs-up, and then tossed the towel next to the sink. "Let's carry on with the magical mystery tour, come on." He was on the move, and I said an awkward goodbye before hurrying after.

"Those two are speechwriters," he was saying without looking to see if I was actually keeping up. "Brilliant kids."

"I've actually said aloud you must have a great speechwriter here."

He stopped dead in the hallway and turned to make an aggressive amount of eye contact. "You have?"

I was taken aback but got my face under control. "Absolutely, yes. To a colleague of mine."

Mom waved his hands at me, gesturing for me to turn around. "We need to tell them!" He marched off back to the kitchen and stopped in front of the two thoroughly confused speechwriters.

"Tell Sig and Viola what you told me," Mom said, arms folded over his chest, shoulders back.

The three of us—the two Draft speechwriters and I—stared at each other for a moment, bound together in the camaraderie of panic.

I recovered first and forced a smile. "Oh. I was just saying to, uh, Mom here that I've commented to colleagues that the Draft has really good speechwriters right now."

"Oh! Oh wow," Viola said, dropping eye contact. Sigmund, oat milk latte still steaming in hand, looked profoundly uncomfortable.

"It's quite noticeable," I added. Their discomfort relaxed me, allowed me to enjoy this. Next to me, Mom nodded approvingly, beaming at them.

"That's—that means a lot. Thanks so much," Sigmund said.

"What have I been telling you. Everyone can tell. You do make a difference. You're elevating us, kiddos. Elevating!" Mom turned to me then, blasting me in the face with his Care Bear Stare of positive energy. "Let's get this show back on the road, shall we?"

The speechwriters' relief was palpable as he turned and marched off, humming to himself, and I followed.

"They hear it from me all the time," Mom was saying. "How great they are. How it all matters. I know they're sick of it and, well, it's hard to believe when it comes from someone like me. But you? Someone on the outside? That matters."

"Outside feedback is important," I allowed.

"It's critical," he said. We passed another clutch of three employees, who also went silent as soon as Mom approached, and I could feel them waiting for whatever it was that was about to happen to them.

"Rhonnie, great work on that press release. Really good stuff. You're settling in great."

"Oh, thanks." Rhonnie looked like the sort of woman who played with the same D&D group she'd had since high school and kept a pet gecko. It was hard not to like her.

"Thanks for being such good mentors," he added to the two coworkers behind her, whose hopes of avoiding whatever this was were immediately dashed. They made bashful and dismissive noises.

"Do you like softball, Rhonnie? I bet you do, I can always tell." He looked to the other two. "Invite her out to one of our games sometime; she'll love it!"

Rhonnie looked like she spent exactly no time out of doors that was not mandatory, but there was no hope of getting out an excuse before Mom was on the move again, like a shark.

"Are you in an especially good mood today?" I asked. I was caught between being annoyed and fascinated by the energy surrounding him.

"Me? Nah, I'm always like this. Bit much, eh?"

"I mean—"

"It's fine, you can say it, I know I'm a lot."

"That's . . . refreshingly self-reflective."

"Here's the thing. These folks? No one's ever believed in them, not really. Draft's been all about squeezing every drop of talent out of whoever comes through here, not caring if all they leave behind's a husk."

"That scans."

"I want more than that for them."

I was turning over a few retorts in my head, selecting one like a fresh melon, when he stopped dead in the middle of the hallway.

"Oh!" He cartoonishly bopped himself in the head. "There's

someone else I really wanted you to meet." His eyes were twinkling, and he gestured conspiratorially for me to follow him.

We wound back through the maze of desks into a quieter, less populated area of the office. I recognized the hum of a server room when we passed it, one of the few rooms with opaque walls, and then we came upon a corner full of boxes of routers, and more cables that seemed plausible, indicating we were in someone's IT domain. Two people, who could have been twins they looked so similar, squinted at the blue glow of a monitor, both standing while one typed furiously, bent at the waist. The room was otherwise almost entirely dark. Mom hesitated the briefest moment before carrying on—even he was able to recognize they were frustrated and focused enough on what they were doing that he shouldn't disturb them.

We turned one more corner and there was a lone desk tucked next to a far wall, near a supply closet. The space was the same as the other little islands, with enough room for three or four people to have a workspace, but there was only one person here. He looked startlingly young at first glance, concentrating on his screen so intently his round face had become almost serene. He was touch-typing incredibly fast, and there were papers and tablets and random bits of tech scattered about him in a seemingly chaotic way that I immediately clocked as being incredibly deliberate.

Mom grinned when he saw him, and walked over to the desk proudly. Despite how bombastic Mom's entire persona was, and how much he telegraphed all his movements and intent, the man we approached was focused enough to still be badly startled when Mom dropped a hand affectionately on his shoulder.

"This," Mom said proudly, with the air of a car salesman slapping the hood of an especially impressive model, "is our auditor!"

The man's focus snapped to me instantly, with a withering laser focus that completely erased the baby-faced smoothness I'd mistaken for youth a moment before. I automatically gave something between a smile of greeting and an apologetic grimace, but the damage had already been done. He glared at me with a pure, naked loathing unlike anything I had seen directed at me in a long time.

That is going to be a problem, I thought.

I opened my mouth to say something, to dispel the tension, but I never got the chance.

"Now, I'm sorry to break up this party as soon as it's started, but I've already dragged her all over the office. But next time! We'll all have lunch!" He waved and started walking away, so I followed, unwilling to lag behind with a man who was very clearly trying to kill me with his mind.

There was an office just ahead of us, one with an actual door. Where the nameplate would have been was a gray sign with flowery gold lettering that said "Mom," the kind of decor you'd find next to a "Live Laugh Love" sign in Bed Bath & Beyond.

I squinted at the sign, trying my damnedest to tell if it was painfully earnest or unironically self-aware, and could not for the life of me settle on which it was.

Mom bustled in and started moving piles of paper around the desk, seemingly at random, and clearing off a chair for me that was currently home to several out-of-season coats. The office clearly belonged to someone who spent almost no time there. Nothing was arranged for actual use, from the stock office chair to the shelving that seemed to have no organizational system whatsoever. It was starkly unlike Leviathan's office, which was meticulously crafted to perfectly serve the needs of someone who almost never left, from the decor to the tech to the furniture. Mom seemed to be discovering the office for the first time, picking up a few memos he'd clearly never seen before. The only decoration was a single, lonely cross-stitch hung on the wall behind his desk.

"Well, gonna have to deal with that at some point," he said, dropping all the memos into a pile on a shelf with the air of someone who planned to never look at them again. "Have a seat, make yourself at home."

I arranged myself carefully into a chair, and finally sipped the oat milk latte in my hand. It was okay.

"You're a lot quieter than I expected," Mom said suddenly. His face was still open and jovial, but there was a glittering intensity in his eyes now that was very different from the breezy demeanor he'd exhibited until that moment.

"I don't know what I expected," I admitted. "But it certainly wasn't you."

He grinned. "Never is."

"Is that your thing, then? Pretend to be the 'World's Greatest Mom'"—I gestured to the coffee cup he'd placed on the desk between us—"while secretly masterminding the Draft, ruling with an iron fist, all of that."

"Not pretending, but I do lean into my natural tendencies. Who doesn't?"

"You just happen to be Saint Nick the general manager."

He gave a loud whoop of a laugh. "That's really good!"

"I guess what I want to know, then, is if you're secretly Krampus."

"I'm afraid not," he said, awkwardly settling into what was clearly an unfamiliar chair.

"So you're the one good one. The single, mythical good apple."

He grew a bit more serious. "They're all good." He gestured toward the door, encompassing the whole department.

I wrinkled my nose. "Does that mean you'd be happy with any of them in charge."

He smiled like I'd said something foolish. "No one's really 'in charge' around here," he said, using exaggerated scare quotes.

I stared at him with practiced blankness.

"I know it might look strange from outside the organization, but—"

"I would appreciate it if you would not insult my intelligence. I have been following the . . . volatile leadership situation you're in for some time."

He chuckled. "You have, huh?"

"It's my favorite TV show."

He put his hands in his pockets. "There've been some shake-ups. I'll give you that."

"And you're doing everything you can to make sure you end up in the best position."

"I want what's best for the organization."

"If you're not going to be honest with you, who can you be honest with?"

He chuckled. He seemed to be genuinely thinking for a moment. "I think I have some pretty good ideas. And, in my experience, the people around me are happier when things are going my way."

"There, that wasn't so hard."

"But it's not for me, Anna."

I managed not to flinch. I couldn't remember the last time someone had used my civilian name in my presence; hearing it now registered like a slap. I considered correcting him. But the way he said it, like a secret we were sharing, made me think saying my old name mattered to him. If it made him think he had something on me, some kind of intimacy, he could use the thing I had worn out and discarded.

I leaned a little closer. "Of course not, no."

"I mean it."

"I am sure you think that."

"I want things to be better. Really, truly better. And I think a lot of people here are . . . stuck in some pretty unhealthy ways of thinking. I want to shake it up." He paused. "I'd prefer that they'd change."

"They won't."

"I can't afford not to be an optimist."

"And I can't afford to be one."

He leaned forward. "I know what you do. That's why I wanted you to come here. To prove that you could come here, walk through the doors, meet with me, and return safely. I just wanted it to happen, and for it to be fine."

"Prove to who?"

"You." He nodded toward the ceiling. "Them. Everyone, really. I wanted to see if it was possible."

"So this is—what? You making a bet with your coworkers that I'd be civil enough not to smuggle a neurotoxin in one of my teeth?"

"Something like that."

"Taking a meeting on the wrong side of the cape isn't that unusual, even if it's off the books."

"Not with you. You don't . . ." He was clearly trying to come up with an inoffensive way to finish the sentence, and settled on, "come out very often."

I turned my head deliberately so he could see the scar winding up the side of my it and into my hairline. "I haven't had the best experiences with field trips, personally."

He visibly flinched. "I know. So I wanted you to have a different kind of experience here. It's safe to say you haven't had the best impression of the Draft."

"That's an understatement so insulting it might be hilarious. But go on."

"I know some of it, but not all."

I assumed he could have put together the big shapes; even if he wasn't privy to exactly what had happened to me, first by repulsive negligence and later by malice, he could make informed guesses.

"I'm sure it's worse than I think it is," he continued, and I realized he was gently pressing.

I didn't dignify this pressure with a response, just met and held his eye contact, hard. I wasn't about to fall prey to his bid for false intimacy, to get me to open up my trauma for him under the guise of helping him understand. Just because he hadn't been in the room didn't mean he was exonerated from responsibility. I thought about the stack of memos in the corner, the ones he would never read, and wondered how many black site torture sessions he'd obliquely signed off on with the same cheerful carelessness.

In the end, he was the one who looked down. "But I've been talking your ear off; you must have a million questions."

"Just one."

"And what's that?" He was absurdly eager, leaning forward and smiling.

"Why am I here? Really. Not the sales pitch. Why did you want to get me here so badly?"

His expression didn't change, but something behind it cracked; the warmth in his expression changed to something brittle. "I wanted you to see for yourself."

"See what."

"What we're really like. What we *can* be like."

I tilted my head to one side. "Did you think it would be harder for me to be your enemy if I went on a take-your-hench-to-work-day tour?"

He chuckled even though he obviously didn't find it funny. "I would have said it differently."

"But I'm right."

"You're not wrong."

"That doesn't seem like enough. Also, it's a bad idea."

He searched my face. Whatever he saw there changed his mind about something, or perhaps more accurately, convinced him of something he'd been considering. "Well. I also wanted to speak to you privately. Not just someone, but you, specifically."

"Oh?" If a table was about to turn, this would be it. I could almost feel the tranq dart hitting me in the neck from some concealed aperture, but fought my discomfort and stayed still. I let myself be comforted, for once, by the certainty that Leviathan was watching.

"You still have time."

"Time for what."

"Let me show you something."

Some fumbling and a brief call to tech support later, and he was sharing his laptop screen on the wall via a projector. On it was a densely nested series of spreadsheet pages. They were all labeled with a series of numbers and letters that certainly made sense to some kind of internal filing system but meant nothing to me. I wondered if he'd done that himself, or if some beleaguered security expert had insisted on changing the file and sheet names before the meeting took place.

"This is you," he said, opening up one of the pages.

I looked at the rows and columns, and after a moment the data began to make sense. I was looking at a vast, complicated debt calculator—not dissimilar from the ones I used to calculate the cost of superheroes to the world—but with very different equations behind the numbers. There were lines for the PR budget funds that had been diverted to cover the blows I'd dealt to heroes' public images. There were the physical injuries, the recovery times, the replacements—and deaths. There was the psychological damage, lines for therapy and reassignments and rehab. It was deeply flattering, in a weird and terrible way, to see all of my work tracked so closely—even if it was incomplete. I felt a swell of pride at the size of my debt, displayed in red.

"Can you send me a copy of that? I'd love it for my next performance review."

He gave me a smile much sadder than anything I thought he was capable of. "It's a pretty big number, eh."

I nodded, and crossed my arms proudly. "Really something."

"The thing is," he said, selecting some columns and running an equation, "you still have time."

A second number appeared, bigger than the first by a decent amount.

"You already said that." I furrowed my brow. "Still have time for what?"

"To change course." He gestured toward the screen, looking at it with a weird longing. "You can do so much good. So much good, in fact, that, well, there's still a chance."

"A chance."

"To wipe it clean. Pay off your debt." We both stared at the spreadsheet for a moment, undoubtedly running a very different series of calculations in our respective heads.

"Is *that* why you want me here? To work it off?"

He put his hands in his pockets. "Doesn't have to be with me. Could be for a different civilian organization, an NGO, heck even a research hospital. As long as we were on the same side, I'm not picky about the specifics."

I sneered and ran some more numbers, playing the calculations in my head. The "paying off" he was suggesting, undoing the damage of the last few years, was a much slower process than doing the damage. It would take me a couple of decades to get back in the black, according to his reckoning. Even if I wanted to—which I adamantly did not—it sounded utterly miserable.

"So you're hoping for a redemption arc. I renounce my villainous ways, devote myself to the side of truth and justice once more, and after sufficient penance I work my way out from under this arbitrary number you've assigned me? You'll forgive me if it doesn't sound very appealing."

"I didn't expect that it would."

I sighed in exasperation. "Then why suggest it to me at all?"

"Not a lot of folks as talented as you have the option," he said, undoing the last selections and hiding my secret capacity for goodness behind the curtain of rows and columns once more. "Or who have worked as hard as you. Most blow through that capacity pretty quickly, and then, well—there's nothing to do but stop them. Take them down, whatever it takes."

"And you, in an act of generosity, are trying to get to me before that fateful day comes."

"You're running out of time." He said it fiercely, so much so that I was startled.

When I spoke again, the sarcasm was gone. "How much do I have left?"

"Depends on you. Honestly, it might already be too late, I only have projections. A few good weeks, or a few bad ones, might be all it takes. Or maybe you have years! Who knows. There're too many variables. But I can tell you this. That window is closing. And one day, even with the most forgiving predictive models, it will be gone for good."

"And you wanted to tell me."

"Before it was too late."

"Why?"

"It's how I sleep at night." He shut down the laptop, and the spreadsheet disappeared from the wall behind him. I felt a pang and almost asked him to put it back, so I could stare at it a little longer, but resisted the urge.

"Is that all it takes? You make the odd intervention and then you can merrily continue violating our civil rights as much as you please, snoozing like a baby?"

"I do what is necessary to protect people. *Whatever* is necessary. And if someone is doing more damage than good–"

"No," I said, holding up my hand to stop him, "I am familiar with your ethics."

"No, you're not." It was the most hostile thing he'd said so far, and I smiled.

He rubbed his forehead. "Sorry, that was rude. I just–this means a lot to me. Look, Anna. I know it sounds to you like I am talking a load of crap."

He paused a second, leaving an opening for me to slip a verbal razor in if I wanted to, but I let it pass.

"But the thing is: I mean every word. You could do so much good. So much more. And I want that for you, if there's any chance at all."

"What if what I'm doing *is* the good the world needs."

"It isn't." His voice was all dead certainty.

"Is this a pitch you make often?"

"Not often, but sometimes."

"Has anyone ever taken you up on it."

A tiny, deeply sad smile trembled on his face. "No. Not a one." He sat up straighter and snapped his fingers, shaking the sadness off. "But I try. I gotta keep trying. One day, someone just might listen. And if even one like you does, well, then it's worth the other disappointments."

He put his hands on his desk with a thump, making me jump. He stared at me intensely, something that might have been threatening in another person but in him just spoke of a vast, desperate kind of hope. "I hope it's you. I'm sure you think I say that to everyone I've tried this speech on, but I mean it. Anna, I really hope it's you."

"SHE WAS HERE again."

Keller wasn't exactly glaring at me. But he was making it very clear that if I knew something and hadn't tipped him off, he would be supremely pissed.

"You mean—who, Quan—Decoherence?"

My answer was clumsy enough that he believed my genuine confusion. "You've met, I think. Great tattoos. Bad taste in men."

"She was *here*?"

He tossed a folder down in front of me.

We'd just finished a debrief of what had happened in my absence. The handoff before I left had been uneventful: Red Sprite didn't say a single word, and nodded to me without making eye contact when we traded places with each other, me passing into Draft custody and her into ours. Keller attended personally, to make sure I knew how mad he still was about the whole thing.

The reverse exchange had been similarly calm, though Red Sprite was in a very different mood. She was furious, and even made the effort to give me an obsidian-grade cut-eye when we were traded back. Her anger was soon explained in the debrief as several members of Research and I&I described her reaction to the "tour" we'd prepared for her. I knew I had left her in capable hands, but I was deeply proud of the experience they'd built for her.

In addition to her unnecessarily large security escort and Vesper's enthusiastic tour guide services, she'd been required to wear a comically huge, neon-pink physical guest pass. While moving through the offices, they also made her carry a small, portable light that rotated and flashed, and played a musical alarm when she entered a new room.

"We told her that it was so people could end their conversations when she was around. And put away documents." Jav could barely get the words out, he was giggling so hard.

"It's actually good operational security," Artem said humorlessly.

"That makes it *funnier*."

She spent the day being chattered at by a bunch of nerds, being stared at every time she entered a room, and made as visible as humanly possible. I figured I'd definitely earned that single glare, and looked forward to the turmoil the experience could be causing between her and her teammates and handlers at this very moment.

After the debrief proper, Keller had asked me to stay back a few minutes—and immediately dropped the bomb that Decoherence had phased into the building again.

Knowing what I would find, I opened the folder to a printed still from a security cam. It showed the end of a hallway where a pair of restrooms were located, and Red Sprite was ducking into one of them. Through the open door, blurry and backlit, I could make out the unmistakable silhouette of Decoherence, waiting for her.

"Thought she'd drop in to talk to your guest."

"Fuck me." I stared at the photo. "How long was she here."

"Three minutes, maybe four. But long enough to talk to your hostage."

I stared at the security photo in front of me, at the deliberate set of Decoherence's shoulders, her wide stance. I tried to imagine what she was preparing to say, what few sentences she was hoping to squeeze out while she had Red Sprite cornered, before an alarm was raised.

"This can't happen again," Keller said, stating the obvious.

"I know, but the fuck am I supposed to do about it?"

"If you *don't* do something about it," Keller said, poking the table, "I will."

He was right, which was additionally frustrating. "You are absolutely within your rights to treat her as a hostile intruder," I said, calling his bluff. I knew that engaging in any kind of confrontation with her would be a colossal pain in the ass for him.

"Which I have only not done yet," he said, jaw set, "because of our former collaboration. That goodwill is spent now."

He'd also not attempted to drop a Faraday cage and phase suppressor on her for my sake, which he would never say out loud, but which I appreciated nonetheless.

"I'll try to talk to her."

"I'll have to report this."

"I wouldn't dream of asking you not to."

He shot me an unimpressed look but let what he likely assumed was a joke go. *If he's watching*, I thought, *I hoped Leviathan liked that*, and then recoiled away from my own internal monologue.

"I *will* talk to her," I said again.

"Try and keep it from being my problem."

I WONDERED IF she'd even kept the phone I gave her, and if it was charged, and if she ever checked it. While it took a few minutes, soon enough the words "is typing" appeared in the secure chat client I had installed.

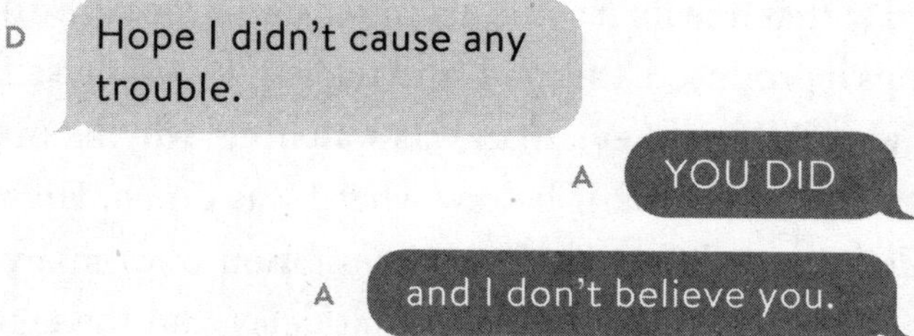

She didn't reply. I started to feel irritated.

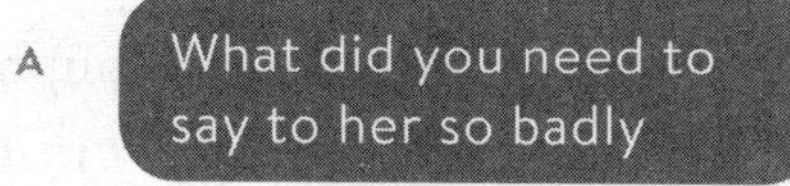

I watched "is typing" appear again and recede several times, as Decoherence tried to explain what the fuck she'd been up to in my absence.

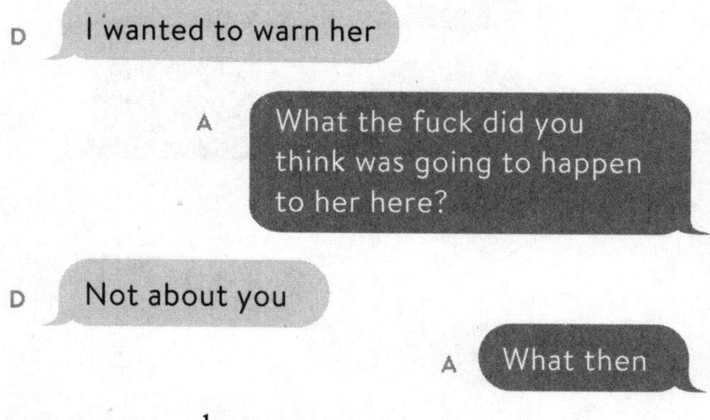

There was a very long pause.

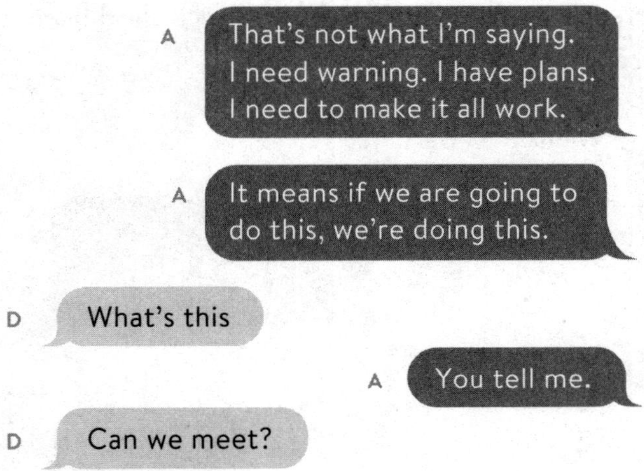

I stared at that line for a while, trying to parse the painful, crackling feelings it produced. I second- and triple-guessed myself before I replied, wondering if Leviathan was watching, why he might be, and what he would think if he saw what I was doing. His surveillance added a new layer of anxious hesitation onto many of my decisions, and I hated the weight of that delay and the emotional sludge that came with it. I felt a spark of anger when I caught myself hesitating again.

If he has a problem with this, I thought, *he can tell me his goddamn self.* It felt good to think angry things in the privacy of my own head, which was still inviolate.

WE MET IN a park in the nearby City. She was sitting on a bench beside the central fountain, and I felt a prickle of vicarious embarrassment at how easy she was to spot.

"Athleisure and sunglasses. Is this the incognito look you all learn in superhero school." The only thing she was missing was a baseball hat with no logo on it.

She glared at me behind the reflective lenses. "You're one to talk."

I adjusted my own tinted lenses studiously. "I actually have something to hide."

She sneered. "I was talking about the cane sword."

"It is a *necessary mobility device.*"

"Also a sword."

"This isn't the Middle Ages . . . It's a Taser."

"Oh, forgive me, that's definitely better."

I sat down on the other side of the bench, performatively fuming. "I assume you wanted to meet for more reasons than just to irritate me."

The playfulness that had put a dimple in her cheek faded. She leaned forward, resting her forearms on her knees and rubbing her hands together.

"I wanted to talk about the Future."

"I assume with a capital *F*, not about us one day renting an apartment together."

"Correct."

"What about it. Them."

"They're—" She paused and recalibrated, looking for the words. "You're going after them, right."

I thought about lying to her, or saying something sufficiently ominous and noncommittal about sharing my plans too early, but it all seemed so cliché.

"They are the primary nexus of many active plans."

"Jesus Christ, stop talking like a villain."

"Think about what you just said."

"I get it's your *job,* but you don't have to be so Renaissance Festival about it."

"When did you get so boring."

"When did you get so—" She couldn't even pick a word and just waved her hand at me in disgust.

"I haven't been able to get out much these days. Work. You know how it is."

We both sat in a comfortable, companionable hostility. I was never able to hold just how much I liked talking to her in my head for very long, like I was incapable of remembering just how much fun it was to banter with her until it was actually happening again.

I set us up another volley of conversation, like a tennis serve. "So. I assume you wanted to meet for more than my charming company."

She answered with a sigh—but a welcoming sigh, one that invited further questioning.

"How did you know where she'd be?"

She seemed to consider not telling me, and decided against it. "A couple folks still talk to me. Not often. But now and again. Probably burned that contact with this one, though."

I sincerely hoped I'd one day be able to find out who that was. "Was it worth it?"

"I hope so."

"And how was your chat."

"Brief." She thought for a moment. "Illuminating. But brief."

"Well, not much time for more than a few words at the sink."

"She's having a hard time," Decoherence said, accusingly.

"I've barely even done anything, you know."

"Yeah. I do know. It's not you. It's them."

She sat back and stared out across the mostly deserted park.

"Accelerator wasn't their first choice," she said, out of nowhere.

"What?" This was not something that I had expected at all.

"For Supercollider's sidekick. He wasn't even their third."

I started to catch up. "I heard he was going through them like used tissues for a while," I said cautiously. Accelerator had become Supercollider's sidekick shortly after I started henching, when I barely knew more about the major players than the average media-savvy civilian. I tried to reach back into the Before Times and dredge up what I knew: he had a string of short-lived (literally) sidekicks over a few years: there were the twins, Higgs and Boson, whose DNA was unraveled by Double Helix; I couldn't remember what happened to Eigenstate, but had the vague sense it had something to do with being dissolved; and Manifold was by all accounts still in a fugue state.

She nodded. "They—the Draft. They planned for not all of them to make it."

"I'm sure there's a whole line of succession."

"Yes, there was. But they burned through them all."

"They ran out of understudies? Then what?"

"They . . . kept looking. At the level he's—he was at, survivability is incredibly low for someone who's not—"

"Like you."

She swallowed. "When none of the candidates they had in mind made it, they cast the net wider. They started looking over rejected profiles."

"When your third-string quarterback breaks a leg, you sometimes go to the practice squad."

"Or the triple As."

I'd always thought Accelerator was too young, dangerously young, when he was elevated to Supercollider's side. Practically no one had heard of the kid and suddenly he was thwarting world-ending incidents. When he kept living, the discourse concluded that Supercollider must have "seen something" in him, rather than just run through options until someone displayed any longevity at all.

I moved more fully into the room. "Alright. I'm following. There's no secret the Draft has a track record of using their own as cannon fodder."

"It's not a new track record. Or," she noted, "a retired one. It's very obvious they're doing it again."

"I don't get the whole 'sacrificial' vibe from the Future, though. It seems like a real bid for a new anchor team."

"Just because it's 'real' doesn't mean they aren't expendable."

"No one knows that better than you," I said, trying to be gentle.

She flinched, but nodded.

"So what do you want to do?" I asked.

She hung an arm over the back of the bench, casual to the outside observer, but I could feel the tension winding ever more tightly in her. "I don't know. But something. I need to ... get to them. I felt like if I could just talk to them, even one of them, and get them to listen to me ..."

"You want to warn them."

She nodded.

"So Red Sprite was amenable–"

Decoherence snorted. "She said what I am sure she was told to say, that if she ever saw me again, blah blah blah. Told me I was a traitor, that my words meant nothing."

"Did she mean any of it?"

"She–I don't know. But she did hear me out. Let me finish."

"That's not much."

"But it's something. And maybe, if I can talk to the rest of them–"

"Do you think *they'll* listen to you?"

"I have to try."

We sat for a long moment, neither of us saying anything. A squirrel trotted up to us and stood on its back legs hopefully; when neither of us tossed a peanut, it ambled away, looking for a new mark. A few feet away, a pair of pigeons chased each other in small circles over the husk of a bagel.

"You realize," I said slowly, "that I'm not trying to help them."

I wondered for a moment if she hadn't realized, and I had instead said something incredibly stupid. But after a moment she sighed and knit her fingers together.

"I figured."

"If you want to protect them, I'm not the best person to be talking to."

"You might be more help than you think."

That was not a pleasant thought, and I wanted to know if she was right. "What are you on about?"

She licked her lips. "I don't expect I'll be able to get you to leave them alone."

"You're smart."

"But you might just be showing them how . . . how fucking stupid all of this is. How little the Draft cares about them."

"That would be ideal."

"While you're doing . . . what you do. If there's ever an opening, like this one. Can you . . . let me know."

I pretended to consider the request. "No more surprise visits from you. And no interference."

She swallowed. "I can't promise not to get involved. Not if one of them is in real danger."

"If that happens, then we treat you like an adversary."

"That's fair."

"But not until then."

She nodded. "Not until then."

And I nodded back.

IT WASN'T LONG after my bewildering first meeting with Mom that things started to go wrong. Nothing catastrophic, but definitely inconvenient. A trusted courier late to meet one of our suppliers, damaging an until that point pristine relationship. We'd finally made a new hire in I&I, a very talented infosec specialist, who had a sudden crisis of conscience and quit, forcing us to do a round of extremely time-consuming and absolutely unavoidable security updates and vulnerability patching. And most personally devastating, the company we contracted to do our catering suffered a sudden plague of supply chain issues, and several of my favorite snacks were no longer available in the break room.

"This," I said to Vesper, pawing through a basket of protein bars I already knew was barren of any good flavors, "is a personal attack."

"Tell me about it," he muttered. "Did you know they only delivered decaf to the hangar last week? I had to straight up steal a bag of real beans from Enforcement."

"No, I mean it literally—I think this is a personal attack." I wandered over to the automated espresso machine and started hunting through the dwindling supply of pods for something I could make us a pair of drinks with.

"I do love a good conspiracy theory."

"Once again, I am actually serious."

"Oh?" He still thought we were playing a game, or at least there was a strong possibility we were, and leaned against the counter, arms amusedly crossed.

I located a couple of pods and started operating the machine. "I regret to inform you that I recognize the handiwork of someone trying, very deliberately, to ruin someone else's life in tiny increments."

"You're saying your bad luck lately—"

"Isn't luck. I know bad luck. And I know when levers are being pulled."

His smile faded a little. "You think someone over there is fucking with you?"

I could still feel the abject hatred of the single glance I'd received from the Other Auditor, the only direct communication we'd exchanged. "I think, at the very least, someone is aiming as close to me as they can, still from afar, calibrating what works, what lands."

"Finding their range."

"Exactly." The espresso machine growled to life and I'd had to raise my voice just slightly to be heard over it.

"This is definitely a stupid question, but any idea why someone might have it out for you, someone with this particular . . . mode of operation? That might be too long a list to—"

"I know exactly who it is." I started steaming the milk, my ancient barista muscle memory taking over as I moved the metal carafe under the steam wand.

"That was fast."

"I'm positive." My latte art left a bit to be desired, the ripples of milk looking like rather lopsided leaves in the tops of our mugs, but it would do. I handed him a mug while he studied my face, his own grown serious.

"So what are you going to do?"

I took a sip, thinking. "Nothing, yet. Nothing that he could interpret as 'doing something about it.' I'm going to watch and track, see if I can intercept any of the inconveniences before they can go off, and see exactly how much of a nuisance he wants to make himself."

"If you wanted to go a more direct route, I am sure Ludmilla would be happy to oblige."

"I'm sure she would but it's a . . . bit of a delicate political situation I am in at the moment."

He made a thoughtful sound. "Right, there is some sort of charm offensive afoot."

"Sort of. Also, I'm not especially interested in letting this person think I have spared a single thought for them."

"Don't want to let them know it's been effective."

"I also don't want to give them the attention."

"Ah, like a tantrum."

"In a best-case scenario, they just burn themselves out in a few weeks, get bored of attempting to give me a new ulcer, and I can continue on my merry way."

Vesper's head buzzed; he was summoned. He tapped one temple in acknowledgment, then gave his coffee one last sip. "Well, just remember you don't have to do this by yourself. You have a team, all of whom will happily obliterate anyone you'd like."

Something moved in my chest, a warmth, and I smiled at him

as he nodded to me once and then quickly left in the direction of the hangar.

As sweet and thoughtful as the words were, something about them stuck between my ribs. I decided not to analyze the feeling too closely, and turned my thoughts to strategy.

I just have to starve him out, I thought. *It's a siege he's going to lose.*

"I HAVE RECEIVED the most extraordinary communication."

Leviathan said it lightly, almost like he was amused, and I looked up from my notes.

"From who?"

"They somehow believe they can hide that from me. I'll know soon." He was watching me carefully. "It is about you."

I realized he was gauging my reaction. "Oh?"

I started to stand, but he motioned me to stay where I was and came around his desk instead, bringing a tablet screen with him. It was an email with the title "THE AUDITOR." The body was composed of a single picture, and the phrase, "I have more."

It was a photo of Decoherence and me, clearly taken from a great distance with a telephoto lens, sitting on a park bench during our recent meeting. She was looking over her shoulder, with an air that might be taken for anxiety about being watched. I was looking up at her with a freshly cracked half smile on my face, with obvious affection.

There was nothing incriminating in the photograph, except for perhaps it capturing more vulnerability in my expression than I would have preferred, but the cloak-and-dagger presentation and ominous message framed it as something completely damning. Leviathan had known about the meeting I took with her, though I started to second-guess myself, wondering if I had left anything out of my reports on the conversation. My heart started to pound in my chest for reasons I couldn't entirely explain.

"What . . . is the point of this," I managed, landing somewhere between amusement and irritation (I hoped).

"They think they have caught you in a compromising position."

I decided to pretend that he was joking and shot him a look. "Yes, clearly I have been caught in flagrante."

He made a little buzzing sound. "Can you explain why I would care about this."

I knew then I was in danger, but in the Schrödinger sense: I would either find what to say and it would be completely fine, or the situation was about to devolve into a complete disaster. I was not helped by the fact that my body was reacting as though things had already gone off the rails, and I was starting to sweat in misplaced panic. I wasn't sure how to explain away the physiological phenomenon I was experiencing in a way that didn't make me seem guilty of an offense that had yet to be identified.

"I think," I said, choosing my words with extreme care, "that they are assuming you would be angry to learn I had been in Decoherence's company."

He frowned at the photograph. "Hmm." He tilted the picture to the right, as though a slightly different angle would reveal more about how the sender assumed he would react. "Implying you compromised Keller's security protocols."

I had the sudden, extremely inconvenient urge to laugh. "No, not at all. Keller supplied an escort." I could see the barest prickle of irritation start to rise up in him as the reasoning eluded him, so I took a risk and pressed harder. "I think the implication is that you would be upset to know I was in her company at all."

He leaned his head back like I had said something absurd. "The Draft used her and spit her out like so many others. Why should her proximity bother me now."

"You two have a . . . significant history. Our conversation might be construed as collusion of some sort. The sender clearly thinks you would not have approved of our meeting, and might find any association with her upsetting." I tried to keep as far away as possible from reminding him she was the one who had physically mutilated Supercollider.

"Do they think I was *upset* by your 'associating' with Supercollider? Decoherence is not a problem. She is a variable." He said it with a lightness that indicated he had no intention of examining his actual feelings on the matter, which was definitely for the best.

"I think there is the implication that you would consider my connection to her some kind of a betrayal."

His irritation seemed to rise another half step, so I decided to be even more blunt.

"They think you'll be jealous."

He stared at me a moment, then squinted down at the photo like he was missing something.

"That you had a conversation."

"A significant conversation, yes."

"Is the implication that you are neglecting your work or betraying my confidence?"

"They want you to think I'm . . . cheating on you."

He made a disgusted sound and tossed the photo on the table. "What a contemptuous thing to care about."

A wave of relief nearly knocked me over. Then, in the pull of the emotional riptide that followed, I felt a kind of immature disappointment. Despite the fact that it could have been incredibly bad news for me and anyone in the blast radius, part of me wanted him to be jealous. On some level, I expected that kind of maniacal possessiveness to manifest itself, and to see him dismiss it so completely, care so little, hurt me.

I also recognized this immediately as extremely disordered thinking, developed over a lifetime of unhealthy relationships and toxic cultural expectations. It came from an irrational place that equated the depth of one's jealousy with how much they cared, and

I knew it was one more thing I would have to undo if I was ever going to be able to accurately recognize what his feelings actually looked like, behind all the constructs he built to hide their unusual shapes.

"Are you going to respond?" I said, to regain my footing.

"Should I?"

I recognized this as a test in the nick of time. "It's up to you, of course, but I think we could use this. See what else they have."

I sense a little nearly invisible tension leaving him, and I knew I'd passed. "Shall I play the role of the betrayed lover?"

He was being playful again, perhaps genuinely so, and I matched him. "You don't like what you see, but it could mean nothing. Let them show you what more they have. Then get more unhinged."

His mandibles rippled. "I am curious what they think to gain by putting a wedge between us. What the next step of this master plan is."

"I'm sure they think we're less dangerous apart," I said, and immediately regretted it; I thought he would take offense at the idea there would any circumstances that would make him less dangerous.

He made a small sound that would have been a snort from anyone else. "That may be the only thing they're right about." He took my hand and almost idly nibbled at my fingers.

ARTEM HAD BECOME my favorite digital surveillance specialist. I'd made it a point to learn his name and seek him out directly after he traced Mom's call for me. He wasn't an especially pleasant person to be around, but I wasn't looking for a buddy; I just enjoyed his analysis a lot more than his personality. I liked the devious, lateral way that he thought, and his instincts were unusually good even for a profession where vibes were at least as important as technical skill. So when he told me there was someone from inside the Draft who wanted to talk to us, I knew it was going to be good, and I immediately asked to be the one to meet them.

"Where did you *find* her," I asked, ogling her profile.

Artem shrugged. "She wanted to be found."

"Fine, keep your dark sorceries to yourself."

He openly watched my face for my reaction as I read her files. Her name was Evelyn. She'd been an administrator at the Draft for nearly twenty years, starting as an intern, working with individual heroes and their handlers, and even a stint in the Workshop's registrar's office–a life full of supporting superheroism; a career built entirely on supporting the good guys. In particular, she'd worked mostly with younger heroes and heroes-to-be, whether it was guiding the fledglings as they made the huge leap from trainees to official named and costumed superheroes, or working with them those crucial first few years on the job. She'd left the Draft to work with a couple of heroes in particular–a year and a half with Salamander and a little less for someone called Chanterelle whom I had never heard of–before returning to her former post. She had all of the hallmarks of someone who had the kinds of jobs where an unknowing buffoon would think she was "just a secretary" when in actuality she ran whatever department she resided in.

"I immediately thought of you," Artem said, watching me read.

"Flirt."

I internally flinched. *Leviathan might not like that.* I shoved the thought away, trying to not be so paranoid, but the anxiety sat in my stomach anyway.

If she was willing to talk to anyone, let alone us, the disillusionment that brought her here would have to be catastrophic. And the Draft would never forgive her for it.

"I want to talk to her immediately."

He nodded. "I knew you would."

"She could be a plant, but it's worth the risk."

"I don't think so."

"Why not?"

He leaned closer. "Do you know who Chanterelle is?"

I furrowed my brow. "I don't." Something was telling me I *should* know.

"I didn't think so. I had to look her up and it was really damn hard to find anything."

I blinked. That was the coarsest language I had ever heard him use.

"I hesitate to technically call her a hero, though she almost got there. She had a name and a costume and all of the branding, but on the very edge of her career being launched, something happened. She had a mental health crisis, the specifics of which she has never divulged, and whatever it was made them decide to just . . . stop supporting her entirely. Demote her from hero class to the civilian power cap and release her back into the wild."

"So what, is she now a deranged botanist with a chip on her shoulder?"

"Have you ever met Cordyceps?"

I gasped. "No way."

"Yup."

"Holy shit. Yeah, at a party once, and I think she spoke at a conference I was at, but I didn't see her talk." I chewed on this new information. "So Evelyn worked for an almost-hero who became a villain . . ."

"I would imagine," Artem said, twirling a pen around his fingers in a startling display of dexterity, "that someone in her position would have considered that a great failure, until very recently."

"Get her in here as soon as you can," I said.

Artem shook his head. "She'll only talk on neutral ground."

Which meant she was competent, which I respected. "Fine, where."

"One of your favorite places: the gym."

"That is a *hostile* location."

"You don't have to *do* anything."

"It's still rude."

"Just meet her in the dressing room."

For some reason, that made me even more anxious.

I ARRIVED IN gym clothes, an outfit I'd had to buy specifically for the mission. I had a healthy supply of yoga pants, but they were all of questionable structural integrity and opacity, and definitely more suitable for working on spreadsheets. After wandering around the main concourse and buying a smoothie—the only thing the gym was good for—I made my way to the changing room, where I knew she'd be. When I entered the humid room, I found Evelyn already there. She was camera ready, undoing the first pearl button on her cardigan. She faltered when she saw me. Ignoring her, I sat on the same bench she'd chosen. I unzipped my bag and started rummaging around the clothes I'd brought; as I was changing back into office attire, she was putting on her workout gear.

Evelyn was very tall, willowy, and made entirely of angles, like some kind of forest creature. I could see instantly how an idiot would underestimate her and pay dearly for the mistake. She had a kind of intimidation force field she radiated that I immediately took a liking to; the feeling was not mutual. When I had sat on the other end of the bench, her entire body had tensed in obvious disgust.

"I'm listening," I said, not making eye contact.

She took off her blouse, which was cream-colored with tiny eyelet flowers sewn into the sleeves. I waited, slowly rolling the poly-spandex blend down over my legs. She took great care in swapping her matronly 18 Hour bra for a sports bra.

I tried to be patient. This was going to be hard for her; even being near me was hard for her, just as every step made her already irreversible decisions so much more real. I slowed down my own actions, and took the opportunity to start taping my leg.

Eventually I heard, "I no longer . . . believe that I was doing any good, working in my former positions. The opposite, in fact. The more I came to face that, the more it seemed like the only real answer wasn't just to leave, but to run in the opposite direction as fast and far as I could."

"That's a direction I'm familiar with."

She pressed her lips together. "I don't have much data I can give you. Documentation, I mean."

"I didn't expect you would." I secured the last piece of tape and pulled up the long sock that covered almost all of it. "I'm here to listen."

She looked at me warily, but then decided she should go on anyway. "I only have my experience, my memory, and what I saw."

"I'm interested."

"Then I can tell you something with certainty, without the data to back it up, but based entirely on my experience: the Draft are failing, catastrophically."

"I'll be honest: it makes me very happy to hear it."

She shot a look at me before turning away, her eyes huge and angry and liquid. "They are ruining most of those kids. Absolutely ruining them. And I have an awful feeling they are sometimes even doing it on purpose."

I adjusted my tights. "Do you want to stop them?"

She did not answer me but pressed forward with her own line of thinking. "I don't know what the answer is. I tried to fix it from the inside, but after nineteen years I gained almost no ground, and I couldn't face it being twenty."

She stood quite still for a moment. Her underwear was remarkably old-fashioned, with high-waisted control-top panties, contrasting sharply with the high-tech fabric of the sports bra; she looked like a kind of mermaid. "So I left," she said. "And I thought it they won't fix it, maybe you could."

"I need to warn you that 'fix it' in this context probably means 'burning it to the ground.'"

She hardened. "I'm here, aren't I?" She traded her underwear for a simple cotton bikini cut.

"You are."

"And I'm not stupid. I wouldn't have come to you and your boss, of all people, if I didn't think that was probably how this was going to go."

"That seems pointed." I couldn't smile, but I imagine I zipped up my skirt with a certain amount of triumph.

Her face, composed of so many sharp lines and angles, hardened; it was like watching ice crystals spread across still water. "Well. There was Accelerator."

"That must have been a difficult loss."

"It was. He had a great deal of promise."

"Everyone has a great deal of promise." I felt like I was watching myself in the third person as I said that; it came out cool and gentle, much more comfortable than I felt. I wriggled out of a moisture-wicking T-shirt that hadn't had the opportunity to gather sweat.

Her hands twisted themselves together. "I brought him up only to say that I would not come to you if I didn't know what you were . . . capable of." She pulled on a pair of deep blue capri workout pants.

"Why did you come to me, though? There are so many others, and a few of them even know what they're doing. Why here, and why us specifically?"

"Because you're the only one who might actually win," she said.

"I appreciate that. Coming from you. It means a lot."

She tensed briefly, then relaxed again. "You aren't deliberately antagonizing me, are you." It was a statement.

"I'm not. But I like being an antagonist. So for someone who has been on the side of the protagonists for so long, it might feel that way."

"Alright." She thought for a moment, and I let her. "I promise I don't intend this as an insult," she said eventually.

"Noted, and you have me interested." I finished buttoning my shirt, and put on a jacket.

"Well. Most of the young people I met, or knew, who went through the Program—most of them don't, you know. Become heroes."

"That tracks."

"I felt sorry for a lot of them, and outraged for a few that I knew should have made it. But the only time I felt I had truly failed . . . well, was when they became one of you."

"Villains, you mean."

"Yes."

"That makes sense to me." I remembered being in an interrogation room in some Draft basement. I could feel again the ache of the freezing concrete against my feet, the shackles on my ankles as Supercollider paced around the room in front of me. *We make our own villains*, he'd said then, referring to me, using the old phrase of his mentor to justify what they had already done to me, and were about to do to me. In the nightmarish moment it felt cartoonishly awful, my fate decided by a superheroic mishap; but there was something about the way this disillusioned administrator in my office was speaking now that made me think this might be the real version of what he had been trying to say.

"I thought you might take it personally," she said, and I snapped back to the present. It took my brain a moment to dematerialize, and put together why she might imagine that reaction. She picked up the last of her clothes and put them into a locker, and patted herself down as a final check.

"Not at all. It can look like failure, from the outside. When I was a little girl I didn't dream about being permanently injured by a superhero and becoming bent on revenge."

That seemed to startle her; I could see her imagining that place-holder little girl, dishwater blond and needing a trip to the ortho-dontist. I saw something in her soften against her will, picturing the weird little kid I must have been.

"Do you regret it?" she asked, and suddenly her voice was kind.

The voice someone might use to talk to an animal, to tell it they intended no harm. Or a child.

"No. Not even a little."

"Did you always feel that way?" These questions weren't conversational; she was about to blow up her life in some very specific ways, even if she was never found out, and was looking for any kind of data to cling to, even if it came from someone like me.

"I've had moments. But I was a very different person then."

"If she—that former you—if she knew the outcome, would she make the same decisions?

Unbidden, I thought about Supercollider, folding in on himself. I saw the way his flesh rippled and contorted, the way he would have been torn apart like wet tissues if his own infernal invulnerability had not worked so hard against him. I thought about Quantum Entanglement next to me, sweating with the exertion, talking unintelligibly to herself as she twisted him beyond recognition into a knot of flesh and mucus, begging until he could only burble and leak. I thought about showing myself, sad and angry and in a white haze of painkillers, an image of that future. I felt myself recoil.

"No," I said. "She wouldn't have had the stomach for it."

Evelyn took my answer and held it carefully. I wondered if I had given too much, and hoped it had been just enough. It had hurt to do, but not unbearably, and would be worth it if I managed to keep a hook in her. I let her sit with my answer for a long moment, gave it all ample time to settle in and find purchase in the softer parts of her, before gently steering the conversation back to where I needed to go.

"So, no. I don't find it insulting at all to consider that a failure. What was done to us, whether through neglect or stupidity or malice, *those* were failures. Any person or process that breaks so many people in so many ways is built of failures. But *we* are not the failures. The Draft is. We took that failure and spun it into gold. Became what we are. That is the part I will never be ashamed of."

I watched the pool of sympathy in her eyes recede as I spoke, but it did not dry up entirely. She disagreed with me but not in any way she could fully articulate or wish to fight on, and so I considered it a victory.

I tried to sound kind too. "I would like to offer you the chance to set things right, in whatever way you can."

If she could have melted my face off with her eyes she would have done it.

I KNEW I was being followed almost as soon as I left the gym. It was a moderate walk to my extraction point and I took my time after letting my security detail know I was on my way. I waited a few blocks before I dropped the first hint I knew someone was there. A quarter of a turn of my head while not breaking stride, and then the tiniest, barely perceptible increase in speed. The footsteps behind me picked up, covering too much ground in excitement. But then they fell back, quieted, and maintained their conservative distance. I maintained my pace as well, feigning restrained nervousness while I considered what to do.

What I should have done—what I'd been instructed to do and done multiple rounds of training on—was to press the alert button on my cane and let the consequences fall where they may. However, I knew that meant our enforcement team would collect me immediately and do whatever they deemed necessary to "eliminate the threat." I felt reasonably confident the person behind me wouldn't survive those necessities.

If I thought they were a hero, I'd have pressed the button the second I clocked them matching my turns, then sat back and watched the fireworks once the concealed tactical van rolled up. But my feeling was that if they *were* a hero, they would have swooped in, caped and suited, bellowing like an idiot. Even if it was someone operating in an official Draft capacity, I'd already be tranquilized in the back of a van. I assessed the threat behind me as a single, nervous person, and that made me think he was just a mugger or a hench on a bad assignment. I wanted to see where this was going before I signed a death warrant.

I changed course and ducked into a parking garage; my stalker veered after me into the echoing, concrete space that smelled of exhaust and old piss. As soon as we were out of sight of the road, I heard their footsteps echo as they ran toward me. I gripped my cane strategically so I could activate the alarm and taser at once, and turned around.

He stopped suddenly, and we looked at each other. He was wearing a worn black trench coat and a trilby pulled low over his eyes. He was tall and broad, which was undercut a bit by the round slope of his shoulders. I couldn't see much of his face, but it was so wormy pale and round it was impossible not to recognize him as the man who had glared at me with pure, raw hatred during my visit to the Draft offices.

"Rather chilly for a light evening confrontation, don't you think."

"The Auditor. At last." He acted like I hadn't spoken, like he had been rehearsing this conversation over and over again.

"What do you mean 'at last'? I saw you a few weeks ago."

He hissed, like an angry opossum protecting a discarded sandwich.

"I'm afraid I still only know you as, well, some kind of bizarro auditor," I said, specifically to piss him off further. "Naughtitor? Does that work?"

"My name," he hissed, "is Black Pill."

"Oh. Really? That's . . . kind of cringe."

He took a half step toward me, the anger building in his body like a physical force. "You have no idea who you're dealing with."

"Hey, what matters is that *you* like it. What can I do for you? Because you're right—I have no idea who you are. I assume there's a reason we're talking in this delightful setting"—I gestured to the concrete and rebar all around us, echoing with a distant car alarm—"instead of you reaching out to my assistant to book a meeting."

"This isn't about work. This is about *you*."

"Alright." I wasn't sure I even made such a distinction anymore, but so be it.

He smirked. "I'm sure you've noticed some . . . things going awry."

I raised my eyebrows in pretend surprise. "Like what?"

His slight smile vanished. "Don't fuck with me."

"Why would I fuck with you? I saw you once for twelve seconds."

"I thought this was your specialty."

"Are we still talking about the 'awry' or . . . ?"

"Making things go *wrong*. I thought you're supposed to be intelligent enough to recognize it when it's happening to you." He straightened a little to make room for the extra superiority. "I seem to have overestimated you."

I made a show of furrowing my brow and thinking hard. "I mean. Things do go wrong all the time, but we pivot, and adapt, and often things turn out better for it." I shrugged. "Can you give me a hint."

He learned closer, wearied by my stupidity but unwilling to let me miss any of his genius. "How did he like the *pictures*."

"Oh. That was you?"

"I wish I could have seen your face." For all the things I wasn't loving about this interaction, I particularly did not enjoy the lascivious way he said it.

Keeping my distaste to myself, I said, "I'm afraid it would have been quite boring. My boss knows about my collaborators, obviously."

He tried very hard to mask his disappointment. "Did he know how . . . close you are."

"A couple of feet? Yeah, he saw the pictures."

"No! How . . . *connected* you two are."

"You may be mistaken about the nature of our relationship."

"I saw how you looked at each other."

"My boss had no problem with the content of my facial expressions."

He gave a toothy, self-satisfied smile. "He asked me to send everything I had."

"And did you?"

He rubbed his hands together gleefully. "I did."

"Well, they must not have contained much to interest him, as we haven't talked about it again."

His smile faltered. He clearly had nothing else yet, and shifted gears to hide it.

"You think the deal with Larvomancer fell through on its own?"

"Yeah, of course it did—that guy is a flake."

"What about the disillusionment of the Necrosis Collective? You called it 'so promising.'"

"Yeah, it was cool—everyone loves laundering money through art—but as soon as the gallery they worked with got busted for selling some antiquities, the bottom fell out."

"Who do you think *sent them* the idea?" He was gritting his teeth now.

"Were they *your* antiquities dealer? Ugh. Figures. Well, good job, I guess, but there's lots of other ways to get the work done."

He flung his arms into the air. "Don't you fucking lie to me, I know it was a setback!" His face was turning dangerously red.

"My life is a steady string of setbacks. I mean, we do similar work—you get it."

He looked utterly disgusted by the comparison. He made a point of looking me up and down, lip curled like he was looking at something vile. "We are *nothing* alike."

"That's not what your boss thinks."

"What he thinks doesn't *matter*," he said in a tone that indicated it did, indeed, matter very much.

"'Adjacent' work? Is that better?"

"No one else is on my level. *No one* can do what I do."

"You must not work in a very collaborative environment."

"I don't need pathetic 'group projects' to get my work done."

It took a lot to not sigh after everything he said. It was clear that he thought he was winning this altercation. I found that curious. He stood a little straighter and lifted the brim of his hat. There would have been some little-boy sweetness to his face if he wasn't so sullen, and at that moment he was staring at me with hostile disappointment. Whatever he was searching for in my face, he couldn't find it.

"I don't understand," he said in a low growl, but there was something petulant about it. His arms were stiff and an odd tension seemed to have crept into his wrists.

"What's that?"

His eyes rolled over me critically. "You're nothing special."

I cocked my head to one side; this was a different kind of game. I shifted tactics. "You're right, I'm not."

"You're just . . ." He gestured toward me with the sweep of one thick hand, heavy with disgust.

"Yeah, not much."

"So why the fuck does anyone care about *you*?"

I thought for a minute, genuinely kneading the idea around. The anxious, self-deprecating part of me wanted to say something like *what makes you so certain that they do?* The egotistical part of me wanted to wax poetic about my accomplishments, say something like *it's not what I am, it's what I do.* That was closer, but still not the right answer. I had to dig under all the fear and self-loathing I carried around with me, discarding each piece like trash before I finally laid my mind on something useful.

"Well?" he asked, impatiently.

"You'll have to ask them," I said. "Not to be dismissive, of course. But I can't tell you what they're thinking, or why they care."

He was grinding his teeth unconsciously—I could practically

smell the enamel dust. "Even people who hate you give a shit. They *know* who you are."

"I might argue that people who hate me *especially* give a shit." I tried to parse his expression. "You don't have many enemies, do you?"

"All I have are enemies." He said it with a superior world weariness that I saw through immediately.

"Do you?"

"Yeah, I fucking do." He tried to tower over me.

"Do they *know* they're your enemies?"

His face contorted. "What a stupid question." Except it clearly wasn't and had cut him deeply.

Now that the knife was in, I decided to twist it a bit. "Hate's a very active emotion. Hard to sustain. I'd wager most people dislike you, but they don't hate you. You're mistaking contempt–or indifference–for hate."

"What the fuck would you know about it?"

I took a step closer to him. "I got *very* good at hating someone. You think about them constantly, especially when you don't want to. You obsess over them. They keep you up at night." I looked him over, sadly.

"So?"

"So, I don't think anyone thinks about you much at all."

I could almost hear the words making contact, and I imagined the same resonant *thunk* that an arrow makes when it sinks into an archery target. He trembled for a moment before exploding into a shower of expletives, like a piñata full of misogynistic slurs.

"You're fucking–you're full of shit–you stupid bi–"

"Look, I appreciate what you were trying to do and all, but–"

"No!" He pointed a finger at me violently, like he was leveling a weapon. "This has only begun."

"Uh, okay." This seemed to be an important moment for him,

so I waited, but he didn't seem to know what happened next. "I . . . wish you luck?"

Before he could answer, the unmistakable rumble of an engine; a large vehicle was navigating down the asphalt slope into the parking garage.

"I think my ride's here," I said, but he was already walking away, too fast, heading toward the stairwell and elevators. He pushed the button frantically when the Enforcement tactical vehicle came into view, and just barely got in before the first boot hit the ground.

IN A PERFECT world, I would never have thought about Black Pill again. I knew the stronger the response, the happier he would be about it, and a deeply stubborn part of me refused to give him the satisfaction. I would have loved to make forgetting about him an active practice, happily winning every minute of the day by shutting him out entirely. But something he said made that impossible: he had interfered with my work too directly, and knew too much about precisely what I had been plotting for comfort. Whether that was good research on his part or something more sinister, it had to be looked into. So, unhappily, I filled out the requisite paperwork, filed my incident report, submitted notes on all of the projects he'd claimed responsibility for interfering with, and advised everyone involved to record any further activity but come to me directly before moving forward with anything drastic. I informed Leviathan, I contacted Artem in digital security to set up an audit for me, and—with great reluctance—I went to HR.

The human resources department was different at Leviathan's organization than it was at most other places, even for most other supervillains. "HR representative" was a remarkably chill-sounding title for some of the politest yet most horrifyingly pragmatic human beings on the planet. They were not there to help you overcome petty squabbles between your colleagues; in fact, a moderate amount of conflict was considered actively healthy, and frankly, each of us was expected to be capable of settling disputes when they arose personally and not putting up with anything beyond an expected amount of bullshit. They'd even conducted occasional seminars on how to "do conflict more productively" rather than avoiding it altogether. They were also not there as a kind of ass-covering mechanism for Leviathan or any of his high-ranking lieutenants (which, though I was still not entirely settled into the idea, included me). We were also considered directly responsible for everyone whom we hired, both for their safety and their conduct; if anyone behaved abominably, or was treated poorly, we were expected to take whatever action was necessary to deal with the situation, as the limits of our powers dictated.

Where the limits of our powers ended—well, that was where HR came in. They effectively sidestepped the hierarchy of Leviathan's organization entirely, answering directly to him. This meant they were able to step in at any point they believed someone in power was not exercising that power appropriately. Sometimes that meant simply having a difficult conversation; sometimes that meant much more extreme action. They served as a kind of internal enforcement, investigating anything that might be construed as treason.

It wasn't a perfect system, but I had to admit it was pretty comforting knowing that in the unlikely event someone got hired who somehow managed to hide the fact they were a violent homophobe or a double agent, in addition to whatever fate befell them, whoever hired them would also have a very difficult conversation waiting for them.

I'd never had any kind of direct encounter with one of HR before, just a few benign exchanges before or after a workshop that reinforced they were both quite pleasant folks and absolutely not to be fucked with under any circumstances.

My meeting was with Emeril, a soft-spoken woman who looked much younger than she actually was. She had perfect gel nails and an easy smile. I knew she'd once ordered an IT mis-hire to be walked out of the building by Enforcement through his own department so all his former colleagues could witness that humiliation. Then, she sent a dossier to the Temp Agency and every hench recruiter in her considerable Rolodex, detailing (with screenshots, time stamps, and extensive documentation) the precise reason for his termination. I had decided some time ago that I both admired her and hoped I would never have to talk to her for any reason.

She smiled, welcoming but otherwise unreadable, as I awkwardly arranged myself on the opposite side of her desk.

"Can I start off by reassuring you that you don't have any reason to be anxious," Emeril said, wordlessly pushing a beautiful pink glass candy jar across the desk toward me.

I gratefully took off the lid, too loud, and pulled out a tiny bag of fruit snacks.

"I will be the judge of that," I said, trying to keep the bravado up.

"We can check back in at the end and see how you feel."

I decided I wanted to get this over with as quickly as possible. "I'm not sure if you've had a chance to go over all of the paperwork, but—"

"I have."

"Ah. Great. So I don't have to—"

"Why don't you just tell me what—or who—you think the problem is."

"What—I'm sorry?"

"Gut feeling. Who is talking about you."

I pictured the faces of several of my colleagues in my head, thinking of the last times we had interacted, if anything about their behavior had seemed off. I thought about Vesper, whom I trusted to lead a superhero around the building in my absence; I thought about Jav and Darla, whom I worked with every day; I thought about Keller, who had never steered me wrong even when we violently disagreed on something. I pushed the idea of any of them betraying me away; I just couldn't see it.

"There's no one."

She looked at me intently. "Are you sure?"

"It doesn't feel right to say any of their names."

She opened a notebook and scribbled a few lines down, underlining something she had written sharply. "Would it have to be someone who works here?"

"It would have to be someone who knew about my specific projects, so yes."

"Now, I have to ask: Could you have talked to anyone outside of work about this?"

"I don't have a death wish."

"I know admitting to violating an NDA has consequences, and you might not be comfortable, but–"

"No. It is actually impossible."

She raised one eyebrow slightly.

"The only people I've spoken to outside of the organization in recent memory are enemies, or temporary allies, and only about whatever pertained to my relationships with them. I did not expose any vulnerability, or talk about any of the projects that have been disrupted. I am sure of it."

She nodded and wrote something else.

"So the information must have come from a colleague."

"Yes."

"Do your colleagues like you?" Her smile continued to be practiced, curated, making it absolutely impossible to tell if she was being funny or robotic.

"That's a difficult question."

"It shouldn't be."

I thought hard for a minute, trying not to let the impulse to self-deprecate skew the data. "I think some like me and some tolerate me. But I don't think I have any enemies here."

She gave a tiny sigh. "Alright. We are going to do this the long way."

I could feel my eyes widen. "What's that mean—"

"We're going to need a list of everyone who had the required knowledge of the projects in question, and anyone who had access to your devices directly."

"What will happen to them?"

"At first, just a conversation."

I imagined Molly getting an invitation to a meeting with HR and the confused panic they would feel. "With everyone? Is that necessary?"

"Without leads, yes."

"I would prefer we not have to do this."

"Unfortunately, that is impossible."

"This feels like I am creating a lot of stress for a lot of people with little evidence, and—"

"There's no way to put this politely, but: this is not a request."

I didn't know what to say to that.

Emeril regarded me for a moment, head ever so slightly tilted, and I watched her make a decision.

"I am going to tell you something I ordinarily wouldn't."

"What's that."

"Leviathan considered taking on this matter personally. But he asked me to do it instead."

Something cold writhed in my chest. "I can't imagine he would have time for that."

"He specifically said he would make time. However, he was concerned that, considering your unique relationship, he might take action too quickly or impulsively. He thought I would be a more impartial judge."

I let the implications of the phrasing "unique relationship" sink in for a moment.

She raised an eyebrow. "So you are aware, he reported the change in your dynamic immediately, to ensure that we had it on record, to ensure your workplace equity and safety."

"He told you—"

"That you're fucking, yes."

I wished very hard for the floor to open up and swallow me whole. "That is—"

"Very appropriate of him," she said cheerfully.

I tried to shift my brain back into the previous gear, anything to move past this horrifying bump in the conversation.

"So for, shall we say, conflict of interest reasons, he wanted me to work with you."

That odd soft feeling came over me again, melting some of my anxiety. There was something about that care, and admitting he might not be fully rational when it came to my protection, that got to me.

She continued. "He didn't want to . . . dismiss someone out of turn."

"A fine euphemism," I said, and she gave me another bespoke smile.

"I'm sure I'll be a much more reasonable alternative," she said. "I'll begin conducting interviews and researching any potential weak points. I'll also be in touch with the team investigating the possibility of an external data leak. And if you think of anything else, or anyone else, in the meantime, please let me know.

"Without delay."

A wintry chill crept into her voice. I heard myself agree, while I knew with a grim certainty that anyone I admitted to suspecting would immediately have a terrible time.

WHILE I COULD not forget about Black Pill entirely, I pushed him into the background of my thoughts with an ease I know he would have hated. He continued to try to get to me, of course, but our security teams shielded me from most of it, unless they thought something was especially funny. Frankly, there were far more important members of the Draft I was focused on. Mom looked more and more every day like he was going to win the race to lead the Draft. His efforts were starting to bear fruit, as the Future were becoming more popular, and the acting CDO was more assailed and overwhelmed every day. Between losing her therapist and several incidents where her prescriptions were accidentally not renewed, Ms. Gentileschi was having a bad time. Our efforts to attack her psychological well-being had been wildly effective, and she had made it clear she wanted to hand the title off rather than hold on to it. Considering her close working relationship with Mom, and how badly Chisholm was holding up himself (his third wife was in the process of leaving him), Mom's candidacy seemed more inevitable all the time.

Meanwhile, Mom's personal threat surface remained irritatingly small. All he seemed to do was work, a quality I begrudgingly respected him for, and so the primary way to get to him was attacking his efforts rather than him personally. It was a stark contrast to what we'd had to do with the rest of his C-suite competition, but it meant that I could focus my effort even more on the work I truly loved: making superheroes miserable.

For this, Evelyn wound up being a gold mine, as her disillusionment overruled her obvious contempt and distaste for me and mine, and she continued to talk to us, just a few innocuous minutes at a time from the opposite end of a bench in that boutique gym locker room. I didn't go every time, leaving some of the delicate conversations to one of our social engineering experts, but sometimes I wanted to ask her a specific question or gain some clarity. I also started using the sauna here and there, and sometimes would do a few idle laps around the pool; it reminded me exactly how little I left Leviathan's compound now, how small my physical world was becoming.

Between our own research and Evelyn's opinions and memory, I started to compose maps of our young heroes' internal landscapes. The members of the Future did not have the smooth, strong narrative arcs the Draft wanted us to believe characterized all of their great assets. Rather, they were messy and wandering and sometimes devastatingly sad; and the vast majority of that tragedy rested squarely on the Draft's shoulders. They had molded the entire lives of all the superpowered young people who fell into their clutches, and almost all of what the heroes suffered was a direct result of Draft action or inaction, one way or the other. In studying the Draft's sins, we gained an ever-clearer image of how to undo the people they had created.

So as our view of their psychological topography grew sharper, it was time to start drawing battle lines.

MOLLY AND I stood at the front of the room together, a pair of monitors thrumming behind us. The large conference room was packed with as many of my remaining colleagues as could make it. In addition to the usual suspects from the research team, there were our favorite data scientists, several folks from I&I (including Menachem, who was hovering at the back of the room availing himself of muffins and coffee), and even Keller himself with a pair of strategists from Enforcement. Usually I played my cards much closer to my chest, especially before I had all of the pieces in place, but what I wanted now was to get our people curious, and even more than that, I wanted them excited. The more creative minds I had in adjacent departments using their spare moments and brainpower and terrible daydreams thinking up awful fates for our enemies, the better the outcome would ultimately be.

Molly and I made eye contact with each other and I subtly raised an eyebrow; Molly nodded in agreement. In near unison, we started our respective slide decks, our dueling cover pages obnoxiously springing to life. The titles of our presentations were the same: "Dueling Dossiers," each of us with a pixel art banjo GIF strumming itself below the text. Our subtitles were different, though; Molly's read "Origin Stories," while mine said, somewhat more ominously, "Death Throes."

"Dearly beloved," I began, and I could hear an audible groan that set off a small ripple of snickers. "We are gathered here today so that Molly and I can share with you just a few details about the unfortunate fucks about to meet their fates at our hands."

"Each of these poor souls should represent one of the best and brightest that the Draft have to offer," Molly said. "Their hope for the Future."

Silence.

"Get it?" I added.

Keller groaned, scratching a few angular words onto a comically tiny notepad.

"They got it," I told Molly.

They continued. "This little show-and-tell is to make you all acquainted with them. There is no detail too small, no coincidence too seemingly inconsequential that we can't find a way to exploit it, and we want to give everyone here, and their department at large, every opportunity to do your best."

"They mean 'do your worst,'" I said.

Keller was talking to himself, unintelligible but clearly aggravated, while he wrote down something else.

"Why do you hate my jokes, Keller?"

He raised his eyebrows and looked up at me. "Your jokes are fine. This situation I hate."

"You love strategic meetings."

"I *hate* fighting teenage heroes."

"The youngest of them is twenty-two."

He waved his hand. "Same things. Unformed cortex. And the hormones!" He shuddered. "I'd rather fish my ex's wedding ring out of a garbage disposal."

I waved my hand dismissively. "You fight emotionally volatile heroes all the time."

"And I'm telling you young ones are the fucking worst."

This was getting interesting. "Really?"

"None of them know what they can do, they're barely in control of what they do know, and the odds of one of them having a meltdown and discovering they have some kind of *Naruto* mega attack is too damn high."

"How the fuck do you know about *Naruto*?"

"One of them sees blood for the first time and turns into a nuke? Pain in the ass."

"I'm not forgetting about the anime—we *will* talk about that later—but I'll bite: It's that they're unpredictable?"

"Exactly. And you know how much I hate not having contingencies in place."

"Do you think it also makes them more vulnerable?"

"It absolutely does; you get a good shot in or surprise them and they might just crumble." He shrugged. "But they might not. And that's the problem."

I added that data to the spiderweb of plans in my head, testing which equations might need rebalancing. "Noted. Thank you. This was incredibly helpful."

Molly cleared their throat. Keller and I both nodded, and they began. Their first slide was a photograph of a handsome young woman with a strong jaw and high cheekbones, looking away and past the camera. The same hero who had accompanied Doc to Supercollider's funeral. She looked at once athletic and melancholy, as though her broad shoulders had been custom-made to carry more than their share of the world's weight.

"This is Thundersnow. The de facto leader of the Future."

"That is really what they are calling themselves?" said one of the Enforcement strategists in near-disbelief, a tall and lanky woman with short, vibrant coral hair. Her companion was silent beside her, a barrel-chested man with his head shaved so close there wasn't even a shadow of his hair left. He was already studiously taking notes.

"Unfortunately," Molly said. "Until the Draft's latest supergroup was unveiled, and her previous dreams dashed, she was going to be known as Polyphony."

Molly advanced to a slide of Thundersnow in action, her fists at her sides and her mouth wide as she screamed. There was some visual distortion around her face, a kind of rippling halo, as the sound she produced warped the air near her.

"She has super-hearing over great distances, and is also extremely good at zeroing in on specific sounds over interference; under other circumstances, she would have been an excellent spy. But unfortunately for her, she's also capable of producing various chromatic frequencies that have extremely unpleasant effects on the human body."

"I get the 'Thunder' part, but why the 'snow,'" the strategist pressed.

"She's Canadian," I said, quoting her directly, as though her stock answer made any sense.

I noticed the strategist whispered something to her companion, who nodded and continued writing things down.

Molly caught my eye. I took my cue and shared my first slide: a picture of Thundersnow embracing her former girlfriend, the two sharing a twilight kiss against an orange and purple sky and the ragged black outlines of pine trees. They'd been camping at the time; this was a personal photo her partner had shared on social media and neglected to take down.

"She was a late bloomer," I said. "She and her girlfriend started sneaking out at night in homemade spandex suits as teenagers, kids playing without any real sense of the consequences. When they were eventually caught, she was 'discovered' by the Draft, one of those rare, fairy-tale-like later-in-life scenarios where someone who seemed barely remarkable as a preteen was actually something extraordinary. She was offered the world, and she took it."

"That offer was only good for one, however. Her girlfriend's name was Solvent, and she was nothing special, as far as powers go. A small-city kind of superhero at best. She and Thundersnow might have grown old together had the latter been ordinary, or even just not quite as extraordinary as she was. But instead Thundersnow was something different, and she left Solvent behind.

"To be fair, it doesn't seem like Solvent especially wanted to go, even if she was invited. She wanted to protect her city, not the world."

Something I didn't say, because I didn't want to engender too much sympathy in anyone, was that Solvent seemed . . . kind of alright. She was the sort who went to bat for the villains she helped capture, weirdly. She requested shorter sentences, spoke at their parole hearings, and helped them with rehabilitation programs. While it all felt supremely distasteful, even slimy to me, upholding and working within a profoundly broken system while still trying to be good along with Doing Good—she genuinely seemed to mean it. She was more than one reformed villain's AA sponsor, and I couldn't find many people who would say something unfavorable about her.

Instead, I said, "Like a lot of small-scale heroes operating without Draft support, Solvent's career was ultimately cut short. A villain she put away eventually got out and held a grudge, and fucked her up pretty badly. She lived, and made a decent recovery, but she decided to retire, permanently, from any kind of heroic activities."

I now showed a much more contemporary photo of the two of them, a candid shot someone captured while they sat in the front window of a diner, talking over brisket sandwiches. "When she was hurt, Thundersnow took a leave to visit her as she recovered. The relationship between them had been strained in the past couple of years; they haven't been a couple in a long time. But it's clear Thundersnow still cares for her a great deal, and is possibly the only person still in Solvent's life who would understand some of what she's gone through."

Molly stepped in to add, "When she returned to the Draft, she expected to be returned to the team she trained with and kick off her career; instead she was catapulted directly to the big leagues, tossed into the deepest end of a leadership role."

"She knows she's good," I said. "And to be clear: She is. She's capable, confident, and not easily rattled. She's also incredibly green, nearly untested, and with much less formal training than anyone else she's working with. It'll be easier to make her team distrust her than for her to lose faith in herself; meanwhile, she's much more likely to be taking her responsibilities so seriously, be so worried about anyone getting hurt on her watch, that cracks should start to appear without very much pressure.

"Let's ruin her life."

I looked over to Molly, who queued up the next section of their presentation. "Who's our next contestant?"

"Riot Shield," they said. An amused murmur moved through the room; the slide displayed a pair of pictures side by side. On the right was a recent portrait, clearly taken during an official photo session. Riot Shield stood with his feet wide apart, hands resting authoritatively on a clear acrylic shield that was, for the purposes of the press kit, there only to visually represent his powers. On the left was an old family photo of the hero when he must have been about twelve, wearing a cheap police officer's costume, the kind that came with little plastic handcuffs and a billy club. He was in the exact same pose, his little face fixed in a serious scowl, with a handmade cardboard and balsa-wood shield positioned in front of him. It was clear he'd been playing at being the same hero since he was a little boy.

"If you recognize this upstanding fellow, it's probably from his relatively brief time with his original team, Siegeworks."

A couple of the I&I representatives muttered to each other;

they'd collaborated with us more than once on disrupting Siege-works' activities, and definitely would have had some *feelings* about Riot Shield's team of origin.

"He's the nicest fascist of the bunch, if it matters," I said.

"It doesn't," someone deadpanned from the back of the room, knocking a real laugh out of me.

Molly waited a moment for my composure to return and then continued. "Riot Shield was the primary support member of Siege-works and really leaned into the role of protector, both with the manifestations of his powers and his personality."

The next slide showed the hero holding his fists out in front of him, feet planted as he leaned forward, brow furrowed in concentration. Behind him, two of his horrible little goblin teammates, Baton and Taser, crouched down for protection. Baton was visibly smirking. In front of the three of them, an invisible air cushion, created and maintained by Riot Shield, held off a group of Meat who were attempting to attack them with improvised weapons and some kind of plasma ray.

"Siegeworks, for the unfamiliar, are the fucking worst," I said. There were vague noises of angry agreement around me. "They're like cops squared."

"His powers were almost benign compared to those of his team-mates," Molly continued. "They are entirely defensive, as he is able to create what he has described as 'insulation' between them and harm. They are most effective against kinetic attacks, though they do repel most forces, and seem to harden in response to the speed and ferocity of the violence directed at them. Riot Shield has to be in contact with these defensive barriers in order to maintain them; he can't project them away from his own reach, though he can expand them to fully cover at least half a dozen people. His situational awareness, speed, and general reflexes also reach to superpowered levels, enabling him to keep up with teammates and react to danger."

I shared an image of all five members of Siegeworks standing together, receiving a commendation from the City's ex-chief of police. He was shaking Water Cannon's hand while she smiled broadly, her teeth an eerie blue-white, while Taser and Baton sniveled behind her. Rubber Bullet stood right next to her, his hand resting too low on her back, almost cupping her ass, but not quite. The "nonlethal combat" expert's limbs all seemed slightly too long for his body, and his face had the cheerful, dead emptiness of a sociopath's. Riot Shield stood apart from all of them, looking down at his feet awkwardly, his big hands clasped behind his back.

"He never really fit in with his playmates," I said with mock sympathy. "Poor little guy thought he really was going to get to be a hero, instead of breaking up protests and pushing the limits of police brutality. While the rest of these monsters naturally found each other, the Draft assigned Riot Shield to Siegeworks as the sole defensive member in this ultraviolent little family. They also, I suspect, chose him because they hoped his generally more calm demeanor might mitigate their worst impulses. They were entirely wrong, but the thought seems to have been there.

"If I had feelings, which I don't, it'd be easy to feel bad for him. They treated him like shit, made him the butt of every joke, blamed him when something went wrong, and never gave him credit for anything he did right. Getting removed from Siegeworks is, unquestionably, the best thing that's ever happened for him."

I pulled up a post from the r/S3ig3works forum, made under a pseudonym but almost certainly written by Rubber Bullet himself. The title was "Fuck F*ggot Shield" and the post itself was a solid wall-of-text rant about how the "least deserving member of the Siege gets elevated of fucking course" and how the Draft were a bunch of "cowards" for passing over "an entire team of alphas" for a "beta cuck" like him.

"That's not very inclusive of them," someone toward the back of the room said, earning a smirk from me.

"His promotion has ... not gone over well with his former compatriots," I said. "He's going to be desperate to fit in with his new team, personally more than professionally. His self-esteem is low, despite his admirable performance over the past few years and the massive boon of being promoted to the Future. He's also primed to be unappreciated, whether that's looked down on for being a support or mistreated for being who he is. He'll want their affection but expect cruelty; with a little luck he'll practically sabotage all of these relationships for us."

Molly advanced to a slide of a short, compact woman wearing a costume that resembled a wetsuit with reinforced legs and boots, and a set of extremely heavy, insulated goggles. Most of her hair was tucked into the hood of her suit, but the few springy strands that managed to escape around her face were visibly frozen.

"You may have had the pleasure of meeting our next young hero in person," they said, pausing for a moment to polish their glasses. "She was a guest here briefly."

"We were co-hostages," I clarified.

"While she might not look like much at first glance, there's more to her than you might think. Red Sprite can fly."

One of the data science team put up a hand, and Molly pointed and stood up on their tiptoes to acknowledge them. "By what definition?"

"All of them. She's a True Flier, best in a generation. Maybe longer."

A few muttered conversations broke out, which we allowed to happen briefly before continuing. Lots of superheroes claimed flight as one of their powers; Supercollider certainly had. But it was actually Quantum Entanglement who kept him in the air and gave him the illusion of flight, when in truth all he could do was launch himself into the air and survive the fall. True flight required a whole suite of powers that rarely manifested together in the same person:

some kind of take-off mechanism; the ability to propel themselves in the air when they were up there; enough cold resistance that they could survive the extreme temperature changes traveling at speed that high up; the ability to breathe in a much thinner atmosphere; a superhuman metabolism to manage the spectacular amount of energy for all these powers to function at the same time; and enough resistance to damage that they had the capacity to survive the landing (or a minor in-air collision).

Of course, you didn't necessarily need every single one of these powers; a superhero could have most of them and be considered capable of genuine flight. But missing one meant a fatal flaw, a weakness that would almost certainly result in an untimely death. Sonic Boom died of exhaustion mid-flight, after pushing himself too far during the Twilight Crisis; Pterodactyl's primary parachute was sabotaged by Regicide, and then his backup chute failed. While it was incredibly dangerous, flight had been one of the most highly regarded powers since ancient history. Now and again, there was even debate about whether a supe with a complete suite of powers was even possible. The last known case was The Vulture, who died in the early thirties, and some skeptics questioned whether his abilities had been exaggerated or oversold.

"She's the real deal, I'm afraid," I said to back Molly up. "She's comfortable at cruising altitude and at most is in danger of injuring an ankle if she comes to a . . . sudden stop. Closest thing to a weakness we can see is her eyes drying out or freezing, which doesn't seem to hurt her, by the way, but does take her vision away, hence the headgear."

"She's been flying under the radar," Molly said, ignoring the room's collective groan at the horrible pun, "in a group called Atmosphere."

"It's so bad," I said.

Molly nodded seriously. "Quite terrible, yes. Her former team members, in contrast to her, can do things like manipulate humidity or create minor electrical events. As with a lot of genuine miracles, it seems most people who encountered her were convinced her flight was more of a parlor trick—because usually it is."

I clicked through to a picture of Red Sprite with her new team; it was a screenshot I'd lifted from one of the videos of their public introduction. While the rest of the group had their best Heroic Faces on, ranging from reassuring stoicism to benevolent weariness, her face was oddly expressionless. She looked blank, and honestly a little lost.

"The Draft haven't downplayed her abilities in the past, but they didn't capitalize on them. Despite the absolute gold mine of a narrative she represented, the full force of the Draft's marketing was never truly behind her. I suspect they weren't quite sure what they were going to do with her yet, so they kept her on the training squad, safe and out of the line of both fire and public attention, until they needed her. And they need her now."

The next picture I displayed might not have been recognizable as Red Sprite outside of the context of this presentation. She was walking to a car with a plastic shopping bag in her hand, wearing a nondescript hoodie, jeans, and sunglasses. She was also wearing a wig; it was a decent one, mid-length and light brown, gathered into a ponytail. She'd clearly chosen it to be unremarkable and to completely cover her much more distinctive curly hair.

"A few of you have heard me say this once before, but it bears repeating: Red Sprite genuinely seems to hate this," I said. "Being famous, being recognizable, even to some extent being a hero. She's an introvert. She doesn't really like talking or being in front of the camera; she hates being recognized in public. Even on a small team the attention she garnered seemed torturous for her; since joining the Future she hasn't been seen a single time, and is probably holed up in their headquarters somewhere.

"There's a great irony here. Someone with perhaps the most sought-after and genuinely rare constellation of powers in the world is emotionally and psychologically completely unsuited for everything that comes along with this life. There are infinite possibilities for finding openings and exploits, and I am positive that as we eventually see her working in the field and interacting with her team, those vulnerabilities will become much more apparent."

"This last one is a double feature," Molly said, advancing to the final section of their slide deck. "The twins: Cartilage and Marrow."

They showed a photo of all four members of Ossuary, the team that the pair used to belong to. Tibia loomed over the group, all seven feet of her, the preternatural lankiness of her limbs and large hands and feet making her look like an oversize teenager. Ball & Socket, by contrast, was built like a weight lifter, all thick waist and neck. The other two were set slightly apart from the others; while Ball & Socket's and Tibia's powers were primarily focused on their own bodies (various forms of superstrength in the case of the former, the ability to stretch and reconfigure their body shape for the latter, and both of them possessing varying degrees of unusual flexibility), theirs were also focused outward, and from the body language of their teammates, something about them made the others more than a little uncomfortable.

Cartilage and Marrow were identical twins, difficult to tell apart even by people who knew them well. In the past, they'd gone out of their way to differentiate themselves with different-colored uniforms and personal aesthetics; in this photo, Cartilage had dyed his hair so platinum blond it was almost white, while Marrow had gone for a vibrant, arterial red. "Cartilage can, rather uncannily, *soften* himself, so his bones become more of a suggestion than an anatomical boundary. He's also frustratingly resistant to many types of damage, conveniently for him. Very unfortunately, he can also drastically tighten or loosen the connective tissue in someone else's body, which is even more horrifically painful than it sounds.

"Marrow's powers allow him to either drastically speed up or slow down metabolic and other body processes, both his own and someone else's. This could allow them to place someone in a temporary coma, or kick-start his own healing, or do many more extremely unpleasant things to someone he's fighting."

Molly advanced to a new slide, showing the twins in their brand-new Futurist costumes. In this photo, they had the same haircut and their natural brown hair color, and their uniforms bore identical symbols. "Looks like they've been instructed to strip out any individuality from their appearances now that they are among the Chosen Ones. This could just be marketing, but also may have some strategic benefit, if part of their gimmick is going to be how hard they are to tell apart."

I queued up a slide that showed a photo of the twins when they were much younger. It was a low-quality photo, a scan of a physical image that had been lightly water damaged at some point. They were nine at the time, small for their age and wearing T-shirts that were much too big for them. Marrow (I think it was Marrow) was holding a ratty stuffed duck, desperately clutching it by the neck, which was so threadbare and had lost so much stuffing that it looked uncomfortably like the toy's spine had shattered. The twins' facial expressions were eerily empty.

"They entered foster care shortly before they were three; after a brief and extremely unpleasant stay with a family member, they were placed with the family who raised them until they were twelve, and who were most of the way through the process of adopting them when Marrow manifested his powers for the first time."

I skipped to a photo of Cartilage, now alone with his foster parents on what must have been the first day of high school. "The Draft stepped in and the adoption process was refused; Marrow immediately became a ward of the state and was removed from the family's custody. He was raised at the Workshop for the next several years. Usually the Draft doesn't get to just . . . take a kid and not have to worry about the families, but with the bio parents' rights recently terminated and the adoption not yet formalized, they saw their opening and went for it."

"They were separated?" someone asked.

"Yes. At first it looked like Cartilage was going to be left behind, but it turns out he was just a little late. His powers manifested just before his fifteenth birthday, barely young enough for the Draft to swoop in a second time, but swoop they did. The brothers were reunited, trained and educated, and came out of the system as rare sibling heroes. I would expect both of them to have severe abandonment issues, obviously, and that a great deal of their early trauma was not treated by the Draft so much as it was . . . weaponized. They love doing that."

"Not to mention separation anxiety," the same talkative data scientist said.

"And maybe even some sibling rivalry, as I'm sure Marrow was—maybe *is*—more advanced than Cartilage for all the extra years of training and 'care.'"

I brought up a final slide of all of the Futurists, standing together. Thundersnow stood front and center, her arms crossed and her feet planted confidently. She was not quite smiling, but one corner of her mouth turned up optimistically as she gazed out over the imaginary horizon. To her left, Cartilage and Marrow stood very slightly back to back, their knees bent and hands raised in delicate, wizard-like configurations, expressions of concentration on their mirror faces. Riot Shield stood to her immediate right, his fists pointed forward as though he was holding an invisible battering ram, his face pulled into a defiant scowl. Red Sprite, goggles on and a short capelet flipping around her shoulders (I assumed the work of a wind machine), was airborne just behind them.

"Their leader is good but largely untested, and most likely terrified by the prospect of her team getting into real danger. Their most potent defensive member is a victim of bullying with severe self-esteem issues, and doesn't know he's nearly as strong as he actually is. We have a True Flier here, who absolutely hates being the center of attention despite being a living fucking unicorn. And twins who are walking trauma collections whose entire lives and identities have been irrevocably fucked up by the system they're in. They're all a collection of hairline fractures."

I let a wave of whispers and snide comments ripple through the crowd before continuing. I wanted everyone in the room to have a moment to snark, feel disdain, and have terrible ideas.

Then I smiled. "We're going to shatter them."

It took over an hour before I got back to my office, after answering questions and having side conversations and being stopped half a dozen times on my way to the door. I knew we'd knocked this one out of the park; I could tell by their enthusiasm, the diabolical excitement in the voices of everyone I spoke to while they asked for clarification about the freezing point of Red Sprite's eyes or Siegeworks' secret social media accounts. I felt almost giddy as I added more notes to my to-do list and promised to pursue different lines of inquiry; it had been a while since I felt so fully on my game, with so much potential opening up in front of me.

When I got back to my chair, there was a single note face down on the desk. I recognized the weight of the card stock as Leviathan's personal letterhead, the same stationery he'd once used to send me a get-well message. This time, whatever fluttered in my stomach had its wings turned to cold lead.

I flipped over the note to see the alchemical symbol for sulfur burned tastefully into the other side, along with the handwritten line: *Today you made me proud.*

The meeting had not been streamed, and he had not attended virtually; I hadn't even formally submitted my slide deck to him yet. There was only one way he could have watched the events of the afternoon closely enough to have an emotional opinion about it. He'd watched me, maybe through my own eye—not because I was in any potential danger, but just because he had wanted to.

I imagined going to the kitchen and finding the sharpest thing in any of the drawers. I thought through my options, long bamboo skewers and forks; a filleting knife might be narrow enough. I pictured myself running into the bathroom, using the magnifying mirror to drive the point into my eye as precisely as possible. I wondered if I would be able to force myself to do it, if I would be able to do enough damage to disable the surveillance devices before he could stop me. I imagined aqueous humor and blood pouring down my face, trailing bits of wiring like optic nerve.

Even as I panicked internally, and imagined mutilating myself, another part of me thought: *He might be watching right now.* He might want to see my reaction to the sweet message he'd sent to me in the moment I received it. So I cradled the letter in my hands, as though it was fragile, and read it over again, as though treasuring it. I smiled at the letter and hoped he would interpret my elevated heart rate as happiness.

Part Four

I SLOWLY GOT BETTER AT THE INTERNAL CHECKS, THE CON-stant self-policing, the new layers of filters I employed between the inside and outside of my body. I expected the disgust and hot fear and the occasional spikes of anger, braided in with soft, comfortable feelings about being cared about and watched over. It was easy to become conditioned to the horror when it was married with a kind of affection and closeness with Leviathan I had not allowed myself to believe was attainable. I'd wanted him back so badly, and forced myself to believe that what I wanted was impossible; but it was here, and better than it had ever been, and it was hard to maintain a kind of vigilant distress about my privacy and autonomy when I was getting exactly what I'd hoped for in so many ways.

I spent most of my time in a perpetual liminal space between happiness and terror. I felt the best, the most at peace, when I forgot I was being watched, but there was danger in forgetting, and a sharp spike of panic when I remembered again. I was constantly anxious that I would let something unintentional or humiliating slip out in an unguarded moment. All of the intrusive thoughts that would emerge to torture me while I was trying to fall asleep involved wondering what he might have seen, what moments of privacy had in fact been observed

When you don't know when you're being watched, you have to assume you always are, and it is exhausting in a way I would never be able to fully articulate. Solitude was no longer replenishing, something in me was always flexed. I could never uncoil, and had to always be awake, on, evaluating and filtering.

If I was entirely unhappy, it would have been easier. I could have rebelled, or escaped, or done any number of things to alleviate a situation that was intolerable. I could have even just told him how deeply uncomfortable I was with all of the technology he had implanted in my body reporting back to him. But I didn't. It wasn't only fear that kept me quiet. The odd intimacy that was still growing between us was so weird and so potentially fragile that I didn't want to disturb it. I didn't want to waste whatever we had together fighting about something, and whenever I was in his company, I felt a kind of calmness I felt nowhere else.

It helped that we were both just so fucked up about intimacy, resentful and suspicious about it while also pressed together by weird, desperate need. We worked together as brilliantly and terribly as we always had, but now sometimes we would lean against each other for a kind of animal support, or he would take one of my hands and play idly with my fingers, like it was a gadget he was repairing. Sometimes, that absent attention would become much more focused.

He got angry, once, because he liked me too much. It was simultaneously hilarious and genuinely frightening because as absurd as it was, the fury was real. He was in a terrible mood to begin with, a series of small stressors adding up into a cascade of frustration, and when it turned out Gary—our head death ray technologist—was on PTO, he ordered the handful of us who'd been in the meeting out of his office.

Typically, I would have done what everyone else did: immediately obeyed the instruction and left. This time, I looked at him carefully, at the line of his shoulders and back, at the tension and psychic weight he was carrying there. I could see him withdrawing into himself rapidly, and I made an executive decision I wouldn't have dared weeks ago.

"It would be better if I stayed."

He flinched when I spoke, almost like I'd startled him. "It would not be." He stood, and moved a half step closer to me, trying to usher me out with the proximity of his body. It was the move only someone who was used to being perceived as both repulsive and deeply intimidating would make; most people were profoundly unsettled by his physical proximity, and it was clear he expected just getting closer would effectively scare me away.

But that didn't work anymore. I felt a very different suite of emotions and sensations about being close to him, so I stayed seated and unbothered, looking up at him. I watched him flex his hands—not threateningly, though, but with a nervous energy, like he wasn't sure what to do now that move had failed.

"Auditor." He meant it as a warning.

I stood up, and his palpable relief was enough that I very nearly turned toward the door. But instead, I took a step nearer to him, to his very obvious confusion.

"I don't want to upset you."

"I am not upset."

I pressed my lips together in the most disbelieving straight line I could muster.

Even he couldn't convince himself that he wasn't lying, and very badly, so he started to bluster. "And if I were, I don't wish to . . . express that in public."

"You aren't in public."

His frustration was like a physical presence in the room. "You know what I—"

I put a hand on his chest and he stopped abruptly, staring at my palm resting just below his collarbone like I'd sunk a knife into him.

"So this is what you want." His voice was strangled and harsh, full of static.

"I want to stay with you."

"You want to see me weak."

I pressed my fingers into him harder, for emphasis. "I want to see *you.*"

"You make me weak."

That was dangerous. I reacted just enough, pulled back the smallest amount, and he knew an opening when he saw it. His hand wrapped around my forearm hard.

"I won't allow it," he said quietly. "Not even from you."

I had to be careful now. I'd pulled something out of him I hadn't expected, tripped a defense mechanism for a kind of vulnerability he was extremely guarded against.

"No, I don't want to see you weak."

"What else could you say." His fingers contracted, clawlike, in a way that was not quite painful but was nearly there.

I fought the urge to pull back, and did the only thing you can do when trapped in something that will cause more damage if you fight it: I pushed further in. I put my other hand on his shoulder.

"I don't want you to be weak because I touched you. I want you to glow, like a bronze statue caressed with gold."

He stayed extremely still for a moment. "Why?"

I was quiet for too long, trying to form words out of the emotional shapes whose edges we were tracing. I could feel him breathing, the rise and fall of his chest, the plates of his biological armor creaking like tectonic plates.

"I don't know. But I want to be next to you even if it's terrible."

"You are going to regret that," he said gently.

"I hope so," I said, and smiled.

He loosened his grip just enough that it became an embrace instead of a threat.

"I expect to be poor company."

"Sounds great."

"Fine." He tried to put as much frustration into his voice as he could, which was very effective, but I detected a tiny bit of warmth underneath. He let go of me and stalked toward the door leading to his apartment, and made it almost all the way there before throwing the smallest glance backward to make sure I was following.

FOR A TIME, a painful tenderness suffused everything, like a bruise that only hurt when pressed. I wasn't even sure I could call our connection "romantic" in the literary sense, but it was deeply intimate, with all of the visceral strangeness that came with it. Our day-to-day interactions didn't change all that much, though they became charged in different ways. We were already close, our lives and ambitions enmeshed. Yet both of us were extremely independent, and needed a lot of our own space and time, and had our own work to be obsessive about (on our own or together); neither of us wanted someone who would overtake those obsessions or become the other's whole life. But when it came to the parts of ourselves we did want to share, we split ourselves open.

There are a lot of clichés about fucking supervillains—most of which are variations of "sure, they're psychotic, but the sex is good"—that ended up being irrelevant at best and actively unhelpful at worst. Leviathan's voraciousness made me question and deprogram a million tiny things I thought I knew about what I wanted and what a partner might want. I saw all of the ways I had always held back for someone else's comfort, all the self-imposed limits I'd pressed on myself, assuming I was too much, too heavy, too anything. I had to accept he meant it when he told me he wanted me to do anything. I could trust his durability easily enough, but

I also had to believe his desire, that he wanted whatever I wanted and whatever my body could do.

I also had to unlearn a lot of the ways I was holding myself back, the internal math that I was running, to make sure I was not initiating too much, or saying yes too much—trying to track some kind of balance, keeping desire within acceptable limits. I had to break those equations and embrace my own "yes" whenever it was there and genuine, and not just when I thought I was within reason. Having a part of my life where I didn't have to worry about balance and moderation was a joy I jealously protected.

I saw my body very differently when I was with him. He wasn't interested in the things about me that any other partners had been—which is to say, only the traditionally sexy parts. He seemed to appreciate all of me, but it wasn't my ass or my eyes or my tits he ever talked about. He was much more interested in the narrative of my body, in the stories that it told. He would refer to bruises as nebulae, a keloid became a starburst. I stopped seeing myself as a collection of things I had suffered, and instead saw what I had become.

Leviathan changed, too. As objectively strange as he was, he didn't have many hang-ups in the places one might think he would. He wasn't insecure about the way he looked, or anxious about any perceived monstrousness—his physicality was a neutral fact he accepted and embraced, and had often used a lot to his advantage. His body was in no way a crux of self-loathing, and he seemed to treat his desire the same way. It might be weird and overwhelming, but he didn't feel shame about that. What mattered to him was that his desire was returned and amplified, and he developed a kind of endless curiosity about the different ways we could explore it.

What he did have an intensely hard time with, though, was casual contact. He was very much not used to nonsexual physical intimacy, and had an extremely difficult time processing it at first. When he touched me, that was one thing, but me reaching out was not something he was prepared for. I'd always drawn a lot of comfort from physical contact when I was close to someone, and it seemed to leave him totally bewildered. It was as though he could accept why someone could want contact with him for a sexual purpose, the same reason he would understand why someone would seek out contact in the form of violence, but to touch him for the sake of touching him was very hard for him to understand. For all that, though, he saw it mattered to me, and worked on it, and though it continued to be something I had to be very gentle and cautious about it—he was, after all, the kind of monster you did not want to startle—he started to accept the idea I just might want to touch him.

This little pocket universe of intimacy we had was delicate enough, and wonderful enough, that I almost accepted what he had done to me entirely. It was not mutilation, but addition; he was watching out of care, not malice. I forced myself to believe that far longer than I should have. For a while, what we were gaining far outweighed what I had lost.

I WAS PREPARED for a lot of complicated, volatile emotions while I tried to process being simultaneously ecstatic and freaked out about most of the things that were happening in my life.

I was not prepared for how desperately it made me miss June.

I had not thought about her in a long time, very deliberately so. I had shut her out systemically, purposefully, turning all the focus and cognitive behavioral therapy I could to training my brain away from turning toward her. It very nearly worked. In the long, terrible months after we'd won, and Leviathan was home, and I thought I had lost everything, I had managed to put my former best friend and roommate almost entirely out of my mind. There were too many new wounds and fresh betrayals to lie awake thinking about, and then the work became ever deeper and more all-consuming, I lacked the space in my head and heart to think of her. With Supercollider's funeral and all that came after it taking up so much of my inner life, it was easy to forget, most of the time, the raw wound I still carried in the middle of myself.

But then suddenly I found myself desperate to talk to her now, to tell her everything that was happening and get her merciless, viciously affectionate advice. She would have never given me a moment's peace about my choices, and I could almost hear her screeching when I tried to describe what had happened and was happening between me and Leviathan.

"You always had terrible taste," the June inside my head said. "But you didn't need to *lean in*." I imagined her rolling her eyes. "Once again you have confused 'I'm in danger' with 'I'm horny.'"

I could perfectly imagine all the mockery as well as the genuine concern that suffused it; she would take care of me, the way that she'd always taken care of me. After Supercollider shattered my leg, when I was delirious with pain and would have been homeless if she hadn't let me live on her couch for months, she was great to me. She set alarms in her phone that went off every couple of hours, even in the middle of the night, to make sure I kept up with pain management or antibiotics or everything else I had to do. Her phone would chime a few bars from "Despacito" and she would heave herself up from whatever piece of furniture she was lounging on with a performative groan, and bring me water and a little cup full of pills.

When I was a bit better, and could get them myself, she would just turn the trilling phone toward me so I could see the screen, every alarm titled "TAKE YOUR DRUGS BITCH" with a walrus and a pill emoji. I remembered her getting little rope baskets, like the kind you might find washcloths displayed in in someone's very fancy bathroom, and filling them with snacks near the couch so I didn't have to hobble all the way to the kitchen when she wasn't home. Even when pain turned me into an asshole, even as I became so blinded by my single-minded antagonism toward Supercollider that I couldn't see how deeply, oppressively uncomfortable I was making her in her own house, fresh boxes of Kleenex and bottles of water still appeared around me like magic. When she was at work, or her unboyfriend's house, even when she was out because she was so sick of my shit she started avoiding her own house, she would still text me, Take your drugs.

Suddenly, all of the months we hadn't spoken rushed in on me at once, and I was knocked over by the force of the longing. It was as though I had been wading, maybe ankle- or calf-deep, in the river of missing her; a constant slog, but a bearable one. Now upstream a dam had broken and I was knocked off my feet, carried along and suddenly afraid that I wouldn't be able to find my footing again. It reminded me how it was possible to drown in just a few inches of water.

So, stupidly, I wrote to her. I had respected her wishes until then, and had not reached out since the first and only time she told me not to contact her again. I didn't write to her formal email address, the one that had contained the cold, legal language forbidding me access to her life. I sent it to her old, embarrassing, middle school address, the one almost no one knew or used anymore, the one from which she'd begged me to just understand that she just couldn't watch me go missing over and over again.

I told myself she probably wouldn't even see it, she probably didn't even check that address most of the time, and surely she'd blocked me or set any messages from me to go directly to the trash folder. I told myself that knowing it was a lie. I had written her dozens and dozens of messages since we had last spoken, but they all stayed safely in my draft folder, messages in bottles never intended for the ocean, just to be kept lined on a shelf.

This time, I hit *send.*

June,

I know I am not supposed to do this. For fuck's sake I am writing 'I am not supposed to do this,' like that exonerates me, and I know it doesn't either. Neither does my knowing it. There are no defenses of self-awareness that I can deploy to cover the fact that what I am doing is not what you want. That's fucked up. If I was better at loving you and being the friend you needed I would have been able to give you what you needed. I'm sorry. I know it's wrong and I am doing it anyway.

I miss you so bad. It's like shrapnel, sharp pieces of iron buried under my skin that can't come out and won't ever quite heal. Sometimes I can shut it out, but it's awful now, and even if you never see this or reply, I can reach out to you. I can stretch and even if I never touch anything, I'll know I tried and in that reaching I was just a little closer to you.

I can't tell if you would be proud of or disappointed in who I am, what I am becoming. I wish more than anything I could ask you and just know for sure. I am afraid that you would hate it, hate me, find me unrecognizable and boring or worse, and want the old me back. It would be awful not to be able to give her to you, be her for you. But sometimes I think, "June would have loved that," and I wish I could tell you the most ridiculous fucking stories you have ever heard in your life, and maybe I could bring enough to the table again to be worth having in your life after all. I don't know how realistic that hope is. I wish I could ask you and know for sure.

You once told me that if a message begins every paragraph with "I" it's not worth a goddamn thing, and I look back on what I have written here and am ashamed of it, but I am not going to change it. I want you to see that I am still selfish, so whatever choice you make you do it properly, with all of the information. I miss you. I wish we could be friends again.

> Supercollider is dead. The world feels different. I am hoping,
> completely idiotically, that it might be different enough that
> you'd want to be back in my life too. I love you, asshole. Come
> back.
>
> Anna

I hit *send* and watched the email blink into the ether, forced myself to wait out the few seconds until the "unsend" timer expired. Then I immediately felt sick to my stomach. I had promised myself I wouldn't lie to her, but I had. Even my signature was a lie. Somewhere between the first time "Auditor" was hurled at me as an insult and I replaced all my business cards with my new name, Anna had disappeared. I had called myself something that wasn't mine anymore, because it was the only name she would recognize; but I was so far from the person I had been it no longer fit, and by writing a message from Anna, I was telling her a person who loved her, who she loved, was still here waiting, when Anna no longer existed.

I started to write a new message. *I should not have written that.* And *I am sorry.* And *Please disregard.* But I sent none of them. Instead I convinced myself that it was all moot, that she wasn't going to read it and if she did she would never reply, so she wouldn't ever get to find out that I was capable of fucking up this egregiously when I was already in the middle of deliberately fucking up.

If she wasn't done with me, I thought, *she might even find that funny.*

THAT EMAIL WAS just one more embarrassing decision to push out of my head, and there was so much to do I was almost able to forget it entirely for a while. I wanted to move in on one of the Future as soon as possible, get them crumbling before their camaraderie could fully solidify. Deciding who to attack first, which weak point to exploit, was genuinely difficult. Like all malicious forces, though, I am extremely lucky, and soon the Draft leadership race heated up again, and two players made moves that made my choice for me.

The protest was about Leviathan. Despite assurances from the Draft that the "threat was contained" and that they were "committed to justice for everyone, especially those who fell in service of it" (barf), a lot of people were furious about their perceived lack of action. "Action," of course, being used in place of "immediate and unrelenting violence." For anyone, civilian or hero, who believed the only appropriate response to Supercollider's death was the complete eradication of his accused murderer without due process, I could see how it looked like the Draft and their heroes weren't doing close to enough to exact retribution.

Despite it being a massive point of contention even at the Draft and among those vying for leadership, they had thus far not been willing to fight us directly.

The truth was, they just didn't have any guns big enough. Sure, if every hero available attacked us simultaneously it would be a disaster, but that meant pulling them all off the other work they would be doing—and I'd been making sure they were being kept busy. None of it was in Leviathan's name, but across the City experimental weaponry was being stolen and more circus-themed cybercrime was being committed at alarming rates—and had been ever since we'd been supporting it. Going after us full force meant everything else collapsing—or it meant throwing their Future away, attacking us long before they stood a chance.

That's not to say a couple of heroes didn't try. Directly against orders and without Draft support, Glass Lizard made it inside the perimeter before security took her down with something Keller called a "gel harpoon." Stoic managed to crash through the roof of one of the food courts before being choked out. Both of them were tied up neatly and dropped off a reasonable distance away, alive when we left them; neither of these incidents were ever openly addressed, but it was clear to everyone involved that these were not serious attempts to accomplish anything.

And that made some people furious. Demands for the Draft to do *something* about the "evil no longer kept in check" got louder and louder, and was starting to spark occasional demonstrations. The largest one yet was organized to coincide with the opening of a new wing at the local community college, for the Cultural Study of Superheroics. People didn't want to see action in the form of a long-game culture war where they could control the curriculum of journalists and analysts; they wanted blood. And that made it the perfect opportunity to take a swing at Riot Shield.

He was the buffer between the Future and immediate danger, someone they absolutely had to rely on, someone who had to believe in himself in order to function at the best of his ability—all of which made him an ideal candidate to tear down.

"We don't need to rip him down to the foundations," I said to the assembled teams, in the opening debrief. "We just need to shake him badly enough that there's structural damage. He's got a lot of hairline cracks in his psyche. We're going to use those to our advantage, make those wounds even deeper.

"And as a treat," I said, grinning already at the prospect, "we get to do terrible things to the remains of Siegeworks."

An actual cheer rose up from around the room, and a couple Meat from Enforcement openly high-fived. It always felt good to be able to deliver work that my colleagues desperately wanted to do; it was, I had to admit to myself, a significant part of the reason I wanted to go after Riot Shield first. The time was right and my own research along with Evelyn's insights made me convinced it was also the correct course, but I also wanted to give everyone working with me a gift, let them take out their frustrations on someone who dearly deserved it, and I could think of few more deserving.

Siegeworks were going to be disbanded, something the remaining members aggressively objected to, and unfortunately for the world their protests had not fallen on deaf ears. They'd been taken under the wing by none other than the chief compliance officer, the repugnant August Chisholm, who saw the potential in their terrible personalities and new resentment. He reinstated their team and promised them access to a "new kind of position" at the Draft, which sounded very uncomfortably like his personal Praetorian Guard and had so far been completely opposed by everyone around him with a survival instinct. But the CCO was tenacious, and kept the four dejected heroes close at hand. He saw the same opportunity that we did for different reasons: the university program was one of Mom's flagship projects, and fomenting as much anger and public outrage about it as possible was to his direct advantage. And there was a lot of damage he could do in the name of "protecting" the work of his opponents, gaining traction with plausible deniability.

He put the four remaining members of Siegeworks in charge of the event, as a "reassuring presence" that the Draft was "taking safety seriously." When questioned by one of his underlings why the four supes were even necessary, especially since civilian law enforcement seemed sufficient, the CCO typed the incredible sentence *Just let the little fuckers blow off some steam.* That was a stolen memo I genuinely treasured.

For all the very bad things that might mean, it put us in a great position for fucking with Riot Shield. Despite how terrible they'd been to him, both while he was on their team and after he left, he had a great deal of guilt about abandoning his former teammates. They were furious he'd left them, so much so that they actively refused to replace him—to prove, extremely ill-advisedly, that they were perfectly capable of great feats of heroism without him. They were so angry at the perceived slight of his absence they thought their collective pride would be protection enough, but luckily for me hubris is a remarkably ineffective shield. When the inevitable consequences arrived, Riot Shield would not be there to save them, and he would never forgive himself for it.

"Your job is not to take out Siegeworks directly," I continued, addressing several of our Enforcement agents as well as a few new contractors who specialized in crowd control and mob psychology. "Your job is to make sure someone else does. Preferably, many someones at once. Put weapons in their hands. Get people pissed off, throw the first rock. Whatever you need to do to get the crowd swinging."

"What if they try and run?" one of the contractors asked, a woman with tattoos covering her neck and above one eyebrow.

"They're the kind who'll run when it's already too late. Slow them down."

"But you don't want us to take a clear shot if we have it?"

I shook my head. "We want Riot Shield to feel, acutely, that what has happened was because he wasn't there," I explained. "With him, they could be invulnerable. Without him, they're just fast, and free from most moral qualms."

"They'll underestimate you," Keller added, addressing both the people he was sending in and the mercs they were accompanying. "You aren't capes, you don't have powers. They'll think they can just kick you around like nothing. But they're not much more durable than you."

"They're going to gamble on you being scared," I said, "intimidated by their reputation and the theater they bring with them. They'll probably look to make a couple of 'examples' early on, to make everyone else's will break and scatter."

"Show the rest of they crowd they don't have to be scared." Keller paused to look around the room, making a brief moment of eye contact with each of the dozen or so Meat and mercs assembled there. "They'll get close and careless looking for someone to hurt. Turn that on them."

It wasn't one of our Meat, who had Keller's finest portable sound cannons or a cleverly deployed can of restraining foam hidden in their backpacks, who kicked things off. It was the merc with the neck tattoos, who'd done a lot of work in crowds before. She knew to wear black, featureless clothes and cover any part of her body that was easily identifiable with makeup, while not looking especially polished or tactical. She knew how to blend; she knew how to get close.

When the protest got a little too loud, a little too angry, Siegeworks dropped into the middle of the crowd at the earliest opportunity. They didn't hesitate a moment to start dispersing the protesters, wide smiles on all of their smug faces. Water Cannon knocked the caps off a nearby fire hydrant and directed the flow with vicious efficiency while Rubber Bullet flung out his hyperelongated arms like whips. Baton, though, with Taser ever at his side, barreled right into the largest group of people he could find. The heroes weren't even pretending to try and just keep people away from the Draft headquarters building and the increasingly jumpy lines of riot cops.

Our merc saw her opening and got close enough to get right in Baton's face—but she didn't go for his face. She went for his feet. She dropped to the asphalt, pulled a modified cordless framing nailer out of her jacket and swung it down on the top of his boot with all the force she could. The nails she'd loaded in were long enough to drive all the way through his foot and deep into the asphalt. When he howled and reached down instinctively toward his leg, she took the opening to drive a second nail through the other foot. It wasn't as neat as the first, the energy from that initial blow having already fed his powers, so it drove through the leather and flesh and rubber at a bad angle. He wasn't affixed to the ground quite as securely on that side, but it was enough. He was momentarily stuck.

The merc knew that was her cue, and she got the fuck out of there.

Everyone around Baton and Taser took a collective step back. He'd been mid-stride when the first nail hit him, so his feet were planted awkwardly, making it hard for him to stand, but neither could he really fall. He wobbled and screamed off-kilter, unable to move or fully regain his balance, while Taser flitted around him. At first Taser tried to push Baton forward, then tug him off the ground, which only caused the trapped hero to scream louder. They probably could have worked him free if they'd had the time and the patience—the nails were deep, but not so much that they couldn't be tugged out in desperation, or by someone with even moderate super-strength.

But the crowd would not let that happen. Without the space and momentum to start gathering kinesthetic energy to redirect back toward whoever he was fighting, Baton was not much stronger or more durable than anyone else. He had to hit you, or you had to hit him, for his powers to work. Unable to barrel his fists first, there wasn't much he could do to generate the energy he needed, and worse than that, he couldn't get away.

You couldn't hit him without giving him an advantage, but you could move in slowly. You couldn't throw anything at him without it bouncing off and making him briefly more durable, but if you approached calmly, with little initial force, there was nothing for him to turn on you. Once there, you could press something sharp right into him . . . if you went slowly. If you increased the force only as much as you needed. If you went in just a little at a time.

Though I'm loathe to give any credit to them whatsoever, Taser did try and protect Baton, initially. The electric shocks she could produce were no joke, and she snatched a water bottle away from a bystander and splashed it over everyone nearby, to enhance the conduction. At one point a dozen people were at the duo's feet twitching horribly, and it looked like she might be able to hold them off long enough for the cavalry to come.

But "cavalry" implies cohesion. Water Cannon and Rubber Bullet were busy. They were catching each other's eye, grinning as they worked, posing and preening and striking the most dramatic poses they could. They paid no attention to the commotion in the crowd where Baton and Taser had disappeared; rather, a frenzied mass of panicked people was a sign to them that everything was going according to plan. Besides, they never had to worry about actually protecting their teammates, that was someone else's job; that was Riot Shield's job.

Someone threw a coat over Taser first, then a fire blanket. With the extra insulation of the layers of fabric and the rubber soles of everyone's shoes, it was much safer to step on the pile of fabric than any other kind of contact. After a while, the muffled shape underneath stopped moving, and the puddles of water nearby no longer crackled angrily with electricity. Then, almost serenely, the crowd returned to the business of taking Baton slowly apart.

THE LAST TRANSPORT vehicle was just pulling in as I stepped outside. Keller was already there, debriefing with the team leader and first lieutenant. He looked serious but satisfied; the lieutenant was doing most of the talking while the commander offered the occasional clarification with a lot of nodding.

The medical team was also swarming the courtyard, sorting every one of the returning Meat into triage. Most of them were fine, or just needed some ibuprofen and some superglue, and were answering the medics' early screening questions with simple clarity.

Did you have any direct contact with a hero?

Do you have any injuries that you know of?

Does anything hurt?

The first vehicle back, the one closest to the medical bay doors, had clearly been used as the ambulance. All the injured Meat had been loaded in and sped away. Only two were standing. Three were unable to walk under their own power, and were being taken inside on stretchers or a wheelchair. One medic had climbed into the back of the vehicle, where two prone bodies lay, and was checking for vitals he didn't expect to find. Two pairs of boots, toes pointing up and profoundly still, hung at the edge of the open back doors.

As I got closer, I heard one medic arguing with a huge, baby-faced bruiser of a man whose face and shoulder was soaked in a truly spectacular amount of blood. It was impossible to tell what color his short hair usually was, or even its texture, as it was stuck down into sodden clumps as the gore slowly congealed. Blood was caked into the shell-like coils of his ears and the folds of skin around his neck.

"I'm fine," he said.

"I am not asking," replied the medic, who was maybe a third his size and deeply unimpressed with his attitude. She was pressing a thick wad of gauze to the side of his head, standing on tiptoes to do so while he awkwardly leaned down.

"I just need a couple stitches."

She snorted. "A couple, yeah. And a full concussion evaluation, and—"

"There's no concussion, I—"

She was done, and called over her shoulder, "Commander, will you tell Gabriel that he's coming with me to medical for a full eval-uation."

Gabriel, who had lifted his hands in a *you don't need to do that* supplication, winced. Keller and the pair of Meat he'd been speaking to all turned, took one look at Gabriel's head, and glared at him.

"Don't be fucking stupid," the team leader said.

Gabriel tried to nod glumly and let himself be hustled away. He was in the best shape of the significantly injured, and by a wide margin. The medic told him to hold the gauze as tight as he could to his head and moved on to someone who couldn't apply their own pressure.

The other injured Meat who was still walking was visibly in shock, glassy-eyed and sweating. He looked like he didn't know where he was, and kept absently starting to wander away from another medic trying to get him to stay, pay attention, answer questions. His right arm was loaded into a sling, where it drooped and sagged like rotten fruit in a plastic grocery bag. I couldn't keep my eyes on it for long, the soft wrongness of it filling me with a kind of existential nausea. I couldn't tell, before I looked away, if it had been crushed or if it just didn't have bones anymore.

As I got closer, Keller took a half step over when I got near enough, indicating I should join the conversation.

"Zub's not getting the arm back," the lieutenant was saying. Her hair was pulled back so tight it lifted her eyebrows.

"That's a real shame." The team leader had an extremely prominent Adam's apple and a deep, resonant voice, and sounded like they meant it.

"You think the other four might be back?" Keller said.

The lieutenant sucked her teeth. "Hard to say. Once they're looked at we'll know better. Gabe looks good, so does Henri if he didn't puncture a lung. Marlon seems all superficial, but it depends on if anything hit his eyes."

"What about Yanez's leg?"

The leader and lieutenant looked at each other.

"Legs," the lieutenant clarified, with obvious difficulty. "And something's fucky with his pelvis."

"Ah shit."

"Hoping it's just a coccyx break or bad bruising."

While they spoke, I automatically ran numbers in my head, calculating everything that day had cost us—had cost the people working for us. The Meat losing the use of an arm probably meant the end of his career, and Zub was barely thirty. He could have had another twenty years doing violence for money; but there was the recovery that lay ahead of him, adjusting to a prosthetic, therapy. Maybe Gabe would be fine in a couple of days, with nothing but a cool scar to show for it; maybe he had a TBI and would undergo an awful personality change, and would be too volatile to do the work. And any possible spinal injury was a nightmare to consider. Even with good outcomes, with two bodies and two more serious injuries at least, the cost in lifeyears was easily in the triple digits.

"Wish them luck," Keller said, though I couldn't tell if it was an instruction or a blessing. "Good work. This was as clean as it was gonna get."

"Thank you, sir."

"Appreciate it."

The team leader hurried away, and Keller turned his attention to me.

"You get what you needed?"

"We'll see."

He made a huffing sound. "Don't know how you can handle it. All that 'wait and see' shit. I want to know if things were a disaster or not immediately. Cut and dry."

"If only. People aren't predictable as ballistics."

"Ain't that the truth."

"How was that for you?"

He took a long look over the people and vehicles scattered around us; everyone who could be treated was inside now, only the bodies and a couple of medics filling out paperwork for them remained.

"You have seen better, or a lot worse. Those fucking Bone Brothers are no joke."

"It sounds like Yanez met Cartilage."

"Yeah, 'met.'"

With Baton and Taser down, the situation rapidly got out of control. Water Cannon and Rubber Bullet finally realized something was horrifically wrong and started to retreat, and might have been in very real trouble had Cartilage and Marrow not arrived as surprise backup. The rest of the Future were off at a training exercise, but the twins got into a fight with Red Sprite and everyone decided it would be better if they stayed behind, at least for a few days, to cool off. They weren't close enough to save all of Siegeworks, but they put a sudden stop to the escalating violence. Our teams had withdrawn as soon as they arrived, but not fast enough.

"I'm sorry."

"Don't be, that's the job. You end up with what you needed, then it was worth it."

I looked at those two pairs of boots dangling out of the back of the tactical van. One was a brand-new pair, barely broken in, probably still giving their owner blisters, but he'd been so eager to wear them he'd put them on this morning anyway. The other pair were well-loved, the leather creased and oiled, with after-market Vibram soles.

I didn't know who they were, but I would look later. I would put everything I knew about them into a spreadsheet: how old they were, how healthy they were, what else they might have done, what they could have been. I'd calculate the years of their lives that they wouldn't get to have anymore, and add it to the cost of those heroes. And the cost of myself.

I thought about Riot Shield, who had been too far away to help, who had left his team to become something more, something better, and would be wrestling with that for the rest of his life. I thought about the whole long, heroic career ahead of him, and all the damage he might do. I thought about how many more people we might prevent him from harming, and weighed that against those two pairs of boots and a man carrying what was left of his arm in a bag.

You had better be worth it, you fuck.

WHILE IT WOULD take a long time to see the equations play out in full, the immediate fallout was more than promising. Riot Shield was devastated, as predicted, and insisted on showing up at the funeral, despite the generally held and very obvious opinion that this was a terrible idea. Water Cannon left as soon as she saw him, screeching for him to be removed, while Rubber Bullet attacked him outright, swinging his flail-like fists for all they were worth. Riot Shield held up some half-hearted defenses at first, letting his former teammate punch ineffectually at his force fields, but then he dropped them. He stood impassive and let Rubber Bullet hit him until several other heroes had to intervene. His nose ended up broken, and there were endless photos posted of a pool of blood on the floor in front of the two caskets.

There followed a deluge of opinion pieces about whether or not a former member of Siegeworks was "stable enough" to bear the responsibility now placed on him. Not to mention, how could he protect an entire team of heroes who were expected to take on top-tier villainy when he couldn't win a fistfight?

It was then that I messaged Decoherence. I thought it was the perfect time for her to speak with him; emotionally broken, assailed by guilt, and being doubted by everyone around him, sometimes silently and sometimes extremely aloud. If he was ever going to be malleable enough to be convinced of anything, including whatever it was she was hoping to say, the timing seemed perfect.

I genuinely expected her to be much happier to hear from me.

"You *lied* to me."

I yelped and dropped the glass of water I was carrying on the carpet. She had materialized directly behind me in my apartment, just as I was getting ready for bed.

I grabbed dramatically at my chest. "And you said you wouldn't *fucking do this* anymore. Christ, D–"

Decoherence stood furiously in the center of my apartment. "You said you would tell me what you were going to do."

"I told you *if there was an opening*, I would let you know. There is now an opening. I am letting you know."

"Don't you fucking play semantics with me! Baton and Taser–"

"Even you can't pretend that was a loss."

She didn't take the bait. Instead, she said, "It didn't have to go that way."

I breathed deeply to get my heart rate under control. "It might not have. But it's how I chose for it to happen. Now Riot Shield is spiraling and things for the Future are looking less stable by the minute," I added. "Both Mom and the awful CCO have had their plans fucked with. Which is a success."

Decoherence's facial expression didn't shift much, but something behind it did. "What did you call him?"

It took me a second to catch on to what she meant. "Mom. You knew I met him."

"I didn't know you were on a first-name basis."

"It's what he told me to call him."

"It's what everyone there calls him."

I bent to pick up the glass from the sodden carpet. "So why are you being so weird about it?"

She frowned. She had the best frown in the business, somehow both grave and intimidating. I studied the downturn of her lips, the way the lines of her expression flowed into her face tattoos, and envied it. "It sounds . . . fucked up, coming from you."

"I promise it's not coming from a place of affection."

"It just—never mind. That's not the fucking point."

"What *is* your point?"

"You could have—I wanted a chance to talk to him *first*. Before you fucked him up. Before anyone died."

"You really should have specified," I said coldly.

"What is *wrong* with you?"

I was starting to get genuinely angry. "Don't you fucking virtue signal to me like you're suddenly squeamish. I know what you can do. You know what I can do. I've *never* hid that from you. I am letting you in, because I respect you and you have been a valuable ally in the past. That does not mean you get to dictate *anything* about how I work and what my plans are."

I spoke from my diaphragm, standing as straight as I could, pointing dead into the center of her chest. It felt good to dress her down; I only wished I wasn't wearing my goddamn pajamas.

She bared her teeth, and looked like she was in some kind of pain. "I expected more from you."

I laughed at her, a quick, mean bark. "That was a mistake."

She squared up in front of me, getting too close; not threatening me, exactly, but definitely inserting herself into my personal space. Like she wanted me to feel the disappointment radiating from her. It also meant her presence was suddenly in my sensorium, and I could feel her body heat—she always felt like she was running a fever. I wondered if it was some kind of hero thing, if her powers made her burn hot. I could smell her skin and deodorant, and had to fight not to recoil from the intimacy of it.

"I don't believe it was a mistake," she said, controlled. "You care about people being hurt. You care about unnecessary violence. Isn't that what you're all about? Or is that what you *were* about?"

I narrowed my eyes and got even closer to her, not quite touching but enough that she could certainly smell the fresh toothpaste on my breath. I resisted the urge to stand on my toes and glared up at her.

"Oh, I do care. I promise you that. Stats don't lie. Do you know what Baton's numbers were like? I can tell you about every fractured orbital and complex spinal injury in the last eighteen months, if you'd like. Everyone who bled to death internally in hours or lived for a couple years before the bedsores got them. So don't try and make me feel guilty for giving him an ounce of what he deserved. I'm *comfortable* with how it all balances out. I'll work it off."

She didn't know what to say to that. I took a half step back and shook out my shoulders to release a little of the tension.

"I thought you were better than this," she said, but with much less fire.

"And I thought you were worse."

"*What?*"

"You aren't a fucking hero anymore. Stop acting like it."

She seemed genuinely surprised by that. "I'm not a villain."

"Well then, you'd better figure out what you are, because right now you are dangerously close to getting in my way."

We stared at each other for a moment. Neither of us could fully believe that I was so close to actively threatening her, when I was just a frail little bag of meat in front of all her immense strength. But a weird sense of invulnerability surrounded me; I knew, without question, that Leviathan was watching this interaction unfold. There had been enough changes to my bodily equilibrium—the sudden scare, my raising temper, even the volume at which I was speaking—to get his attention. For all I knew he was already on his way or directly outside the door, and that made me feel like I could say just about anything I wanted to her with impunity.

For her part, Decoherence seemed genuinely startled by how aggressive I was. She wasn't mad about it, exactly, but was displaying the confusion of someone who usually had people watch their words very carefully around her.

I took a step back from her, deciding that I had won. "Talk to Riot Shield. You're not going to find a better time to get past his defenses. If you play your cards right, now is the best chance you have. Take it."

She would have said more, but from the next room I could hear someone with security clearance opening my door. I turned instinctively toward the sound, and as soon as I wasn't looking at her directly, Decoherence vanished again.

WITH THE FUTURE dealt a significant blow, and possibly even more destabilized by Decoherence scaring the hell out of Riot Shield, I wanted nothing more than to continue on with that momentum. I had a few different ideas for how we might pit Cartilage and Marrow against each other, and Thundersnow was already shouldering so much weight keeping her team together that I was eager to add more to her burden too. But before I could capitalize on what we had accomplished and make things even worse, Black Pill finally found a way to gain my attention again.

I'd managed to quite effectively compartmentalize his attempts to get to me for a while, and had even allowed myself to think, on the rare occasions that he did cross my mind, that he had lost interest. But then I got a search engine alert on my name—not the name I used, the only one I had been called for years, but the old, worn-out civilian name that only lived on a few pieces of expired ID I had tossed in a drawer somewhere. I got fairly regular pings on "the Auditor," from articles replete with phrases like "suspected connections" and "rumors of involvement" and "nefarious schemes." And usually when my old name appeared, it was from very rare mentions of my old website, *The Injury Report*.

Until this alert, which was actually a cluster of alerts, all of which included both of my names together. This hit me with a disorientation uncomfortably close to nausea. A podcast episode had gone up very late the night before, a show called *Behind the Masc*. The hosts were the type of guys who ironically used the terms "alpha" and "beta" in context that had nothing to do with werewolf erotica and could say "looksmaxxing" without snickering. They were clearly superhero fanboys in the most annoying possible sense; they had an entire episode devoted to the best superhero jawlines, and modeled their ideas about ideal manhood on what was sold to them wrapped in a cape.

To my utter horror, one of the guests on the latest episode, "The Myth of the Sexy Villainess," was Bracken, the young investment banker I'd gone on a single, disastrous date with during my earlier days as a desperate hench.

Listening to them talk about me, or at least the person that I had been, was excruciating. I hated the way my name sounded in their mouths, hated hearing it at all. I could only listen in short bursts before I would have to put my headphones down and curl into a humiliated ball for several minutes.

Attempting one more time, I hit *play*. "So we gotta ask," one of the hosts, Trevor, said.

"Fire away." That was Bracken, his good-natured tenor voice exactly as I remembered it.

"Did you know she was, you know, one of the bad guys? When you booked the date?"

"Be honest, you can tell us," said the second host, Brad.

"Truly, no."

"It just never came up?"

"That's surprising, from a high-agency male like you."

"Wish I had," Bracken said.

"Alright, alright."

"So what was your first impression when you saw her, then. Was it the mystery?"

"Or, yeah, the intrigue."

Bracken chuckled. "Disappointment."

The two hosts laughed and I felt like crawling under my desk.

Bracken went on to describe the date in horrific detail. Not just the end of the night, where our cab ride back to his place was interrupted by a detour to take an injured Meat to a Butcher for treatment. Bracken had gotten enough blood on his clothes that night to want nothing else to do with me, which was entirely fair. But he was equally merciless about the first half of the night, the part I thought had gone well, where I didn't think I had done anything wrong, just listened intently while he talked about work and didn't ask me a single thing about myself. I'd come to be vaguely embarrassed about what a pushover I was, that I was still interested in him at all when he had done nothing to earn it. But apparently even that was too much and not enough in equal measure.

"She looked nothing like her pictures," he said.

"Did she catfish you?"

"She should call herself the Catfish," Brad said, clearly thinking he was brilliant.

"That's a good name," Trevor agreed.

"Thanks."

"No, they were of her," Bracken admitted. "She just picked good ones, you know? Maybe there was a filter. In person, she was just kinda. Eh."

"So she didn't show up in, like, a black PVC catsuit?"

"Or, like, a power suit but carrying a whip?"

"She had on, like, slacks or something. And a sweater."

I was forced to remember being on the other side of that exchange, all the desperate optimism I felt, how I just wanted someone to like me and for something to go well, while he felt nothing but contempt. I had agonized over that sweater.

They spent the better part of ten minutes dissecting my lack of appeal, from my awkward attempts at conversation to my "drugstore" makeup (which I wore too much of, apparently), and how I was a perfect example of how "women villains" were not just morally bankrupt, but we weren't even hot.

It was a stupid podcast with repulsive hosts whose opinions didn't register in my universe, but that didn't mean listening to three people talk about how boring and ugly I was didn't feel like shit. It felt so bad, in fact, that something in my brain told me to pay attention.

This meant something.

So, I tried to listen differently. I started to look at my feelings a little closer. Aside from the garden-variety embarrassment of being torn down in public, I had to admit I hated the specific kind of vulnerability it exposed, the way it might change the way someone out in the world saw me. This was the sort of thing that eroded the mystique around a person, made them more human. This wasn't really a segment about the Auditor, a name that made a lot of heroes flinch now when they heard it; this was about a weaker, sadder crea-ture I had once been, a part of my backstory previously unexposed to the light of day. It made me feel terrible, and damaged some of the natural dread I had painstakingly accrued over my career. That was just too effective to be an accident.

The slithering embarrassment in my chest evaporated as a hot surge of anger—and even just a small bit of respect—took its place. The entire thing stank of Black Pill's doing; it was too thoughtful not to be. It was his best work yet, and by a wide margin. I pushed my discomfort to the side and started the podcast from the begin-ning, while opening several new search tabs for further research. If I was right, there was data here, and if I listened carefully, I was sure I could uncover something that would help me find who was pointing him toward my crit spots.

I started with Bracken himself. He would not have been hard to find, if you knew who he was, but you would have to know who he was. Before the podcast episode, there was not a single piece of information available that connected the two of us. He'd blocked me after the date and I'd deleted his contact info; there wasn't so much as a picture or a post online to commemorate our unfortu-nate meeting. Bracken could have set up the podcast interview himself, of course—it wouldn't have been outside the realm of pos-sibility for him to listen to manosphere podcasts; he could have approached *Behind the Masc* himself, offered to tell the story. But he was embarrassed about it. I could hear it in his voice the entire time he talked about how much sushi I ate and how weird my laugh was. The whole story, in his mind, reflected badly on him. He told it through a self-deprecating lens, reprimanding himself for making such a bad choice. This was not something he was proud of—not something he would have volunteered.

I thought about everyone I had told the story to. Very few of my current colleagues, I realized. Soon after taking a job for Leviathan,

I stopped trying to make myself seem smaller and more ridiculous to the people I worked with; being nonthreatening was no longer an effective survival technique. I told far fewer unflattering stories than I had before, and made fun of myself less. When I looked over the mental list I had of every potential link, I found myself crossing off a lot of names, many with a great sense of relief. But in the process, I added a few more, and some of them made my stomach drop.

There were others, of course. There was my boss, the Electric Eel, who had interrupted the date in the first place; I dearly wanted it to be him, as any excuse to obliterate him for the way he'd treated me would be nice. There was my driver, Oscar, whose cab got blood all over it. But right after that awful date with Bracken, I had gone out to karaoke with two people who were very close to my only friends at the time: June and Greg. They saw firsthand how destroyed my self-esteem was, and laughed both with and at me about it. They were there when it happened. They would have known enough, could tell the story well enough, to someone who could do some damage with it.

I was not yet ready to face the idea June might be involved, so I decided to rule out Greg first. I opened our old chat, which I saw with a pang I had not touched in months. Before that it was just a string of emojis, first batted back and forth like we were playing badminton, but slowly Greg's serves were returned by me less and less, until there was just a string of waves and smiles, little pings reaching out for the smallest bit of attention that was never returned. It broke my heart, seeing what an asshole I'd been. I'd been so busy and so in my head for so long I'd neglected our friendship entirely. This would be a turning point, I decided. A reality check. I would talk to Greg, neatly rule him out as a possible leak, because of course he would not be, and then make sure we spent time together.

But the smiley face I sent to him didn't go through; and it was only after trying and failing repeatedly that I finally realized his name was grayed out. He was no longer a "valid user" in our internal messaging system.

"HE'S BEEN GONE for a couple months," Emeril said.

"*Months*," I repeated with a calm horror.

She nodded, tapping on her keyboard to tab through his employee file. It was clear acrylic, glowing with pink RGB Lights. "He did all the offboarding, handed in his laptop, signed all the NDAs, and we gave him a nice reference. Haven't heard a thing."

"Did anyone ever call in the reference."

Tap, tap. "Nope."

I rubbed my temples and stared down at the surface of her desk. "So you don't know where he is."

Emeril shrugged and clicked around with her mouse a few times, almost idly. "I can find out."

"Do that." I stood up.

"You're hoping it's not him."

Her eyes were fixed on me now. Her gaze had a kind of gravity, like she was sucking in all the possible data from the world around her, drinking in my body language, my expression.

"I would deeply prefer it not be."

She looked back at the screen, typing some notes. "Right now, it's not looking good."

"Just make sure."

"I always make sure," she said dispassionately.

AR   I got another message from your boyfriend.

I SCOWLED AT the chat client priority window that had just popped up on my screen, interrupting my workflow. I was confused, thinking for a moment Artem meant to relay something about Leviathan, before a screenshot of Black Pill's email address appeared.

AU Don't you dare call him that.

AR It's more esoteric than his usual work so I thought you'd want to see it.

Artem sent through another attachment, a photo of a physical document he'd clearly taken with his phone. He included his own caption, *this mean anything to you?*

It was a photo of a low-rise building on a residential city street, close enough to a main thoroughfare that it was always noisy. I was looking at a view I could have drawn from memory: the outside of June's apartment. It was taken from across the street, from the perspective of someone standing on the opposite sidewalk. While it wasn't especially zoomed in, the photo was clearly focused on a third-floor walk-up apartment with frilly curtains in the dirty windows.

When I saw the photo I doubled over like I'd been punched, and a wave of nausea so intense gripped my stomach I thought for a horrible moment I was about to vomit into my own lap. The last time I saw that street, I was about to be grabbed by Draft goons, tossed into the back of a van, and tortured for several days. Moments before, as I left her giggling between sobs on the couch after a catastrophic breakup, was the last time I saw June.

I'd had enough security audits to know where my weak spots were and weren't. I hadn't spoken to my parents in so long they were merely vague shapes, and our losing touch was a relief to us both when it happened. There were no great first loves, just a string of misaligned connections that were pleasant at best and regrettable at worst (and Bracken at third). I had never been good at keeping friends. All my deepest vulnerabilities were firmly in my present, the people I kept around me now, the weird, spiderweb-strong network of relationships I had built since becoming whatever I was now. My past, for the most part, felt like it belonged to someone else.

Greg and June were the only two old wounds worth exploiting, and it seemed that Black Pill had found them. If he could do damage to me via one's presence in my life and the other's absence, he would.

It was no longer an option to starve him out with lack of attention.

AU Tell me where he lives. Immediately.

I EXPECTED TO feel anxious as I waited, sitting in the dark of Black Pill's dingy kitchen. Instead, I felt almost giddy. I chattered more than usual over the comms, to the point where Keller had to warn me to keep it down. When the Meat we had running surveillance confirmed he'd entered the foyer to the building and was on his way up, and radio silence descended, I was overcome with a sudden need to giggle. It took a mighty effort to put away the smile that split my face and resume my poised, vaguely bored expression. And as the door opened, even as a bit of the old fear of fieldwork came back to me, it was weak and distant.

When he flicked on the light, it took him a moment to register he wasn't alone in the room. He'd dropped his messenger bag and was shrugging out of his coat when he finally noticed me. He let out a weird, startled yelp, much louder than I expected, and got caught in his sleeves.

His utter dismay dissolved the last vestiges of my nerves, and I relaxed, hands resting confidently on my cane. "Oh, calm down, that's not necessary."

He fought his way out of the garment and started to back up, groping for the door. "The fuck—" he spluttered. "You're in my house."

"Such as it is," I said, looking around. I picked up the paper bag I'd placed in the middle of his kitchen table earlier and waggled it enticingly. "I brought doughnuts."

He was jiggling the knob now, more and more frantically, but it refused to yield to him. His eyes somehow got even wider, his face gray with bright pink spots on his cheeks. He was starting to sweat.

"You're not in any danger . . . at the moment."

"Let me out."

"Sorry, that's nonnegotiable."

A tiny spark of anger appeared in the middle of his fear, and he tried taking a step toward me. "Let me out." I could see why he thought physical intimidation might be a good idea, since he was much taller than me and I had a prominent mobility device.

He was, of course, profoundly mistaken, as I was neither limited by my own base physicality nor interested in playing fair. One of the Meat I had working with me showed an impeccable sense of timing and turned on their laser sight at Black Pill's first significant move forward. They started it low, in the middle of his chest, and trailed it up slowly until it centered on his forehead. He reacted as though it was a tarantula crawling up his torso; the clawing horror to get out of his own body unsatisfied, he pressed himself back against the door as tightly as he could. The laser sight disappeared when he was still, but we both knew while it might be off, the person aiming it was still paying very close attention.

"I'm just here to talk, but only as long as you don't do anything stupid. Well—stupider than you've been doing."

"Fuck this." His voice was low and tight.

"That's fair, I might not believe me either, but it's still true." I gestured to the chair across from me. "Have a seat."

"And have my head blown off?"

"Nah, probably not. They don't want to get blood on me. Have a doughnut."

He refused to move. I shrugged, fished around in the bag, and took out a small circle of fried dough covered in cinnamon sugar. While he watched, I went to the fridge, fished out two bottles of limeade, then went through his drawers until I found a bottle opener. Once I'd popped both the lids and placed one on the table near the empty seat, I took my own drink and sat back down.

His breathing grew less ragged while he watched me. He was still sweating and his hands shook, but the immediate adrenaline spike was loosening its grip. After a long moment, watching me nibble my doughnut, he slowly made his way to the chair. I gestured encouragingly for him to sit, brushing sugar off my lap.

"These are great," I said.

"What the fuck is happening?" He rested his hand on the back of the chair and very slowly sat down, making sure that none of his movements drew the ire of the laser sight.

I shrugged. "Nothing."

He stared at me. He was absolutely furious but had no way to express it in a way that might not be fatal.

"Oh, to be clear, it's a very particular kind of nothing," I said helpfully.

"Fuck off with your villain dialogue."

"Aw, but I worked so very hard on it."

"What are you doing?"

"You should be proud, you know. This is exactly what you wanted. You got my attention."

He didn't say anything, just stared at the table, leaving me to make the conversational moves.

"Unfortunately for you, that means I've been forced to leave my extremely comfortable office, put on real pants, and do something about it."

He was regaining, if not confidence, at least some of his arrogance. "So this is, what? You confronting your nemesis?"

I stared him down with brutal contempt. "No."

He was taken aback. "What?"

"You are not my nemesis."

He sneered, liking that he'd got to me in some way. "You don't have a say in the matter."

"I am literally the only one with a say in the matter."

He snarled. "I have declared our enmity. I am determined to thwart you in whatever ways that I can. I—"

"'Thwart'? Now you sound like a fucking hero."

His lip curled. "You can't just reject my hatred."

"I assure you that I can."

His voice became more shrill. "We are enemies! You being here proves it! That means *I'm your enemy*!"

"What a scintillating tautology." I cocked my head to one side. "You are, at most, very irritating. However, I will concede that while being an irritant, you have now fucked into a realm of my consciousness where I must take action."

I pulled out a copy of the photo he'd sent, of June's house, and laid it on the table next to the greasy paper bag. A smile spread over his face, slowly, like mold across a petri dish. He was genuinely proud of this one.

"I knew that would get you."

"And unfortunately for you, you were right."

It finally occurred to him that his success might, after all, be having some negative consequences. "Are you. Are you going to—"

"I already said you are not going to be harmed in any way."

His relief was visible, a physical shudder and deflating. He was immediately embarrassed by it and tried to recover. "I don't believe you."

I lifted my littlest fingertip. "What if I pinkie promise."

"So what, you're going to *ask* me to leave you alone? Buy me off?" He sounded deeply disappointed.

"I'm old-fashioned, I guess. I wanted to be able to give you the terms in person."

He learned forward, almost excitedly. "The terms." Clearly that phrase made him feel like we were negotiating, like he was a part of this.

"In exchange for remaining alive, you stay the fuck away from her, and you never bother me again." I waved my hand over the photo of June's house.

"I—"

"To make sure that you don't already have something unpleasant in motion, you're going to stay here, in this house, in a nice little bubble, for the next few days. Just until we can confirm nothing unfortunate is going to happen. I'm sure you have enough groceries to get you through. And now you even have doughnuts. Your phone and internet won't be available, sadly, so it might be a little boring, but I'm sure you have a few gigs of pirated anime on a hard drive somewhere that you've been meaning to catch up on."

"But—my job—" He sounded genuinely worried.

"You won't be going."

"Do they know?"

I almost felt bad for him. He'd learned only a few minutes ago he was under super-illegal house arrest, and he was worried about how that would go over at the office. For all the fuckery I'd suffered there was never a moment I worried that Leviathan would be upset at me for being kidnapped.

I worked to kill the sympathy I felt. "Would you like me to send a sick note?"

"You can't—"

"I really can."

"But—"

"Oh, also: If there was anything you had in the works in regards to my former associate here, you should definitely let us know and call it off. It would be *very* unfortunate for you if anything were to happen to her. At all."

"This is—you—" He looked like he was trying to say five things at once, each fighting to be the first out of his mouth.

"You look like you're going to hurt yourself."

He flushed deeper. "You fucking bitch."

I licked some cinnamon sugar off my fingers. "I could do a lot worse, you know."

He didn't reply, and I could see he was caught between rage and fear. He wasn't afraid of me personally, which was a shame, but the entire situation, its unpredictability, was keeping him pinned in place.

"Don't be too worried, though. I'm better than you. If I were one of the good guys, I'd have lobotomized you already. Classic hero stuff."

I stood up. He watched me closely, tense.

"I just want you to take some personal days and reflect on your actions. You deserve it, don't you think? A little staycation. And after this, neither of us will ever have to think about the other again."

He flexed his hands, looked around the kitchen. The linoleum floors had an unpleasant stickiness under my shoes, and his sink held a small pile of forgotten dishes encrusted with old tomato sauce.

"Try and enjoy yourself," I said, squeezing as much distain into the phrase as I could. I nodded to him, then moved past him toward the door. I passed close enough that I could smell the sour brine of fear on him.

When I turned the knob, he made a small move, as though he was thinking of lunging after me, using this opportunity to launch himself through the door. The laser sight immediately became visible again and I pointed to it on his chest. He looked down and was once more stuck to his chair as sure as a pin through a bug. Once I was certain he wasn't going to actually try anything stupid, I left, letting the door close behind me. I didn't intend for it to open again for the next seventy-two hours.

I walked into the apartment next to his. Conveniently empty, we'd commandeered it for the next few days as a base of operations. Three of our Meat were in the room and all of them looked up when I entered. One was wearing a pair of headphones and was hunched over a laptop displaying video feeds from the various cameras we'd hidden throughout Black Pill's apartment. Another was lounging on the leather couch of unknown origin, a rifle leaning across their knees and chest.

"Feel good?" the third Meat asked, standing near his surveillance colleague.

"Excellent," I said. "Spectacular work on the laser pointer."

Surveillance cranked a thumb toward a window. "Lane's on the opposite roof."

I kissed my fingertips.

"What now?" That came from the Meat with the gun.

"Very easy and boring. Make sure he doesn't leave, talk to anyone who's not one of us, or have contact with the outside world. Thursday afternoon, just pack up and let him go."

"What kind of prevention you looking for?"

"Just keep him in there."

They all nodded.

My earpiece crackled and I touched the side of my head, adjusting it.

"You're being way too nice to that fuck," Keller grumped.

"I'm doing a thing."

"I got a few things I'd like to do while we're at it."

"I'm trying to come across as sophisticated and better than them—it's a whole vibe I'm cultivating."

"No one's even paying that much attention."

That stung for some unknown reason. "Rude."

"Don't you like heads on pikes?"

"I also like leaving a survivor to relay the terrors they experienced. Besides, this feels more like winning."

"I get to say I told you so when this bites you in the ass."

"As long as you'll still ride in with the cavalry."

"Of course I will, how the fuck else are you going to say I was right if you're dead?"

I smiled widely. "Get fucked."

THE NEXT MORNING, I woke less stressed than I had felt in weeks. For the next seventy-two hours, everything would be mercifully uneventful. I would have no one else who once mattered to me endangered. My colleagues off campus would suffer no DDoS attacks, my sources would not have their relationships outed to their intolerant families, and I would not have to waste the energy and cycles of brain uptime trying to put out any fires. And if everything went the way I wanted it to, June would stay safe, and I would not have to live with the guilt that I was directly responsible for putting her in the line of danger again. I was feeling downright cheery about the whole thing until I received a text from Keller.

> MISSION ABORTED

My throat felt like it was closing in. "Aborted" didn't mean he'd escaped, or that things were going sideways, but that someone had canceled the mission mere hours in. There were very few people with the authority to do so, and I couldn't fathom why they would. Gripping my phone with both hands I texted Keller.

> wHAT HAPPENED???

The three little "I'm typing dots" dots hovered on the screen for a suspiciously long time.

> You Should Probably
> Come Down Here.

The immense frustration I was feeling began to be dampened by worry.

> Is everyone alright?

> Ours. Yes.

Any further questions were left on read, so I hauled my ass all the way down to Enforcement, hovering between concern that would boil over into fury as soon as I needed it.

Keller was waiting for me at the security checkpoint, and his face had an unusual softness I didn't recognize. It alarmed me, but not enough to wipe out how frustrated I was.

"What did he do, did the fucking Draft—"

He looked at me with an expression I would have thought was sympathy had it appeared on someone else's face. "I'll show you." He gestured for me to follow him into his office.

I was starting to get really worried now. "Are the Meat . . . Is everyone okay?" He ushered me into the room and closed the door behind me before answering.

"The extraction was completely uneventful; they're on their way back now."

I felt a helpless confusion, and hated it. "Did something fail? Why didn't you tell me before you called it off?"

"I didn't call it off." He gestured for me to sit in the chair in front of his desk, and then took up a position behind it.

"Stop being so fucking vague! Who the fuck else—"

I didn't finish the sentence, because I knew, of course, what that meant.

"But . . . why?" I hated how upset I sounded.

Keller didn't answer me, too focused on hunting-and-pecking out a few words on his keyboard.

I sifted through my last few conversations with Leviathan in my head, looking for evidence that his faith in me had wavered, that he had a reason to believe I couldn't pull this off or that it was a bad idea. "Why would he—"

Then Keller turned his monitor to face me. It was a recording of the security footage from inside Black Pill's apartment. The camera was somewhere in the ceiling, probably a light fixture or a smoke detector. The video was paused, showing Black Pill standing in his kitchen mid-stride.

"Listen first," Keller said. He hit *play* on a second window, which held no video but an audio file.

It was quiet for a moment, just breathing and shuffling, then the sound of a door opening.

"Deep, you're not on for another—" The Meat who was speaking cut himself off with a gasp. "Sir!"

There was the sound of chairs scraping as everyone in the surveillance room sprang to their feet.

"You are dismissed," Leviathan said gently. His voice was light and casual, though with a little more buzzing interference than usual.

"Um, is the mission—"

"It is no longer necessary." I heard the click of his footsteps. "Take your things with you. Extraction will meet you at your fallback point."

I heard Leviathan close the door behind him and then a burst of frantic activity, hushed voices speaking over each other as they began packing frantically.

Keller stopped the audio. The arrow of his mouse crawled across the screen horrifically slowly—his sensitivity was clearly turned down to some unfathomable level—and then hit *play*.

Black Pill paced his kitchen, clearly talking to himself. There was no audio feed from the room, just the video file, but I could see his lips move and his arms swing angrily. He stopped suddenly, and looked toward the door. He sneered and called out, squaring his shoulders.

Then, it was as though his body collapsed into itself. His eyes went wide and he backed up until he hit the edge of his kitchen counter. He gripped the edge with one hand and held out the other in front of him, in a desperate gesture of supplication.

Leviathan stepped into the frame. He moved with a casual grace, no threat at all in his body language. He stood in front of the cowering Black Pill and let him talk, regarding him with an amused curiosity.

When Black Pill finally ended his monologue, Leviathan took a half step closer. I guessed he had spoken, because Black Pill redoubled his pleading, sinking most of the way to the ground.

The video paused. Keller stared at me until I looked at him.

"Do you want to see this?" His voice was neutral, neither kind nor patronizing.

He was offering me an out. Despite the sick cold feeling that was gathering in my chest, and the part of me that very much wanted to take the mercy he was offering, I turned it down.

"Yes. Play it."

He didn't ask me to reconsider, just clicked and let the video run.

Leviathan had shifted his body language slightly, standing in a relaxed contrapposto, so that he appeared almost bored. Black Pill was still talking, but appeared slightly less panicked now. He dragged himself up to his feet, and splayed out both of his hands, as though trying to appeal rationally to the supervillain standing in his kitchen.

There is a particular kind of speed that only spiders have. You can be staring right at one, utterly still on the wall, and almost without out seeming to move, it is suddenly, terrifyingly somewhere else without seeming to have needed to move its limbs. That was the way Leviathan moved now, and then Black Pill was in his hands.

It was quick, but not quick enough. The man came apart for him like paper, like dough, like a little bundle of sticks. I tried to think of him as an object, to process what I was seeing in terms or relative strengths—that was as easy as cracking an egg, that was like tearing Plasticine in half. It was almost as though I wasn't looking at a body at all, because a body would have presented far more resistance, but I could not dissociate completely. I hated how long it took him to stop moving.

Then there was a little pile of Black Pill left in the center of the room. Leviathan used a dishcloth from the sink to wipe off his hands and forearms, and then dropped the soaked cloth on the body on the floor. As he turned to leave, as unbothered as he'd come in, Keller stopped the video.

"Well." He heaved a sigh. I waited for the second half of whatever he might say, but he remained silent.

"Where is he?"

"He's on his way back." He sucked his teeth. "I might wait a bit before you go see him. Let him take a shower first, at least."

I WAS WAITING in Leviathan's office for him. He wasn't surprised to see me—the security system would have informed him the second the door opened and his office was occupied. He brought with him a slight increase in humidity and a fresh, herbal scent from the shower he'd just taken, and there was a lightness about him that was almost cheerful.

I'd been around enough people now, heroes and villains, right after they'd killed someone to know that very rarely did they behave like you'd expect. I would have assumed taking a life was something that left a palpable impression, a weight that followed you at least for a while, like a gravity well formed at the site of such a huge change in the universe. But that was almost never the case. Sometimes, usually after the first time, you could feel the huge weight of their guilt—it was something I'd seen in fresh Meat from time to time. But most of the time, very little changed, especially if there were no significant consequences.

There was no weight at all clinging to Leviathan. If anything, something had been lifted, and I realized as I watched him that he was genuinely happy to see me. "Has my surprise been spoiled?"

"You killed him."

He nodded, then sighed in theatrical disappointment. "I'd hoped to tell you myself, but no matter." He watched me like I was opening a present in front of him and he was eager to see my reaction.

I struggled to find a way to communicate with him. "I am experiencing . . . complicated emotions."

There was a thoughtful ripple of his mandibles, and he came to sit near me. "Unfortunate but understandable."

"I just wanted to . . . contain him for a while."

He put a hand on my shoulder. "Your restraint was working against you. Harming you." He spoke like he was telling me something I might find slightly embarrassing.

"How so?"

"His most recent escalation caused you significant distress. An opportunity he should have never had."

"I would have handled it."

"You would have. Admirably. However, I found it unacceptable . . ." He thought for a moment, trying to filter the words properly. "That he destabilized you."

"You killed him because he upset me."

He shifted in his seat and crossed his legs, settling into a more languidly comfortable position. "It was clear your own internal rules of engagement would not allow you to take the necessary next steps."

He wasn't insulting me, exactly, but there was a bit of fond condescension I picked up on. "I was not afraid to kill him. I just didn't think killing him was necessary."

He waved a hand. "And you would have continued suffering for it. Giving him power over you. So I took the liberty. Now you may continue your work unobstructed and also get a fresh measure of peace."

"I wanted to handle it myself." I hated how my voice sounded almost petulant, and I felt my cheeks start to burn.

"Handle it yourself?" He uncrossed his legs and leaned forward. He brought a hand up to his chin. Something had occurred to him he hadn't considered. "You do not need to prove your capabilities in a vacuum, Auditor. The issue is one of mercy, not competence."

He was trying, very hard, to figure out what was bothering me, and had hit upon something that would have bothered him were our places reversed. And he wasn't entirely wrong; some part of me bristled at the idea that he felt it necessary to step in and take more dramatic action my "boundaries" prevented me from taking. I flailed internally, trying to find a way to say *it's fucked up to kill someone like you did just for upsetting me.*

"I am having a hard time processing the . . . extremity of your reaction," I finally said.

He gave a single short hum. "Did you access the surveillance feed?"

"Keller showed me."

That seemed to irritate him, but the feeling, I suspected, was directed at Keller, not me. "I did not wish for you to witness the specifics." He shifted his shoulders. "I would have planned to bring you with me if I thought you would have enjoyed it."

I was suddenly worried I'd placed Keller in danger, and tried to backpedal. "He wanted me to know what happened to the mission when I received the auto-alert, he—"

He waved his hand. "Keller's judgment may not match my own, but it is always sound." Which was his way of telling me his head of

Enforcement would survive my admission. "Regardless, you saw. I wish you hadn't. Don't allow the details to matter more to you than the outcome. That is what you should focus on."

I took a deep breath and let it out. "Looking at the outcome, it doesn't seem . . . enough of a reason for him to die."

His face lit up, like something had clicked into place in his head. "Ah. I see." He leaned forward again and took one of my hands in two of his. He held it like it was an injured bird, something very delicate he didn't want to harm and was also preventing from hurting itself by keeping it still. "Auditor. You care deeply about fairness. It is one of your finer qualities. And to your calculations, his life was not enough of a price to pay for troubling you."

He loosened his grip slightly, so he could touch the back of my hand with his fingertips. "But you see, I don't. And I have no interest whatsoever in being fair."

He smiled at me, in the way he could smile, a happy fluttering of his mouthparts. And I felt myself smile back, over the horror, as part of me contorted with guilt and disgust and the rest vibrated with an awful kind of gratitude.

MOM CALLED ME, once they'd found Black Pill's body. It took a pitifully long time. I wondered how many weeks the Draft would have just kept sending him automated warnings about not filling out his timesheets if a downstairs neighbor hadn't repeatedly complained to a recalcitrant super about a smell.

"He didn't deserve that," Mom said, without saying hello.

"I beg to differ," I said, presenting a united front.

"He was a civilian. An auditor."

"He wasn't playing civilian. More, he had personally targeted me. The Auditor."

"That's . . . partly my fault, I think."

"So you knew?"

"I did."

"You should have warned him not to pick a fight with me, then."

"He was so focused on you, and learning how you operate; it was good for him. And he was just doing his job. Just like you."

That was a cheap shot, and I refused to let him get away with it. "He sent me a picture he took of my best friend's house, with a clear threat. She's a civilian, too."

He sighed, deeply. "Is she?"

"She is, you piece of shit."

"Hey, there's no need for that."

"You're the one who called me up to *chide* me for that son of a bitch when he was willing to fuck with a person completely not involved, an *innocent bystander.* I know you love those."

"Not to victim blame here, but I know her work history. If she's your best friend, how innocently can she be standing?"

"*Former* best friend. I should have clarified."

"Ah."

"Did he have to harm her before he deserved it?"

He took a few deep breaths before answering me. "I know we don't use the same formulas. I don't fully expect you'll understand. Douglas . . . he was a lot, as a person, and could sometimes stray further than we liked from the good work. But he did much more good than not, overall."

It occurred to me I'd never known Black Pill's government name, and I felt weirdly offended on his posthumous behalf that Mom had used it now.

"I was unwilling to let my ex-friend be a part of that *balancing.*"

"I hope she's worth it."

"She is," I snarled. I knew he would have considered her work and life an unfair trade for that repulsive human he thought was working for the good guys, and I hated him more for it.

"You're really racking up the numbers lately, Anna." He had a bone-deep disappointment in his voice now. "You had a much better chance at a different life before, but now you're . . . It's really getting close."

"Your concern is moving."

"I wanted—I still want better for you."

"You know. I have to give you some credit. You almost got me."

"Oh? What did I almost do?"

"Your act. Your entire performance. I thought I knew what you were doing, but it was even better than I guessed."

"It's not an act, Anna. What you see really is what you get."

"So you're just a monster who likes cardigans and casual Fridays."

"I think I'm a little better than that."

"How many people have you killed?"

He sounded completely taken aback. "I've never killed anyone, Anna. I'm not a *villain*."

"How many people have died because of decisions you've made."

"That's . . . a very complicated question."

"It's really not."

"How many dead are *you* responsible for?" he spat back.

The number that I conjured behind my eyes was quite different from the one he intended. He wanted a clean body count; but my answer was just as complicated as how many people I'd fucked. What counted, according to who was asking, was relevant, as was the context. But I knew the lifeyears I had cost the world, could even whittle it down to months; given enough time and data, I might have been able to round it to the nearest day.

"Enough."

He flinched. "I'm sorry. That was mean of me."

"Not at all."

"Anna, I know you don't agree. But you're wrong. You're really smart, one of the smartest I've met, and that's saying something." He sighed. "But you really got life all wrong, kiddo."

"I can tell how much you care."

"Thanks."

"You know that makes it worse, not better."

"Since we're both being honest here, yes. I know."

"I don't think we have anything else to say to each other."

"Alright, Anna." There was a faintly choked quality to his voice, like the emotion was getting to him.

"I'm going to miss talking to you," I said, intending it derisively, but I found in a small way I meant it.

"I know we're not talking about the same thing, Anna. But I am really going to miss you, too."

KELLER DIDN'T LOOK up as I pulled myself into the mobile command vehicle with the help of one of his Meat. She was broad and blunt-featured, and closed the door behind me hard. I took a seat next to him and put on a headset without being invited.

We were parked in a corner of the large central courtyard, surrounded by a handful of other armored vehicles. In front of us, visible on the wall of surveillance screens in front of us, three huge cannons were being rolled out onto the grass. Their wheels cut troughs into the manicured sod; if I looked carefully, I could just barely see huge lighter patches of grass scattered throughout the yard, where enormous chunks had been torn out and blasted open when Supercollider and Leviathan last fought here. Even the ground had scars.

Keller stabbed one of the screens with a finger, breaking me out of my brooding.

"There she is."

I squinted and saw a tiny silhouette, flying fast toward us. Several of the screens jumped and refocused as the cameras were turned toward her.

Keller unmuted his headset. "Southwest, coming in hot."

As the cameras zoomed in, I noticed something about her shape wasn't quite right.

"She's got something in her arms."

Before anyone could answer, Vesper's voice came over the comms.

"I have visual. It's Red Sprite."

Keller switched channels to address the Meat positioning the cannons. "Load cannon number two with a retiarius." The gunners acknowledged the order; one started prepping the barrel while the other two selected a mortar packed with what they called an "energy net." Named after a type of Roman gladiator, the retiarius was much more like firing a chain-link fishing net wired to a car battery out of a cannon than some glittering grid of light.

I turned my mic on with a quick tap. "Vesper, can you see what she's carrying?" I asked.

There was a crackling pause before he answered. "Looks like a duffel bag." Vesper was in one of the smaller, highly maneuverable recon vehicles that moved suddenly and erratically, like a wasp. The cloaking on it was good, most effective from a distance, but the heat shimmer of it was recognizable up close. It was covered in quantum panels that "bent light" around the shape, and it made me weirdly uncomfortable to try and look at.

"I have a clean shot," Vesper said.

I shook my head as though he could see me from the cockpit. "No, I need her."

Keller frowned but didn't argue. "Scan the payload."

"Not getting anything from it. Nothing electrical or chemical, no heat signatures."

Keller spoke again to the gunners. "One and three, load with mortars. Anything she drops, shoot it down. As soon as she crosses into our airspace, net her."

I resisted the urge to reiterate I wanted Red Sprite to live through whatever spectacularly stupid gesture she was presently in the middle of.

Keller angled his body slightly toward me. "So. Your friends over there say anything about this visit."

"No." I watched her silhouette get closer, a stark, determined little outline of a person in an obnoxiously gallant flight pose. "But she's not acting alone." I'd expected Mom to fire back, and this was right on cue.

"She seems like the kind to listen to orders," Keller observed.

"She does."

"So why send a single one of your flagship heroes to certain death."

"They sent her in before; she's clearly the one they're willing to gamble on."

Before Keller could answer, Vesper's voice was in my ears. "She's stopped."

"Did she see you?"

He took a second to consider before he answered. "I don't think so. She's just outside the border."

I watched the screen intently. Red Sprite had pulled up suddenly, a dozen or so meters from our no-fly zone. She had her head tilted to one side, as though listening to instructions. After a moment, she hefted the duffel bag into her arms, and threw it toward the center of Leviathan's compound.

She was stronger than I was prepared for. I knew she had some superstrength, it was necessary for her to be able to fly, but I'd underestimated how that would translate to other kinds of athleticism. The bag flew in a strong arc, like an expertly thrown football, beginning its decent over the first few buildings on the southwestern edge of the compound.

The three cannons in the courtyard fired in quick succession, two toward the bag and the third toward Red Sprite herself. The retiarius net opened, the weighted ends spiraling toward her like a bolus. She didn't dodge to the side to try and escape, but suddenly dropped in a way that made me feel nauseated. It was like gravity suddenly regained a grip on her, and she was falling with horrifying velocity. Just as quickly, she stopped herself and bobbed back into a hover midair.

Both mortars narrowly missed the bag, one high and one slightly wide.

But Vesper doesn't miss—breaking cloak, he fired on the bag, which exploded like it had been filled with confetti.

Red Sprite zoomed upward, matching the altitude of Vesper's angry wasp. She stopped when she was level with the cockpit, and she and the insectoid vehicle seemed to make eye contact with each other, goggles to windshield. Whatever Red Sprite was considering, whether it was her own volition or a handler screaming in her ears through a communication device, she abandoned her inclination to throw hands with a helicopter. With a final glare, she turned and sped off.

"Fire or pursue?" Vesper asked.

He might have been asking Keller, but I answered. "Follow her but let her leave. And break off if you meet any resistance."

Vesper acknowledged the order and the wasp sped off in pursuit.

Outside the command vehicle, it was snowing paper. Mostly tiny scraps, many singed from the mortar, but many larger pamphlets had survived. Keller called for a hazmat team to contain and clean up whatever they were, and the gunner cleared the field. Shortly after, the first few cleaners in full-body PPE start rolling out industrial hoses.

One of the phones mounted to the console in front of Keller started to ring, and I got to witness a small argument between R&D and Enforcement, the latter of whom wanted to collect and analyze what was falling out of the sky before it was hosed down into slush.

"It doesn't matter what it is," Keller groused. "It needs to be neutralized."

I could hear angry squawking on the other end of the phone. I put a hand on his shoulder, and Keller covered the receiver with one hand so we could talk.

"I want a sample," I said.

He scoffed. "It's either toxic or nothing. There's your data."

"No. I want to see what it says."

He stared at the screen for a minute, processing, and then nodded. He pulled his hand away from the receiver and agreed to collect a few of the sheets of paper and bag them for analysis before spraying everything down with denatured water and neutralizing foam.

The sheets were not toxic. There were no acids or hallucinogenics embedded in the pages, no toxins or viral loads. The only thing on them was a message printed in waterproof ink that read, YOU CAN ALWAYS COME HOME. On the reverse was a QR code.

The code led to a press release about what the Draft was calling the Amnesty Initiative. They were offering a brief window of immunity to any hench working for Leviathan who wanted to leave. There would be no prosecution, no societal debt to work off. If they wanted out, they just had to say so, and they would be given protection, career counseling, "anything you need to get back on your feet and walking a new path."

Leviathan's sins don't have to be yours. It might be a terrifying prospect to leave, and you might feel like you have no choice.

We want to acknowledge that we, the Draft, have contributed to that. We have been all too eager to see the world in black and white. But we all know the world is complicated, and while it might seem like there is no way out, we want to assure you that there is.

There is hope. This is an offer for anyone who wants to get out, to start over. We want to open the door.

But forgiveness wasn't going to wait forever. The Draft didn't state outright how long the program might be available, with the "evolving and volatile" situation with Leviathan—but right now, anyone who left was guaranteed safety, repatriation, whatever help they needed to get back on their feet and start a new life.

I wondered, at first, if it was all a ruse. I could see the Draft pulling such a deception, luring a cohort of stressed, desperate henches out of hiding, only to imprison and interrogate them, or worse. But, to my increasing horror, the offer seemed to be genuine.

The physical flyers were, of course, matched with a public digital campaign. It was important to get public buy-in on the amnesty program, to paint many of the henches in Leviathan's employ as good, talented souls who had gone astray for one reason or another, and who now believed that there was no way out of those bad decisions. They needed to humanize us if the initiative was going to have a real chance at working.

"If there's one thing we know about prodigal children," said one of the voice-overs in an ad spot, laid over a stock video of a sunrise, "it's that they should be embraced and welcomed home."

Mom himself appeared on morning news shows and high-profile pro-hero podcasts, repeating the same infuriatingly effective messages. Every appearance featured a new cardigan over a new T-shirt with some kind of inspirational, inclusive message. "We know how it looks. We know it seems we have not done enough to bring justice to those who took justice from us. But in our hearts, we knew we couldn't live with ourselves if we took everyone working for Leviathan down with him." I bit my lip until I tasted blood while I listened to him talk about all of the reasons someone might be "driven" to make such a terrible choice as to work for a supervillain.

"It's easy to sit here and say, 'Everyone who has thrown their lot in with a villain deserves whatever they get,'" Mom said, talking to a late-night talk show host. Both he and the host were drinking out of World's Best Mom coffee mugs, which Mom had brought as a gift. "But we know in our hearts that's not true. Henches are just people who are in a bad situation, who think this is the only choice they have. We don't know what's led them there."

"But this is a serious situation," the host said, adjusting his hot-pink tie.

"It's because the situation is so serious that we have to show mercy," Mom said.

"At the end of the day," Mom's voice was somehow mournful and parental at once, "we didn't want a single person who would have left Leviathan to stay because they thought there was nothing else left for them. We had to show them that there is a way, there is always a way. And if we wanted to be telling the truth when we said that, then we had to make that way for them too."

Soon, the heroes returned. This time it was a pair of them; Tungsten Man used Elasta's body like a slingshot to launch several bundles of pamphlets into the courtyard before Keller's artillery fired a pair of massive glueballs in their direction and chased them off. A few days later it was Orbweaver, who slung them in using webbing that clogged half of the vents and gutters of the compound. By the end of the week, Recoil had also made an appearance, ripping the package apart high over the compound with a kinetic blast. It was clear they had orders to withdraw at the first show of force or resistance, to just deliver the latest batch of propaganda and run. New flyers every day, not that they were needed. Everyone working under Leviathan's employ knew about the offer by then, either from the messages directly or the endless stream of social media announcements and advertisements in the world at large.

The Draft's offer of amnesty wasn't just benevolent, of course. Behind it was the at first implicit—soon explicit—threat that those who did not take the offer would be considered lost, and whatever fate befell them was entirely on them. Not taking this chance meant recommitting to the forces of evil, and that would be something that would not be so easily walked back. Leaving during the amnesty meant protection and forgiveness; not leaving was its own kind of declaration of war. There would be no mercy for anyone who stayed behind.

"This isn't a door we can leave open forever," Mom said during the very last interview he would give on the subject. It was a serious one-on-one interview with a long-form news program. This time, the cardigan was gray, and the shirt he wore beneath had buttons. "As much as I want to say that everyone should take all the time they need, that's not true. I can't say when, but the door is going to close, and when it does . . ." He paused, as though overcome with emotion, and when he continued, his voice was hoarse. "When it does, we won't be able to protect them anymore."

IT WORKED. THE talent bleed we'd experienced turned into a hemorrhage; more and more people were leaving every day. Anyone who might have stayed because of ease or inertia, or the relative safety and security the job meant alone—that was no longer enough. Entire wings, then entire buildings were shut down as the remaining employees relocated into the center of the compound, the buildings immediately around Leviathan's office.

When a person experiences hypothermia, eventually all of their blood leaves their extremities and pools in the organs, keeping the most essential tissue warm. We retreated to the core of the compound, keeping it and ourselves alive.

It wasn't long before the heroes weren't coming to deliver propaganda anymore, but rather to help escort anyone who wanted to leave off the premises. They weren't hostile—they seemed to have pointed and specific orders not to be—but they were insistent. The heroes had the names of everyone who had applied for amnesty, and they would not leave without them. It was clear that they expected this to be a rescue mission, and were ready to force their way in, if necessary, to lead these misguided waifs to safety. Instead, they were greeted by that day's batch of payroll clerks and sysadmins, blinking and bewildered in the sunlight. No one was stopping them. The Draft could have sent Uber drivers every day and saved themselves considerable cost and headache.

Leviathan's reaction was consistent and unwavering: Anyone who wanted to leave was not just permitted to go but actively ejected. As soon as someone expressed anything resembling an intent to depart, their digital and security access was revoked. They were treated as little more than trespassers, and afforded the one chance to get out as quickly and passively as possible. It was not something anyone was permitted to be unsure about. You were in or you were out, and if you weren't wholeheartedly, unreservedly in, he would make the rest of the decision for you.

I expected Leviathan to be furious at every departure, to see each as a betrayal, but he was almost eerily calm.

"I will force no one to work for me. I will hold no one captive, nor threaten them into staying."

"We can't lose everyone," I said, my nerves humming with anxiety.

"We won't," he said, serene. We were walking through one of the now-empty buildings, which had become an echoing liminal space of silent cubicles and empty conference rooms. "If someone wishes to leave my service, they are welcome to. Soon they will learn they are on a path that only flows one way."

I pressed down the impulse to scream at him with well-honed skill. "While I appreciate your desire to respect everyone's autonomy, there are practical concerns–"

His delicate little mouthparts quirked up on one side, something like an amused smirk. "It is more than that." He ran the tips of his fingers across the wall as he walked by, the pads of his fingers hissing against the plaster. "This was a crucible. A filtering process. I welcome it, despite the inevitable delays and . . . inefficiencies we might experience. It will be worth it."

I thought back to my conversation with Menachem, shortly after Supercollider's death, when the first waves of my colleagues quit. When we lost Tammy. He'd told me this was a part of a cycle, an ebb and flow that always happened during major crises. I tried to see it as part of the same process, one further manifestation that we just had to get through, that we might even be stronger for. But it did not feel like the same thing; this was the Draft taking advantage of that cycle and using it to do as much damage as they could with it.

"I would never suggest we force anyone to stay," I ventured. "I don't want anyone who would waver here either. But there are so many who would have stayed, who would have been loyal, had the Draft not pressed them."

"Loyalty that crumbles under pressure is not loyalty. Devotion must survive inconvenience and threat to matter." He made a soft hum. "When you came to me, I had been successful for a very long time. You had not seen us at the beginning."

"That's true." I felt a pang of loss; I would not have even been an adult when Leviathan was established as a villain, but I wished I somehow could have been there, to see what he would have done with nothing, when he was so much younger and incandescent with hatred.

As though sensing what I thought (and, maybe he was simply reading my vitals), Leviathan reached out and took my hand, squeezing my fingers. "You would have loved it then. But now, in a way, you will get to see how it was in those early days.

"It is inevitable," he continued, "that when one thrives as I have, not everyone inside these walls would be heart-and-soul devoted to the enmity of all heroes."

"How could they be," I agreed.

"This is a winnowing event. When it is done, only the most committed will be the ones left behind. And so far, no one has truly disappointed me."

"No?" That surprised me. I had been disappointed many times already: it seemed every day someone I delighted in working with stopped replying to their IMs, and their emails started to bounce.

I thought again, with horrified betrayal, to Greg, and shoved the thought away forcefully.

"Everyone I knew would stay has stayed," Leviathan was saying, with a surprising amount of affection. "You see loss, and you are right. But many have surprised me with their commitment, as well. Many more are here than I would have counted on. Some may yet go. But those who do not, especially those I might not have guessed would remain—I will not forget this."

He stopped suddenly and took my chin in his hand, quickly enough that it startled me. Even though his grip was gentle. I froze, and he placed his other hand on my shoulder to steady me, and simultaneously kept me from pulling away.

"You are, as always, exactly where you are supposed to be," he said.

"FUCK," I SAID.

Emeril didn't apologize when she set the dossier in front of me. She had nothing to apologize for; she took pride in her work, and it shone from her. She had done a thorough, exceptional job, the only kind of job that she knew how to do. The fact that she had done exactly what she needed to didn't make the delivery of that data feel any less terrible to me.

"Would you like me to walk you through it?" Her voice was citrus bright.

I wanted to snatch the documents in front of me and run, to read them in the peace of my office so I could scream or cry unobserved (*no, not completely unobserved*, I reminded myself). I wanted to destroy them. I could do neither of those things for a host of different reasons, so instead, mechanically, I said, "Sure."

She flipped open the cover of the folder in front of me, so I was looking down at a pair of photographs paper-clipped to the cover page. One was Greg's official headshot, taken in the first weeks after I'd gotten him hired on. It had been a moderate favor I'd called in to even get him the interview, which he was so nervous about he nearly bombed, but I convinced the sysadmin to give him a chance. He did exactly as well as I expected him to, which was perfectly competent after he settled in and stopped being so goddamn nervous about everything. He'd been good to me when I was at my weakest, and when I'd bent the universe into a shape that suited me better, I'd wanted to return the favor in whatever small ways I could.

The second photo was much lower quality, a still from what looked like someone's door surveillance camera. It was much more recent, taken within the last couple of weeks. He was walking down a sidewalk with a pair of new colleagues, far away from Leviathan's compound. He had a fresh haircut, more standard business-casual clothing than the "literally whatever" dress code he would have followed while working here. All three of them were wearing visible lanyards and employee IDs. Emeril had conveniently zoomed in on his, highlighting that part of the image, which while grainy, unquestionably bore the Draft logo.

"I'll give you the highlights," Emeril said. "He left long before amnesty was offered. I suspect he may have been a sort of . . . prototype for the program. He was unemployed for a short while, and seemed to be a little lost, honestly. He submitted a résumé to the Temp Agency but pulled it just a couple of days later. The reason he gave on the form was 'received another offer of employment.'

"They reached out to him first, if it matters to you," Emeril offered primly.

"It does," I said, more viciously than I intended to. It meant that while he might have left under his own volition, he did not run to them on purpose. He might have walked through a door they opened in front of him, but he hadn't knocked. It wasn't much, but it was something.

"Looking through your chat logs," Emeril continued, directing me again to flip forward, "it seems like you hadn't had much contact in the months before he left."

Guilt tried to rear up in me and I crushed it back down. "That's right."

"Was there anything he *couldn't* have known? Any details that might have had another source?"

Emeril was not looking for any kind of an out for him; she merely wanted to know if this was the only loose end that needed tying, or if there was anyone else in the organization who could be a secondary leak. So I thought carefully, thinking over every inconvenience, every foiled plan I had suffered at the hands of Black Pill.

"No," I said, after a while. "The biggest blows were personal, and a lot of the smaller ones had either been in motion for a long time—something I might have mentioned to him—or could have been gleaned from tendencies, preferences."

"The problem was that he *knew* you," Emeril said.

"Knows me," I corrected, then looked up sharply, in case her past tense meant something more violent.

"I have not acted on this information without confirming everything with you first," Emeril said coolly, not in any way that could be construed as comforting, and yet I still cared enough to feel relief. "Of course, if you are comfortable that the results of this investigation are conclusive, I can move to take care of it."

"He's left the organization. Doesn't that make him outside of your jurisdiction?" I tried very hard to keep my voice calm and even, as though we were not discussing, in her beautifully appointed office, murdering one of my oldest friends.

"Usually, it would," she allowed, "since no contact was made while he was still employed by us. But there are exceptions, and he has hit on two of them. One, he's discussed details of active, ongoing projects, which is very clearly covered in his NDA. Not dealing with the matter places every operation at risk, and our policies are very clear.

"More importantly, however, is that he is an ongoing security threat because of the sensitive nature of additional information he possesses."

"Information about what?"

She looked at me with a patience she clearly did not feel. "About you."

The knots in my stomach tied themselves tighter. "You mean about me personally."

She nodded crisply. "He is clearly privy to a great deal of personal information that exposes vulnerabilities."

I thought about the podcast interview about me on *Behind the Masc*, the one that dredged up Bracken, whom I had merely gone on one bad date with. I thought about how much that had rattled me, and how much worse it could be if Greg gave them an interview. I tried to imagine the worst he could say, all of the sniveling things I had ever told him in moments of weakness because I trusted him, in the way you trust people who are just as pathetic as you are not to break that mutual confidence.

"Let me handle this," I heard myself saying. "I want to take care of it myself."

Emeril leaned back in her chair and steepled her fingers, showing more surprise that she'd ever displayed before. "My entire job exists when things have progressed beyond the point where someone can handle it themselves."

"True," I said, "but that was when we thought the situation had to be internal. But since the call is coming from outside the house, things have shifted."

She did not agree with me, but she didn't immediately argue back either.

So, I pushed forward. "Now that we know what happened, I would like the chance to take care of it on my own terms. If possible, of course."

"My current charge, as always, is to Leviathan," she said. "He told me to handle it."

I was about to launch a counterargument, but then I heard Keller's words in my mind then, when he was angry at me for trying to go over his head: *He'll pretend to seriously consider all angles and then just let you do whatever you want while making it seem like it was his idea to begin with.* I hadn't believed him fully at the time... but a great deal had happened since then.

"By all means, take this to Leviathan," I said, as casually as I could manage. "Inform him I would rather take this task on personally. If he maintains you should handle it, as per your orders, that's fine, of course."

"Hmm." Emeril took out her phone and tapped out a quick note. "Certainly. I'll let you know what he says."

When the assent arrived in my inbox a few hours later, accompanied by Emeril's gorgeously designed email signature, I should have felt relieved. I had not doomed Greg to summary execution by HR, but I had not saved him. At best I had bought a tiny bit of time to figure out what I wanted to do, what I could do, at the expense of taking on the entire burden myself.

It did not feel like winning.

WHEN YOU BUILD something that needs to work under extreme conditions, and the stakes are high—say, a robot sent to explore the surface of Mars—it can't be delicate. The robot needs to crawl forward, take pictures, collect samples, and relay messages with an almost dead battery and a single functioning limb. Similarly, a gun you need to fire from a trench can't require careful handling and cleaning; it needs to fire reliably when caked in mud and blood and half rusted out. There's an incredible beauty to these systems and machines that can adjust and recalibrate and find new ways to work while broken.

Leviathan's organization was such a system. Departments whose populations were depleted fused into new configurations; unnecessary projects were abandoned, tied off as with tourniquets and left to wither so those remaining could thrive. This meant there were things we could not do, but also things we could do better than before. Plans could be put into practice quickly, sudden pivots could be made, resources reallocated. This was not to say Leviathan and his organization had not been dealt significant blows, but in some ways it made us significantly more dangerous.

It was easy to see, from the outside, how the Draft were ready to declare themselves immediately victorious. The amnesty program was being heralded as a massive success, and the Draft loved to talk about how many people were choosing a different life, a better life. How many were getting job placements, how the different agencies were banding together to get everyone resettled, finding places where they could fit, where they could belong. After the disaster that had been the literal and metaphorical dismemberment of Siegeworks (and with it a cornerstone of the CCO's bid for Draft leadership), Mom's ascent into the role of CDO was all but assured.

I wished I had the time to make things worse for him, personally, in those moments. I wanted to follow up on everyone who left us, to track their retention, their trajectory, what that acceptance would really be like when the cameras weren't rolling. I wondered how many of them would have their profiles back in the Temp Agency's databases in two years.

I did not have that luxury. Time was the only resource I could not manufacture more of on demand, couldn't bargain or barter for it. I could only use it as it sped by, and that meant not allowing my enemies even a moment to breathe or revel in their success if I could afford it. And even with limited resources, it was crucial we press forward, keep going. The best reason to apply pressure was always to disrupt, to make what they were doing harder, make them doubt themselves. Continuing to move forward, even weakened, even greatly impeded, was the greatest act of defiance I could muster.

Also, I knew the pressure was working. My access to information from inside the Draft, especially as it pertained to the Future, was reduced but not entirely severed. I knew Riot Shield was speaking to a Draft counselor more regularly than the mandatory check-ins, and was trying a course of EMDR therapy; I knew that Red Sprite had started asking many people she'd been close to—a few former classmates, an early mentor, even a few trusted handlers—if they had any idea why the Draft would have chosen her for the Future. Anytime I could knock someone off course I knew I had succeeded. With Mom and the Draft trying so hard to slow us down or stop us completely, the most demoralizing response we could offer was to stubbornly persist.

In other words, it was the perfect time to execute a bespoke kidnapping.

Well, technically, a pair of them.

Cartilage and Marrow were the weakest members of the Future, and simultaneously the strongest. Their powers were—or perhaps more accurately, would have been—the most formidable of all of them, especially when the pair used them in concert. But they were nowhere near to maximizing their potential. The structure and scope of their powers were far outside of what were typically considered "good" or "heroic" definitions. If they weren't so talented, and if the Draft weren't actively expanding their repertoire out of desperation, it was easy to see an alternate reality where they were destined to become villains from the start. People whose powers were innately tied to dismantling the human body weren't usually destined for being the good guys. As it stood, the Draft didn't have long-established models to guide their training, and it showed.

Being woefully underprepared, plus a combination of trauma and insecurity, meant that they eternally saw themselves as being in much more of a support role, even when their actions starkly belied this assumption. They often stuck close to Riot Shield (who was dropping the "Riot" more and more these days and going strictly by Shield, in what was clearly an effort to distance himself from his former teammates), almost certainly feeling that they needed protection when they had, in fact, the greatest capacity to inflict damage of any of their newfound comrades.

I also found myself wondering if, consciously or otherwise, they were making themselves seem smaller and more vulnerable to their teammates, to keep everyone else from realizing how terrifying they were.

It might have seemed obvious to attack these insecurities of their directly, to agree with their internal assumptions about themselves and deepen those wounds. But there was a risk there; they knew those insecurities so intimately, and used them to hurt themselves so often, that it might backfire.

"The danger," I said, pacing Leviathan's office, "in repeating the same things they say to themselves is that they are *too* familiar."

"Are you overthinking it?" It was not a hostile question, but one he asked both himself and all his lieutenants about plans, to make sure unnecessary complexity was not introducing unnecessary weak points into an operation.

I slowed, considering what he asked, then discarded the idea. "No. If they hear the same things they're saying in their own heads come out of the mouths of their enemies, it might give them what they need to reject both ideas. Then they have a moment of character growth and confidence and we're much worse off."

He nodded. Content I'd given the problem enough thought.

I held up a finger. "Compliments, though . . ."

"What about them?

"Weaponized compliments can destroy them completely. When someone you've been coached to hate for most of your life tells you something good about yourself—what does that say about you?"

"You believe they will reject flattery because of its source?"

"It can't be flattery. It needs to be true."

He tilted his head, as though the words were shifting weights in his mind. "So the compliments cannot be dismissed."

"Exactly." I stopped pacing and came to stand close to him. He was sitting on his desk, watching me, and I positioned myself directly in front of him, between his knees. "Whatever we tell them has to hold up to scrutiny. It's got to be something they can't just throw away. It's got to be good, and true, and worm its way into their minds—and preferably their relationships."

"Do you intend to make them jealous of each other?" He was no longer making eye contact with me, but rather looking all around my face, studying the details.

"The opposite. I don't want them to feel the other is better; I want them to shoulder the guilt of being special. They are uniquely powerful, and their twin is not. I want to see how each of them navigates being told that they are the better half."

"Something like survivor's guilt."

I nodded and placed one hand on his leg. "Their talents split them apart once. What if it happens again? There's so much trauma to dig into there. Both live in fear of the other being left behind, or leaving them behind, and raising the specter of separation will make them cling to their own insecurities even tighter. They'll do most of the damage to themselves."

He beamed at me, his admiration like its own kind of light. It was a struggle not to look down and succumb to the discomfort of being perceived.

"I am glad," he said, "that you are on my side. And only mine."

If I hadn't been holding on to him I might have fallen over; I could not imagine him paying me a higher compliment. I stared back at him, unable to control whatever emotion I could feel radiating from my face. Being glad I was on his side implied, however obliquely, he would consider me some kind of threat (or even a nuisance) were I not; it was an honor I couldn't fully process.

Weapononized compliments can destroy you completely, my awful brain echoed.

Pattern recognition was one of my finest skills, a literal superpower, and even I couldn't escape its sharp edges. If he did mean to use compliments to undo me, planting a seed now to utterly dismantle me in the future, the way he seeded it was perfect.

Mercifully, he saved me from having to dwell on that miserable idea by leaning over and tenderly biting my shoulder. Then I didn't have to do any thinking at all for a very long time.

"I'M NOT GOING to sugarcoat it: this mission is going to cost us," Keller told me when I brought him the plan. It wasn't intended to discourage me; he wasn't arguing about the necessity of what we were doing. But it was true, and he had to say it out loud. These were all his favorites, the best Enforcement had to offer, from the most basic goon to the most talented tactician. The best, after all, were all we had left. Every loss would be a hard one.

"Let's make it cost us as little as possible," I said, and he nodded. While the sentiment was valid, that was not going to be fucking easy to accomplish.

To start, actually kidnapping Cartilage and Marrow was a logistical nightmare, even more so than the usual problems with fighting assholes with laser eyes. Keller and I sat together in his office, reviewing reports and watching endless tapes of the two of them in action, looking for weak points. They were both effectively impossible to deal with physically; one could fuck with your metabolic processes and the other could turn your joints into slime. In a one-on-one, or two-on-fifty, you did not want to straight up fight them. Dealing with one was also quite different from handling the other, as their powers operated very differently. Cartilage needed physical contact with an opponent to properly melt them to jelly, while Marrow required line of sight. You needed two teams and two sets of tactics, splitting all of our resources even further.

Complicating matters was the fact that they were identical twins, and unlike their old branding, their new looks emphasized that fact rather than trying to set them apart. Their outfits were identical and they were styled the same, and so while there were small differences, it took someone who knew them well or studied them intensely to really tell. Which, when you are trying to stay alive and intact in a melee, is not realistic. Dealing with one often meant dealing with both of them, since they were rarely apart, and even if you could isolate one it was extremely likely you weren't sure whom you had isolated, so anyone making contact needed to be prepared for taking both of them on at once.

Drugs would have made things a lot easier, but Marrow could prevent anything from being metabolized by either him or his twin, so that ruled out any helpful substances. So you could not let them touch them nor let them see you; a literal nightmare scenario. I'm not sure anyone but us could have done it.

IT STARTED WITH a handshake. I briefly considered something like a glitterbomb, but I didn't want anything that would alarm them at all, even something so relatively benign. So instead we sent in one of our more genial Meat posing as an admirer, who excitedly shook Marrow's (and only Marrow's) hand when the twins made a brief appearance at a charity event. His hands were covered in invisible UV-activated dye.

After that, it was a matter of setting a trap. This wasn't difficult so much as it had to be well calibrated; we had to use their talents and training against them. The Draft did many things well, and one of them was ensuring that their heroes had finely tuned, well-honed heroic instincts. This made them powerful, efficient, and if you looked at it from the right angle, intensely predictable. We could pick a bit of theatrical evildoing that required immediate intervention, but wouldn't require them calling for any kind of backup.

We settled on a nice mugging. One of our Meat posed as a pedestrian, her muscles covered by a smartly tailored jacket. We had her act distracted, talking just loudly enough about the dry cleaning she needed to pick up, the kids who needed to be retrieved from day care. She seemed put together but frazzled, devoted but distracted. An excellent victim. We ensured that the twins were watching (they were bored, trying not to fidget, while a Draft representative gave a "candid" interview nearby), when another pair of our Meat grabbed her and, hands over her mouth, dragged her into an alley. I don't know if they managed to do it on purpose, but they handled the almost-silent scuffle in such a way that they left a single high heel toppled over at the entrance to the alley, like a tooth knocked out of a mouth.

The twins, good little do-gooders that they were, did precisely what had been drilled into them: they reacted without saying a word. A couple of other bystanders saw what happened and were squawking and pointing awkwardly where the three Meat—the attackers and our victim—had disappeared. There was no danger to the twins, not according to their internal risk-assessment calculations they were always unconsciously running. Even if the muggers had half a dozen friends waiting in the alley with bats and chains, that wouldn't have remotely resembled a problem.

What was a problem, though, was that the alley was empty. Assuming the victim they saw had been dragged all the way through and away, the twins sped up in pursuit, breaking into a run, only to find themselves unwittingly stepping into a massive snare trap. Before either could react, they were neatly swept up into a carbon-fiber blackout bag. Careful to stay well out of reach, more Meat used poles (sort of like those used to maneuver rabid dogs) and cables to drag them into the back of a waiting tactical vehicle, manned only by Melinda and a copilot. The rest of the Meat evacuated separately for safety, and to split any pursuit. But things went even better than all but the most optimistic of my time estimations; everyone was so certain that the twins were about to emerge from the alley with a grateful victim and two would-be muggers reduced to bone slurry that no one so much as checked on them until we were long gone.

My heart was in my throat the entire time Melinda drove back with her pair of volatile payloads. The back of the van was entirely dark, and there were multiple barriers between her and the cargo she carried; it would have been spectacularly unlikely for one of them to be able to get eyes or hands on her. But still, when she finally arrived, a few minutes behind the rest of the Meat, I could have wept with relief.

That feeling, however, was extremely short-lived. Because once we opened the doors, separating and containing them with minimal loss to life and limb was a new problem. We'd considered putting them in one containment chamber and sorting it out after, but scrapped that early; any time they could have together, whether just to plot or for emotional support (the latter arguably being worse), would actively be working against everything we wanted to accomplish. Even the transport itself was riskier than I would have liked, but separating them in the field had too many X factors. We needed them here to control as many variables as possible, and we needed to get them apart quickly, so they had no time to assess and regroup.

So we cut the damn bag in half. This was a dangerous process, separating and then isolating their bodies while trying to make no direct physical contact and closing the gap between them as quickly as we could. It was somewhere between pinning an insect and dissecting a frog, except with no harm involved—well, no harm to them. One of the techs cutting through the bag with a diamond-tipped bit didn't pull back quickly enough when Cartilage got a pair of his fingers through, and ended up with an arm and part of his spine melted; Marrow caught a glimpse of another through a gap that was missed, and two of our Meat collapsed, one spewing bile into her helmet, before someone stomped on the gap and held it shut.

These were planned losses; if I was an even worse person, I would have called them "acceptable losses," in that they were considered and accounted for. Part of the actuarial table that precedes any of my plans. That didn't mean that they didn't hurt. In the state we were in, we felt every loss more acutely than ever.

All told, it cost us one career and two extended recoveries to get the twins here and contained in separate rooms, physically unscathed except for a few bumps from being loaded in and later lightly stepped on. A relative bargain in today's market.

More, we had the UV paint to tell us who was who, so we knew to keep Marrow visually and Cartilage physically separated from anyone who needed to interact with them. We let them cool off for a few hours, let the adrenaline run its course and leave cold fear and exhaustion behind, yet also not so long that despair set in.

It was a fine line, but my team excelled at fine lines.

Besides, I had a promise to keep, and some texts to send.

I AGONIZED OVER how to message Decoherence, typing and deleting messages over and over. There was no reason to believe that Leviathan would be watching at that specific moment; there was also no guarantee he wouldn't be. He had not specifically instructed me to let him know every time I contacted her, but not doing so also felt somewhere between poor judgment and an active betrayal. In the end, I decided to control as many variables as I could. I would rather be uncomfortable, even to the point of crawling horror, than uncertain.

AU If I'm going to keep my commitment to Decoherence, now is the time to message her.

L Do you wish to keep it?

I thought a long moment before typing a reply (not alarmingly too long, I hoped), trying to find a way to say "I want to" that didn't convey too much of that wanting.

AU Not communicating now would sever that tie completely. Keeping it, for now, has more benefits than losing it.

L I trust your judgment

While unquestionably a compliment, there was also a warning in that message. Trusting my judgment was not the same as sharing it, and there was an implicit "you will answer for it if you're wrong" hidden inside it.

AU Thank you for your trust.

I tried to wrap my discomfort in affection.

L Tell me when you intend to speak to her.

AU Right now.

Then, I put down my primary phone and pulled out the companion to the burner I'd given Decoherence, an action that felt loaded with a frankly irritating amount of symbolism.

AU You busy?

She started typing immediately.

D This a booty call?

I flinched, knowing Leviathan was looking out of my face at the same moment I was.

I had tried hard to pay attention, to the best of my considerable abilities, but there was no perceptible signal when he was there or when he was not. Even with my enhanced senses, there was no hum or heat or imperceptible internal switching on to give it away. I wondered if he had done that on purpose, made sure none of the senses he'd enhanced would pick it up, and hated the thought instantly.

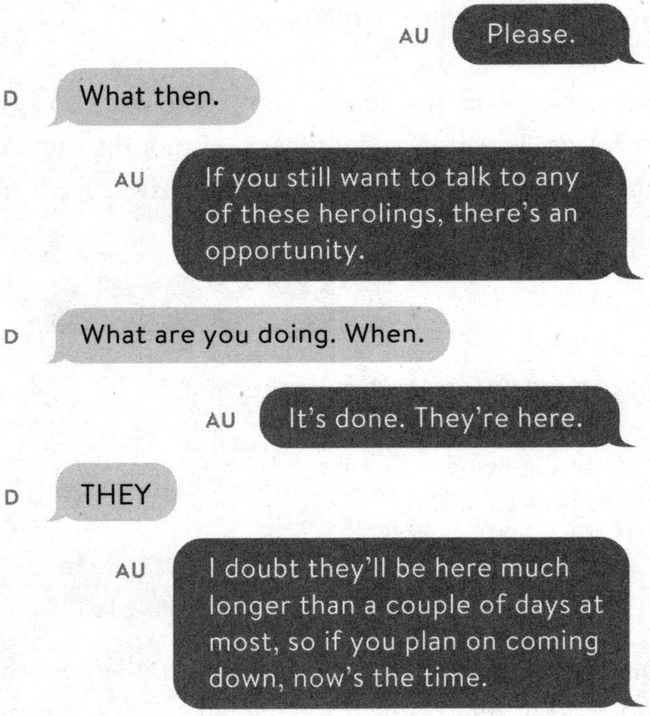

There was a long pause before her next reply, "is typing" flashing on the screen as she drafted and redrafted her next message.

It did not escape me that she was offering her own kind of olive branch by even vaguely insinuating a time. After a moment, I decided to take it.

I spent time psyching myself up to see Decoherence again. I spent extra effort on my makeup, getting the wings of my eyeliner and angle of my cheekbones as sharp as I could. I found myself jittery in a way I very rarely did; I spent almost all of my time in high-pressure situations and there was no awkward social encounter or public-speaking moment that had much power over me anymore. But the prospect of seeing her again made me feel like I'd swallowed a bluebird, feathers in my throat and wings beating in my stomach.

Now that I knew when she'd arrive, rather than her just spontaneously appearing, I had the time to really get nervous. I realized that there'd been some benefits to her just manifesting out of the air at inconvenient times: I didn't have the chance to get in my head about it. But knowing she would walk through the doors of the observation room in the next few minutes was harrowing, and made me suddenly wish I'd just let her keep crashing my parties.

Instead, she showed up respectfully seven minutes late, escorted by a couple of pieces of Meat who could have done less than jack shit if she decided to hurt someone. It was symbolic, letting herself be led, like accepting the "guest pass" device she'd have been asked to swallow. Things she could have easily circumvented, but did as signs of good faith. Almost certainly for me. Despite my nerves, I felt myself smiling when I turned to face her.

"What did you do to them?" she said icily, and I twisted that convenient smile into a sneer.

"Nothing. They might have a scratch or two from the ride over, but they're otherwise completely unharmed."

Her face was iron, her frown as deep as the tattoos around her mouth. She stared at me a moment as though she could burn the truth out of me with her eyes.

She looked like some kind of avenging angel, and the pair of Meat on either side of her shifted uncomfortably.

"Give us some privacy," I said, providing them an out, and waved it off when one of them dutifully tried to protest. They left after that, relief palpable, and took up positions on the other side of the door.

A bit of stiffness left Decoherence when we were alone together, and her eyes shifted to the young hero in the room beyond. Marrow had eventually stopped pacing and was sitting in the very center of the room, as far away from all of the walls as he could be. There was a reinforced one-way glass panel on each wall, and two more set up high near the ceiling; he had no way to know which might have observers behind them. So he picked a spot where, if any of the panels opened, he could see all of them.

"He's genuinely alright," I repeated, and she gave a small nod of acknowledgment.

"Thank you for . . . telling me. Letting me talk to him."

"I did promise."

I watched her consider that for a moment; I imagined her doing some math in her head, adding the fact I'd kept my word to her to her own internal ledgers. "I appreciate it."

"Well. It's like you said. You might not be able to get through to them. But at least you can try."

She looked deeply uncomfortable and turned away from me, looking through the two-way glass. "Where's Cartilage?" she asked, changing the subject.

"Elsewhere. You can talk to him first if you'd like."

"No. This is fine."

There was now something off about her demeanor, even considering the circumstances. It was starting to make me twitchy in response, and suspect there was something she might not be telling me. "What's wrong with you?"

"I wish you'd have done this differently."

"Oh? A moment ago you were thanking me."

"I would have preferred—"

"I've done exactly what you asked. No one was hurt—except for some of our own people, not that I would expect you to care much about that—and I've let you know they were here before so much as speaking a word to them. Isn't that precisely what you wanted?"

"I thought—" She struggled for a moment to articulate her own expectation. "I thought you would tell me *before*..."

"Before."

"You kidnapped them."

That made me relax a little. I heaved as theatrical a sigh as I could manage, shifting my cane to my other hand so I could gesticulate more effectively. "Listen, you're either scandalized by my loose morals or mad you didn't get invited to the kidnapping. You can't be both."

One of her fists clenched unconsciously. "Go fuck yourself, it's not about being invited."

"Are you sure."

"Yes, I'm sure. It's about being in on this or not."

"You know what I think," I said, getting up close to her. "I think you wanted to keep an eye on me. I think you didn't trust me not to vaporize these twerps and wanted to supervise me, and you're pissed off that you didn't get the chance."

"It has nothing to do with supervision."

"Or are you mad that I *didn't* do anything untoward and proved you wrong?"

She turned her eyes upward. "Why the fuck do I ever try and talk to you." It wasn't exactly a question.

"I'm very charming."

She didn't reply, but I could see from the muscles in her jaw that she was clenching her teeth.

"Details aside," I continued, "you're here, and so are they. If you're going to talk to them now's your chance."

Her mouth twisted into one of those snarls only superheroes seemed capable of, one that showed her teeth. "I'm sure Leviathan isn't *thrilled* to have me here."

"He honestly doesn't mind."

She made a derisive noise. "I'm sure he would, if he knew."

"First of all, you need to fucking learn not to say shit like that aloud in a literal *lair* that has *very good surveillance*. And secondly, he knows."

That shocked her. She took a step back from me. "He *knows*?"

"About the Draft's offer and that you entertained it. Yes."

"How—"

"How do you think?"

"You *told* him?"

"Of course I told him."

She turned in a slow circle, surveying the room, suddenly certain it was a trap.

"Oh, calm the fuck down. The Draft made the offer, they tried to take out a literal hit—but you didn't. To him, then, it's over, and at the moment he is much more interested in working toward a common goal than punishing you for thinking about it."

She turned her attention back to me, a different kind of concern spreading across her features like a bloodstain. "We do not have goals in common."

I didn't flinch from her. "I know you hate the idea, but you and he are on almost the same side right now," I continued, moving a bit closer. "All three of us want the Draft to be immolated. All three of us think these heroes have been lied to and deserve better. Our tactics might differ, and our far-future outcomes may not be fully aligned, but the sooner you come to grip with the fact that we should be working together on *this*, the better off you will be."

A speech was welling up in her, a righteous one; I could see it. I might have settled into a long, engaging argument with her, but in that moment my head started to buzz; Leviathan was calling me, his signature bone-conduction ring vibrating through my skull. So instead, I watched Decoherence gather all her righteousness into her diaphragm; then, just before she could speak, I interrupted all the energy she'd built up, like a ruined orgasm.

"Intercom's on the table there. Have a nice chat," I said, and left the room. I heard her kick a chair behind me, and I smiled at her frustration.

"YOU WORK WELL against her," Leviathan said out of nowhere. We were in bed together; I was propped up on a small nest of pillows while he bent over me, applying tiny dabs of antiseptic to my chest and inner thighs. I was covered with a new constellation of star-patterned bite marks, and a few of them had slightly broken the skin.

"What?" It took me a minute for what he said to sink in. My head was still fairly cloudy with endorphins.

"Decoherence."

"Oh." I couldn't quite get a handle on what he was trying to say, let alone how to safely respond, so I settled on the safety of "thank you."

I shifted a little to test a spot of tenderness. Leviathan followed my movement and turned his attention to my hip. None of my extraordinarily minor injuries required doctoring, but it was a ritual we'd fallen into and both deeply enjoyed. "I tried to handle myself well," I added.

"Hmm." After another moment of fussing, he helped me flip over, so I way lying on my stomach and he could examine the length of my back.

"That's not what I meant," he said, after a long moment.

"What did you mean?"

"The way you two are in conflict—does this hurt?"

"No, not at all."

"Mmm. The way you two are in conflict," he said again, "it suits you."

"Is this one of those 'you're pretty when you're angry' things?"

He buzzed. "No."

I considered being playfully offended by that, but before I could bluster he made a thinking noise, and I instead gave him the space to finish the thought.

"You are good adversaries," he settled on at last. "It brings out qualities in you that I appreciate."

"I didn't set out to be her adversary," I said, and was surprised by the amount of emotion I found there.

"We never do."

With a final sweep over my body, he picked up the cotton pads and antiseptic and placed them on the table nearby. I stayed where I was, face turned away from him while he moved around behind me. After a moment, I felt him climb back onto the bed and return to perching over my body.

"You wish her to be an ally," he said. His voice was very gentle, but I still felt like the conversation was approaching dangerous territory. That may have been my own hang-ups rather than his, but it still made me feel tense.

"It's like I told her: we are . . . much more closely aligned than we are opposed. She's also been wronged deeply, over and over, by the Draft—there is so much potential there."

"The enemy of my enemy."

"It's a powerful thing."

"It is."

I propped myself up on my elbows and looked at him. He was sitting up against the headboard, legs stretched out in front of him, one of his antennae directed toward me in pointed curiosity.

"I feel like I am . . . so close to getting her on board. She is so close to understanding. If I can just get her to see the vision . . ."

"The greatest divisions are a single degree from perfect understanding," he said, no longer only talking about Decoherence and me. "Don't shy away from that, if it comes to be. She could be the great hatred of your life."

His voice grated at the end of that statement, ending on a rasp. For the first time, I detected something like real jealousy from him.

I DIDN'T SEE Decoherence again before she left the compound, but later I reviewed every minute of tape from her visit. She spoke with both twins from the safety of an observation room, though she let Cartilage see her, briefly, through the glass, to prove she was who she said. For Marrow she produced a tiny force field, a little violet bubble, and delivered a bottle of water to him through the solid wall. I listened to her talk to them—her was voice conspiratorial but firm. She was offering, not convincing. She told them, very briefly, what happened to her; the way she had been sacrificed on the altar of public opinion, the way she had been discarded and vilified to protect their most important asset.

"They are lying to you," she had said, "the same way they lied to me. I am not what they say I am, and you are also not what they say you are, what they are trying to make you into. You can be whatever you want to be, whoever you want to be. You can be more than their hero. And no matter how much they claim to love you, they will not hesitate to throw you away if it means winning."

The identical twins did not respond the same to her. Marrow (who had been taken first by the Draft when he was still sleeping with stuffed animals) was silent, offering nothing but a sneer, not deigning to even look in the direction of her voice. But Cartilage (who had been left behind and spent years nursing that abandonment) inclined his head while she spoke. And when she had left, he wrapped his arms around his knees and sat very still for a long time.

I made a mental note to thank Decoherence, the next time I saw her. The way they reacted, the subtle differences there, helped me talk to them when my turn came. I learned a lot from her few minutes alone with them. My own conversations with them would not have gone as well without those new insights.

We didn't want to keep the twins confined long; the lengthier their absence, the greater the chance of retaliation, sanctioned or otherwise, from the Draft and their heroes. I was confident we'd left no damning evidence behind when we took them, and we certainly weren't gloating about it, but it would only be a matter of time until they knew what we'd done even if they didn't know how. So as soon as I dragged myself out of bed and reviewed the footage, I was back into an observation room.

Now that exhaustion had made them vulnerable and Decoherence's strange visit had enough time to really sink in, it was my turn to get under their skin. I spoke to them each alone. I chose not to let either of them see me; risky, it's not easy to connect with a disembodied voice. But I wanted the experience of talking to me to be as similar as possible for both of them. For each of them, consecutively, I turned on the audio feed in the rooms we were keeping them in by way of an introduction.

"I had hoped to be the first to talk to you," I said over the intercom, using the same words for both of them, "but I see a . . . guest made it to you before I did."

Neither of them responded; in fact, they reacted so little, if I didn't have their rooms mic'ed with a feed displaying the audio levels, I might have worried they couldn't hear me.

"I'm sorry for the security breach," I said to both of them. "It's difficult to keep out someone who can walk through walls."

"Who are you?" Their voices had the same pitch and timbre; speaking to them in sequence gave me the oddest sense of déjà vu.

"I'm the Auditor."

"Ah." They both leaned back, expectant, tense.

"I'm flattered you've heard of me."

"We've been prepped to deal with you." They both delivered the line like a clear threat.

"I doubt it'll do either of you any good." *Especially considering I'm not going to get any closer to you than a disembodied voice.*

"Where is my brother?" they both asked.

"Perfectly safe," I reassured them, and it was clear from their body language that neither of them believed me.

"I want to see him," the twins both said.

"We won't keep you apart long. As soon as I can, you'll be re-united. You have my word."

"Your word," both of them said with contempt. "And what is that worth?"

"A villain's word is everything. More than a hero's, if you think about it. If we didn't make good on our threats, we'd hardly inspire any fear."

What they said next had a small but crucial divergence. "What do you want with us?" Cartilage said coldly.

"It's not what I want with you *both*," I said to Cartilage. "It's what I want with *you*."

He sneered at me, taking refuge in self-deprecation; he felt himself the weaker brother, so he didn't believe me. "And what could you possibly want with us?"

But Marrow let the tiniest bit of real concern slip through when he replied, "What do you want with *me*?" Because he *had* been the special one before, and it had been terrible for him.

"You're extraordinary," I said to both of them, letting a little awe color my voice as I spoke to Cartilage while keeping it very matter-of-fact with Marrow. "Some of your abilities have never been documented before, let alone fully mapped. That's very rare, and very powerful."

Their reactions converged a little, though Marrow remained more tense. "My brother's powers are just as rare as mine," they both said.

"Maybe," I allowed, "but they're not like yours. You can do things that they can't. In fact, you can do things *no one else* can, and possibly never has before. It's your potential, and how much further you have to go, how much better you can be."

Now it was Cartilage's turn to be uncomfortable, whereas this was easier territory for Marrow, who had been praised for his potential since he was a preteen.

"I know what I can and can't do," Cartilage said.

"Yeah, I know all about my 'potential,'" Marrow said.

"Do you?" I asked. "Or do you know what the Draft has told you that you can do?"

"Are you suggesting they're hiding my own powers from me?" they both asked, a different blend of incredulous and wary in each of their questions.

"Not hiding, exactly. But holding you back? Definitely. They need to be able to control you, after all. And I'm not just suggesting all this; I've seen the documents myself."

Both of them retreated into little fortresses of distrust. "And you just thought you'd tell me, out of the goodness of your heart?"

"Of course not. It's very much for my benefit."

They raised their eyebrows, eerily the same way. "You thought one of your enemies should know they could be much worse for you to fight?"

"Yeah, that makes a ton of sense," Cartilage said, answering his own question.

Marrow was harsher in answering his own. "That's fucking stupid."

"I am telling you," I told each of them, "because you're not my enemies. The Draft is."

"Isn't that the same thing?" Cartilage asked.

"That's the same thing," Marrow said.

"Not at all. Or, at least, it doesn't have to be. You're only my enemies insomuch as you do their bidding, but you, yourselves? I have no problem with you. In fact, I feel sorry for you."

And this is where the conversations broke apart. Cartilage didn't like that; he bristled, and his shoulders took on a protective hunch. "You don't get to feel sorry for me."

I had to tread carefully, feeling acutely that a misstep would cause Cartilage to wall himself off completely. "I don't mean it to be insulting. I don't pity you; not like you think. It would be more accurate to say: I'm furious for you."

He audibly snorted; it felt very performative, like he wanted me to hear.

"Yeah, you were so moved by my plight of *being a superhero* you just had to abduct me to this glorified conference room. This is much better than my regular life, thank you."

"The sad part is that I think it really is."

He stood up and faced a wall he guessed (incorrectly) I was behind; his hands were curled into loose fists. I watched him from his left side, and I could see his jaw clench. "You'd think fucking wrong then. And I want to leave. Now."

Marrow, on the other hand, was more nonplussed, having less experience being pitied, and a far less negative reaction to it. "That's rich, coming from you. You're not as smart as they say you are."

I could push him a little harder. "Thank you. I love it when people underestimate me."

"Show me I'm wrong. Come in here. Look me in the eye. Shake my hand." He extended his palm, offering a handshake to the empty air. He liked this line; he'd used it before.

I laughed. "I'd like my mitochondria to stay functional, thanks."

"So you know what I can do to you. Then you also know it's only a matter of time before I break out. So let me go now, for your own sake."

I pulled the two conversations back in sync, and gave them the same reply. "Listen. I don't want you here any longer than you have to be."

"Then why am I here at all?" they both said, Cartilage audibly more annoyed.

In this moment, I told them something completely true. "There was no other way to speak to you. It's impossible to get close through any sort of legitimate channel, no way to get a message to you that your keepers wouldn't intercept. If we ever met, you'd attack me instantly, and I wouldn't survive that."

They both wanted to argue, but they couldn't. Marrow looked sullen; Cartilage carried more guilt.

I gentled my voice as much as I still could. "I understand that you have no reason to listen to me, and this is probably futile. I knew going into this you would most likely discard anything I had to say, and I made my peace with that. But . . . Well, I'm selfish. So I did this for me.

"You're special. You have something no one else does. And I mean your powers, but not just your powers. You care. You listen. So if talking to you means kidnapping you, okay. It was worth it."

I took a step closer, which neither of them could see; but when you're acting, it's important to fully commit, even for a moment. "I believe you are what you think you are," I said, with as much depth and meaning as I could conjure. "I think you might just be what you're pretending to be. More than anyone else on your team, and more than your brother. And because you mean it, I wanted you to know that the Draft is worse than any of us. Much worse than me. No matter what you do with that information, at least you'll have it.

"Can you prove it?" they both asked the question, though Marrow's voice held a little more of a sneer, and Cartilage spoke with a bit more pensiveness.

"I can. Would you like to see the data? I have it. I can show you how much harm they cause to ordinary people, to villains and their henches, though I suspect the latter matters less to you." I paused for a moment, like I was weighing whether or not I wanted to share the final piece of data I held. "I can show you how much they hurt heroes, too."

"I am who I am because of the Draft," they said, Marrow vehemently and Cartilage with sorrow.

"Do you want to know how much harm you've cause the world because of them?"

They both allowed for a long, awful pause. I recognized that space, where they both desperately wanted to know and needed to look away.

"Does my brother know that you're talking to me?" Both of their voices were filled with profound loneliness, and I could feel them both wishing they weren't so alone.

"No," I lied. "He's here, but he doesn't know why. I trust you with everything I've said, though, whether that means sharing it with your brother . . .

"Or not."

I didn't ask either what their intentions were; I could feel in the profound loneliness and discomfort that both of them held in their bodies they weren't going to say a thing. I left them both with their thoughts, and when they realized they'd been quiet for a very long time, they found themselves trying to pick up a conversation with the empty air.

RELEASING CARTILAGE AND Marrow was almost as risky as capturing them; weakened and disoriented, they were still dangerous as hell. As with any big predator being released from captivity, you couldn't fully trust that they'd just run into the trees once you opened the cage; they might try and eat you instead. The plan was to drive them, separately, away from the compound, and then evacuate the drivers. The locks on their transport would be released remotely, once our people were safely withdrawn, and we'd let the Draft know where they could be picked up. Not easy, but straightforward, and—without something going catastrophically wrong— potentially even safe.

Luck was on our side, and the release went like clockwork. Everyone hit their marks like it had been rehearsed a thousand times, and soon the twins were squinting and blinking in the sunlight, one at the edge of an abandoned industrial park and the other near a remote soybean field. I sent Mom a message with their respective coordinates from my personal email, just to be an asshole about it.

He replied within minutes, but I was already lost in a string of debriefs with our teams, confirming with Keller that the twins had been retrieved and setting up monitoring for any potential retaliatory action once the twins had the opportunity to tell their handlers whatever version of events they decided to share. It was much later, in my final recap meeting with Leviathan, that I finally dug Mom's message out of my inbox as part of the final report.

We'd been in the midst of a conversation already, but I suddenly went quiet, reading the message several times over, trying to figure out what I could be missing.

From: CMO@DRAFT.SPR
To: Auditor@Leviathan.org
Re: I had something(s) that belong to you

Anna,

I know we won't speak after this; not like we have. I'd make a plea for his life if I thought it would do anything, but considering all the effort you've gone through, I can't imagine a scenario in which that does any good.

It's breaking my heart to do what you asked; he doesn't deserve this. And I know what I had to do to protect my kids (I know they're grown but they're all my kids), but he's one of mine too.

This is over the line, kiddo. I'm not even talking about the numbers on this one, because if it was just one more tally on the sheet, I could work it out. There would be hope.

But there's no coming back from this. Not if this ends the way I think that it will.

I can't say I hope you're happy. I don't. I can't say I hope it's worth it. Because it won't be.

You won't ever be able to come home again, Anna. And whether or not you believe me, that's the saddest thing I've heard in a long time.

Mom

What the fuck is he talking about, I thought to myself.

Leviathan saw me frowning in confusion at my tablet, and came to stand behind my shoulder.

"This makes absolutely no sense at all," I said, angling the screen so he could see it more clearly. "I just gave him a set of coordinates. He's acting like I demanded . . . someone?"

Leviathan clicked in annoyance, crossing his arms. I'm not sure if it was his body language or just the energy he had in that moment, but I knew instantly that something was deeply off. Before he even spoke, my heart had already started to sink.

"He ruined my surprise," he said.

BEFORE I SENT my catty message with a set of coordinates and a little friendly gloating to Mom, Leviathan had instructed Emeril to contact Draft HR. In her signature polite, wicked efficiency, she had let them know that the twins were safe and sound in our care—and if the Draft wanted them to remain so, there was a bargain that needed to be struck.

A former member of my staff has, regrettably, made the decision to join yours. During their time working for you, this individual has violated a number of confidentiality agreements. In order to rectify the situation, I must insist that you bring said employee to the enclosed location, so that I may collect them and conduct a more thorough debrief to ensure no additional issues arise.

She made a hostage exchange sound as tedious as recovering a company laptop. But she was not asking for property; he was asking for a person.

For Greg.

Draft HR, similarly dispassionate, did, to their credit, ask if there could be a different solution. But Emeril did not negotiate. She made it clear that either the Draft delivered Greg, healthy and whole but entirely alone, to the specified drop-off location and not interfere when some Meat retrieved him, or the twins would never be seen again.

Draft HR did not put up much of a fight after that. As far as they were concerned this was easy math; and it was their job to make these kinds of calculations, what civilian lives were worth dedicating superheroic resources to. As far as they were concerned, a mediocre network administrator was an excellent deal for a pair of flagship heroes returned safely. He wasn't even a part of the Amnesty Initiative, as he'd quit and been hired well before it was put into effect, so there would not even be any ugly paperwork to process about it. The head of HR, the horrifically titled chief people officer, whether out of merciless efficiency or active spite, signed off on the exchange, and only then informed Mom.

By then, Leviathan had called me to his office for a "discussion" that very quickly turned into the two of us devouring each other. I thought we were having a breathlessly spontaneous moment until it became clear his actions were deliberately calculated.

"I had to keep you busy," he said languidly. "I didn't want you to know about my gift before it had arrived."

I stared at him, still trying to process what was happening.

"Greg is here. Now."

"Yes. The exchange would not have happened if he wasn't delivered as instructed."

I felt like the world was tilting. A few moments ago, this was an operation I had in my complete control. I had drawn the timeline down to the minute, and thought I knew exactly which pieces were in play, from the personnel to the vehicles deployed. It was going *beautifully*. I thought the only communication directly with the Draft was coming through me, and I'd held that control deliberately. I was going to be the only one to delicately press that *send* button. I *owned* this entire series of operations.

But just as Cartilage and Marrow had underestimated me, so had I underestimated Leviathan. As was his wont—and as he was extremely good at—Leviathan was operating on a completely different level, spinning his own outcomes, pulling whatever levers he wanted. He'd used my meticulously planned, perfectly balanced scheme as a stepping stone to one of his own. This wasn't even him taking the reins and accelerating a timeline, the way he had in the past, when he had baited Supercollider into a fight before I'd managed to weaken him sufficiently. This time, he'd just seen it as an opportunity to get something else done.

I felt the anger heating up in my chest like an iron bar starting to glow, incandescent with rage. Leviathan took the emotion he saw gathering in my face as a different kind of upset, and put a hand on my shoulder in support.

"This must be shocking to you."

"Yes." I managed the word, only a rasp, but didn't trust myself yet to say anything else.

His fingers squeezed my shoulder sympathetically. "You have

worked yourself to exhaustion and have had no time to tie up this loose end."

"I had *worked*," I hissed, "on a kidnapping and unconditional release. Not a hostage exchange."

"More of a prisoner exchange." He said it lightly, as though expecting me to enjoy his pedantry.

I stared at him with the closest thing to open hostility I had ever conjured. "This was *mine*."

My anger slid off him completely. "Auditor." He bent down so we were eye level with each other. "This could not wait."

"It had already waited! What would a few more days—"

"Everything." There was something about the way he said it, final as a cinder block dropping, that cut through to me. "He had been left alive too long. Every moment he was with them was a moment he could do more damage."

I focused on what he just said, zeroing in on a single word. "Alive." I couldn't get more than that word out.

"He still is," Leviathan said, "and unharmed. I would not have taken that from you."

I felt a twist of guilt. "This isn't—"

He saw my distress, and softened. "That was not to wound you. You said to Emeril you would handle it. I recognize you have been overwhelmed and unable to take this on yourself. I am making sure you have what you need to keep your word."

The anger I felt was draining away, replaced with something wet and cold. I had not given my conversation with Emeril, my request, or even Greg himself a moment's thought in a long time. It had become entirely lost under a tidal wave of other machinations; my brain was too full to even consider it. And some part of me wanted to simply forget; let whatever retribution was required fall to the wayside.

"I had not . . . decided how to handle it," I admitted softly, looking down. "I hoped it would come to me."

"I know." My eyes darted up, but there was nothing but patience in his face. His complicated mouthparts rippled with an alien sympathy. "It is not an easy task."

"What if I let it go?"

"You know you can't."

"But what if I did?" I was starting to feel panicked now. "I don't believe he did this maliciously."

"The impact is the same."

"He can't have known what the impact would be."

"How many people hate you, my Auditor?"

His voice was as gentle as I had ever heard it, and being referred to as "his" anything made me freeze in place. I wasn't sure what this feeling was, something like panic yet warm, but I thought if I stayed very still it might not immediately leave.

"How many?" he prompted.

I tried to speak. "More than I can track now."

"How many people hold knowledge of you that could hurt you?"

I flipped through the Rolodex of humiliation I stored in my head, from every kink I'd shared with an undeserving partner to every middle school bully who had wrung tears from me. He felt me physically flinch, and held me carefully in place.

"If you let this go," he said, "anyone who holds something you might be vulnerable to has nothing to fear. They will sell it or even offer it freely to our enemies. We need to show them that any harm that comes to you will be returned tenfold."

"Make an example of him."

"Yes."

"He was my *friend*."

"That does not make his sins against you better. In fact, it makes them worse."

"What if I—" I paused to take a deep breath. "Will you let me be weak?"

"No." His voice was soft, and final.

"I don't want to kill him."

He thought for a moment. He'd been focused on me completely for our entire conversation, but now I felt him pull away slightly, really considering my statement. A coil of anxiety started twisting up inside me, and I wondered if he thought less of me for admitting this.

"I see two outcomes," he said after a while. "If the act itself is distasteful to you, that can be overcome easily. Emeril will take care of the task as originally intended, and you can be given as much or as little information about it as you wish. The second outcome is less desirable, in every possible way, but he can be contained here, permanently. The Draft and everyone in his life will be led to believe he is dead as promised, but he will be housed here, where he can't do anymore harm."

I inhaled to protest, but he stopped me, holding up one hand to my lips. "There is no scenario in which he returns to the world."

"He'll be too scared to ever talk to anyone again. I know him, he—"

"The harm now is not his sharing any of your confidences. It is his continuing to live."

"I—" I tried to formulate a question, but I couldn't get the words out.

Eventually, softly, I said, "I cared about him. I wanted to protect him by bringing him here."

"And look how he repaid that kindness."

"He just doesn't know—"

"Auditor." He gave me a small shake, to regain my full attention before I could spiral. "You are allowed to be angry that he harmed you. You *should* be angry."

I tried to find the anger he wanted from me, but it was still small and scared. I felt a lot of the same complicated writhe of emotions I had when Leviathan had killed Black Pill. That harming me, inconveniencing me did not seem like a capital offense. It was easy to find the anger when someone else was harmed—when Leviathan had been captured, I would have torn anyone apart if it meant freeing him. But finding those emotions, the towering rage and indignation, for harm that had befallen me was harder.

"I don't feel angry."

"Ah," he said, like a connection had just been made in his head. "That is a problem. We will find it."

"Find it?"

"The rage you will need." He thought for a moment. "Talk to him."

"*What?*"

"He's in perfect health, even comfortable right now. He will remain so until you choose. Take as much time as you require to talk to him. If you find the anger you need, then you can see to his end yourself. If not, I will have it taken care of."

The finality of that statement felt like a door closing. I tried to find it in me to protest again, to beg for my friend's life, but I could not find the conviction to do so. A part of me, an ever-growing part, was aligned with Leviathan's perspective; at the very least, speaking with Greg, both to sort out my own emotions and determine what fight to take on, seemed like the only way forward.

"I've never done this before," I found myself saying. I flexed my hands. "Myself."

He nodded. "The first time will be fraught. But that itself is also important."

"We will have to work out how."

He released his grip on my shoulders and took one of my hands. "We will find something perfect for you."

LEVIATHAN, AS ALWAYS, was true to his word. He didn't have Greg hanging by his thumbs in a dungeon somewhere or even in a high-security room; it wasn't as though the poor idiot had powers, and even his knowledge of our security systems wasn't deep enough or recent enough for him to have much luck even escaping anything more advanced than a locked conference room. So Leviathan picked a room with actual furniture and good environmental controls, so the only thing causing Greg any discomfort was sheer terror.

Leviathan agreed to wait in the next room, out of sight; Greg had been terrified of him during the best of times, and there would be no way to have any kind of a real conversation while he was there.

I knocked softly on the door and then Ludmilla walked in ahead of me. Greg had leapt to his feet at the sound, and I got to watch the raw fear turn into stupid relief as soon as he saw me walk in behind her. Part of me bristled at the sight of me making him *less* afraid. He literally ran to me, and I had to stop Ludmilla from tackling him when he went to throw his arms around me. I stood there stiffly while he sobbed into my hair.

"Anna, god, Anna, I am so glad you are here, explain to them—"

"Shut up," I said gently.

He pulled himself back and sniffed. "Right, right, yeah, sorry." He ran a hand through his hair, which was too long again but not terribly so. He had a short, neat beard now, and looked like he was making an effort to dress and groom himself like a professional adult person.

"Greg," I said softly, "I am going to ask you some questions."

"Yeah, of course, anything. Does it have to be here, though? Can't we—" He looked longingly toward the door.

"It has to be here."

He was visibly disappointed. "Okay. Okay, yeah, of course."

Ludmilla shifted her toothpick from one side of her mouth to the other. "Why don't you sit down," she said. It was not a suggestion.

Greg hesitated, then folded himself onto one of the chairs around a small table. Ludmilla continued to stand by the door, arms crossed, looking a very particular kind of bored that was often the last thing someone saw.

I sat in a chair opposite him, keeping the table between us. He was fidgeting and awkward, not sure where to look or what to do with his hands.

"Greg, I need you to tell me, in as much detail as you possibly can, everything you have said about me to your new colleagues."

He had the gall to look startled. "What?"

A little spark of anger shot off me, like a flint being struck. "Anything you said about me," I repeated.

He was starting to panic already. "I–I don't–"

"Look. This is very important. Someone at the Draft had information that only someone who knew me very well would have access to."

A thought came to him, and he flushed visibly in embarrassment. "Is this . . . about the podcast?"

The sparks were catching now, and little baby tongues of anger were licking up inside me. "Yes, Greg. And a lot of other things. But it is about the podcast."

He laughed. He actually laughed, in a terrible kind of relief. "Holy fuck, okay, that's what this is about."

I did not share his mirth. "We need to know if there is a security leak. If they got it from you or someone else."

He slowed to a few chuckles. "Fuck, you scared the shit out of me."

"Greg. I need you to pay the fuck attention, okay."

Greg looked at me, annoyed. "Anna, this is–"

"That is not my fucking name, Greg."

"A–what?"

"My name."

He deflated a little. "Oh. Uh. Auditor."

"That's right. I'm the Auditor." I said it slowly, as though explaining it to a child.

"Okay. Sorry." He was subdued again, unsure how the energy had shifted between us.

"And I need you to tell me what you told them."

He twisted his fingers together. "I didn't, like, tell them anything." Except, because he couldn't help himself, he added, "Not in the way you mean."

"What way do I mean?" It was a steady burn, now, low and under control but unquestionably crackling.

"I didn't tell them anything about you on purpose. I didn't, like, do an interview or give a report or whatever; it wasn't anything like that."

Oh my god, he actually thinks this matters.

"Okay, that's helpful," I said to him. "But you said something."

"Sure, but, like, just the way anyone would talk in an office."

I folded my hands together. "Give me an example."

He thought for a moment. "Well, like, we were out and talking about bad dates. And I didn't really, like . . . have a ton of stories myself, but, uh, I had that story about you, you know, and that guy and the cab—"

"Right. So you told the story."

He gave the awkward cringe of someone who realized they might be in a little bit of trouble. "Yeah."

"To your coworkers."

"Right. I didn't think anyone would—"

"Did I come up at other times?"

I could tell before he answered that he didn't want to tell me the truth ". . . I mean, some people thought it was wild I worked with you."

"Right."

"And at first they didn't believe me, like this guy from IT, I think, he called bullshit and told me to prove it. So I, like, gave him some details to—"

He stopped. He could see on my face that he had said something very wrong, though he couldn't quite pinpoint what yet. I didn't carry the conversation, however, or try to fill the space and make him more comfortable. I let him hang there, thinking on his own, until he finally broke eye contact again.

"Sorry. It sounds fucking stupid now that I am saying it out loud." His self-deprecation was genuine, but that didn't make it any less infuriating.

"It was very stupid," I said softly.

"I'm sorry. I didn't think it would cause trouble for you."

"I don't think you intended to do any harm."

That made him relax. He even smiled a little, and rolled his shoulders back to let some of the tension out. He thought that meant I was forgiving him. That his intent was all that mattered; that the outcomes I'd experienced were unfortunate but not his fault. As long as his heart was pure, it would all work out.

I squeezed the handle of my cane unconsciously; instead of feeling the familiar warmth of the polished wooden handle, I heard the gloves fitted over my hands and arms creak gently in response. The handle of my cane cracked under the magnified pressure, and part of it broke off, falling to the floor with a muffled thump.

"Oh shit, are you okay," Greg said, with a nervy jump of surprise. He reached toward me ineffectually.

I set my broken cane aside and flexed my hand. Inside the glove, it didn't feel any different. Moving was a little bit stiffer, perhaps, because of the carbon-fiber armature and chitin-like ceramic plating, and I couldn't feel all the usual tactile feedback through the ultralight armor. The gloves went all the way up my arms and fitted over my shoulders, meeting at my back, where the hub of the hydraulics system nestled against my spine.

"It's very much like the legs of an ant," Leviathan had explained to me when he helped me put the gauntlets on. "It is how they can lift things many times their own weight."

Of course I could not lift anything massive wearing only the gloves; I'd need to be wearing a full-body version for that to work. But this lightweight piece would let me exert more pressure than my body ever could have done on its own.

Greg was standing now, wanting to come closer to me but darting nervous glances at Ludmilla. She, however, was looking only at me. I nodded, and she gave the tiniest incline of her head in acknowledgment.

"I'm okay," I said. "You can come here."

He walked around to my side of the table with palpable relief. He thought it was almost over, that everything had been explained and there was nothing else for him to worry about. That was what I wanted. If I could give him nothing else, it was to spend his last few minutes unafraid.

"I'm sorry," he said again, and this time it was because he felt it, not because he was afraid.

"I know you are. I believe you."

"It . . . doesn't seem real."

I allowed a tiny smile. "What doesn't?"

He swung one gangly arm around us. "All this. And, well, you. Look at you. I bet if five-years-ago you saw you right now, you wouldn't recognize yourself."

"I bet I wouldn't."

"It's almost like you're a villain or something."

"Almost."

He smiled and put his hands in his pockets. Under his beard, it was the same bashful smile he'd always had.

"Let's get you out of here," I said, and opened my arms.

Without a moment of hesitation, he wrapped his arms around my shoulders. I hugged him back, wrapping my arms fully around his rib cage.

I felt him relax, and sigh.

I squeezed.

I WAS SHAKING so hard I could not hold anything; not the shattered remains of my cane, which I tried to take with me for some inexpressible reason, nor the glass of water Leviathan tried to place in my hand. It was as bad as it had been when Supercollider first shattered my leg, when I was in complete shock and puked in the ambulance. After I spilled the ice water for the second time, I broke into ugly sobs.

Leviathan watched me carefully, not offering to touch me until I reached out for him. Then held my body with a deep, steady pressure like he was holding me together.

When I stopped weeping and quieted, he still waited a few more minutes before asking, "Would you like me to talk to you?"

"Yes," I said, my voice wet and strangled.

I couldn't process or retain anything he said, but the steady cadence of him speaking gave me something to anchor to. The slight buzz his voice always carried helped even more, like a kind of soothing white noise. He kept talking, first to me, and eventually simply narrating what he was doing, what he wanted me to do, as he led me back to his office and then the apartment above. I found a brief bit of peace in deep disassociation.

Leviathan helped me take the armor off, which I doubt I could have managed myself even if I hadn't been in shock, and placed it in a large biohazard bag for cleaning. He helped me into his shower, and kept talking when the sound of the water spraying made his words completely unintelligible.

". . . so proud of you," were the first words I was able to pick out clearly, when I was wrapped in a robe and sitting on the edge of his bed. Something about those words threw me back into my body, forced me to pick up the reins of myself again. Everything was suddenly sharp and vibrant and awful, and I grabbed his wrist hard enough that he was startled into silence.

"I need a minute," I whispered.

"What do you need?"

"I need . . . to be alone, I think."

He was not at all offended by my request; in fact, he nodded sagely, as though this was one of the reactions he was expecting.

"Of course. Take as much time as you need. Solitude is valuable."

"Please," I added, "don't watch."

Leviathan lowered himself to one knee, and tilted my face up to ensure we made eye contact. He was deeply earnest, and wanted me to see it. "You have my word you will have privacy."

I nodded, but could not quite find the words to thank him. Taking that as a sign I could no longer process company of any kind, he simply escorted me back to my apartment in silence.

I'd moved, again, when the exodus of Leviathan's employees was at its height and the entire operation was consolidating into fewer buildings. The new suite I had been offered was in Leviathan's tower, a few floors down. There were no other residences in that building, aside from Leviathan's own apartment. He'd pretended like that was a perfectly normal space for me to occupy, like the rooms were just sitting there and happened to be vacant at the right moment, instead of completely remodeled for me to move in. I'd pretended back that this was just a pragmatic decision, with nothing to do with affection, despite the fact it made my stomach ache with what I took for a kind of happiness.

But when I was alone in those rooms, once Leviathan had made sure I was safe and comfortable and had courteously left me, I was hit with a wave of claustrophobia. I was alone, but I was not *truly* alone. He'd given his word he would not be watching, and I believed it, but that was something I had had to *ask* for. I had to fight back an awful, vivid impulse in that moment to find something sharp and dig the implants in my eye out myself.

All those sensations hit me because, in that moment, I wanted to wrestle with what I had done entirely by myself. I wanted to process all of my awful, complicated, and hideous emotions in the privacy of my own head, without the interference of anyone or anything. But I couldn't. Not out of fear of him watching at that precise moment in time, but because I knew he *could*.

I needed him out of my head. Not just in the sense that he might be watching, but also how he was impacting every decision I made. I was constantly checking myself against his imagined reactions, adhering to what I thought he would want me to do, and I could no longer bear the weight.

Despite the fact that the only hands that had just been bloodied were mine, that I'd had several choices (even if all of them were bad), and moved forward with the power of my own agency. Some part of me, though—either looking for a way to escape some of that awful responsibility or out of sheer horror at all the time I had spent constantly examining and reexamining my actions—screamed that I might not have killed Greg if Leviathan hadn't been watching.

I knew that it was not true—at least, I did not think it was true. But I had second- and third-guessed myself so much—and ran my action through the filter of his imagined approval so many times— that I could not conquer the fear completely. Yes, I could have chosen differently. I could have let Emeril or Leviathan or anyone else kill Greg instead, and never have to see or smell or feel a moment of it. I could have agreed to an indefinite imprisonment, and found a way, eventually, to free him—or not. I chose none of those things. And the choice I'd made was mine. It *had* to be mine.

But after hours of screaming and sobbing and whispering to myself, trying to make the equations of guilt balance, I could not shake the last bit of uncertainty that my will was entirely my own. But it had to be. If I was going to become what I was already becoming, I could not live with that doubt for another moment.

[Part Five]

DECOHERENCE'S BUILDING WAS AWFUL. THE LOBBY WAS LIT BY a fluorescent light that washed everything in an anemic gray green, and the tile floor seemed perpetually wet. Once I actually went inside it was even worse, reeking of industrial cleaner and wet winter boots.

It hadn't been hard to find her. She did a decent job hiding from anyone who didn't make OPSEC something of a study, but she made enough mistakes that someone who really wanted to could track her down. And I needed to find her, and quickly, while my request for privacy would give me more time than I would have had otherwise.

There was no one there to stop me as I walked purposefully for the elevators. I made my way to the fourteenth floor like I knew exactly what I was doing, but I stood in front of her door a long time before knocking, wondering if, even that far in, I was actually going to do this.

At that moment, I could still turn back. I could take the long, exhausting journey back to the compound and pretend I hadn't almost committed what would only be seen as a massive betrayal of the one person I'd promised never to betray again. I could go back to pretending that I could live with the horror and implicit duress of someone looking out of my eye whenever they wanted to. I could change my mind.

I closed my eyes and felt Greg's rib cage collapse in my embrace, the way he'd broken in my arms like I'd squeezed a quail egg. The way his mouth had erupted with blood, covering me. If I was going to be a person who could do that, then I would need every scrap of agency I could carve out of the world. There could be no doubt in my mind who was behind anything I did anymore; if I was going to be coerced, I wanted it to be overt, not implicit. If I was going to enact horrors, they would be my fault and mine alone.

I wondered if Decoherence had felt something like this in the moments before we properly met. I thought of her in the entranceway to the safe house, when I first saw her on Keller's security cameras, face obscured by a hoodie and her hair. I remembered how defeated she looked while she waited for us to respond to her request to be buzzed in, how tense she was. Thinking of how that moment must have been for her, what it would have felt like to push that button over and over and wait to see what happened, gave me the courage to finally knock.

It was an ugly door, battered and scuffed and reinforced with steel at the corners. There had been no attempt to make it look less grim and institutional, and metallic numeral stickers like the kind usually found on exterior walls and mailboxes displayed the number. There was no peephole.

No one answered the door. After a long moment of not hearing so much as a scuffle from inside, I started to quietly panic. *Why would I think she was home?* Hell, she could have even moved in the last few days and vanished into the ether again. Even if she was inside, it would be in the opposite of her best interests to answer an unsolicited knock.

I was ready to walk away when a perverse idea struck me. I knew when she'd said it to me, she was just being an asshole, but what the hell.

I started to whistle.

I got through a few bars of a quarter-speed rendition of "Sandstorm" before I devolved into a wheezing laugh that came dangerously close to hysteria. I felt like I might be losing it. Disappointed and relieved, and completely unsure what the fuck to do next, I turned to leave.

Decoherence's head and shoulders phased through the door. I yelped in surprise and she glared at me like an angry ghost. "What the *fuck*," she whisper-yelled at me.

I had managed to drop my cane, which banged shockingly loud on the floor. I winced. "Can I come in?"

"Shit." Her head disappeared inside, and I heard her unlock the door and slide back a chain. A moment later she reached out and dragged me in, practically hurling me into her living room. I kept my footing but was badly off-balance, and barely managed to totter a couple of steps to the couch before collapsing into the cushions.

"Auditor." Her face was incandescent. "You'd better explain."

"My cane is still in the hallway," I said.

She stared at me, then stalked back to the door. She didn't bother opening it again, just reached through and brought the cane with her as her atoms slid cleanly past each other, reordering themselves again after she was safely back inside.

I held out my hand. "Could you have pulled me through the door?" She dropped the cane and I caught it, glad it was one of the lighter, acrylic models.

"The fucking audacity." Her voice made it clear she had indulged me far enough and was not going to do so for very much longer at all.

"I—"

I'd rehearsed what I was going to say to her, but now with her scowling down at me, I drew a terrible blank. It occurred to me that showing up here, to the apartment where she lived, was in fact very different from her showing up at my established safe house populated by security staff. I had Keller with me back then, waiting and eager with a canister of nerve gas. She had only herself, which made her much more vulnerable . . . and therefore dangerous. It certainly didn't help things that she was wearing ratty sweats and looked unshowered, and was in no way at all prepared to deal with me or anyone else.

"I need to talk to you," I managed stupidly.

"I have a phone. That you gave me. Remember?"

"That . . . wouldn't work." It sounded even worse spoken aloud.

She was unmoved. "Why were you making so much fucking noise in the fucking hallway?"

"You said to whistle."

Her face hardened. "Auditor, I swear—"

"This is important."

"Then *what is it*?"

I'd kept things so tightly locked up in my own head that I couldn't get the words out. I tried to find a place to start, scraping through my brain like I was trying to find the edge of a roll of tape. I could feel whatever scraps of sympathy Decoherence might still have draining away the longer I took. I stared at the floor, trying to focus.

The place she'd been staying was grim. The laminate tile that delineated the part of the main room that was the kitchen was peeling up, and there was a sour mildew smell that pervaded the place over the stink of some industrial cleaner that clearly was losing the battle. The couch I was on was more accurately a slouchy futon, with a brown velour chair next to it. I was already acutely aware of a couple of different springs jabbing me in the legs. She wouldn't be in this place if she didn't have to be. And right now, I was compromising even that.

"*Could* you have pulled me through the door? I promise it's relevant."

She wanted to punch me. I could see the tension in her body, the way the unthrown blow gathered in her shoulder. But she let it go, let the violence lose its tension and fall from her fingers.

"I could. Yeah. It's very unpleasant, though."

"How unpleasant?

"Have you even been in shock?"

Very recently. I winced. "Yes."

"That's the best possible outcome."

"That's too bad."

She stared at me after I said that. "You said it was relevant."

"It is." I swallowed. "If there was something . . . inside someone else. Could you get it out?"

"What?" My question clearly made her deeply uncomfortable.

"Could you take something out of someone's body?"

"*Something out*?"

"Yeah."

That must have tipped off something in her hero brain, because some of the hostility and confusion left her, replaced with a kind of efficiency. She started to look me over, as though searching for a wound. It was an unnerving but not unpleasant way to be looked at. "Is this an emergency?"

I hesitated. "Yes."

She took a deep breath. "Alright. Aside from how it would feel— which is extremely bad, you may remember—it depends a lot on where it is, what it is, and how it got there."

"Okay."

"Say if you swallowed something, then yes, I could take it out. But go for the charcoal first if you can."

"Not swallowed."

She looked more alarmed, and came a bit closer. "Is there an entry or exit wound?"

"No."

"If it's healed in, then that's a problem. Something lodged in you, like a bullet, or something bigger—yes, I can take it out. Technically. But the more bonded it is to flesh, the harder it can be not to mess something else up."

I was starting to feel defeated. This was sounding more and more like a complete disaster of an idea. "Does that make it harder to remove, or impossible?"

She uncrossed her arms, reached out with one hand and manipulated something imaginary, trying to find words for something that existed mostly in her muscle memory. "You still have pins in your leg, yeah?"

"And a rod."

"I could take that out. But all the holes would still be there, and their stabilization would be gone. You've healed around it."

"What about—"

"For the love of *fuck*, Auditor, what is happening?" She wasn't annoyed anymore, just afraid—and she was scared for me, specifically, a fact that made me feel ashamed.

"I have . . ." I took another deep breath. *Please don't let him be watching.* "It's about my eye. The cybernetics there."

She immediately shook her head. "No. I can't. See a specialist. I assume you have access to—"

"I *don't.*"

The line between her eyebrows deepened. "I thought it was a custom job."

"Just assume I can't."

"I still won't do it."

"But could you?"

"No. I haven't done anything like that before, but I can tell you *I* would hate it. But more succinctly, I fucking would not want to attempt it. This isn't like your leg. Something that complicated—that's hooked into your eye and nervous system—there's a good chance it's not survivable."

"Could you break it if you can't remove it?"

"Auditor. Please—"

"Leviathan put something in my head."

She froze. The annoyance and confusion on her face was replaced by a blank serenity. "What kind of something?"

"Nothing that could hurt me. Directly."

"You sure?"

That took me aback, and I froze for a moment. Then for my own sanity I decided in that moment that there was *not* a bomb in my head and refused to consider it further. "No. Nothing like that. There's. Something like a camera in my head."

"A camera."

"He can hear and see what I do, if he wants to."

"And right now?"

"I don't think so."

"But you're not sure."

"He said he mostly wouldn't."

"He said he mostly wouldn't."

"But he *has* done it. More, much more than I . . . would like."

"How much."

"Enough."

She nodded once.

"Who knows?"

"You."

"You've told no one else?"

I nodded.

"Why are you telling *me*?"

Why are you here, Quantum?

I could hear my own voice somewhere in hers, the weary exasperation and confusion, the same way I had felt when our positions had been reversed. I remembered how I just needed her to *get to the point* so I could figure out whether I was going to let Keller try to exterminate her in the safe house kitchen. I had needed her to give me just enough information so I could spin it into kindness, and I tried, very hard, to do the same for her now.

"Anyone else I would tell either works for him, which would put them in a terrible situation, or is in direct competition or enmity with him, which would be a horrific betrayal. You're . . . something else."

"Am I." She wasn't sure that she liked that.

"You are. And you're strong enough, you might—"

"I might give you enough time to run?"

I glared at her, much more offended than I would have expected to be. "You might know what's it's like to disobey someone like him."

Something softened in her face. Because she'd been at Supercollider's side, in his shadow, for a huge part of her adult life.

"You get it," I said softly. "You're smart. Your powers are amazing. And you might be able to do it before he finds out."

"Don't you think he'd notice that your router wasn't connecting?" There was a gentleness now in her humor that almost made me want to cry.

"Of course. I just—it would give me time," I settled on.

"How much danger are you in right now?"

I looked up, and her expression was still calm, coolly evaluating, but sympathetic, too. There was something else behind it I couldn't quite identify.

"None at this exact moment, but that could change."

"Because he doesn't know."

"Yes."

"Do you want to leave him?"

"No! Not at all. That's part of why I'm coming here, so I don't have to leave."

"Is that the truth?"

She stared at me a long moment, in case I changed my answer.

After a while, she nodded, and walked into her horrific kitchen. She returned with a chipped mug full of hot water and an Earl Grey tea bag.

"So. He pulled the old plant-an-AirTag-in-your-car—the super-villain version." There was a lightness in her voice that told me, even if she had no idea how, she had decided to help me.

She wouldn't help you if she knew what you just did, I thought, just to hurt myself.

"Yeah." I swallowed.

"That's fucked up."

"I am . . . deeply uncomfortable about it."

"When did you find out?"

"A while ago. Long after it had been installed. Too long."

"Can you tell when it's on, or—"

"No." I cupped my hands around the hot mug. I bobbed the tea bag up and down a few times by its string, glad to do something nervous with my hands.

"I could take you somewhere," Decoherence said. She sounded like she hated her own idea, and so I called her on it.

"Why did you say it like that?"

"Because it's not a good option. But it's *an* option."

"If it's better than an ice pick in the back of a van, I'm in."

"It might not be."

"I'm still in."

THE CAB DELIVERED us in front of a seemingly deserted collection of grim commercial facades. There was an abandoned dentist's office, a convenience store at the far end that looked like it still sold looseys and lottery tickets, a desolate bank, and a bakery. The largest storefront, Romano's Fine Meats, had a broken sign and the windows were papered over.

As soon as we paid and got out, the cab sped off

"Ever been to one?" Decoherence asked.

"No. Dropped someone off once, though." That had been my only exposure to any of the Butcher Shops where injured Meat went for under-the-table medical care. I remembered that disastrous, bloody cab ride—what ended up being my last civilian date, with Bracken—as I rushed a sobbing young man to very similar doors. I couldn't remember his name—I remembered asking, but not his answer—and felt a pang of shame for that. We weren't really supposed to learn their names, which was part of the joke, why we called them Meat. I remembered his glassy, panicked eyes. I hoped he'd lived.

"They're all basically the same, really," Decoherence was saying.

"I've never been inside."

"You were, like, a secretary before, right?"

"Data entry."

"Not doing the punching, is all I meant."

"Punching in numbers." She glared at me. I couldn't even manage to smile back.

She looked at the building. "I've only been in one a couple of times myself."

"That makes sense."

"We—heroes usually pretend they don't exist."

"Usually?"

"Yeah. It's an unwritten rule. Like not bombing hospitals."

"That rule is definitely written down. It's quite a famous document. But I understand you might not be familiar with it."

"I meant for the heroes, not in wartime, asshole."

"When *did* you go in?"

She pressed her lips together. "This guy, a courier, I think, he swallowed something that we needed to unlock this—You know what, it's not a very good story."

We reached the locked doors. The windows were covered by layers of newspaper and butcher paper, making it impossible to see anything inside. At the bottom seam of the door where it met the sidewalk, I thought I could see the faintest glow from a faraway light.

"Wait here," Decoherence said, and stepped directly through the wall and inside the building.

After a few minutes, I started to hear something from inside the door: two sets of footsteps walking quickly down the hallway. One set was Decoherence's confident, authoritative stride, her Super-hero Walk, while the other was uneven and heavier. Then I heard panicked jabbering, at first unintelligible, then gradually resolving into a steady stream of pleading.

"...kids, I got kids, and I'm behind on child support, do you know what that means? Child support? Do you know what it's like to—"

The person speaking cut themselves off as they turned the lock and opened the door. The entrance and hallway beyond were still dark, with a faraway room casting a bit of backlight behind Deco-herence and the man standing in front of me. He had the kind of narrow, tragic face that could have belonged to someone who was twenty-seven or fifty-two.

"My friend just needs a hand," Decoherence said, speaking slowly and reassuringly.

"A friend." He squinted at me. He was pale, but his cheeks were dangerously flushed.

"Can I—"

"Get in here." He waved his arm at me and stepped to the side, locking the door behind me as soon as he could. He turned the mechanism with shaking hands, which did not fill me with any ad-ditional confidence.

"It's a quiet night, but keep it the fuck down. Yes, okay, I'll look, but it's not like I have any choice." He shot a sideways look at Deco-herence, both irritated by her and terrified at her presence. He quick-marched back to the one room with a light on, expecting us to follow.

The room was, I was extremely dismayed to discover, indeed

the back room of a former butcher shop. The drains in the floors, occasional hooks on the walls and ceiling, were extremely unsettling next to the stretchers and hospital beds. All of the medical equipment looked like it had either been stolen or purchased in a foreclosure sale. Many of the pieces had broken clamps still partially attached or bolts marking where they would have been fastened to a floor.

The medic with us wore an apron with leather straps and a coverall, which made him look a lot more like a mechanic than someone adjacent to a doctor. He led us over to one corner of the room, where there was a desk and a battered laptop, and a vinyl-covered "examination" chair that had definitely once belonged to a hairdresser.

"In and out. That's the goal here. We're going to get you in and out as fast as possible, alright?" He gestured for me to sit, then dropped heavily into his sagging office chair. He slapped his legs and looked at me over the rims of his wire-framed glasses. "Let's go. What's the problem."

"Do you know who she is?" Quantum asked, her voice still gentle.

He flinched. He'd clearly been trying to pretend she wasn't there anymore and disliked being reminded of her presence. "What kind of question is that? Everybody's somebody. And it's generally better in this business not to recognize anybody if I can avoid it."

"It's relevant. I promise."

He sighed, taking a moment to clean his glasses. "No. No idea. And I do not care. I would like both of you out of my damn office as soon as possible, so please. What the fuck can I do for you here?"

I took over. "I have some aftermarket parts."

"Yeah?" His eyes darted over me, curious despite himself, lingering a bit on my face and arms.

I tapped the side of my head next to my left eye.

"Ah." He picked up a headset, which included a headlamp with magnifying lenses attached, and fitted it over his face and head. He moved a lever next to my chair and it dropped several inches suddenly. The light was bright and I struggled to keep my eyes open. "Just the one?" he asked.

"Yeah."

He examined the skin around my eye, holding the eyelid open. He then felt around my orbital bone and pressed the skin around my temple to feel for the edges of what might be underneath.

"It's good work," he said eventually.

I felt a little pang, thinking how hard Leviathan must have worked on me, and how carefully. "Thanks."

"Well, what's wrong with it? Looks great to me."

"Can you take it out."

He snorted. "Not on your life. And definitely not on *my* life. You think I'm a transplant surgeon? Have you seen where you are?"

"Can you damage it?"

"What the hell for?"

"Can you fuck it up or turn it off?"

"Why can't the specialist turn it off for you?" He sounded deeply suspicious.

"The person who put it in is . . . disinclined to take it out."

He pulled back and fixed me with an intense glare. "Who put it in? Tell me or you leave now." There was a very short list of places I could have gotten work close to this good, and he clearly did not like the implications of any of them.

"I did ask if you knew who she was," Decoherence said.

He peered at me, as if some clue might trigger his recollection. After this went on for a bit too long, Decoherence decided to rip off the Band-Aid for me. "Leviathan put it in."

He stood up suddenly, almost knocking the headset off in the process. "No." He wrestled it off his head, knocking off his glasses. "Get out."

"Doctor—"

"*Nope.* I'm not your fucking doctor. The two of you should never have come here. Get the fuck out." He groped on the floor to retrieve his glasses while trying to scramble back but also sound authoritative—none of which was working well for him.

"I wouldn't be here if I had a choice," I said. "I just . . . I need it turned off. It's important."

"And *I* don't have a choice, because my life is important." He stood back up, balled his hands into fists.

"I'm not threatening you—"

"It wasn't a question. I'm saying I don't have a choice about whether or not I want to do it—I *can't* do it. You think I'm going to piss off your boss? You think I'm stupid? Look, I don't want any trouble with the supe here, but no. You need to leave and forget this address."

Decoherence took a step forward. "We're not leaving." There was a lot more danger in her voice than there was before.

The Butcher put his glasses back on with both hands. "Why fuck with me, huh?" It wasn't quite a whine, but close. "It's not going to change the fact that L—your boss will kill me."

"He's not here." She shifted her weight and the man's shoulders slumped even further, his body a defeated crescent. "*I am.* So weigh your options: me now or him later."

"Fuck." He reached back for his desk, used it to steady himself. "Fuck me."

"I'm sorry, if it matters," I said.

"It doesn't. Shut up." He tried to glare at me but didn't really have it in him. He put the headset back on and took another look at my face. I could smell his fresh sweat and late-night breath as he panted over me.

"It's really in there."

"Yeah."

"Just the eye, or is it deeper?"

"There's a lot in there."

"Great. S'what I thought."

He backed up and I blinked frantically, tears running down one cheek while huge pink spots of light blindness temporarily obscured my vision.

He looked up to Decoherence before looking back to me, and I almost admired the bravery of this craven man. "I couldn't take it out if I wanted to."

"Are you sure?"

He made a sound that was supposed to be a laugh, but sounded just like a coughing sob. "If I could, then I'd do it just to get rid of you."

"What about damaging it," I tried again.

"I told you—" He stopped. He looked me over, and back at Decoherence once more, and made a decision. "Alright. Come here."

He laboriously got up and led us over to a different station, this one with a slightly better chair. There was a huge, mechanical arm hanging from the ceiling, holding up a device that looked very vaguely like an enormous camera but much more broad and boxy. The arm was made of metal and that yellow-gray plastic of most aging electronics.

"Hold still."

"What's this?"

"Just an X-ray."

"Should I leave the room or something?" Decoherence asked. I thought it was odd she even asked—I'd never read anything in her files that indicated X-rays would bother her. I filed that piece of data away in the depths of my brain, then focused back on the Butcher.

He shrugged. "If you want." Then he pressed a button and the machine gave a deep, shuddering click before she could possibly react. She startled, and seemed ready to hustle out of the room, but then stopped and stood very still, pretending to be unbothered. That interested me, but I kept still and quiet while the Butcher worked. He took a few images, moving the X-ray around my head.

When he finished, Decoherence shuddered in relief and rubbed her upper arms, as though trying to shake off some terrible sensation.

The Butcher turned to Decoherence. "I have to go and get the images. Can I do that?"

"Of course!" she said, cheerfully. "I'll go with you."

"Sure." He made no effort to hide his lack of enthusiasm.

A few minutes later he returned and we gathered around his desk while he attached the X-rays to a nearby light board. Three images of my skull looked back at us, each from a slightly different angle. I could see the fillings in my teeth, the outline of my weirdly pointy chin, the lines in my skull from a bone saw, and an intricate blossom of machinery on one side of my head. My left eye was lit up; I remembered at one point Leviathan's doctors explaining that they'd managed to save some of my original "wetware," so my own retina and lens were cradled against delicate mechanical ellipses. My eye socket was reinforced, as was the side of my skull that had been opened, with delicate plates. Coils like wires or roots ran along my optic nerve, reaching out much deeper into my brain than seemed plausible.

"I got good news and bad news," he said. "Good news: this is an incredible piece of work."

"It is," I said, and my voice almost caught. I fought against the sudden pang in my chest; the obvious care and delicacy of the work that was done to me, and the alien beauty of the final result, gutted me.

"So now the bad news. I ask that you excuse me, as this is a technical term, so I understand if you don't quite follow me, but this tech: it's incredibly fucking complicated."

I couldn't say anything. A pit had opened deep in my stomach. I deeply regretted ever coming here, ever finding my way to Decoherence's apartment. I should have just taken an Ativan and coped, because while this was much worse, it suddenly felt no less futile than trying to blind myself with a ballpoint pen in the privacy of my own apartment. At least that could have been ascribed to some kind of a mental break under stress.

"If I wanted to—and to be clear I don't—but even if I wanted to, and I was somehow fucking stupid enough to attempt it, well . . ." He pointed at the tendrils that reached the deepest into my gray matter. "See these squiggly bits."

I didn't respond, but stared at the X-ray he pointed to.

"You need all that stuff. I'm a blunt instrument. The only things I could do would not be conducive to that all working."

I nodded. I suddenly didn't trust myself to talk, afraid that I would start weeping.

Decoherence saw my face and lowered herself so she was closer to eye level with me, squatting with her weight on her heels. "What do you want to do?"

I took a few deep breaths to make sure my voice wouldn't shake when I spoke again. When I was just about to say some version of *I have no fucking idea*, a distant scraping noise, followed by a mechanical clang, echoed down the hall.

Decoherence stood.

"Fuck," the Butcher said, pushing himself back from his desk. "Another client. Okay. You"—he pointed at me—"stay in the chair and shut up. You"—he pointed to Decoherence—"get in the back. I'll get you in a minute."

Decoherence looked like she was going to argue but then she nodded and started making her way out of the room.

"Stop." I said. Decoherence slowed and turned to look back at me. The Butcher rolled his chair back and forth in nervous agitation. It was still too loud.

"Shut up." They both went still to listen to what I had heard. In the quiet, we could all hear the footsteps.

"I thought you locked the door after us." Decoherence sounded irritated.

"I did," he said.

They sounded like they were both speaking somewhere very far away. My heart was trying to throw itself out of my body. I recognized the footsteps: odd, slightly muffled clicks, like thick ceramic.

The Butcher wore an irritated frown and Decoherence was saying something to me, but I couldn't hear her. I could only hear the footsteps in the hallway, footsteps I would have recognized anywhere in the world. I tried to calculate his precise emotional state from those footsteps, but his gait was deliberately measured and careful. There was no stalking aggression, no quick march of annoyance or the long, encompassing stride of rage that covered as much ground as possible. Just a calm steadiness, purposeful and easy, and there was something about that gentle stoicism that was terrifying.

Decoherence grabbed me by the shoulder, trying to get me to pay attention to her. She shook me once, but I didn't respond. My entire awareness narrowed to a single point, and the rest of the room became an indistinct blur as the heavy door to the examination room opened.

Leviathan stepped into the room.

"Take your hand off of her."

Decoherence stared at him. There was no rush to obey, but then there was no rush to anything; it seemed like they had all the time in the world to consider each other. She looked down at me, at her hand, her fingers around my shoulder, as though carefully studying the amount of pressure she was exerting. She looked back at Leviathan thoughtfully, evaluating, making the kind of calculations one makes if they hold the power in their bodies to destroy anything that might be in front of them, if they wanted to.

Leviathan was running his own violence calculus and waiting on her choices.

The Butcher, for his part, had slid to the ground and hid behind his desk. I thought how pointless that was, how little it mattered—but then, what else was he supposed to do?

Decoherence decided, for the moment, to comply. She gently

loosened her grip and took a single half step away from me, enough to signify no current ill intent to either of us.

"Thank you," he said, politely, as though she had humored him by turning off the air-conditioning.

"You are unharmed." Though he didn't take his eyes off Decoherence, that was addressed to me, and it was not a question.

"I'm alright," I said, my voice scratchy.

"I noticed a radiation spike," he said, and I immediately felt stupid. Of course significant X-ray exposure would immediately raise concern; while a sudden shift in GPS location might not set off any literal alarms, that certainly would.

"Can you explain that?" he said, while the literal X-ray of my skull was still displayed on the light board next to me. But he was waiting again, clearly expecting an actual response.

"I had an X-ray," I said.

"A recreational X-ray." There was an edge to his voice now. The calm was still there, but beginning to frost over at the edges. Time reengaged in that moment; it no longer felt like we had all the time in the world. In fact, at least half of us in the room might not have very much time at all.

Despite my being in the wrong half, I needed to direct his attention back to me. "I didn't want to put anyone in a difficult position."

"So you brought the difficult position here." I most definitely had. I felt suddenly guilty about the man hiding behind his desk, who was doing this shitty job to pay his child support.

"I didn't want their loyalty—"

"Don't say the word 'loyalty' again."

I tried to take up as little physical and psychic space as possible.

Leviathan softly kicked one leg of the desk, to let the Butcher know he was being addressed.

"Did you know who she is?"

"Oh god," he moaned.

"God's not listening," Leviathan answered. "But I am."

"Please."

Leviathan waited, with the kind of infinite patience that only accompanies an infinite capacity for violence.

"Yes. Yes. Okay. They told me. I knew. But I didn't want to help. She made me." He pointed a shaking, accusing finger at Decoherence.

Leviathan tilted his head slightly to one side. "Did she." He was no longer speaking to the man behind the desk.

"He's telling the truth," Decoherence said. "I was here and you weren't. He had a bad choice to make."

"Hmm." He gripped the edge of the metal desk with one of his hands, and it crumpled like a soda can. "I trust now you would choose differently."

"Yes. Yes yes yes." The Butcher repeated it like the word might keep him safe.

Leviathan nodded once.

"We're leaving now," he said, almost cordial.

I stood from the chair and steadied myself on my feet, bracing to follow him.

"She's not going anywhere with you," Decoherence said.

I stared at her in horror, while Leviathan turned slightly to face her more fully.

"What was that?" he asked.

Decoherence had spoken with her chest; there was no question that he'd heard her perfectly. He wanted her to backpedal or dig in.

She chose the latter. "I said, she's not going anywhere. Not with you."

She took a half step toward me, inviting me, with the angle of her body, to step behind her. I didn't move. She looked pointedly at me, as though I might have missed the signal.

"You," he said softly—an extremely bad sign, "don't have a say in the matter."

"Neither do you." Decoherence squared her shoulders.

"Don't do this," I said, feeling the situation rapidly spiraling out of control.

"It's okay," she said to me, while not looking away from Leviathan.

"Just let us leave."

"You don't have to go with him."

"Yes, she does." The volume of his voice was still low, but the smoothness was gone, replaced with a grating buzz.

"She can go wherever she wants. With whoever she wants."

"I want to leave now," I said, desperately trying to de-escalate this. "With him."

Decoherence swallowed, and I could feel the disappointment emanating from her. "You don't have to say that."

"I *am* saying it."

"I don't think you feel safe enough to say what you really want."

Panic and frustration coiled around my throat like a pair of snakes. "I want this to stop."

She stepped forward and took hold of my upper arm. She was much stronger than I was, but her hand was not the only thing that held me. The ultraviolet hum and ozone smell of her force fields spun around us, and I knew that I was not going anywhere she didn't want me to.

By the time her fingers were closed around my arm, Leviathan was somehow behind me, his own hand locked around my wrist. Though he must have moved in response to her, it still seemed like he somehow got there first. As well as physically holding me in place, this prevented Decoherence from just teleporting us away. He knew her powers well enough to be certain that as long as he held on, anywhere we went, so would he.

"Let her go," Decoherence ordered.

"She said she wants to leave." The buzzing in his voice was thicker now, like he was speaking through guitar distortion. Hearing him speak right behind me, unable to see his face but feeling him radiate with anger, made me shake involuntarily.

Decoherence noticed and read the situation like a hero would. "You think she wants to go with you? You think she can be honest about what she wants around you, ever? She's *terrified* of you."

"That's not true," I said.

"You see." Decoherence gestured toward me with her chin.

But it wasn't true, and I hated the thought that she might convince him my affection for him was compelled. "Stop," I tried again.

Yet neither of them loosened their hold on me. I felt my bones starting to hum with whatever Decoherence was preparing to do, while Leviathan's sharp, chitinous hand on my wrist was like a steel cable, an immovable and merciless strength.

"You're the same as you always were," Leviathan said, drawing up closer behind me. He brought his other hand down possessively onto my shoulder. In response, the arm in Decoherence's grip pulsed with the first visible flash of purple light. "You don't care what she wants, only what you think is good for her."

"And *you* care what she wants?" Her voice was thick with contempt. "You're incapable of caring about anyone other than yourself."

"You seem to know so much about me. Would you like to learn more about my capacities?" Leviathan's voice was almost seductive with the promise of violence.

"I've seen enough." Her disgust was palpable. She tried to pull me closer to her, but my body was anchored in Leviathan's grip, so instead she drew closer herself. Their faces were only a few inches apart, with only my body in between them now.

"We are leaving," he said. I knew it was for the last time; his next reply would be an action.

"You're not taking her anywhere."

I felt both of them steady their grip on me subtly, preparing for whatever it was they each intended to do; and I wondered if I was about to be ripped in half.

I reached as far down into my body as I could and found a place to scream from.

"Get your fucking hands off me!"

I thrashed my body to get out of their respective grips, not expecting to be able to, but demonstrating I was fully willing to hurt myself trying to get away.

My shriek and sudden movement made them both start back, breaking a little of the tension between them and reminding them of the relatively frail bundle of skin and nerves they were about to fight over.

"Auditor–" Leviathan began.

"Don't–" Decoherence spoke at the same time, trying to be calming.

"Let me fucking *go."*

They both released me slowly, like duelists lowering their pistols but not uncocking them. I jerked away, out of breath and dangerously close to tears.

Decoherence spoke again first, talking directly to me this time. "It's okay, it's going to be okay–"

"Don't use your hero voice on me."

"I'm sorry." She cleared her throat. "Do you really want to leave with him?"

I didn't answer. Instead, I looked at Leviathan. We stared at each other, both waiting for me to say yes, the words already hanging between us like a bell to be rung.

"You know why I came here," I said to him.

"I cannot fathom."

"I bet you can't–" Decoherence started to say, but cut off with my glare. I turned back to Leviathan.

"I can't live with this"–I touched the side of my face–"the way that it is."

"It is for your benefit and protection. It is a gift."

"It's making me . . . deeply unhappy."

"So you want to hide things from me?" His voice was strained now.

"No, I want my agency and my privacy. There's a difference."

"Do you think me some kind of degenerate—"

"I want my dignity back."

"I am almost never watching."

"But *sometimes you are,* and there is no way for me to know when, so you may as well *always* be watching."

"Do you not trust my judgment—"

"I trust you, but it's *your* word and *your* judgment, and that does not always align with mine."

"I suggest you bring it into alignment." The threat was back, but not as merciless as it had been.

"You don't think I've tried?"

Though still carefully controlled, he raised his voice. "I will not have you outside my reach in an emergency, and I won't have you harming yourself."

"Then, *you* help me with this. Because it can't stay the way that it is."

There was a long quiet. I could hear the Butcher shifting his position behind what was left of the desk, sniffing a few times. Decoherence was watching the conversation play out, her face unreadable. Somewhere down the hall, I could hear the hum of an aging vending machine that needed to be serviced. I knew I was imagining it, but the room around me suddenly smelled like old blood.

"Come home with me," Leviathan said quietly. "I will make the necessary adjustments myself."

I nodded and took a small step closer to him. Decoherence didn't try to stop either of us again, but I could feel every instinct in her body screaming for her to do something. I stared at her for a long moment, holding eye contact for as long as I could, before I had to turn away and leave. I knew I should say something—thank her, reassure her—but nothing came.

And eventually, I turned away.

"AUDIO AND VIDEO off entirely."

"Out of the question."

"It's the only question. That is a hard boundary."

He stewed for a moment. "Let us move on."

I refused to let it go. "Is that agreement?"

He fought against his own frustration. "That is a temporary pause on that point of the discussion."

I didn't like it, but I allowed him to move on so I could know which battles to choose.

"Location tracking stays on."

That was easy to agree to. "Yes."

"I assume the same is true for your vitals."

I pushed back on that one. "What are you tracking?"

"Heart rate, blood pressure and oxygenation, cortisol levels."

"You are not allowed to use that while we are interacting."

That surprised him. "What?"

"You don't get to polygraph me every time we talk." *Or fuck*, I thought, but could not quite figure out how to say.

"Polygraphs are quackery."

"That was a metaphor to explain how I don't want the data used."

"That isn't . . . something I can turn off mechanically."

"Can you limit *your* access to the data?"

He thought a moment. "I can refrain from accessing the interface in your presence."

I considered that. "I want to think about it for a moment, but that should be acceptable."

We spent the better part of two hours negotiating over the gear he'd put in my head, discussing edge cases and figuring out where my comfort levels were. We were in the lab space of his apartment, and as we spoke he slowly assembled the equipment he'd need to do what I was asking. The sticking point remained the primary points of surveillance: his ability to see what I did and listen to what I said.

"It has very narrow directionality and range," he tried to reason about the audio component.

"So you can only hear what *I* am saying?"

"A close conversation would be audible."

"How much of tonight's conversations did you overhear?"

He looked up from the tools he was laying out. "How is that relevant?"

"When did you start listening?"

He thought about his answer. "You were having a cup of tea."

That was much earlier than I had expected. I realized I was gritting my teeth and deliberately unclenched my jaw. "So as soon as my GPS was showing a different location."

"Describing it as a GPS is inaccurate and oversimplified."

"Again, that is not the point."

"I wished to know the reason for your absence. Considering your state of mind, I was concerned."

"I asked to be left alone. You agreed."

"You were no longer in the 'alone' I agreed to."

"That is still not an emergency."

"I beg to differ."

"It was not—"

"Would you have preferred I had let you be, and allowed that Butcher to lay his hands on you?"

"He couldn't do it anyway!"

"He might have *tried*." He placed a bin of cables down considerably harder than necessary. "The fact that you even went there was an unacceptable risk, one you would not have taken if you weren't—"

"The *point* I am making is that, at the moment you chose to listen, nothing more sinister was happening than an off-site conversation."

"My instincts were correct."

"Your instincts are not an emergency. Nor is 'I don't like what is happening.'"

Leviathan crossed his arms. "Tell me, Auditor: What would have happened if I had not arrived? If he could have met your requests?"

"I would have . . ." I faltered, genuinely unsure how to answer. I thought back to the feeling in my chest, knowing what I was doing was stupid and futile, regretting it before the Butcher even turned me down. "I would have left, with the new data I had."

"Would you have pursued your intent elsewhere?"

I looked down. "I don't know."

He sighed and came a few steps closer to me. He took my chin in his hand, tilting my face up, and looked carefully at one of my eyes, and then the other.

"It was good that I came," he said. "I am glad I stopped you."

As quietly as I could, I reiterated, "But *I'm* not glad. Not because of what might have happened, but because of *how* it happened. It doesn't matter if you were right. The only person who can look out of my eyes should be me."

Something about that resonated with him; he tilted his head in a way that showed me my words had landed.

"You have . . . been through a lot, in recent days."

"Don't," I said. I suddenly felt like I was choking.

"You should take some time. To think if this is truly what you want."

"I have been thinking about it since the first moment you told me it was there. This is what I want."

He chose not to fight me on that point any longer, but that didn't mean he gave in either. It took a long and exhausting time before he agreed to settings on the implants I was comfortable with, and only after I conceded to "minimal functionality" when it came to his access to my vision.

"Whenever you're watching," I said, "I have to know it's happening."

It was a long and complicated process, much of it deeply unpleasant, that required several different procedures to complete. The worst of it came right as he began, when he had to insert a needle-like device into the center of my eye to make some physical adjustments. He fitted me with a halo for that, the metal device clamped as tightly as possible around my head and shoulders, so that I couldn't make even the smallest movement.

"I would be remiss," he said, just before the needle pressed into my artificial cornea, "if I didn't ask you one more time. Allow your enhancements to remain as they are. We can discuss your . . . boundaries about their usage and I can adjust my behavior accordingly."

I would have shaken my head in admiration if I'd been capable of moving; of course he waited until I had a needle hovering a few centimeters away from my eye before giving me a final chance to give in to him. He was, after all, very good at what he did.

It turned out so was I.

"While your timing is impeccable, no. This is what I want to happen."

"So be it," he said, and as he pressed forward I heard the sound like a hot needle on glass.

"IT'S DONE," HE said, sadly. He moved as though gravity had suddenly doubled its force on his body.

"Thank you," I said, rubbing my scalp where the sharpest points of the halo had dug into my skin. When I lowered my hands and looked at my fingertips, there was a tiny bit of blood from where a couple of the screws had pierced skin. "I am sorry to have disappointed you," I said, though I wasn't sure where the apology came from.

He did not look at me. "I thought you wanted—" He stopped himself, shook his head, and reset. "You wish to retain your agency. I can't fault you for that."

"Don't you also want me to have agency?"

"I wished for you to be my right hand."

"I want to be more than your appendage."

He turned away. It was easier for both of us if we didn't have to look at each other.

"It is an honor, not reductive. You are—you would be an extension of my will."

"I want that, too."

He paused, his back still turned toward me. "Then why ask me to do this?"

"So that my will is not *subsumed* by yours. I choose to lend it to you, every moment."

He hated that. "In a perpetual state of noncommitment."

"In a perpetual state of *choosing* to commit."

"What use is a hand that might decide not to obey at any moment?" He tried to sound derisive, but there was a genuine question there, so I answered as though it was asked in good faith.

"Trusting that it will even if it does not have to."

He finally turned around and looked at me fully. I had eased myself off the chair and was standing, one hand resting very lightly on his workbench for balance. The pinprick marks on my forehead ached, my eye throbbed, and I was profoundly exhausted. He looked drawn and subdued, but he was listening carefully.

"I want to be a whole person for you. Not a limb."

I watched him flush in the infrared; I found myself relieved I could still see the extended spectrum I'd become used to. I watched the heat of the emotional wave he was experiencing pass over his whole body. Whatever was happening between the two of us, it was deeply difficult for him. I felt grateful he'd left those abilities wholly intact, and I found myself grateful he had not turned that part of my vision off, out of spite.

"You would have me trust you. Over and over. To choose to obey, until you don't. To exercise your own will, and trust that it will be in service of my own if you tell me so." It was on the border between a statement and a question and I chose to answer, to make it clear that I couldn't dictate how he felt any more than he was to dictate how I felt.

"Yes. I would."

I could see him grappling with the loss of control like it was a physical force, like he was wrestling a sea serpent. "Why would I open myself to such a risk?"

"I can't—explain why." The absurdity of me trying to explain the value of vulnerability to anyone was not lost on me. "But I just know it will be better if it is given, and is always a choice."

"How is it better?"

"You will know that everything I am doing is because I choose it." I paused for a moment, wondering if I should flip that coin so he could see the other side. "And I will also know everything I do is because I choose it."

He looked momentarily confused. "You doubt your own will?"

"I have been … running myself through a filter, consciously and unconsciously trying to adhere to what I think you would want."

"You should be doing that anyway," he scoffed.

I suppressed a frustrated sigh. "It's a matter of degrees. How fine the sieve is. And this is unsustainable."

"I would not express displeasure for every minute disagreement," he said, and there was something about his tone that made it clear he had many such moments. I refused to let that bother me.

"But it shackles me, nonetheless. And if I am—" My voice caught. Speaking was horrifically difficult again. "If I am going to do this, be this person, I have to do it under my own volition. I can't for one moment be making choices because I think it's what you want me to do or because I am cornered into it. I have to be doing this for me."

"Does this mean you would not obey me?"

"It does not mean I won't do what you command, no. But if I am doing something for myself, it has to be for me alone."

"I should have simply ordered you to kill him." There was a sullen regret in his voice.

I pushed away the scent of blood, the feeling of a long, final exhalation, and clawed my way back to an answer. "No. You should not have. You presented me with a choice and I made it. I am going to be making more of those choices and I need to be making them as free from duress as possible, even imagined."

"The outcome would be the same."

"But the path is not. I need to know my choices are only mine. Especially when they are ugly."

I was just beginning to make sense to him again. "The coercion you felt was an illusion."

It wasn't, but that wasn't worth going into. "Even if it was, I knew it impacted my decisions, and that is what matters."

"So your evils will be your own." He began it in an almost mocking way, but partly through the phrase, his tone shifted, as if he realized what he said was true.

"And no one else's, not even yours."

I was winning this conversation, and he didn't like it. "And so you place me at the mercy of your decisions. Starved of data. So much less able to predict where your agency will take you."

I softened a little. "You'll always know that I want to be here. That I want to be with you. That I want *you*."

We'd been slowly, unconsciously moving toward each other. We were close enough now that he only had to take a single step before he could put his hands on my shoulders. He gripped me with a steady pressure, as through trying to feel if I was solid. Real.

"And what if you choose to leave?" His voice was as quiet as he could make it, and I would have missed it if we had not been so deep in each other's space.

"I could always choose to leave. It might be more difficult, or result in worse options, but there's always a way out."

He didn't reply. I could see that part of him wanted to make sure I could never leave. But a greater part of him wanted me to be a whole entity, with or without his control, and I saw a deep sadness move through him. I felt it pass through his body like a wave, brushing against me as he continued to hold on to my shoulders.

"Do you *want* to leave?"

"No. I just need to know I would survive if I did."

He adjusted the grip he had on each of my shoulders, evaluating them. He tightened his hold slightly, letting the rough pads of his fingers dig into my skin. I felt a bit of the old fear ripple deep in my stomach, an automatic response in my body to a reminder that he could, if he wanted to, tear me to pieces.

I spent a lot of time around people who could kill me. Heroes and villains alike, and the various sidekicks and henches and others who worked with them. Everyone has the capacity for violence, of course, no matter how physically weak or restrained they might be; everyone has their own ways of getting around their limitations and doing harm. I had just proven that, vividly, to myself. But there is a different feeling when someone is so much stronger than you are and you are both acutely aware of that imbalance; it's yet another thing entirely when someone has a significant body count, when the horror of a single death has faded away into a series of obstacles that had to be overcome.

Leviathan was known for his impossible invulnerability, but his raw strength matched or exceeded that of almost any hero he'd ever fought. While more than one high-profile death had been pinned on him inaccurately—Supercollider only the most recent—that didn't mean there weren't plenty he *was* responsible for. He did not languish in misery for what he had done; he would, unquestionably, do harm again, directly and indirectly, whenever he had to in order to achieve his goals.

Supercollider had the opportunity to kill me numerous times: he'd wrapped his huge hands around my throat once, fully intending to squeeze until my eyes went dark, but he was stopped—not by his own choice, but by external pressure. Other heroes arrived on the scene, and he couldn't just kill me in front of them. He cared enough about what the world thought about him to stay his hand, to keep things hidden until no one important was watching.

Leviathan was different. In this moment we were alone, but it would not matter who was watching. The only thing that prevented him from crushing me at any moment was the choice not to. He made that choice, over and over again, every moment I (or anyone else) was in his presence. I kept living because he wanted me to. It was impossible to be around him and not be acutely aware of that fact that my continued survival was an active choice that could be altered at any moment.

I was very good at managing these feelings in his presence, acknowledging them and respecting them as my brain tried to protect me, while carefully compartmentalizing its warnings so that I could interact with him as normally as I possibly could. I had even learned how to relax into it. I imagined he was also acutely aware of my vulnerability in his presence, though he had never drawn deliberate attention to the fact that he was completely capable of obliterating me with a trivial amount of effort. But now we both stared at that fact—and the way it could impact my decision-making—dragged out of that constant background radiation of subtext and placed squarely between us.

"This"—he lifted one hand, briefly, gesturing toward my eye—"was meant to keep you safer. Never place you in danger."

"But I can't ever be safe from you." I said it softly, like a sweet thing. I supposed that it was.

"No," he agreed. "You can't. But I do wish you to be safe. Is that enough?"

It was.

I WISHED I could have taken weeks to heal and decompress from everything that had happened. Leviathan had been extremely careful, but my eye was dark with broken blood vessels and I was racked with a terrible headache that made it hard to concentrate on anything at all. I wanted nothing more than to sleep and nurse all of my various hurt and confused feelings, but "no rest for the wicked" is much more than a clever phrase. I couldn't falter now. So I took some extra painkillers and turned down the lights in my office, and did all I could to push through.

I no longer had the privilege of a well-thought-out and perfectly structured plan unfolding as it should; with my rather chill kidnapping of the twins turning into a very fraught prisoner exchange that not everyone survived, my ability to predict the next set of outcomes was not nearly as precise as I'd intended it to be. I could make very good guesses, of course, but it was still far outside of my control, and the margins for error now yawning chasms. It was one of my least favorite of all possible places to be:

Waiting to see what would happen next.

LEVIATHAN AND I were, predictably, incredibly awkward around each other, both of us wounded and raw, though only one of us was physically hurt. Regardless, he had to make sure everything was healing properly, so we couldn't even avoid each other and nurse our complicated emotions. The disappointment I felt radiating from him also reminded me of how Decoherence must have felt. Once again I had used her when I needed help, placed her in real and immediate danger, and then still left with Leviathan, leaving her to whatever fate she chose. As angry as I was at her inability to not be a hero in a goddamn emergency, I knew I had also let her down. But there were only so many emotions I could manage beyond my own, and while I felt deep and complicated things about her, it was Leviathan I shared space with.

Every time he looked at me there was a profound sadness in his eyes. For him, this was a huge rupture between us, both because of my actions and the loss of what I imagined to be a unique kind of intimacy he had enjoyed; for me, there was a vast, terrible relief tinged with guilt for the pain I was causing him, inextricably bound up in every misshapen, ugly feeling I had about Greg's death.

No, not his death. The feelings I had about killing him, the unfairness and necessity of that, and my absolute need to hold on to my own agency through it. For all of the tumultuous uncertainty that I was feeling, that was my one anchor point: that I knew now I'd chosen it for myself, and could not hide behind any real or imagined duress.

Even though it had been my decision, it was just as important to me that I did as right by him as we could. We returned Greg's body to the Draft in a dignified manner. We had a private ambulance that often worked with dubious clients deliver him, neatly covered and bagged, to the Vet, where we knew the message would reach who it needed to as quickly as possible. We knew that they'd waste no time in making him a martyr, and decided to give them as little ammunition as possible, not that it mattered in the end. I just wanted to know, when I looked back on it, that I had handled things as well as I could.

For all the performative wailing and gnashing of teeth that was to come, we had given the Draft an incredible gift. And to their despicable credit, they did some of their finest work. I was not at my best, and my team had been whittled down to only Jav and Veronique (who I had just stolen from Molly), and so I could not pinpoint the exact moment someone said that he'd been "Audited" for the first time. But like any excellent phrase, it did its work beautifully. It was repeated in articles and sound bites and pull quotes, and I found myself deeply admiring whoever had deployed it. I wondered if Mom might even have written it himself.

When the Draft began to release their own statements, a carefully considered thirty-six hours after the wider campaign began, something happened that had not before: my face was a part of the messaging. That didn't surprise me, but the images they used did. I might have expected some decent long-range surveillance photographs from my rare journeys off the compound, or a few recent professional headshots they'd scraped up. They chose, instead, a surreptitious photo another villain had captured (and then either sold to them or had seized) during Supercollider's funeral.

What shocked me most was how flattering it was, catching me mid-sneer, leaning toward Leviathan's shoulder as though I was about to whisper something sinister, my cane looking like a theatrical embellishment instead of a mobility device. I looked better than I ever pictured myself looking in my own head, strange and scarred and deeply intimidating, and it felt *good* to be seen that way while newscasters fought tears or barely contained their rage, talking about what a monster I was.

That same day, Mom was on the air. He wore a suit for the very first time in his professional life, and possibly at all, but it had been chosen well and fit him perfectly. It was black; a stark contrast to his usual kindergarten teacher palette. He appeared on broadcast and simultaneous livestream as a man in profound mourning, as though reaching the apex of his career was the worst thing that ever happened to him instead of the best.

He should be sending me flowers, I thought, watching on my laptop from bed, alone in my apartment.

The title card beneath him identified him not as the CDO, as I expected, but as CEO of the Draft. Again—a move I hadn't anticipated, as it signaled not just a regime change, but a tectonic shift in the Draft mindset. By occupying the position that had been symbolically left open for decades, Mom destroyed the fiction that the Draft was ruled equitably and no one in the C-suite had more power than anyone else. To drive the point home, the former acting CDO, Carmel Gentileschi, and the CCO, August Chisholm—his greatest rivals for the position he now occupied—stood at his left and right respectively, presenting a united front.

Mom was triumphant beyond even the scope of his original ambitions, and he had the audacity to act heartbroken about it.

"This is not the job I wanted," he began, his voice carefully hoarse. "It's not an honor to stand here with 'CEO' next to my name. If we're enacting these emergency measures, it is because we have failed."

"Please," I said aloud, to no one.

"It has been made clear—abundantly, horrifically clear—that a stalemate is no longer an option. We can no longer delay direct, decisive action against the forces of evil that darken our door."

He took a moment to gather himself, looking down at the podium. Chisholm clapped him on the shoulder once, as though offering him support. Mom nodded in solemn thanks, and I had to wonder how often they'd rehearsed that.

"When we announced the Amnesty Initiative," he continued, "many of you were reasonably skeptical, and I understand those feelings completely. I know a lot of you felt we were making a mistake at the time, and now, many more of you may feel the same way. But I don't regret it, not for a moment. This . . . tragic, despicable, and utterly unnecessary incident has driven home, for me and the rest of our organization, just how necessary it was. If there was anyone we could get out and to safety, we had to.

"I am sorry—" And here his voice broke. He turned briefly away. Gentileschi reached for him this time, and he briefly squeezed her hand back, before facing forward again. When he continued, it was past a lump in his throat. "I am sorry we could not save all of you. Please know that we tried."

He paused again, gathering a different kind of energy. He cleared his throat, and his voice was clearer now, and with an edge of iron.

"We always knew the Amnesty Initiative would have to be temporary. We'd keep the doors open as long as we could, but *only* as long as we could. Now, with this unprovoked attack on a civilian to send a message—in direct opposition to that amnesty we offered—that door has to close. We must choose to protect everyone who has already walked through it, and everyone else the Draft has sworn to keep safe—which is all of you," he said with a nod toward the cameras, including everyone watching into his fold. "There will be no more opportunities and no more extended deadlines. As of this moment, anyone who has not claimed amnesty will find there is no mercy left for them. Not from us or anyone.

"We resisted the call for retribution against Supercollider's murderer for many reasons," Mom continued, "mostly because we knew retribution was not his way."

"How fucking dare you," I said to the screen.

"In his name, we wanted to avoid any unnecessary violence, and until inevitable conflict did come, we wanted to prepare our surviving heroes as best we could. We aren't going to say that was a mistake, because all of those reasons are good; but sometimes when you are dealing with monsters, you can't do what's best for everyone. The kindest options don't work. You need to do anything you have to, to get rid of the monster."

Finally, I thought, *something we can agree on*.

"We gave as much time and mercy as we could—many of you will still say too much. You might even be right. But we had to let as many people as possible turn their lives around, if that's what they wanted. But to anyone who is still there, anyone who chose to remain with that Villain—well, you have also made your choice. We will respect it, even as we mourn for what could have been."

As reporters clamored to ask questions and many in the audience started to clap, I felt a cramp in my cheeks that worsened my headache, and I realized I was smiling. I had initially detested how he framed things, how he made his lies feel so believable. I also thought I might feel some fear or misplaced regret at a moment like this, when I was reminded I'd finally crossed a point of no return. I thought I might have a moment of panic, and perhaps a different version of me would have. But now I felt nothing but pride, and a bit of relief that no one would harass me about a misguided redemption arc ever again.

It was at that moment, warmed by a deep, new kind of satisfaction, that I heard the first explosion.

THIS WAS NOT the first time I had experienced the compound going into a complete lockdown; when Supercollider and Leviathan fought outside, every blast door and secure server was locked and sealed shut to weather the storm. That time, it was a relatively standard superheroic attack, in that most of the henches just had to mine their emergency protocols and duck and cover. The heroes' main concern was the climactic battle outside, and no one was especially worried about the accountants and janitors sheltering in place or fleeing with their laptops.

This time, however, nobody was getting out. There were no off-site safe houses to evacuate to, no tedious paperwork to start, no ordered furloughs of nonessential staff until the Lair could be rebuilt. While we might have been reduced to a relative skeleton crew over the last months, everyone left was now already considered acceptable collateral damage.

Instead, we all went deeper into the compound. Moments after the first awful sounds, a pair of Meat showed up at my door. Rather than the escort I expected, I found myself unceremoniously picked up and carried while they ran through dark halls, the floors barely illuminated by emergency lights. I'd been safely deposited in the main Enforcement bunker, surrounded by colleagues I felt certain, in that moment, I had completely failed.

I paced the bunker miserably, viciously picking at my cuticles. I couldn't fathom how I had gotten this so catastrophically wrong. I knew that the Draft would react to Greg's death, they had to; but this was wildly disproportionate and completely outside the band of all my simulations. I expected the press conference, but sending in the Future to attack Leviathan directly was nothing like what I had predicted. Greg was, at the end of the day, a single civilian and a former hench, and not even one covered by the beautiful promises of amnesty. I expected the incident to be held up as a perfect example of why all the Draft's programs were necessary, not used as an excuse to sign a death warrant for everyone I worked with.

"I fucking love a good siege," Keller said, hands on his hips, as he watched the security feeds arrayed before him. "Good for the heart." He took a bite of an energy bar.

I felt nauseated. "You know you might not live this time," I said, and the truth of that statement scared me more than most things could have. I'd never before considered Keller was capable of dying, and now I hated it was a reality I had to consider.

He grinned at me. "Nah, I'm a cockroach. Not getting rid of me."

"You're one of those 'they'll never take me alive' assholes, aren't you."

"I am offended you even have to ask."

My response was cut off by another huge smashing sound. Shield and Thundersnow blasted the east observation tower to pieces, leaving hunks of burnt concrete and rebar scattered across the yard below. I watched on the security monitors as they nodded to each other in satisfaction, before walking back to their teammates, who waited by the wreckage of the main gate. That tower had been empty for weeks, except for occasional maintenance—one of the casualties of all the employees we had lost—but there was no way for the heroes to have known that. As far as they knew, they had just crushed to death whoever was on guard duty or monitoring the radar without a second thought.

"That was to get our attention," Keller noted, far too cheerfully, and adjusted the angle of a pair of massive sound cannons he had pointed toward the entrance.

A moment later, Thundersnow stepped forward. She strode past the smoking, twisted gates—that had been the first explosion we had all heard—like she owned the place. The rest of the Future followed in carefully choreographed positions. Shield walked on her right with the broad-shouldered swagger of a bouncer. The twins were to her left, and shared a moment of meaningful eye contact. Red Sprite came last, almost floating, her feet still technically making contact with the ground but not in a way that looked like they were bearing her weight.

One of the comms crackled to life. "She's heading toward Leviathan's tower."

Keller poked the *talk* button aggressively. "Do not engage without direct order. No first shots. Against *people*."

Various security cameras recorded their movements from multiple angles, as they stepped deeper into the heart of Leviathan's compound. It felt deeply wrong, watching the five of them walk right through the front doors unopposed. Just seeing their boots on the ground of that beautiful lobby, walking across the same mosaic of the Dragon devouring Saint George I did every day, made me irrationally angry. They moved slowly, scanning the huge, echoing space for threats that did not manifest.

"We can do this one of two ways," Thundersnow said, amplifying her voice like a biological megaphone. The effect was deeply intimidating, like listening to a storm. "Leviathan and the Auditor: Come out and surrender yourselves. Once you have been secured, anyone who surrenders peacefully or is taken in with nonlethal force will be treated fairly."

"Eat my entire ass," Keller snarled at the monitor, as though she could hear him. Almost giddily, he radioed one of his Meat to make sure the rapid-expanding foam guns were loaded.

"If you do not surrender now, we will bring to bear whatever force is necessary to capture these villains. We will take this place apart brick by brick if we have to, and nothing—and no one—will get between us and them."

The way she said it was hard and emotionless, with no real anger behind it—just a nonnegotiable finality. If she felt uncomfortable about threatening the lives of every person on the compound, she didn't show it, which of course was why she was in charge. The rest of the Future, though, did not look nearly as confident or sure about what they were being ordered to do. Shield's shoulders were set, but his face seemed troubled, and the twins looked at each other intensely, as though having a silent argument. Red Sprite even grabbed Thundersnow's arm at the end of the speech and tried to talk to her, but the taller woman shook her off and shut her down with a quick glare.

Thundersnow, as if to drive the point home to everyone and her teammates, added, "Whatever your choice, do it quickly. Even this opportunity is more than we were told to give you. But I want to give you one chance to do the honorable thing and do right by your people . . . if you even know what honor is."

Behind me, I heard the sound of the bunker's massive, vault-like door unlocking. I stood and turned in time to see Leviathan appear in the door, lit from the light of the hallway behind him. He was radiant. His invulnerable body, his own living suit of armor, was covered with additional layers of plates and blades that took his silhouette from insectoid to demonic. Everyone in the room fell completely silent when they saw him.

He looked around the rest of the bunker, filled with members of Enforcement but also researchers and data scientists, engineers and project managers. There were a few more bunkers like this, scattered throughout the compound, with similar eclectic collections of talent, everyone undoubtedly in various stages of panic or acceptance.

"They attempt to cast you into doubt," he said to the room, his voice filling the reinforced space. "Every one of you is safe here, and will remain so as long as your loyalty remains, as it has held fast until now. Remain here until I return."

Leviathan turned to Keller, who stood.

"No interference," Leviathan said, "regardless of what you see."

"You don't want any backup?" Keller asked.

"No. Only I will engage with them," Leviathan said, to Keller's visible disappointment.

"Understood."

He looked down at me, his eyes unreadable.

"Come with me," he said, extending a hand to me. I was surprised, but I took it.

"Shouldn't I stay with everyone else?" I asked as he led me out of the room.

"Absolutely not." His tone had no humor in it whatsoever, and I stayed quiet as we walked down the corridors.

We stopped in front of another massive, reinforced door; this one had a biometric lock that Leviathan operated by placing his entire hand up to the wrist into an aperture, gripping something inside, and turning. The door seemed to think for a minute before the lock groaned open. Leviathan pulled himself free of the keyhole and gestured me inside.

"Why here?" I slowly stepped into a much smaller bunker, also outfitted with an array of security feeds as well as a computer terminal. "I would have been able to see everything on Keller's—" There was a bench that might also have been a bed attached to one wall, and I immediately noticed a small pile of my clothes was laid out on top, along with one of my canes. I felt a spark of gratitude for this, as I had been evacuated still in my pajamas.

"These are my accommodations," Leviathan said, turning on the monitors and ensuring the feeds were all live and functional. "There is no more secure location on the premises."

"Are you . . . worried?"

"Not in the slightest," he said, completely calm.

I was certain then that his composure could only mean that he was catastrophically disappointed with me, and that I had placed him, myself, and every part of the plans we had made in mortal peril. That I had made a series of miscalculations so dire every-thing he'd built, and that we had built together, might have already collapsed.

"This is my fault," I said miserably. "I don't know how I got this so wrong."

"What?" He stared at me with a confusion so deep it was suspi-cious.

"I can't figure out how this could have happened." I started to pace again, though I had much less room in the smaller bunker. "Why would they escalate like this, in response to–" I couldn't quite manage to say *Greg's death*. I let it hang there.

"I'm sorry," I said at last, knowing it was a pathetic response to the gravity of my error. "I didn't know this would happen."

"This isn't yours to bear." Leviathan took hold of my shoulders to stop my pacing. "I knew," he said.

I didn't know how to respond. I just stared up at him, every glit-tering synapse and beautiful neuron in my brain rendered inert and useless.

"You knew? Knew that they would send the Future?"

"Yes," he said. "You have done nothing wrong."

I hated the feeling of knowing I had missed something, like a chasm was yawning at my feet in the dark. "How–"

"I ask for your trust," he said, taking one of my hands in both of his. "It may be difficult. But I ask you now, for whatever comes: trust me."

I wanted to refuse, and I very nearly did. I came very close to ripping my hand free from his fingers and screaming everything I had ever wanted to yell at him. How he wasted my time and effort and intelligence every time we went over and around one of my plans; how excluding me from his real agenda made it impossible for me to completely trust him the way he asked; how he had no appreciation for how terrifying and infuriating it was to be this vulnerable all of the time. My head and face still ached from the changes he'd recently made to the surveillance system he had installed in my goddamn head without my permission, which I had not yet even been allowed the space to be properly angry about. As I looked up at him in that bunker, I almost quit.

But he was looking down at me with an awful kind of hope. He had seen an opportunity, something I could not see, and he had pursued something I could not follow. Now that he could invite me in, he wanted to, desperately. And for all my righteous and extremely justified anger, if what I was so furious about was that he was not letting me in, how could I slam that door shut when he finally opened it. I had demanded that he trust me, and it would make me the worst kind of hypocrite not to trust him now.

So I swallowed that rage and I nodded, not yet about to speak. He pulled my hand to his mouth and held it there, and I found I just could not hold on to the rage I had felt the way I wanted to.

"We can do more than ruin them," he promised. "We can do more than simply win. And I cannot do it without you, could not do it without everything you have built so far. Let me show you."

"I trust you," I said, this time aloud.

I felt, rather than heard, his hum of satisfaction as the vibration was conducted through my hand. With a final soft ripple of his mandibles over my knuckles, he turned and swept out of the room, locking the door behind him. When the mechanism latched and settled into silence, I wondered if anyone else knew where I was, and if it even mattered if they did. Locked in a room that only he could open, I was only ever getting out again if he returned in triumph.

IN PERSON, SUPERHEROIC standoffs don't look anything like you think they will. They're depicted with dramatic, swooping wide shots and then intense close-ups, every squint and sneer meaningfully captured. In reality, it's just a long wait or a long walk toward someone waiting for you, trying to look important and intimidating the entire time. You don't get to directly observe their reaction to first seeing your silhouette, you don't get to see most of their expression as you draw closer. You just have to wait, horribly, until you can finally communicate with each other, usually with violence.

While I slowly got dressed, I had a moment of almost-sympathy for the Future as we waited, together, for Leviathan to meet them. At least I had multiple surveillance angles to watch and a comm in my ear, with Keller narrating to distract me a little.

"The big guy looks like he's going to shit himself," Keller said. "Those kids, the twins? They hate this. Thundersnow's keeping it together, best face of the bunch. Sprite looks relieved he's coming out and she doesn't have to drop a bunch of civvies on their heads from low orbit."

The Future had a lot of time to get nervous, and even though they were braced for it, every single one of them jumped or visibly tensed when the armored doors to the main elevator slid open. The musical chime sounded almost mocking as Leviathan stepped out with slow, languorous menace. Only Thundersnow had ever been physically near him before, at Supercollider's funeral, and even that was from the considerable distance Doc had banished her to. For the rest of them, this was their first time, and it showed. It was easy to take for granted, as someone who actively enjoyed his physical presence, the bone-deep unease he could cause someone who'd never experienced it before.

He stopped walking quite close to them, close enough that he could speak without projecting. Much too close for any of their comforts. Marrow actually started to take a step back before he caught himself.

Leviathan spread his hands, showing them empty, as though it mattered. "I am deeply sorry," he said, "that your handlers have put you in this position."

"That's not all you'll be sorry for," Shield said, and I was impressed that he managed to get the words out, even if they rang hollow.

"I am not surprised, however," Leviathan continued like Shield had not spoken. "They were once my handlers, too, so none of their cruelty shocks me anymore."

I watched as the twins both looked away from each other, as if those words distressed them.

"If you are here to surrender," Thundersnow said, lifting her chin, "turn around." She held a pair of restraints in her hands, mitts that would fit over someone's entire hands and forearms, connected by a thick, solid bar. I recognized them from the Dovecote archives I'd read; they were made of a superalloy of austenite, nickel, and chromium usually reserved for nuclear reactors.

"You expect that to hold me." Leviathan sounded disgusted.

"Think of it as a gesture of good faith," Thundersnow said, without flinching.

I felt a pang of nervousness, and bit my lip. She was smart and confident and hard to rattle, even now. I didn't get the chance to break her down and get under her skin like the rest of them, and it showed; I began to worry if that would be another horrible misstep, an undoing about to happen.

"Ah," Leviathan said, striding forward suddenly. "There is no 'good' here."

Shield tried to launch forward to protect Thundersnow, though she held up an arm to stop him. Leviathan took the opportunity to snatch the restraints out of her hand, and tossed them casually to the side, without looking. Almost like a bride tossing a bouquet. They punched a hole through the concrete wall like a bullet through a soda can. The hole left behind let in a ray of light from outside, swirling with mortal dust.

There was a long silence from the Future after that. Shield was still standing with one massive arm protectively in front of Thundersnow, the air around them thick and blurred with a readied kinetic shield. But he looked a lot less comfortable now with any part of him being between her and Leviathan, though he tried very hard to appear stoic.

"Five against one," said Shield, rolling his shoulders. There was a casualness that didn't quite reach his face; he'd been practicing his patter. "I like those odds."

Thundersnow, however, had different concerns. "So that is your choice. For everyone here." She gestured around her, taking in the entirety of the compound. That sweep of her hand included anyone still on the premises, everyone confidently or nervously or in a state of terror sheltered in a bunker.

Leviathan smiled, the segmented pieces of his mouth rippling. "And what is the fate of 'everyone here,' as I am not inclined to surrender?"

Thundersnow's face twisted. "You know very well—"

"I want to hear you say it," he said.

Thundersnow's face radiated anger, and she shoved Shield's arm out of the way to take a menacing step closer. In that moment I could imagine how much she hated this, and how much she resented being confronted with everything they had been sent here to do.

"I will do whatever is necessary to bring you, and everyone who is loyal to you, to justice."

Leviathan cocked his head to one side with an infuriating kind of curiosity. "And what does that 'justice' look like? Tearing these buildings down a brick at a time, as you said. And what of the people? That's really why you came here, isn't it? To salt the earth? To guarantee we cannot rebuild again? To make sure no one gets out alive?"

Leviathan took another step forward. This time, no one backed up. "No one in this building is going to surrender to you," he said. "Neither I, nor a single person in my employ, is interested in your dubious mercy or pathetic justice. If you wish to carry out your mission, you will have to do as you threatened. Pull these buildings apart, find everyone sheltered within, and let them break themselves against you. Carry out your mission. I invite you to do so."

Every member of the Future was putting on their best game faces now, but it was not hard to see that each one—except Thundersnow, who remained steadily furious—found the idea repulsive. They wanted to punch someone that could take it, not murder humans with no powers.

"Or," he said, lifting a hand as though it held a physical representation of the offer he was about to make, "I can show you just how much the Draft has lied to you."

Thundersnow made a decision on behalf of everyone. She took a deep breath, and she screamed.

Every window, every computer in the lobby shattered. I ripped the earpiece off immediately, but my ear still rang from the weaponized noise. I realized I could still hear her, faintly, not just from any of the speakers, but through the building itself. The ghost of her scream reached through the concrete and lead and steel, a horrible vibration that brushed against me as deep in the heart of the Lair as I could be.

After the sound faded, I didn't dare put the earpiece back in right away. The four members of the future behind Thundersnow all had their hands instinctively over their ears, even though sophisticated sound filters were a mandatory part of their uniforms. Leviathan was no longer directly in front of them; the force of the sound wave had blasted him backward, into the elevator that he'd entered the room from. The elevator car was hanging askew in the shaft, emergency lights flickering, swaying from a partially detached cable.

Without so much as a dramatic pause, Leviathan climbed back through the now-broken doors. Then, he grabbed hold of the elevator car by the exposed frame and pulled it out of the shaft and into the room. I could hear, tinny and far away from the comm in my hand, the horrible metal-on-metal screeching sound as the car was torn free from the metal guardrails and pulled through the disintegrating walls, and then the deeper scrape as it was dragged across the marble floor. There was a slight pause when the cable had been stretched to its limit, but then with a final tug it snapped.

"Unfortunately," Leviathan said, shifting his grip on the elevator car, "you're going to have to try a great deal harder than that."

I expected Leviathan to swing at Thundersnow, who had attacked him. Clearly the Future did as well, because Red Sprite grabbed the twins and rocketed out of the way, and Shield immediately threw up a defensive barrier around her. His muscles clenched and his hands curled into fists like he was holding up a physical object, instead of projecting a force.

But Leviathan didn't swing for her; he slammed the car directly at Shield himself, who in his eagerness to cover his teammate had left himself much more vulnerable, with only a whisper of the barrier extending over his own arms and torso. The overhead arc of the elevator made contact with them both, but while it crumpled around Thundersnow harmlessly, the experience was very different for Shield. When Leviathan lifted the car off of them, like someone picking up a rock to look at the bugs underneath, Thundersnow sprang up, furious.

Shield didn't move.

As I watched on the monitor, riveted, alone in the completely secure bunker, a hand fell on my shoulder. A second hand was instantly over my mouth, stifling any instinctive scream I might have made. I was in the heart of inconceivable destructive power, all of which would move the world to help me or was within my authority to command, but I couldn't reach any of it. It was one of the loneliest moments of my life.

Then I recognized the grip on my arm and face, and the smell of skin and ozone, and relief flooded my body when I realized it was Decoherence who held me.

"Stay calm," she said, slowly releasing her grip on my face to make sure I would comply.

"You scared the shit out of me," I said, with a tremble of nervous laughter in my voice. I started to turn toward her, but she held me still.

"Is this what you wanted?" She shifted her grip so she was holding both of my upper arms, forcing me to face the scene in front of us. "Is this what you meant to happen all along?"

"They attacked *us*," I reminded her, trying to engage her in the game we usually played.

This time, she did not return my serve. "Just like you wanted them to."

Leviathan had set the elevator car down on a furious Thundersnow, who was fighting wildly to lift it off of her, and picked up Shield by the ankle. He was dragging him, rather nonchalantly, toward the elevator shaft. Something twisted in my chest, as the relief I'd felt retreated. "No," I said. "This is not what I intended."

"I don't believe you," she said, and there was a tight quality to her voice that sounded close to tears. She meant it.

"I understand why you wouldn't." I let my very real disappointment color my voice.

"You never wanted better for them. You wanted to destroy them, like you do everyone."

The fear I'd laid aside started to creep back in, cold and sour. "I wanted this to be different for them. Leviathan . . . had different ideas."

Her hands tightened on my arms. "Is that how it works with you two. You pretend like you're trying to enact some kind of villainous harm reduction, then he conveniently escalates."

"It's actually very inconvenient," I said viciously.

"Then leave," she spat.

I drew breath to hiss something back, but her grip on me shifted. She was no longer restraining me, she was holding me.

"Leave," she said, and her voice was completely different. "We can go right now."

"What . . . ?" I found myself at a loss.

"By the time he notices you're gone we can be out of here. Farther than you can imagine."

"Decoherence—"

"If this isn't what you wanted," she said desperately, "if you're as disappointed as you'd want me to believe, do something about it."

I hated the fact that still, now, there was some tiny part of me that considered it. That wanted to say yes, to close my eyes and let her teleport me wherever she mistakenly thought would be safer.

"Fuck them," she said. "Fuck *all* of them. Leviathan and the Draft are just opposite ends of the same fucking spectrum."

She drew in a deep breath, like she was about to take a huge risk. "I know you. I know you didn't do what they say you did. I know they set you up for that guy's death, it's so obviously—"

"True."

"What?"

"It's so obviously *true.* I killed him."

A vast silence followed. While screams and thuds and platitudes echoed out of the broken speakers, all I could hear was Decoherence breathing.

"No. You couldn't have."

"Decoherence."

"No. You're not—you wouldn't do that." She was never good at believing me, especially when I told her something true about myself.

"Listen to me," I said. "Listen very carefully. If you think I'm on some kind of fucking redemption arc, you are dead wrong. And that would mean you're the same as Mom."

She flinched like I'd hit her and I fought the impulse to recoil.

"*He* made you do it. He must have. Auditor—"

"Don't you *dare* undermine my fucking agency like that again."

She was shocked into silence, her hands on my arms going limp. I could have shaken her off, but I wanted to keep her close enough to hear me.

"No one is making me do anything. Not Mom, not you, not even Leviathan. The only thing making me worse is me."

"He was a civilian."

"You sound like Mom. Don't give me that shit. I know down to the body how many civilians the Draft has killed. How many *you've* killed. I know the numbers better than you do."

"It's not the fucking same, and you know—"

"Don't you dare sneak up behind me, in a fucking security bunker, knowing I am beyond help, and threaten my life—which is absolutely what you are doing—and let yourself believe you're still taking the high road. You know your fists are haunted."

She was still for a very long moment, processing, while a restless frustration started to gather in my chest.

"Please come with me," she said one last time.

I was not prepared for that. I was gearing up for another fight, another round reminding her she still had far more blood on her knuckles than I did, that we were closer in alignment than she would let herself think. I was not prepared for a genuine plea, a bid for a real connection.

"Decoherence—"

"Not because it's the right path. I don't know if it is, for you. But you—you don't have to do this. I don't know what to do next myself. But we can figure it out. Together.

"Please."

I knew in that moment I had been wrong. It hadn't been Mom holding the door open for the last time; I had rejected that eagerly, with a twinge of awareness for what I was doing but no real possibility of regret. But she was not asking me to suffer for repentance.

This wasn't a door Decoherence opened, trying to tantalize me through with promises of a redemption arc, with good to do and bridges to rebuild. It was her straining with all her might to keep a door that was already closing open just one moment longer. She was fighting with all her strength to give me time, a little more time, just in case I could make it through.

I didn't expect it to hurt so badly. I had to close my eyes against it. Of all the times I had disappointed her, this was the worst. It hurt, perhaps, even more because she wasn't even hesitating to offer me a choice, which is all I ever wanted.

"No."

I thought at first it was a sound, like a deep, sub-bass hum. But then I realized it was some sort of vibration, the kind generated from a force field. I'd been this close to Decoherence's powers spinning up once before, very recently: in the Butcher Shop, when she thought she was about to fight Leviathan. That time, I would have just been collateral damage again while the two of them ripped me apart to get to each other; this time, her powers were focused entirely on me.

"No," I said again, but this time with a little bit of real fear.

"You'll forgive me," Decoherence said, half to herself, "I know you will."

I thought about Leviathan coming back, having fought off the Future, exhausted and triumphant, only to find me gone. To find nothing here but an empty room, and the smell of shattered atoms.

"If you do this," I swore, from the very depths of my being, "I will hate you for the rest of my life. I will do everything to escape you and then hunt you down again."

We stared at each other. There was nothing in that moment but her own conscience, her own free will, keeping her from taking me wherever she wanted me to go. But she was hesitating—which meant I still had a chance.

"Why," I asked, my voice shaking, "aren't you helping them?"

The vibration stopped; suddenly it was just the strength of her own grip again that held me, and I could have wept with relief.

"What the fuck did you say?"

I pointed at the monitors. Leviathan had dropped the unconscious Shield down the yawning elevator shaft and was now crushing the elevator cab itself with his hands, like you would ball up a piece of paper to toss into a wastebasket. Red Sprite sped into view, and tried to grab hold of him to stop him, but he very casually backhanded her out of frame. Once the elevator cab was crushed down small enough, he tossed it down the shaft after Shield.

"You want better for them? Go help them."

She looked between me and Leviathan fighting all the young heroes.

"I'm here to help *you*."

"The only help I need," I seethed, "is putting the Draft in the ground. If you're not interested in helping me with that, then leave me the fuck alone."

The disappointment in her face was devastating, and her eyes met mine with a huge, repulsed sadness. I knew, without a doubt, that she would never help me with anything again.

"Don't you dare let the Draft fucking win," she snarled.

"I won't."

She thought about threatening me once more, I could see it in her eyes. She thought about saying something else, maybe something softer or meaner, something that would hurt. But instead, she just blinked out of existence, like a bubble popping, leaving me alone again.

I watched the fight continue at first through a haze of tears. As I blinked them back, I saw the confrontation had taken a turn. Really looked at those five young heroes who have been prepared their entire short lives for this moment. I thought about them. They were the best and brightest of their class, maybe their generation, the greatest untested hope the Draft had in a direct conflict with Leviathan. They'd also, in their brief and tumultuous careers, had their teams disbanded and re-formed, had their confidence in themselves and the Draft shattered, and had been turned against each other. Those were the blows I had landed, long before this physical fight began. They were confused and scared and filled with growing resentment, and should never have been put in this position to begin with.

But they were, in fact, the best, and it showed. I watched Marrow reach out, as though he was miming the act of grabbing some invisible lever inside of Leviathan's body, his face twisted in concentration. His hand rotated and Leviathan slowed, wavered, and briefly went to a knee, and some terrible sensation seemed to pass through him. But he shook it off, and stood, moving toward the slim young man. Before he could get a clawed hand on him, Red Sprite literally swooped in and got a grip on one of the pieces of armor on his back, and flew straight up, as fast as she could. A moment later there was a spectacular noise as they smashed through the ceiling; then Leviathan had freed himself from the offending pauldron, and plummeted to the ground like a meteorite. Even though I knew what his endurance was like, my stomach still dropped as though I was the one falling.

He made an awful sound when he landed, his armored boots carving deep wounds in the fractured marble. But he stood a moment later with a rakish kind of ease, and walked, very calmly, back toward the heroes, who were regrouping for the next exchange.

The Future was a strong team. They were putting up a good fight. I had to give them the credit they deserved.

But this was nothing like Leviathan's fight with Supercollider. The hero had many advantages. His powers were unmatched by those of any other hero in his generation (and many others) and were amplified by expectations: if someone thought he could do something, he was vastly more likely to succeed, in a kind of self-fulfilling prophecy. He'd also been Leviathan's nemesis since they were adolescents, and before then they had trained together at the Draft. They knew each other intimately, knew each other's strengths and weaknesses and vulnerabilities, and were uniquely deadly to each other.

These young heroes had no such experience. They had documents and videotape and testimonies to study, simulations and other heroes and each other to fight, but not the real thing. Had it been anyone else, even with their major defensive team member taken out, they would have been a nightmare to deal with. Because even though they were strong and clever and creative, and had learned to work well together, it became more and more apparent that they were losing, and it was not close.

Leviathan, I noticed, was now fighting the young heroes almost *gently*—more gently than seemed possible. He punished their attempts to hurt him, but just with discomfort, not permanent damage. The immovable object to all the world's unstoppable forces, he let them fight him to exhaustion.

It was Red Sprite who went down next. She might have been the greatest flyer in memory, but she had her own limits, and flight was one of the most grueling things any hero could endure. She simply ran out of energy, and even Marrow, desperately trying to overcharge her cells, couldn't stop her body from eventually just shutting down.

When it came to the twins, Leviathan's anatomy was alien enough that neither Cartilage nor Marrow could get enough purchase to break him apart or shut him down, so they focused on supporting Thundersnow as much as they could, powering her past the limits of *her* usual endurance. But that sapped both of them, too, and eventually they folded.

Which left Thundersnow, but not really. Soon she was on her knees, and it was wasn't clear she was going to be able to get up again. In the relative calm, Leviathan moved toward her slowly. He was exerting himself, breathing deeply, but there was joy in the set of his shoulders that I could see even on the monitors. It made my heart squeeze to see him so happy. This might not look like my plans, beautiful as they had been, but I found it in myself to let that go for this moment of triumph. It might not be mine, but it could be ours.

Red Sprite was curled on her side, her hands in gentle fists, like a little kid asleep. Marrow could not stop dry heaving, and Cartilage had the glassy, unfocused calm of someone who had gone into shock. Thundersnow crawled over to put herself between Leviathan and her teammates. This admirable—if ultimately pointless—gesture took a mighty effort, and she was barely able to sit upright. Leviathan approached her slowly, hands extended and open like the statue of a saint bestowing a blessing. I tilted my head to one side—that was interesting. I put the comm back in my ear to try and hear their conversation. The mics had been damaged by Thundersnow's scream, giving everything they said a distorted, almost dreamy quality, but still I could hear enough.

"Will you listen for a moment," he said, using the softest voice he was capable of.

"Do I have a choice," she said, but there was no fight in it.

"No."

She stared at him, but then nodded in assent.

"I have won," he said simply.

"You just wanted to gloat?" she asked, suspicion under the exhaustion.

"I didn't want to *fight*. I wish to start from the facts." He paused, in case she had something to say, but she just stared at him. He took that as acknowledgment and continued. "I have won. I could kill you, easily."

It would have been inaccurate to say that his straightforward calm was more frightening than anger, but it was certainly more unsettling. Thundersnow's facade finally cracked, and she looked at him with a deep fear that made her seem much younger than she was. "Is that what you're going to do, then?"

"No. I meant what I said when you arrived. That you should never have been made to come here. That it was cruel."

"We weren't *made* to do anything." Behind her, Marrow retched again.

"Really?" he said, not unkindly. "You're telling me you had a choice? That you could have said no?"

She didn't know how to respond to that. Like all heroes, when there was something heroic to do, options were never presented. Their action was expected; their willingness or consent was never a part of the equation.

"That," he said, with real sadness, "is what I thought."

"We knew what we signed up for," she parroted.

"You knew you would be beaten this soundly, and you came anyway? Surely you're much smarter than that."

She didn't have the energy to verbally spar with him; she barely seemed capable of holding her head up.

"We knew . . . we knew what we had to . . ."

He was looking down at her with a such profound pity that she didn't know how to process it. So she dug deeper inside herself and found a scrap of anger she could hold on to, like a bit of debris she could fashion into a crude weapon.

"I would have fought you no matter the odds. Even if it was hopeless, and I knew it, it would still be worth it to take a stand—"

"Perhaps you would have," Leviathan interrupted, "but what

about your teammates? They are your responsibility. Would you have willingly led them to their deaths?"

She wanted to say something brave, something meaningful—I could see the defiance in her face. But she made the mistake of looking behind her, hoping to bolster her convictions, and was visibly devastated by what she saw there. Marrow had finally stopped heaving and was instead sobbing quietly, while Cartilage, staring into the middle distance, was absently rubbing his brother's back. Red Sprite was going to need eighteen hours of sleep and an IV bag of electrolytes before she'd be able to so much as hold a conversation. Shield, still down the elevator shaft, was alive, probably—he was if nothing else incredibly durable—but not in much of a position to help anyone either.

"No, you would not," Leviathan answered for her.

Thundersnow sat up straighter, eyes blazing, and found a last bit of conviction to cling to. "I would do *anything*," she snarled, "to bring Supercollider's murderer to justice."

Leviathan froze; for a long moment he was eerily still, carved from onyx, and as far away as I was, I still felt like instinctively recoiling from the monitor, as though even through the screen his reaction might reach me. I wondered, in that moment, if she had said enough to make him abandon whatever his plan was and just kill her instead.

Instead, he slowly lowered himself, until he had taken one knee in front of her. Thundersnow attempted to crawl backward and put more distance between them. Leviathan ignored her completely. He passed one hand, briefly, across his face.

"Then you would have failed."

"Maybe this time—"

"I did not kill him," Leviathan said quietly. The weight of his grief was palpable, and a familiar guilt bit down on me again.

"You're a liar," Thundersnow said, with no real conviction behind it. She said it because it was the thing to say.

He looked down at her. I could not clearly see his face on the various camera angles capturing the scene, but I could see the set of his shoulders and the way he held his hands. I could imagine the horrific sadness she saw there.

"It should have been me," he said, almost too quietly for me to hear. The audio quality was getting worse and worse, as the blow-out mics struggled to carry anything intelligible. "Of all their lies, it is this one I wish most fervently were true. But, to my ceaseless regret, I did not kill him."

He sounded so deeply miserable about it, the loss in his voice so unmistakably genuine, that Thundersnow didn't know how to process it.

"You . . . you expect me to believe that all of those eyewitnesses at the hospital, everyone at the Draft, that they're all lying."

"Is it easier to believe that I rose from the dead, while in storage at the morgue, just because I sensed his presence in the building? That I, at my weakest, was able to kill the invulnerable man, whom I nor anyone else had ever before been able to harm, as he recovered from an unspecified illness in an unspecified hospital bed?" He shook his head. "Not a single part of their story is acquainted with the truth."

She clearly did not like how much sense he was making. "You expect me to take *you* at your word."

He rose to his feet. "Oh no. I expect—"

And then the audio died completely. I tried switching feeds, connecting a fresh comm, but all of the mics in the room had died at last. I could only watch in silence as Leviathan and Thundersnow continued to talk, wishing I could read lips. Leviathan did most of the talking, Thundersnow occasionally interjecting and then visibly hating everything he said in response. Then there was a long stretch in which neither of them spoke.

Finally, Thundersnow tried to stand. Leviathan offered her a hand up, but she snapped something at him that made him politely withdraw. She struggled up on her own, and staggered over to the twins. The three of them spoke quietly, and after a moment, they stood, too. Thundersnow went to check on Red Sprite, who did not respond; the team leader checked her vital signs and put her in the recovery position, then laid a hand briefly on her chest before walking toward Leviathan. He gestured for them to follow him. The twins hesitated, briefly, by the huge hole in the wall where the elevator doors had once been, then followed Leviathan and Thundersnow off-screen, where I could not track them.

WHAT FELT LIKE hours later, I heard the deep, mechanical groan of the vault door as it was opened. But it was not Leviathan's face I saw when I turned; it was Thundersnow's. Her brow was furrowed and her shoulders down, and she stalked into the room carrying rage with her like a physical object. I took an alarmed step back. Behind her, Marrow and Cartilage clung to each other like a pair of closed parentheses. As the three heroes approached me, I was suddenly aware of how small and claustrophobic the room was, how there was nowhere for me to go.

Then Cartilage and Marrow stepped to one side, and Leviathan walked in the room, calm and triumphant. Thundersnow gave him space, grudgingly, but she did, and he came to stand next to me. I was caught between a cool waterfall of relief at the safety he represented and a vivid spike of rage for his frightening me so badly.

"Show me," she said, her voice very low. It was not immediately clear if she was speaking to me or Leviathan. She pointed toward the computer terminal mounted into the wall above the narrow desk that ran down one wall of the bunker.

Leviathan rested a hand on my shoulder. He steered me gently toward the console, echoing Thundersnow's agitated gesture.

"Auditor," he said calmly, "we have guests."

I stared at him for a moment, and wanted to scream. This was the safest spot in the entire compound, he had said; but then he brought three of the most powerful—and currently deeply emotionally unstable—heroes on the planet right in. Hell, he had even unlocked the door for them. He had led them to me and my frail, squishy human body, so confident in his control of the situation that he deemed (what I thought was) the very real risk to my person inconsequential. He could have spared me this, and so many other moments of terror, by simply telling me what the fuck was going on, which he flatly refused to do.

"*I ask for your trust,*" he had said, immediately before he'd left me. I felt him squeeze my shoulder slightly; this was not just an instruction. There was affection there, and reassurance, but something else: a silent reminder of, and a request that I keep, my earlier promise.

I gripped my cane and steadied myself. "What do you want to see," I said coolly, conjuring up my Auditor voice, the voice of someone known for their merciless hyper-competence and not at all for their anxious vulnerability. Leviathan beamed down at me, not trying at all to hide his affection, and I tried very hard to remind myself that I was still extremely angry with him.

"He said . . ." Marrow spoke in a curdled rasp. "He claims he did not kill Supercollider."

"No," I said, with my own deep regret. "He did not."

"Prove it." Thundersnow pointed at the computer terminal, and I obligingly sat down in front of it, entering my employee password and opening the intricate, branching tree of my file structure.

I had only one real option when it came to showing them proof. I had untold gigabytes of data about Supercollider's hospitalization, the attempts to unknot him, and the failure of those efforts—but that was the kind of data that needed careful explaining, and time, and reinforcing, and none of those were resources I had in that moment.

What I did have was Keller's dashcam footage from Decoherence's confrontation with Supercollider, which captured his undoing in awful, silent detail. That was the only thing that would land the way I needed it to: visceral and incontrovertible proof.

While my hands moved steadily, and my eyes didn't falter, inside I hesitated. The videos I had would expose the Draft's lies, but they would also reveal everything Decoherence had done. There was no way to prove Leviathan's word as quickly and completely as I needed to without exposing her.

I tried to tell myself I was finally giving her the credit she deserved, that she had been denied all the responsibility for his death that she was owed. She'd been the vessel of Supercollider's destruction just as much as Leviathan had; it was not stolen valor, it was earned. I knew that the glory had been denied her long enough. But I couldn't lie to myself. In exposing the truth, I would be ripping away a lie that had shielded her from retribution up until now and there was no way I could frame this as anything but a betrayal. The right thing to do would have been to ask her first. There was no time for the right thing. *I wish we had more time.*

I felt a deep flush of something that was not quite guilt, something that hurt more, for showing the Future the video.

I also wondered if, the next time we met, it would even matter.

I thought of the way she looked at me the last time, just before she had vanished from the same bunker I was in; the soul-deep disappointment. She had expected so much more of me, and the person she hoped I would be was so drastically different from the one that stood in front of her it was wounding.

How long will it take before she gives up on me completely?

I heard Marrow cough softly; it occurred to me that it must look like I was dispassionately searching my archive for exactly the right file, not agonizing over whether I should show them at all. I straightened up a little. I remembered: Leviathan had defeated them. *We* were victorious. I was now part of the worst loss they'd ever know.

They didn't see Anna. No, all that they saw was the Auditor.

"I do need to warn you," I said coolly to the three young heroes hovering behind me, "this is going to be very hard to look at."

I didn't wait for any of them to reply. Instead, I looked at Leviathan. Even though my words and tone were directed toward the Future, he was the only person I was actually concerned about. I had no idea if he had ever watched this footage; if he had, it was in complete privacy, and we had never talked about it. In my eyes, I held a silent question out to him—*do you want to see this?*—and he answered with an almost imperceptible nod.

I thought about Decoherence one last time. *I can give her this*, I thought. *I can make her hate me.* I could drive the knife in once, cleanly, so she would never have to worry if I was worth saving again.

I hit *play*, stood back so the heroes could see the screen clearly, and watched as all their worlds fell apart.

[Acknowledgments]

WRITING *VILLAIN* ALMOST KILLED ME. I know sequels are hard; I know second books are hard; I am not afraid of difficult things. I am in fact one of those annoying people who likes to be challenged, falling somewhere between "amusingly masochistic" and "there is something deeply wrong with you." This was different. It was harder than any other project I've taken on, creative or otherwise, by an order of magnitude, and I can't even exactly say why. All I know is that it took me writing the book four times (not four drafts—I mean starting anew, from scratch, four different times because the story I had was just not working) before I had something I was happy with. But I got there, and I am a profoundly different person than I was at the beginning; I think, in a lot of ways, I had to become the person who could write this book before I could actually do it, and that sure was an annoying and painful process. But here I am, still alive, and here this book is, to my shock and joy and relief.

So thank you, firstly, to everyone reading this. Thank you for entering this world with me, and for falling in love (or hate) with these characters as much as I have. Thank you for sticking with me while I worked through a task I genuinely thought might be impossible. Thank you for being delighted or horrified or both, and coming back. I have never cared much about what anyone thought about anything I did, but you have given me that as a gift too: I genuinely hope you enjoy it. Thank you all for teaching me what that particular kind of hope (and terror!) feels like.

Thanks from the very core of my heart to my editor, David Pomerico, who displayed superhuman (complimentary) patience through this entire dire process and never lost faith that I could finish it. He has an incredible knack for difficult-story husbandry and gave perfect, timely advice every time I needed it. He has relentlessly championed my books, and stuck up for me personally, and I don't know if I can ever thank him enough for that steady, unwavering support. I wish every creative person could have a David in their lives.

Thanks to my agent, Ron Eckel; rights manager, Hana El Niwairi; and all the incredible folks at CookeMcDermid, who continue to be the best team I could possibly have in my corner. The last few years have been a wild ride, and I would not have wanted to be on it with anyone but them. Thanks also to my film and television agent, Joe Veltre, and the team at Gersh, who opened so many doors I could not possibly have imagined I would ever be able to look through.

Thanks to my team at HarperCollins, who I still remain convinced are sorcerers of some sort. Everyone I have worked with has been brilliant and hilarious and greeted the arrival of my manuscript in their inbox with unbridled joy, and I cannot ever express how much their positivity has sustained me.

Thanks to Mark Goffman, who loved *Hench* as much as I do, and who has gone to bat for that book and its future in ways I could not have imagined. I have learned so much getting to work with him, and his generosity and friendship are things I will always be deeply grateful for. Thanks also to the original Content Superba team: Joel Stillerman, Owen Shiflett, Anisha Manchanda, and Soleil McGhee, who saw something special in *Hench* and were absolute joys to work alongside. I could not have asked to try, and fail gloriously, with a better group of people.

Thanks to my beloved friends who witnessed my suffering, treated me with care, and continued to believe in this weird universe I have created, especially Madeline Ashby, Braydon Beaulieu, Gennie Catroppa, Izzie Colpitts-Campbell, Oliver Cossette, Heather Cromarty, Chris Dart, Stacey May Fowles, Haritha Gnanaratna, Lauren Jane K., Rachel Kahn, Jessica Kaya, Maxwell Lander, David Nickle, Josh Pryor, J. P. Robichaud, Mariko Tamaki, and Audra Williams. Special thanks to J. P., for having a crucial conversation with me that finally got me out of my own head; and my deepest gratitude to Audra and Haritha, who let me take the time I needed holed up in their magical camper to finish the manuscript, and possibly saved the whole thing with their hospitality.

Thanks to my dear friend Trez Lanz and the entire crew at DoubleRex, whose collective camaraderie and creativity have been the highlight of the past year. Getting to work with you all and make cool shit together has been a complete delight, and thank you all for trusting me to give voice to the worlds we're making.

Thanks to my parents, Harry and Margaret, who have always been proud of me. Thanks to my brother, Michael, and my sister-in-law, Kacy, who both possess that rare combination of being genuinely kind and also hilarious; I look up to both of them immensely. Thanks to their son, Oscar, my first nephew, who reminds me all the time that we have a responsibility to leave all the spaces we move through better than we found them, and that the future is worth fighting for.

As I was finishing the copyedits on this manuscript, my uncle Ricky Pepin passed away unexpectedly. I wanted to thank him, as well as my aunt Shelly, and my cousins Carly, Genevieve, and Christian. His creativity and drive were traits I always admired, and some of my happiest childhood memories were made visiting them all. I will always be grateful for that.

Above all, thanks to my partner, Jairus Khan, the cornerstone of my heart's cathedral. He is my greatest cheerleader in every creative endeavor and my favorite person on this blasted planet. He is a daily reminder that no one should settle for less than a fairy tale, and of all the many reasons I am lucky, getting to spend my time with the love of my life has got to be the greatest one.

—— [**About the Author**] ——

NATALIE ZINA WALSCHOTS is a writer and game designer whose work includes LARP scripts, heavy metal music journalism, video game lore, weirder things classified as "interactive experiences," and, unfortunately, experimental poetry. Her first novel, *Hench*, was a finalist on the 2021 season of *Canada Reads* and nominated for a Locus Award for Best First Novel. She plays a lot of RPGs, participates in a lot of Nordic LARPs, watches a lot of horror movies, and reads a lot of speculative fiction. She lives in Nova Scotia with her partner and four cats.